The Brea File

The Brea File

Louis Charbonneau

DOUBLEDAY & COMPANY, INC.
GARDEN CITY, NEW YORK
1983

All of the characters in this book are fictitious, and any resemblance to actual persons, living or dead, is purely coincidental.

Library of Congress Cataloging in Publication Data

Charbonneau, Louis, 1924–
The Brea file.

I. Title.
PS3575.O7B7   813'.54
ISBN: 0-385-15508-5   AACR2
Library of Congress Catalog Card Number: 80-698

For Bruce Mellett, again,
and for Bruce, Michael and Jennifer

PROLOGUE

It was cold that February morning, in the hours before dawn, high in the foothills of the Sierras, and he moved with caution among frost-brittle branches. Pine needles swept across his face like trailing fingers. Very gently he pushed the branch aside.

There were patches of snow in the woods where the winter sun could not reach, and he skirted around them. Through an opening in the trees the lake gleamed below him, the dull silver of an old coin. He paused a moment to verify his bearings. The cabin was not yet visible. He saw one light, far across the lake, glittering like a single star. That would be the light at Boulanger's boathouse. Sighting on that star, he judged himself no more than a dozen yards off his plotted course.

The wooded slope dropped steeply toward the shore of the lake, and as he started down he made his way even more carefully, testing the ground before each step, making no sound, his vaporizing breath the only fleeting sign of his presence. He was dressed in the black of the night from head to toe; even his face was blackened.

Peering along the shoreline, he felt a moment's concern that he had miscalculated. Then he took two steps to his left, changing the angle of view, and the momentary tension eased. He saw the cabin, completely dark, isolated on this eastern shore, twenty yards from where he stood.

He raised his left arm and pressed a button on the side of his watch. Green numerals glowed briefly: 4:52.

He crept closer to the cabin, staying within the cover of the trees, until he could make out the finger of a small dock pointing into the lake and a small rowboat moored at its side. Everything was as he had known it would be, but he had had to satisfy himself.

In a hollow among the trees on the windowless side of the cabin he waited.

Vernon Lippert rose early from long habit, but this morning for another reason. He was a troubled man and had slept poorly.

The cabin was cold; he had let last night's fire die out, not wishing to waste wood. Crouching before the stone fireplace, he paused a moment, staring at a small pile of blackened paper ashes, a stain against the whiter ash from his wood fire. In a sudden, angry move he mashed the dark pile with the back of a fireplace shovel. Then he scooped them up and dropped them into a pail on the hearth. Over them he piled the white ashes left over from his wood fire until the pail was almost full.

Working quickly in the stubborn chill, he stacked kindling, a tightly rolled wad of newspaper, and logs cut from his own trees. He struck a long wooden match into flame and held it against the wadded newspaper.

The fire had begun to blaze cheerfully as he dressed. He used the toilet—the cabin's one concession to modern comforts—and washed his face with cold water. Then he put on a pot of coffee.

He was a tall, lean man, and only a slight roll about the waist betrayed a lifelong struggle against excessive weight. He would be fifty-five on the sixth of May—the compulsory retirement age for an FBI agent.

Vernon Lippert had spent almost his entire adult life as a Special Agent with the FBI. Looking back on his career, he considered himself a fortunate man. He might have spent thirty years as an accountant with a badge. Instead he had had a stimulating, exciting life. He had handled just about every assignment that came to a field agent. He had worked all over the country, in large offices and small ones. He had spent eight years in Los Angeles, where there was an average of a bank robbery per day every day of the year, and three years in a small New Mexico town where the only bank robber of record was Billy the Kid—and that was more legend than fact.

He had liked it all.

In time he had been lucky enough to be assigned to his office of choice at Sacramento, and for the last six years he had been the

Senior Resident Agent in San Timoteo. An RA's office was an extension of the parent field office, but to a large degree Lippert had been on his own. He investigated everything that came up affecting his territory, which encompassed a number of small northern California towns in the area surrounding San Timoteo. He came to know the area intimately, its people and its places. Liked and respected, he was proud of what he was and of the Bureau he represented. Warts and all, as he sometimes said, it was the best.

His glance flicked toward the pail on the hearth with its hidden layer of black ashes, and his mouth pulled into a tight, bitter line. The documents he had burned last night recorded evidence that would damage the agency he loved. Undermine public confidence and hold the Bureau up to harsh criticism, to the wild excesses of those who were always looking for something to tear down. All because of the one extraordinary event in the otherwise placid history of San Timoteo, a disastrous confrontation between a bunch of radicals and the San Timoteo police.

Vernon Lippert had been at the scene. He had seen with his own eyes the violent explosion that, for millions of Americans, was the climax of the top-rated television show on the evening of August 28, 1981. Whether the cache of explosives in the radicals' hideout had been hit by police gunfire, as some civil libertarians had later charged, or been set off by the revolutionaries themselves as a last, defiant gesture, was not for Vernon Lippert the subject for a suitably grave panel discussion on public television; it was a personally agonizing question. Because he had stood there as pieces of bone and flesh, splintered wood and metal and glass rained down over a two-block area for several minutes after the blowup. He had witnessed the scene of desolation that slowly emerged from the curtain of dust and debris—the blackened, smoking stumps of the foundation, the stunned silence broken by the racking sound of a policeman retching, the emptiness where moments before a cadre of defiant human beings had flaunted their contempt for a society they believed irredeemable. He had stood there and asked himself the unanswerable question: How could such a thing have happened?

It was a question that would not go away. Eventually he had been compelled to begin a quiet but persistent search for the answer. It led him through months of increasingly intensive investigation, working on his own, resisting the truth that gradually took shape, resisting but coming back to it inexorably, until the conclusion was undeniable: The annihilation of the People's Revolutionary Committee had been no accident. It was a setup, arranged by an agent of the Federal Bureau of Investigation.

That agent for a long time remained invisible. He had operated under the code name of Brea. No such code name existed in FBI files. But by this time the case had become an obsession for Vernon Lippert. He was near the end of his career. The betrayal had taken place in *his* town; in a peculiar way he held himself responsible. He wouldn't let the question go away. He had run down all the threads, woven them together, made sense of them. Documented everything, with lab reports and interview sheets and duplicated records. And found, finally, just two days ago, the last missing piece of the puzzle.

He knew who Brea was.

That was why he had come to the cabin alone, at this off season of the year. To be alone with his thoughts and his pain and his unwelcome knowledge. He suspected this would be the last peaceful time he would know for a long while.

It wasn't safe to wait any longer.

He had conducted his investigation without authorization from Sacramento or FBI Headquarters. He hadn't dared ask for it, suspecting what he did. But you couldn't conduct an investigation without asking questions, revealing a particular interest. There was always the risk of a chance remark, an expression of curiosity that would reach the wrong ears— "What's Vern Lippert up to?"

Brea must know!

Lippert had been quiet, careful, circumspect, but you could never be sure.

It was shortly after six o'clock that morning when Vernon Lippert shrugged into his mackintosh, opened the cabin door and stepped outside. He glanced up at the sky, gray but already lighter than the darkness that still hugged the land. He thought he spotted a hawk above the lake, also up early, wheeling slowly as it peered down. And in that moment Lippert felt the first intuition of alarm, the feeling a hawk's prey might have when the predatory bird launched into its dive.

The man with the blackened face started to move as soon as he heard the bolt slide back on the cabin door. He came around the corner just as Vernon Lippert stepped through the doorway onto the narrow wooden platform that served as a porch. He saw Lippert glance up at the gray sky, eyes narrowing behind his glasses as he sighted on something small and distant. Then a whisper of warning alerted Lippert, a slither of boot over soft earth or a stirring of air, and his eyes widened and focused as his head jerked around and he tried to leap backward through the open doorway.

He was not quick enough. What his shocked glance revealed was a flooding awareness of danger, recognition that came like a blow from a fist, and a swift darting sense of the precise immediate threat: a peculiar kind of gun in Brea's hands. It was held in both hands like a medieval crossbow, though it was much smaller and lighter. It was made of polished metal and had a long barrel. It made a small popping sound as gas escaped when Brea pulled the trigger.

Stumbling over the threshold of his cabin, Lippert took the dart high on his temple. He jerked sideways against the doorjamb, stunned by a sharp electric shock. He didn't fall. He sagged against the doorjamb and sank slowly until he was half sitting in the opening, his long legs sprawling over the wooden porch, twitching like a man with a seizure.

Brea closed in swiftly, while Lippert was still stunned and paralyzed from shock. He jerked the probe from Lippert's temple. It remained attached to the weapon by long, thin, plastic-coated wires. The gun had been devised by the burgeoning technology of the security industry as a non-lethal method of immobilizing an attacker. Lippert would be dazed for only a few minutes. Brea wanted no struggle, no sign of violence.

He picked up the lean figure in the doorway as if he were lifting a child in his arms. He carried Lippert almost gently to the shore of the lake and without hesitating waded out into the water. The lake bottom dropped quickly, and at the end of the dock he was almost waist deep in the cold water. He lowered Vernon Lippert's body and, in the moment of thrusting his head underwater, saw the FBI man's eyes pop open.

There was a brief, feeble struggle, but Lippert had not yet recovered from the jolt he had received. In a minute bubbles broke the surface of the water. Brea waited another thirty seconds before he lifted the limp, sodden form from the water and laid it in the small boat tied to the dock. He found a tarpaulin wedged beneath the seat at the stem and dragged it out to cover the body. When he pulled the tarp clear and swung around, the flat paddle of an oar slammed against the side of his face.

The blow slashed a cut high on his forehead. Blood poured into his left eye, half blinding him. The oar rose and struck again and he caught it and yanked, pulling Vernon Lippert into the water with him.

Not unconscious! Not drowned! Lippert had tricked him!

Through a red haze he wrestled Lippert under the water. The lean man still gripped the blood-streaked oar with both hands, refusing to let go. That was a mistake. He was caught between the boat and the dock, and Brea used the oar to pin him beneath the surface, wedged between boat and dock. Brea held Lippert there, his face only a few inches underwater, his eyes open and accusing.

This time, standing in the water near the edge of the lake, the cold seeping through clothes and flesh and striking to his bones, Brea held his accuser for several minutes, not moving, the muscles of his back and shoulders straining long after there was no need.

He pulled the body into the boat, threw the tarpaulin over it. In spite of Lippert's brief struggle, there was no mark on his body to raise questions. Brea's own cut was at the edge of his hairline; it could easily be disguised while it healed.

His gaze swept the lake. Though the sky was paler than it had been only a few moments ago, not enough light had come to the far shore for anything on land to be seen clearly. And this eastern side, with the thick woods and the mountain behind it, was darker still. No boats were visible, no early lights. The nearest neighboring cabin, a quarter mile away, was empty at this time of year. So were most of the houses and cabins on the eastern shore. All was quiet.

He carried Lippert's wet mackintosh into the cabin and draped it over a chair in front of the fire. Then he began a methodical, painstaking search of the cabin. He neglected no possible hiding place but left no sign that anything had been disturbed. In the small, simply furnished cabin there were few places of concealment from an experienced eye. Within fifteen minutes he knew that what he was searching for was not here.

A blind rage seized him. He had to fight the terrible urge to smash and tear everything he could lay his hands on. His whole body shook with the fever of his fury.

When the spasm passed he continued to search, no less carefully but now without real hope. He sifted the ashes in the pail on one side of the hearth and found some blackened, pulverized ashes beneath layers of whiter wood ash. There his search ended. The black residue meant only one thing. Lippert had burned the documents he brought with him to his retreat.

For a moment something went out of the black-clad figure. Then he straightened up. Lippert would not have destroyed the evidence of what he had learned. The Brea file still existed, hidden in a place Lippert had considered safe. The papers he burned would only have been copies.

When he rowed out onto the lake in the first light of day, wearing Vernon Lippert's mackintosh, his face scrubbed clean, he felt a grudging admiration for the dead man in the boat with him. His rage was buried deep, no longer visible even in his eyes. His thoughts already ranged ahead, sorting through the possible places of concealment Lippert would have chosen, planning his next moves.

If anyone saw the solitary figure rowing slowly toward a far corner of the lake, he would have been a familiar sight, even to the plaid mackintosh he wore.

In a private cove he forced the mackintosh over Lippert's stiffening arms. Then he slipped into the water, ducked under the boat and flipped it over.

As the boat drifted slowly away, the dead man's body broke the surface once and sank out of sight. Brea struck out for the nearest shore. He carried with him a single oar taken from the rowboat. To the casual eye it had been cleansed of blood by the cold water as he rowed, but Brea knew better. The oar could not be left behind.

Spilled blood was not so easily washed away.

The Brea File

1

A light, misting rain muddied the windshield of the blue Ford Fairmont sedan. It had rained almost every day during May, turning Washington, D.C., into the world's largest steam bath.

Special Agent Harrison Stearns, attached to the Resident Agent's office at Dulles International, had left the airport shortly before eight o'clock in a Bureau car. In its trunk were four sealed boxes of documents shipped in that day from California for delivery to FBI Headquarters in downtown Washington. Stearns was off duty at eight, but a shipment of classified documents was not to be left at the airport until someone found time to deliver them. Stearns was nominated. "It counts as overtime, Harry," the Senior Resident Agent told him with a grin. "And there's bound to be extra Brownie points for overtime on Friday night in the rain."

Just before leaving the office he had called home to tell his wife Patty that he would be late. His voice was worried when he asked about the baby.

"She'll be fine. Dr. Kosco said it was just a little throat inflammation. Could you stop and pick up a prescription on your way home? I can call it in right now—Kosco said it's a mild antibiotic."

"Okay, I'll pick it up." Patty gave him the name of the pharmacy where they usually had prescriptions filled. It was in a discount store. These days, especially with a young baby to feed and clothe and keep healthy, you had to watch every penny. "They close at nine," Patty reminded him.

Stearns drove carefully even though he was on a wide, divided highway. Driving into downtown Washington on getaway night in the rain *deserved* Brownie points. It occurred to him as he neared the Beltline that a short detour would allow him to stop at the Fedco store on his way in. Then, if he were held up in downtown traffic and didn't get back to the suburbs in time, he would have the prescription anyway.

He parked in the big Fedco lot off to one side of the building. Rain or no rain, the spaces out front were jammed. Everyone was watching pennies.

The rain was light but steady, a soaking drizzle, pools forming in shallow pockets of the black macadam. He pulled his jacket up over his head as he ran toward the store entrance, weaving among the rows of parked cars. Like O.J. going through Dulles, he thought.

The image was still in his head when his foot hit something slick on the glistening pavement and he went sprawling.

Stearns skidded against the base of a light standard. He lay momentarily stunned by the hard fall. He pulled himself shakily to his knees. One hand had lost some skin and, worse, he had torn a hole in the elbow of one of his two good suits.

The young agent swore softly. Climbing to his feet, he waved off a couple with an umbrella and another helpful shopper, thanking them. Then he limped on into the store, wondering sourly about the economy of ruining a good suit while trying to save two dollars on a prescription.

When Stearns emerged from the store and headed around the corner toward the back part of the parking area, it was still raining. He walked. What the hell, a little rain couldn't do any more damage to *this* suit. He was struck by the fact that this portion of the parking lot was not as brilliantly illuminated as at the front of the store.

At first he thought that he had mistaken the aisle where he had parked. But as he looked around he saw the light post where he had taken a tumble.

With his eyes he tracked back across the lot. In the half hour he had been inside, many of the cars had left. It was now quarter to nine, almost closing time.

He spotted a sign on a post at the far end of the next aisle: M2. Yes, that was it. He remembered seeing the sign when he turned past it. He had parked in that aisle.

For a long minute Harrison Stearns stood in shock, staring through the soft curtain of rain. His heart seemed to have landed down around the pit of his stomach. Impulsively he jammed his hand into his right pants pocket. The search became frantic through his other pockets, his jacket.

He stopped suddenly. The car keys weren't there. He must have lost them when he fell.

And the FBI car was gone.

The young driver of the blue Ford sedan headed southwest on 66 and swung west onto Highway 50. Ironically, his route took him within two miles of Dulles International Airport. Traffic thinned out as he drove on through Middleburg. He kept watching the rearview mirror, his thin body tensed against the sight of flashing red lights.

He watched his speed. No point in getting stopped for speeding now. The theft of the car would have been reported, the license plate numbers fed into the old computers. He would have to find a place where he could switch plates.

He grinned exultantly. The guy outside Fedco had practically handed him the car keys. Scooping them up, he had offered the victim a helping hand as he tried to rise. The good Samaritan, that was him.

At the small town of Paris, near Ashby Gap on the Appalachian Trail, he stopped for gas at a self-serve station. While the gas was pumping on automatic, he walked around the car and opened the trunk with the key. The interior of the car was clean but the trunk might hold something interesting.

There were four compact cardboard boxes, each about the size of a file drawer, tightly sealed with plastic tape. With a pocket-knife he ripped open one of the boxes. He pawed through the contents—tightly packed file folders stacked upright—and pulled a file out at random. As the cover fell open his gaze riveted on a letter-head: Federal Bureau of Investigation. And in one corner a bold black stamped word: CLASSIFIED.

He jammed the folder back into the box, his heart thudding. He slammed the trunk lid shut and looked around. There was no one close enough to see into the trunk. Christ, what had he done? Stolen an FBI car?

He stopped the pump hastily. He was going to have to dump this car. He wasn't going to give them any more of *his* gasoline.

He doubled back from the station, remembering that he had passed the intersection of Highway 17. He had to get off the main road fast.

At an empty roadside stop he pulled off once more, curiosity tugging at him. He made sure no cars were approaching before he opened the trunk again. This time he withdrew a fistful of the file folders. They were of varying thickness, but each contained report sheets and forms, each one numbered. He scanned some of the pages carelessly. *"—the perpetrator then proceeded to his vehicle and was observed . . ."* Cop jargon. Routine stuff—Dullsville.

He started to return the sheaf of folders to the opened carton when something caught his eye: the corner of another folder lying flat on the bottom of the box, hidden beneath the upright files. He reached down and pulled it out, wondering what one file was doing out of place. It was only chance that he had seen it at all.

He pushed the other files back into the carton and examined the one which had been on the bottom. More of the same—memos, interviews . . .

A gust of wind whipped the file folder open. Papers spilled out. He scrambled after them, cursing. The only thing that kept them all from blowing away was the rain. Quickly saturated, the papers stuck to wet gravel, mud, a patch of macadam. He gathered them up, peering around anxiously. He didn't want to leave anything behind.

He bunched the wet papers together and jammed them into the pockets of his nylon jacket. After a moment's hesitation he thrust the empty folder back into the carton, burying it among the other files.

He got back in the car, shivering from the dampness and from excitement. He started down the long, twisting grade on Highway 17, heading southeast.

He drove without headlights, flicking them on once when a car approached, then turning them off again. Invisible in the darkness, he felt alone on the road. But no longer safe.

Ben Thomason, driving an eighteen-wheeler bound for Richmond, swung the big rig ponderously off Highway 50. He could take 17 all the way through to Fredericksburg and intersect with

95 going straight south. That way he would bypass the Washington area and its heavy traffic.

Starting down the long grade a few minutes past ten in the evening, he seemed to have everything under control. The pavement shimmered black in his headlights like a pool of oil, but the light rain had almost stopped. His speed was calculated precisely so that his momentum would carry him well up the next rise before he would have to downshift. Near the bottom of the grade he saw the black carcass of a retread that had peeled off the tire of some luckless trucker ahead of him. For a moment, speared in his headlights, it looked like a body. He did not feel the bump when he ran over it.

He didn't see the Ford sedan that was running without lights until he had it right between the horns.

Ben Thomason was a good driver, and he did the only thing he could. He put the big rig into a deliberate skid.

At first the trailer swung out slowly. It gained speed and jack-knifed inward toward the cab. The whole rig drifted on the slick road surface. Thomason swung the steering wheel against the skid and it seemed for a moment as if the truck might avert disaster. But the rear trailer wheels had skirted too close to the shoulder, soft from days of intermittent rain. When the tires plowed into the wet ground the loaded trailer tipped over in ponderous slow motion.

The man in the Ford was lucky. The right front wheel of the big truck nudged the car, flipping it off the road. The driver fought the wheel as the car slewed across the wet shoulder. It crashed through a rusty barbed-wire fence guarding an empty meadow, careened down the side of an embankment and slammed to a stop, nose down, front wheels buried to the hubcaps in the sandy bottom of a shallow ditch.

Miraculously, the truck's cab was still almost upright. Inside the cab, still gripping the wheel as if he were holding the tractor up by sheer strength, Ben Thomason swore steadily. His adrenaline was flowing and there was an oily sheen of sweat on his brow. That had been close—too damned close.

He flipped his CB switch and put in a breaker call to the nearest listening state police. The call was answered within ten seconds. Smokey was less than five miles away.

As Thomason climbed down from his cab, he discovered for the first time that he had banged his left shoulder and arm against the door when he was bounced around in the cab. He flexed his fingers gingerly. Nothing broken. He looked around for the Ford. Its rear wheels and trunk stuck up out of a creek bed where the car had ditched. The trunk lid had popped open on impact and a white light glowed.

Thomason was registering the fact of light where there had been none before when a curious motorist pulled onto the shoulder a short distance above him. The newcomer's headlights slanted across the field below, catching the ditched Ford and the open meadow beyond it.

That was how, Thomason explained a few minutes later to the Virginia state trooper, he happened to see the driver of the Ford loping through the tall grass toward the dark woods beyond the field.

Paul Macimer, Special-Agent-in-Charge of the Washington Field Office, had been about to leave at the end of a fairly typical fourteen-hour day when the call came from Special Agent Stearns to report that an FBI vehicle en route between Dulles International and FBI Headquarters had been stolen. The agent on the night duty desk switched Stearns over to his boss, feeling a twinge of sympathy as he did so. The RA office at the airport came within the jurisdiction of the Washington Field Office.

Macimer blistered the young agent's ears before he caught himself. Stearns already sounded demoralized. Heaping on more coals wouldn't help. "All right, see if you can find any witnesses," he said finally. "I'll send somebody out to drive you home." He paused and added, "Try not to get lost. And report to me in this office on Monday morning."

Stearns was going to have a lousy weekend, he thought, but he had earned it. The night he had an FBI car stolen from him would be one he would never forget.

At nine-thirty, when there had been no further report on the stolen vehicle, Macimer at last shrugged into his raincoat, said good night to the night duty agent and left the office. "If anything comes through on that car, I want to know it," he said at the door. "No matter what time it is."

He was almost home, which was in a Washington suburban development southwest of the city called the Meadows, when the call came through on his car radio. The stolen car had been found. A Virginia trooper named Edward Riggins was at the scene, just off Highway 17 north of U.S. 66. Macimer made a quick calculation. He had just crossed the Beltline himself. Route 17 was about forty miles west. "Patch me through to him," Macimer said.

A moment later he was talking to Riggins. The state trooper had answered an accident emergency call at 10:09 P.M. The driver of a Ford sedan involved in the accident, Maryland license number CAE-281, had fled the scene of the accident under suspicious circumstances. Acting upon this suspicious behavior, Riggins said with exaggerated formality, he had put through an inquiry to the NCIC—the FBI's National Crime Information Center. At that time he had learned that the car was out of the FBI's vehicle pool and had been reported stolen earlier that evening.

"Anything else I should know?"

"Yes, sir," Riggins replied. "There are some cardboard file boxes in the trunk of the car. One of them has been broken open. It's full of documents." He paused significantly. "FBI documents, sir."

"Sit on them," Macimer said. "Don't let anyone near that car. I'll be there as fast as I can."

Forty-five minutes later, from the highway overlooking the patch of meadow which had been cordoned off around the stolen vehicle, Macimer stared down at the car. Crazy kind of accident, he thought.

He read the statements given to Riggins by the truck driver and the motorist who had stopped. He questioned Thomason closely. "You're sure the car was driving without lights when you ran it down?"

"I didn't see any lights," Thomason insisted, aggrieved. "I know how it sounds, like I'm makin' excuses for not seeing him, but that's the truth."

"Can you describe him?"

The trucker shook his head. He stared balefully at his beached rig, which resembled a huge whale on its side. "Hell, he was halfway across that field before I saw him. He was tall, I guess. Kind of skinny. I could see his hair flying, so it must've been long."

"What color was it?"

"Huh? Oh, dark . . . brown, maybe. And he was young."

"What makes you say that if you only saw him running away from you at a distance?"

"Well, that's just it. The way he was running. I mean, he was *flying.*" He glanced at Macimer. "Men our age, we're joggers, not sprinters. We don't run like that."

Macimer smiled. "Not if we can help it."

Accompanied by Riggins, Macimer climbed down through knee-deep wet grass to the creek where the runaway Ford's flight had ended.

"You didn't touch anything?" he asked Riggins.

"No, sir!" the trooper said. "I wouldn't have seen those boxes if the trunk wasn't open already when I got to it. I opened the trunk lid all the way to get a good look, but that's all."

"No one else has been near the car? You're sure of that?"

"I got here before anyone went down to the car. Both the salesman in the car that pulled up, name of Woodruff, and Thomason swear to that. And I never let it out of my sight after I found those boxes."

Macimer nodded thoughtfully. He gave the interior of the car a quick visual inspection. Then he came back to the open trunk and peered more closely at the four cartons inside. He gave a start as he read the shipping labels. The files were from the San Timoteo office.

San Timoteo. The PRC massacre.

San Timoteo was a small, sleepy farming town in northern California. It had known one brief, searing moment in the national spotlight before dropping back to obscurity.

Macimer remembered that the one-man Resident Agent's office in San Timoteo had been shut down that spring, not long after the death of the RA, Vernon Lippert. The documents must have collected a little dust in the parent Sacramento office before being shipped back to Washington for disposition.

Something else nagged at his memory. He stared down at the opened carton, noting the knife slashes in the cardboard. It was this that triggered his memory. The San Timoteo office had been broken into after Lippert's death. There had been a temporary flap over the incident, remindful of the Media office break-in a dozen years ago which had resulted in the theft and later leaking of FBI documents, with damaging revelations of domestic surveillance, unauthorized wiretaps, COINTELPRO operations. Nothing like that had come out of San Timoteo, but . . .

Could there be any connection?

Macimer doubted it. This night's business had all the earmarks of a routine auto theft. Until the thief opened the car's trunk, he had probably been unaware he had taken an FBI vehicle. The discovery must have scared hell out of him. Perhaps he might have tried to make something of the stolen files of documents if he'd had the chance later, but the accident had intervened.

Macimer felt a deep ache between his shoulder blades. It had been a long day, he was bone tired, but there was nothing for it. He would have to drive these documents back to Washington. He couldn't leave them here.

"There'll be some agents here shortly to look after the car," he told Riggins. "Can you stay here until they arrive?"

"Yes, sir."

"Good." Macimer started to close the lid of the opened carton, noted one folder protruding slightly and pushed it down, his curious glance recording the name on the tab: BREA. It meant nothing to him. "Help me get these boxes up to my car . . ."

It would be long past midnight before he would get to bed this night.

2

The first Saturday evening in June was a fine time for a party, and a fine time was had by all—except one. Paul Macimer suspected that Jan's silence on the drive home was a reflection of his own distracted performance through most of the evening.

He glanced sidelong at his wife. Jan was leaning back in the seat, her head against the padded rest, eyes closed. She looked quite beautiful in repose, her face appearing out of shadow in the repeated flicker of passing headlights like the images in a slow-motion film.

There had been a moment this evening on the Fishers' patio as she turned toward him, the thrust of her bosom in profile, the line of hip and thigh modeled by the thin, silklike texture of her loose pants-and-blouse outfit, when Macimer had felt instant desire. Score one for twenty years of marriage . . .

Heading west of the Capital Beltway on Little River Turnpike, Macimer was driving in the center lane at freeway speed when the Long Valley Road exit loomed up. At the last moment he swung sharply across the intervening lane and raced into the off-ramp loop, tires biting out a protest. Jan's eyes popped open. She grabbed the overhead passenger bar as the Buick leaned into the turn. Then the loop straightened out as the road dipped southward into a broad green valley.

Macimer's glance flicked at the rearview mirror. The Chevrolet had not followed them down the off ramp.

He had probably been mistaken about the car being the same

one he had noticed earlier when they were on their way to the Fishers' place. A brown Chevrolet was a clone among cars.

His glance strayed again across Jan's face. Her eyes were closed once more, but he knew she was awake.

Jan had enjoyed herself tonight. She had been the one sparking lively discussion of the President's new energy plan, the latest GSA scandal, the male backlash she scornfully documented. She relished Washington society, where the outspoken opinions which had once raised eyebrows in Omaha and Atlanta were accepted, even cheered.

The Janet Houghton he had married twenty years ago had been a pale, undeveloped image of this animated woman at his side. She had been more awkward then, less confident, less defined. As she matured her features had grown leaner and more striking, the cheeks hollowing out under more prominent bones, the eyes seeming to grow larger and more dominant (was that a trick of make-up?), the mouth more certain of its generosity and humor. Her body at forty-one was firmer, sleeker, more elegant and more sensual, as if it had only become aware of itself belatedly and liked what it found. Her mind had followed the same direction, shedding unwanted fat and girlish softness while it sharpened the edge of its perceptions. Paul Macimer admired this woman he had married. And she could still awaken his love with a glance, a tilt of her head on slender neck, a gaze of thoughtful absorption at a fingertip burned on the stove, an unconscious frown as she examined a bill that had to be paid.

Macimer was conscious of a disturbing irony in these reflections. Their love had endured and deepened through all the normal crises of marriage for couples of their generation, including raising three children through particularly turbulent times. They were still good together. Even desire-at-a-glance was true for her as often as for him. But the isolating silence of their drive home tonight was not unusual. If anything, it was symptomatic of a steady drift.

Macimer had a remembered image of two giant ships moving very, very slowly apart in a harbor, so slowly that for a time it seemed as if they were not separating at all, until at last a small gap appeared. And then, once made, the rift widened swiftly with each passing second . . .

He shook off the vivid impression with irritation.

They weren't in any real trouble. Couldn't be. Jan was too independent and intelligent to fit meekly into a stereotyped role as the model FBI Wife, but Paul had never really expected her to. It was true there had been more arguments lately, more contention over seemingly small things, sharper disagreements over the children. Two nights ago he had overreacted when Jan expressed caustic concern that Chip, their eldest, was turning into what she called the Worst of Jock. But those were normal dips in the broad plain of any twenty-year marriage, he thought. Viewed from the perspective of distance, they weren't visible at all.

Jan sat up, reacting to a familiar bump in the winding road that told her they were close to home. "Did you hear what Carole said about her appeal? She lost. She doesn't even get visitation rights. Can you believe that?"

"I'm sorry to hear it."

A bright, articulate woman, at thirty-five a successful Washington interior designer, Carole Baumgartner had become Jan's best friend. She was also an ardent feminist, and during the past year she had helped Jan to revive long-buried teaching ambitions, lost in the years of child rearing. At Carole's urging Jan had taught an adult evening class at a local community college in what she called Workplace English. Most of her students were young black working women. Paul remembered the intensity in Jan's voice one night when she said, "The hardest part is getting them to realize what they *can* do if they really want to." The class, Macimer knew, had been good for Jan as well as her students. He was grateful to Carole for that, even if he wasn't so sure of some of her other ideas.

The decision on Carole's appeal, anxiously awaited in recent weeks, had to do with her attempt to contest the awarding of sole custody of her only child to her former husband. Just into her teens now, the girl had been ten years old when Carole walked out on her husband, determined to "find herself." She had taken the child with her and fled her native North Carolina for the nation's capital. Her daughter's tenth birthday had coincided with Carole's thirtieth—and with a traumatic feeling that her life was slipping out of her control. A conventional role as a cheerful domestic had begun to smother her, and in panic she had broken out.

Two years ago a private detective hired by the father had snatched the child from the street while she was on her way to

school one morning. Unable to see her daughter since, Carole was
not even sure where she was, the father having denied her any
kind of access. At one time she had even appealed to Paul Macimer to become involved in the case. "It was a blatant kidnapping!" Carole had insisted. "Isn't that one of the things the FBI is
for?" It hadn't been easy to explain that it was not a federal crime
for one parent to steal his own child from another. Even the private detective who grabbed the girl could not be prosecuted under
any federal law.

In the custody hearing, Carole's initial flight with the girl had
apparently been held against her, the father arguing—and the
judge agreeing—that she couldn't be trusted not to do it again. "I
didn't do it the right way," Carole had admitted. "I just didn't
know any other way."

Her husband, Macimer suspected, had not listened to the signals. He wondered suddenly if he could have been missing some
from Jan.

"The appeal was heard over in Charlotte," said Jan, "and
Carole ran into another elderly southern male judge. I guess he
was going to teach her a lesson."

"Maybe it wasn't that way," Paul said without conviction.

"Oh, Paul, you know damned well it was! The real reason she
lost is that she wouldn't stay in her place. She rocked that safe little chauvinist boat, and you don't do that in Charlotte. She's still
the girl's mother. What the judge is saying is that, because she
wouldn't stay with her husband and play the obedient bride forever, she has no rights to her own daughter. Is that fair?"

"No," Macimer admitted.

He turned into the Meadows onto Laurel Tree Lane. It was
nearly midnight and the street was dark. The big trees lining both
sides met overhead, forming a long nave that blocked out the light
from occasional streetlamps. The car's windows were open to the
early-summer breeze, and a million crickets filled the night with
their music, the din like a million tiny unending screams.

"Where were you tonight, Paul?" Jan asked quietly. "What's on
your mind?"

They were close to the house and he turned to stare at her, his
mind only dimly registering something he had seen. He knew better. Anytime you feel that something is wrong, or even in the
slightest way *different*, you don't open a door and walk inside.

You don't ignore the subliminal warnings even if there is no clear physical evidence that something isn't quite what it is supposed to be. But her question distracted him. "Nothing," he said. The truth was that San Timoteo had been on his mind all week, reawakening memories of that long hot summer three years ago, and bringing a vague uneasiness about the coincidence of files from the San Timoteo RA's office being in the trunk of a stolen FBI vehicle. "Nothing I can talk about, anyway. And certainly nothing that has anything to do with us."

"I see," Jan said. "You spend the entire evening off by yourself, brooding over something that's obviously important to you, and when I ask you what it is your answer is that it has nothing to do with *us*."

He swung into the drive, listening to her instead of to that small warning voice that was trying to tell him something. "It doesn't, Jan. Believe me."

"If it doesn't," she answered, "maybe there isn't any *us* worth talking about."

"Jan—"

"Let's not talk about it anymore tonight. You're just locked into the nineteenth century, Paul." She spoke with something like resigned affection, as if she could not really excuse his condition but was still able to view it with a degree of exasperated understanding.

"How can you say let's not talk about it anymore and then drop that little bombshell?"

She didn't answer.

The garage door rose in response to its electronic signal. Macimer drove inside and cut the engine. Behind them the door swung smoothly shut. Jan stepped out of the car on her side with brisk independence and walked quickly toward the door that led from the garage into the kitchen. She had her key out, not waiting for him.

Macimer frowned as he started after her, belatedly wondering what it was about the front of the house that had caught the edge of his vision.

"Wait a minute, Jan," he called after her.

But she was already up the short flight of steps. She unlocked the door and stepped inside. Then it was too late.

Macimer saw Jan stiffen. She gripped her purse with both hands and gave a stifled gasp. He cracked a knee against the Buick's front bumper as he charged toward the steps. Jan stood rigid in the doorway. He couldn't see what had caused her reaction. He wasn't even sure why an alarm was ringing so loudly in his brain.

He vaulted from the garage into the kitchen, heart thudding.

The knife stopped him as if he had crashed into a wall.

The knife poised at Linda's throat.

A thin, muscular brown arm was around the girl's slim waist, gripping her tightly. With a father's irrational perception Macimer was aware of how the arm pressed upward against the swell of a young breast. The trained cop also noticed that the man wore ultra-thin rubber gloves, the kind you can buy in any surgical supply. Linda's face was slack with terror. Her eyes rolled upward, white crescents showing, toward the man who held her. The knife had nicked the soft flesh of her neck, leaving a fine horizontal thread of red more than an inch long.

Macimer's hot anger must have shown clearly in his eyes. The young-old face that leered over Linda's shoulder was suddenly wary. "That's it, Pops. Let's stay cool, huh?"

Macimer had not worn his gun—he had no reason to carry it during an evening of dinner and drinks among friends on the Fishers' patio—but he doubted that it would have made any difference. The threat to Linda was too naked and immediate.

Carefully Macimer stepped into the room, halting at Jan's side. He put a hand on her arm in an instinctive gesture of reassurance. She was trembling.

"Daddy . . ." Linda's voice quavered and her eyes filled.

"Let her go," Macimer said huskily. He had trouble meeting the liquid plea in his daughter's eyes.

The young man had the burnished skin and jet-black hair of a Hispanic. He shook his head, grinning. He had large, very white teeth. "All in good time, Pops. Close the door, huh?"

Macimer obeyed. His anger was under control and his brain was beginning to function more clearly, but one question engulfed everything else. *Where was Kevin?* Macimer knew that Chip was not yet home—he always parked his car out front, and in any event he could hardly be expected before midnight on a Saturday—but Kevin had been in the house with Linda.

The question was answered almost immediately.

The youth holding the knife at Linda's throat backed off a step, turning sideways while maintaining his grip on the girl and the frightening position of the blade. He gave a brief jerk of his head, as if he wanted to look over his shoulder but couldn't risk taking his eyes from Macimer. "Hey, everything's cool," he called out. "Bring the other kid out."

They emerged slowly from a corner of the family room, which was a half flight below the kitchen and visible through the open counter. There were two of them, holding Kevin between them. They were also Latins. One was a man, older and more heavily built than the youth with the knife. He held a gun in his left hand, tipped upward so the muzzle rested lightly against Kevin's temple. He also wore the surgical rubber gloves. The third member of the group, a slender twin of the one with the knife, was a girl. She had long straight hair, jet black. She wore a bright red satin blouse over jeans—and a pair of white cotton gloves. Hardly older than Linda, she would have been strikingly pretty if her expression had been less sullen and defiant.

Kevin's face was flushed, as if he were embarrassed to be found this way, a helpless captive. Macimer saw that the boy was fighting tears—whether of fear, anger or embarrassment was not clear.

Too late, Macimer remembered what it was about the front of the house that was amiss. The front porch light was off. It had been turned on when he and Jan drove off earlier that evening. It was always left on until the last member of the family arrived home. The draperies were also drawn over the front living-room window—uncharacteristically. Neither Kevin nor Linda paid much attention to such details as open draperies. Jan often chided Linda about parading about the house half dressed with the windows open to everyone in the Meadows.

Macimer's glance brushed Kevin's. No reason for *you* to feel chagrined, he thought. The old man is supposed to know better than to be surprised by a trio of punks.

He remembered something Gordon Ruhle had once said to him. "If you're gonna take someone and you think it might be rough, do it when he's feeling safe." Gordon Ruhle had been Macimer's mentor, the calm and encouraging voice of experience, during his early days with the agency—teacher, backup, ultimately his closest friend in the Bureau, although their assignments had not brought them together very often in recent years. "Do it when he's relaxing in his favorite chair with his feet up. But not if he's got a bottle of beer in his hand," Gordon had added with characteristic attention to detail. "That can be a weapon. Do it when he's tying his shoelaces or feeling up his wife."

Or quarreling with her, Macimer thought grimly.

"What do you want?" he asked. "You don't need to play rough with these kids. You've got the gun."

The youth with the knife snorted derisively. "Hey, you hear that? He's telling *us* what to do."

The older member of the group did not smile. He was about thirty, Macimer guessed. He was blocky and powerfully built, thick-chested, with a broad, impassive face. His two companions had the lean, underfed quickness of a couple of street sparrows. "Let the girl go," the blocky man said.

"Hey, I can have some fun with her. Maybe she likes it, you know? And Pops there—"

"Let her go."

It was a command. After only a second's hesitation the youth pushed Linda away and in one swift motion slicked the retractable blade into its long handle and wedged it into the pocket of his tight jeans. With a sob Linda stumbled across the kitchen into her mother's arms.

The heavyset bandit released Kevin. The boy retreated to the bottom of the steps. Defiantly, he did not run. His glance went from the trio of intruders to Macimer expectantly, as if he were waiting for his father to take over and thrash the villains. *It isn't that easy, son, when they're holding the weapons—and hostages.*

The family was herded in a group down the stairs into the lower-level family room. It was a large, warm room with wood paneling, a used-brick fireplace, a wall of built-in shelves that housed books, stereo equipment, family memorabilia. The blocky man with the gun quickly established himself as the leader of the trio. The other two were quicksilver; he was stolid, careful, in control. "Sit on your hands," he ordered Macimer. "And do not be brave. It wouldn't help nobody." His English was accented but fluent. American-born, Macimer judged, unlike the youth with the knife. The girl had not yet spoken.

Linda huddled on a corner of the Naugahyde sofa, Jan sitting beside her protectively. Jan tugged Linda's sweater down where a portion of bare midriff showed. The youth with the knife grinned.

Kevin, still defiant, flopped into a chair. Macimer sat at the long harvest table used for family dining. There were two facing bench seats and a ladder-back armchair at one end of the table, Macimer's regular seat. Out of habit he took his place there. He sat on his hands as ordered, hoping that the table might prevent the three young robbers from watching his hands too closely.

He knew that he would resist an attempt to tie him up along with the others, leaving them completely helpless. A dangerous psychology began to work in such situations, and he was not about to risk it without a fight. Quixotically, his memory dredged up a fact from FBI statistics on robbery: robbers working in pairs or small gangs were far more dangerous than the lone assailant, far more prone to violence—even murder. The presence of one or more companions tended to goad any unstable member of the gang into a need to prove himself, to show off, to dominate help-less victims.

The youth with the knife was the most volatile member of this trio. Nitro poured into a pair of jeans. Especially dangerous if his slender companion was his girl.

"Where is the safe?" the stocky leader demanded.

"There is no safe," Macimer said. "You're welcome to what money we have—"

"Empty your pockets on the table," the other said curtly. "The lady's purse, too." He turned to the slender girl in the bright red blouse. "See what else you can find in those rooms upstairs. Stick to the small stuff—we don't have all night."

"What about Xavier?" the girl protested. "You gonna let him feel up that girl again—"

"*Cállate!*" the leader cut in sharply. He released a torrent of Spanish at the girl, too rapid for Macimer to follow with his limited smattering of the language, although the gist of it hardly needed translation. The leader was angered because the girl had used a name. Sounded like "Habier," Macimer thought. Xavier. Only one name, but it was a small piece of information that might prove useful—as the gang's leader knew.

Macimer concentrated on the stocky man's Spanish, trying to isolate any peculiarities of accent, inflection, choice of words. Stationed for five years in Atlanta, Macimer had been involved in a number of assignments that took him down into Florida's Cuban community. This man's accent might have been Cuban. His speech was very rapid and clipped, with a tendency to eliminate some of the *s*'s. *Etá* instead of *está*.

The black-haired girl disappeared around the landing and up the short flight of steps to the bedroom wing. The house was a tri-level, living room, dining room and kitchen on the main floor, bedrooms a half flight above, with the large family room and a small den beneath the bedroom wing. As the girl moved from one bedroom to another upstairs, everyone below looked up at the faint sounds of her movements.

After a moment the stocky Cuban—if that was what he was—gave Xavier his gun, ordered him to watch the prisoners and left the family room. He went into Macimer's den, once an extra bedroom which Macimer had converted into an office for himself. Macimer heard desk drawers being pulled out carelessly, their contents dumped on the floor. Books tumbled from shelves. Something splintered when it fell—glass from a picture frame, Macimer guessed.

In the family room there was silence. Linda had stopped crying. She remained in a curled-up, protective posture on the sofa beside Jan. Kevin watched Xavier with obvious fascination.

Macimer spoke quietly to the boy. "How long have they been holding you and your sister?"

"No talking!" Xavier shouted.

"What harm can it do? You're holding the gun."

"You are not giving no orders now. This is not the F-B-I head-quarters." He spaced out the letters with heavy sarcasm.

Macimer spoke sharply. "What do you know about me and the FBI?"

The young man was suddenly disconcerted. His face became blank, more Indian, a mask. "What do you mean? You tol' us."

"I didn't say anything about being with the FBI."

"You didn't have to," the stocky Cuban said from the doorway of the den. "We can look at pictures. There is a picture in this room in which you are being given the glad hand by Mr. J. Edgar Hoover himself. And . . . there is this." He held up the black leather wallet Macimer had placed on the harvest table when he emptied his pockets. Casually the Cuban flipped the wallet open, displaying Macimer's identity card and badge. "Special Agent for Uncle Moneybags," he said mockingly. "Such a man must have more money than we have found, eh?" He threw the wallet onto the dining table and turned to Xavier. "I will have the gun. Go find our *amiga* and come back here. It seems we must reason with Señor Macimer. I think he will tell us where to find what we want. Soon . . ."

It was going to get uglier, Macimer knew. He felt a spasm of self-disgust. He had been looking over his shoulder at phantoms tonight. Reality was not a phantom. Too often it was something as familiar as a reckless, hotheaded kid with a knife and a young lifetime's worth of stored-up rage.

Xavier returned with the girl in the red blouse. She carried a plastic bag stuffed with items she had taken from the bedrooms—and, held aloft like a trophy, Macimer's .38 Smith & Wesson in its hip holster.

Macimer had been waiting—hoping—for a moment's carelessness on the part of the three intruders. So far they had not been careless—and now they were better armed, even more in command.

The leader raised his voice. "You must have a place where you keep the real goodies. A box or maybe a safe, eh? Where is it? In the garage? The attic?"

"I told you," Macimer answered evenly. "There is no safe. We keep valuable papers and other things in a safe-deposit box."

"*Mentiroso!*" Xavier shouted. "You lie!"

The stocky Cuban stared at Macimer. "You are making it hard on yourself . . . and not only yourself. Xavier, tie him up." He used Xavier's name himself this time, carelessly, perhaps deliberately. The suggestion that it no longer mattered was chilling.

With a broad grin Xavier started toward Macimer. The FBI agent rose, scraping back his chair to give himself more room. They wouldn't use the guns unless they had to, he told himself.

"*Espéra! Uno momento.*" The leader of the gang studied Macimer with eyes like black marbles. "Señor Macimer does not believe that we will do what we say. I hope it will not be necessary to prove it." At his sharp command in Spanish, the black-haired girl flipped quickly through the stack of records on the shelf beside the record changer. She selected one with a flourish. Seconds later hard rock music pounded through the room. The girl turned up the volume.

At another swift command Xavier turned back toward the sofa. Linda shrank from his approach. Jan rose to her feet, blocking his way. The Latin girl, armed with Macimer's gun, began to circle behind him. The stocky Cuban raised his voice above the pounding of the music. "You must choose, Macimer. We do not wish to harm anyone—you must take my word for this truth. But we cannot leave you with your hands free while we continue to search this house. You are the . . . professional, is it not so?" With a nod toward Xavier he said, "Xavier has a fondness for your pretty daughter, señor. Tell her that she can scream if she wishes. In such a place as this, on a Saturday night, who will notice, eh? Even if she could be heard above such music. Now you must tell *la señora* to step aside. . . ."

"No," Jan said. "I won't."

The stocky Cuban sighed with exaggerated emotion. *"Ah, como son protectivas las mamás! Que sentimiento tan bonito."* Abruptly he dropped the mockery, turning angry. "Do you expect us to go away with a few dollars from your purse and some worthless trinkets? What is so important that you will not tell us where the safe is? *Xavier—la muchacha. Agárrala!"*

The slim youth edged closer to Linda, grinning. Jan refused to be intimidated. Suddenly Xavier lunged forward. When Jan threw out an arm to ward him off, the young man grabbed her wrist and, with a neat twist, flipped her backward onto the sofa. The thin fabric of her blouse tore, a long rent from shoulder to waist. Xavier's laughter froze. He stared at her. Jan wore no bra, and the dark nipple of one breast peered back at him.

With a cry Kevin rushed forward. At his leader's sharp warning Xavier turned. He sidestepped the boy's blind charge and, laughing again, spun him to the floor.

Two guns were pointing at Macimer. He could only stand rigid as Kevin's accusing gaze found him.

Xavier swung back toward Linda. "Please . . ." she whispered. The plea was drowned in the rocking rhythm of Elton John's piano.

Suddenly something in the husky Cuban leader's dark eyes underwent a change. He barked a command. *"Cállense!"* Instantly his two followers were still. *"Escuchen."*

Macimer had heard nothing, but the stocky man glared at him suspiciously. "You are expecting someone else?" he demanded.

"Yes. My oldest son—and a carload of his friends."

The Cuban scowled. He ordered the black-haired girl to see

what was happening outside. She shot up the half flight of stairs and disappeared down the hall toward the front of the house. The stocky man moved with surprising agility across the family room to the stereo, keeping his eyes on Macimer. He switched off the record player.

The sudden silence was heavy, thundering with unheard music as real to the senses as feeling in a missing limb.

Then, clearly, came the sound of a racing car engine, voices, laughter. Macimer had told Chip to keep it down when he and his friends came to the house late at night, out of consideration for the neighbors. For once he was grateful for sophomore exuberance.

The girl returned on tiptoe. "Three cars," she said with a scowl. "There are eight, maybe nine men." She sneered. "They are throwing a football on the grass."

The stocky leader hesitated for only an instant. "You are most fortunate, Señor Macimer," he said. There was more rapid Spanish addressed to the two younger Latins. They started toward the glass doors that led to the rear yard. As the door slid open the leader said, "You will keep the college boys here, señor. If there is anyone chasing us . . ." He let the threat hang there, more vivid for being unspoken.

There was a burst of noise as the front door of the house banged open. Voices tumbled over each other, hoots of laughter, heavy footsteps. The gang leader ran across the room, still pointing his weapon in Macimer's direction, and fled with the others through the open doorway. They disappeared into the shadows of the yard as Chip appeared on the landing, grinning. He stopped, startled by the scene in the room below him. "Hey! What's going on here?"

Sheriff's deputies arrived some ten minutes after Macimer's call. The older of the two officers seemed tired and bored. Robberies were not novelties in the Meadows, and Macimer did not suggest that the trio who had invaded his home were anything but ordinary thieves. The younger deputy could not stop grinning. The idea of an FBI man and his family being held up by a trio of young Latinos would be a source of considerable merriment down at the sheriff's station.

Macimer promised to come down to the station in the morning

to go through the local mug file. He agreed to make a list of anything found missing.

When the deputies had gone Macimer went upstairs. He found Jan in their bedroom angrily remaking the bed, jerking fresh sheets taut as if she were taking her feelings out on them. The used sheets were crumpled in a pile on the floor.

"Didn't you just change those yesterday? What is it—?"

"Yes! I changed them yesterday." She marched over to the sheets she had thrown aside and picked up the top one. "Do you know what those two . . . those *animals* were doing up here while we were gone? Do you know what that is?"

Macimer stared at a stain on the sheet. "I'm beginning to guess."

"It's not funny! Paul, they . . . they *used* our bed!" She was still breathing hard but her anger was cooling as she talked. "Oh, my God—listen to me."

"Take it easy. I know how you feel."

"It had to have been those two youngsters . . . Xavier and his girlfriend. When I came up here and looked at those sheets, I just felt . . . violated."

"It's a normal way to feel. Most people do when they know that strangers have been in their house, poking around in their private places." He took her in his arms and held her gently. "That's a very private place."

After a moment she tilted her head up and let herself be kissed. "I'm all right now," she murmured.

While Jan was undressing Macimer went downstairs to his den and inspected the damage. The room was a mess. It would require an hour's straightening up before he could be sure if anything was missing. Fortunately, he didn't keep anything important here.

He mused over the different reactions people had to a crisis. Jan was angry. Chip's friends had gone off bemoaning their late arrival and missing out on the "fun." Linda looked as if she would have nightmares if she slept at all. Kevin had withdrawn into a morose silence—disappointed, Macimer guessed, in his father's lack of heroics.

As for Macimer himself, he was . . . curious.

They were not ordinary hoodlums, he thought.

It was not a rationalization for his carelessness in being so easily taken hostage, risking his family's lives. There was just something not quite right about the whole operation. Smoothly professional in some ways, amateurish in others—like wasting too much time in the house when they had had only two youngsters to contend with, instead of striking fast, taking what they could find and getting out. And the insistence that there had to be a safe, when they had had time to assure themselves there was none.

They had been role playing, Macimer thought. The swaggering and shouting had been in character, the threats, the leering stares at Linda's maturing beauty or Jan's exposed breast. But even the leering had been perfunctory. It was as if the invaders had been trying to frighten their victims, but that was all.

So what were they really after?

3

At forty-two Paul Macimer was young to be the Special-Agent-in-Charge of over three hundred agents in one of the largest field offices in the Bureau. Less than two years ago he had been with the Criminal Investigative Division at FBI Headquarters, directing the Internal Security Branch, whose special responsibilities included sedition and sabotage, civil unrest and violence, and the actions of revolutionary groups against the United States. He had felt stifled in his job.

On September 7, 1982, a bomb exploded in the office of Carey McWilliams, SAC of the Washington Field Office, which was then located on Half Street in the southwest part of the District. The office door was blown thirty feet across the outer offices. Glass shattered everywhere. The ceiling collapsed directly over McWilliams' office, a picture window exploded, and a five-foot section of brick wall was blown onto the street below. The building itself was so severely stressed that it had to be abandoned. It seemed miraculous that the bomb had been so strategically planted that only McWilliams was killed in the blast.

Macimer had headed up the special investigation of the bombing. A number of radical groups, including the Eagles of the Palestinian Revolution, had claimed credit for the incident, but six months of intensive investigation had produced no proof of responsibility. The case remained open. The FBI has a tradition that an unsolved case is never closed, and that was especially true of the McWilliams bombing, the first case in FBI history in which a Special-Agent-in-Charge was murdered.

Macimer had worked on the bombing investigation out of improvised headquarters for the Washington Field Office found by the General Services Administration in a federal office building on C Street, not far from the FBI Identification Building and within a few blocks of the U.S. Capitol. Nearly two years later the WFO still occupied those "temporary" facilities.

After six months Macimer was unexpectedly named Special-Agent-in-Charge of the office, succeeding McWilliams. The assignment elated him. Like most middle- and upper-level people at Headquarters, he was seldom in the field while with the Investigative Division. His job there was to approve or disapprove investigations initiated in the field, to order an investigation or action by a particular office in specific circumstances, to coordinate leads that came in from various offices, and to pass important questions on up the chain of command. It was a position with a great deal of responsibility, and Macimer had chafed in it. He had spent most of his career in the field. What he had at FBI Headquarters, in spite of its prestige, was a desk job.

Then, by a twist of fate, he had got what he really wanted, the goal of any ambitious Special Agent of the FBI. He had become the SAC of one of the busiest and most sensitive field offices in the country.

The case load of the WFO differed from those in most field offices. There was a heavier than normal concentration on security threats, terrorism and espionage. There were highly sensitive special inquiries for congressional committees and other government agencies, and for the White House, including background investigations of presidential appointees. There were investigations under the aegis of the White Collar Crime Task Force, with special attention to bribery and corruption in the federal government. For all that, the office was understaffed, a complaint heard at most field offices under the President's stringent budget.

And in its temporary quarters, WFO was cramped for space. Macimer's own office was small by normal SAC standards. Jerry Russell, the Assistant Special-Agent-in-Charge, worked out of an even smaller office. There were the usual large squad rooms, supervisors' cubicles, a large area for the staff of clerks and stenographers, the highly secure cable room, a separate room for the

computer terminal linked up with the NCIC and other law enforcement networks, a "radio room" where wiretaps and bugs
were monitored and a real radio communications room, and an interview room—the latter with a door opening off the outer corridor
and close to the elevator so that anyone brought in for questioning
did not see the rest of the offices. There was also a reception area
with the usual bulletin board displaying various notices and
posters, including the "10 Most Wanted" display with pictures. It
was an active, overcrowded office with, Macimer liked to believe,
good spirit and morale. He didn't attribute that fact to his own
leadership, as some did, but to the feeling in the Washington Field
Office of participating in important matters, working close to the
heart of the nation's government, responsible for preventing
threats that would affect the entire country and its people.

On Monday morning Macimer was briefed as usual by the
ASAC on important cases in progress. Heading the list was an air-
plane hijacking in Miami early that morning. "The plane's on the
ground now and Callahan's down there." Callahan was everyone's
idea of a genial Irish uncle. White-haired, dapper and sincere, he
had a marvelous knack for listening and conveying sympathetic
understanding. He could have a stranger spilling out his life story
two minutes after meeting him. He was the head of the FBI's national hostage unit, which included at least two trained hostage
negotiators at each of the FBI's sixty field offices. In between
hijackings and major terrorist incidents, Callahan taught at the
FBI Academy in Quantico.

"Where's the hijacker from?" It was the key question for WFO.
If the hijacker came from the Washington area, Callahan might
want immediate backgrounding here. That would mean a team of
agents to interview friends, relatives and associates to put together
a psychological profile that would help a negotiator.

"He's Cuban, been living in Miami. Says he wants to leave the
country but he also wants money."

"Okay, have our hostage team on standby. You know what
happens when you have one hijacking."

"Yeah. Imitators."

"What else do we have?"

A long-range scam operation looking into suspicion of bribery
in government construction projects involving GSA was not close
to breaking. A major arson case had been turned over to the U.S.

Attorney for prosecution. Jerry Russell left several other files of developing cases with Macimer, along with a stack of 5×8 cards synopsizing less important cases. These were provided by the field supervisors in the office—the sergeants of the organization, each of whom directed a squad of from fifteen to twenty agents.

At nine-thirty Macimer had a conference with Joseph Taliaferro, the agent spearheading an investigation into the passing of secret documents from the Energy Research and Development Administration to a suspected foreign agent. The investigation had narrowed down to a half-dozen clerks of ERDA known to have access to the documents. All six were under surveillance. One of them, Taliaferro said, had lost the surveillance on two different occasions.

"The first time was a week ago Friday when he ran a light. Our people couldn't jump the red light without revealing themselves. We had three cars playing leapfrog with him this past Friday night. Two of them got hung up behind him when he made a left turn at the last second just before another light change. Either he got lucky twice in a row or he knew what he was doing. Our third team stayed with him—they were out ahead of him—until he got onto the George Washington Parkway heading south. He went by our car at an estimated seventy-five miles an hour. There was no way for our agents to go after him without being burned."

Macimer got out a map of Washington, D.C., and environs. It covered the entire area within the 495 Beltline. Taliaferro pointed out the intersections where the clerk had lost his tail, each time by timing a light. He had used two different bridges to cross the Potomac, Taliaferro pointed out, but both times he had ended up on the Parkway heading toward Alexandria. And Washington National Airport, Macimer thought. Some of those documents had shown up in New York.

"What do you think of him?" Macimer asked.

"Maybe I could buy accidental red lights," Taliaferro said. "Some guys just like to run lights, they hate to wait. But I can't swallow the Richard Petty routine on top of those two lights. I'd say he's our man."

"Did you check the airport Friday night?"

Taliaferro flushed. "No, sir."

Macimer said nothing. He didn't need to. Some of the agents in the office said the boss's "silent treatment" was a lot more effective than scorn or shouting. "Keep him under light surveillance this week. Let's shoot the works Friday night. We'll use a dozen cars if we have to. If he goes down George Washington Parkway all the way, we're in luck. There aren't many places he can make left turns once he's moving down that way alongside the river. We'll station a car at every major intersection he might use. And let's get the agents at the airport in on this. See if your boy—what's his name? Molter?—see if he's been taking the Eastern Airlines shuttle to New York. Go back a couple months at least."

"Friday nights?"

"Every night."

Macimer studied the map. The clerk might be going to the airport or on south to Alexandria. He could be getting off somewhere en route to take a different direction, or he could double back. Every possibility had to be accounted for, with radio cars monitoring the clerk's route. If a beeper could be attached to his car, that would make it a hell of a lot easier to track him. Even if he were lost, it would be possible to pick up the signal again from the beeper unit without too much loss of time.

"Shoot for Friday night," he repeated. "We'll track him as far as we can. But I don't want him to know we're onto him, so we'll risk letting him get away from us if he can. But each time he does it we're going to stay with him a little longer. Sooner or later he'll take us to his drop—or to the person he's meeting."

They discussed the plan for Friday night a few minutes longer before Taliaferro left the office. Willa Cunningham, Macimer's secretary, brought him a mug of hot coffee. He had a few minutes to think. A Sunday visit to the local sheriff's office to look at mug shots had been unproductive, but Macimer remained curious about the strange actions of the trio of robbers who had invaded his home. He wondered if it was worth sending a fingerprint team out to the house. The three had worn gloves—unusual in itself for break-and-enter thieves—but they might have made a mistake somewhere. He wondered if Xavier wore gloves when he took his girl to bed.

Xavier. Without photo identification or fingerprints, the single name was all Macimer had to go on. A name search in the huge General Index of the Records Management Division at Headquarters was impossible with only a given name, no numerical identifier to go with it.

The Internal Security Branch had its own Name Index, however, as Macimer knew well from his own assignment with the Branch. It was drawn from the files covering the activities of dissident and revolutionary groups, including a variety of Spanish-American, Puerto Rican and Cuban activists. And the WFO had its own files. It meant a manual search, pulling out every Xavier under, say, twenty years of age. A tedious job but worth trying.

With a grin Macimer called Pat Garvey into his office. A second office agent at twenty-eight, Garvey was one of Macimer's favorites, which meant he was harder on Garvey than on most. "When you're through solving the Orioles' pitching problems," he said, "there's a little project you can handle for me."

Garvey, he thought afterward, had done a fairly decent job of hiding his dismay.

Shortly after ten o'clock, when Macimer had nearly finished a quick review of the stack of 5×8 cards Jerry Russell had left with him, the intercom buzzed. "You've got a call on line five," Willa Cunningham told him. "It's from Headquarters."

Macimer punched line five. "Paul?" a crisp voice said in his ear. "This is Russ Halbig."

Macimer was immediately alert. Halbig was an Executive Assistant Director of the Bureau, one of the Director's three top assistants. At one time a Hoover favorite, Halbig had walked a very thin line since the old man's death. There had been pressure on succeeding Directors to ease out the "Hoover men." But Halbig had never been a highly visible member of Hoover's inner circle and he was also very nimble on his feet. During Macimer's early years with the Bureau he had known Halbig well. They had gone through the Academy together, graduating in the same class. They had both worked for a time in the Omaha office and again, during a long and dangerous summer in the mid-sixties, Halbig, Macimer and Gordon Ruhle had worked out of the same office on a civil rights assignment in Mississippi. Macimer remembered something Ruhle had remarked about their colleague: "Don't ever worry about Russ. He can dodge the raindrops as good as anyone I ever knew. Hell, he could walk through a cloudburst and come out without getting wet."

"Is everything all right at home, Paul? I heard about Saturday night."

"Sure. Just a little excitement for a while, that's all. Chip is sorry he missed the fun." Macimer was not surprised that Halbig knew about the robbery. Any such incident involving a Special Agent would be carefully examined.

"How's Jan taking it? Shook up, I suppose." Halbig often had a way of answering his own questions, as if he were too impatient to wait for a reply.

"She can handle it. She's more worried about Linda than anything else. They were rough on her."

"I can see why Jan would be worried. How old is Linda now? Seventeen?"

"That's right." Trust Halbig to have verified her age.

"You'd think the Meadows was far enough out of the jungle to escape that sort of thing, but . . . there aren't any safe places anymore, are there?" The courtesies out of the way, Halbig's tone became more businesslike. "Something's come up, Paul, about those files you brought in a week ago. I have a meeting with the Director within the hour. I may be getting back to you."

"I'll be here," Macimer said, surprised.

"Good. And listen, Paul, be sure to tell Jan we're all sorry this thing happened at home. We really must get together soon. Erika was saying just the other day, we never see you and Jan anymore. We shouldn't let that happen."

When Halbig rang off Macimer wondered about the real purpose of his call. He took the vague suggestion about getting together as politeness. It was true that he and Jan, the Ruhles and the Halbigs had once been frequent companions—more so when Halbig had been married to his first wife, Elaine. But that had been many years ago, before different assignments took the three men in separate directions, and before Halbig's spectacular rise in the Bureau's hierarchy.

Macimer frowned. Had the investigator's instinct which had been nagging at him the past week over the San Timoteo files been sound after all?

What had come up that might involve him?

4

Those who had worked for and with Russell Lewis Halbig during his twenty years with the Federal Bureau of Investigation were of one mind in the opinion that he had never committed an impulsive act in his life. That made him the perfect bureaucrat at "the seat of government," Hoover's favorite term for FBI Headquarters. If there was one thing that characterized any action taken at Headquarters, it was caution. No directive initiated by a desk supervisor ever went out to a field office without bearing at least a dozen initials approving the action. And it was not approved without minute and painstaking consideration of every possible ramification, including concern for the Bureau's image and possible embarrassment.

His colleagues were wrong. Halbig had made one impetuous decision in his life, risking J. Edgar Hoover's wrath. Halbig divorced his wife, the mother of his three children, with the full intention of remarrying as soon as possible, taking as his new wife a much younger woman, the beautiful blond daughter of a Minnesota congressman who was not running for re-election. Halbig simply could not face the thought of Erika Lindstrom going back to Minnesota and out of his life.

As it happened, Hoover was preoccupied with more serious matters inside and outside the Bureau at the time. Halbig was not certain that Hoover had ever heard about his divorce, an action which, in the old man's prime, would have jeopardized a Special Agent's future with the Bureau. Halbig married Erika two months after Hoover's death. He had regretted his headlong behavior ever since. He was less clearly aware that for the next twelve years he had been punishing his much younger wife for his indiscretion.

Halbig's telephone buzzed. The light blinked on line seven—the private circuit connecting the Bureau's hierarchy with each other, bypassing secretaries and go-betweens. Henry Szymanski was on the line. Szymanski was the Executive Assistant Director in charge of the Identification Division. As such he presided over the largest and most used collection of records in the Bureau—and the one that, more than any other, had given the FBI its early reputation for being able to perform miracles in identifying criminals. No other law enforcement organization in the world could equal Ident's 200 million fingerprint records. Most had been computerized in recent years, including some 25 million in the Master Criminal File and twice that many in the Civil Fingerprint File. Successful automation of the fingerprint identification system had been Szymanski's ticket to the top job in the division, a job that also made him responsible for the Training Division and the FBI Laboratory.

With all that, Szymanski was surprisingly unambitious. His rise had been a kind of accident, a result of seniority, others retiring, and his skill as a technician during a crucial period of conversion. He was uneasy with the nuances of power politics. His attitude toward Halbig was almost deferential, reflecting an awareness that Administration had traditionally carried more clout among the Bureau's higher echelon.

"I was just going to go upstairs," Szymanski said.

"I'll see you there in about five minutes, Henry."

"Do you have anything on the slate this morning?"

"Yes, I do."

"Oh?" Szymanski was curious. "Anything to do with those lab reports?"

"Yes, it does." Halbig hesitated. "You'll have to wait, Henry. I've sent a memo to the Director on it. I'm not sure how far he'll want to open this one up."

"Sure, I understand," Szymanski said quickly. He sounded aggrieved. He was going to have to smooth off some of those rough edges, Halbig thought. If he was going to play hard ball, he had to know when to swing and when to take a pitch. "I'll see you there."

Halbig's thoughts drifted briefly back to his marriage, wondering if it had been as disappointing for Erika, after all, as it had been for him . . .

He had been ridiculously infatuated with her. He remembered the way his hands shook the first time he was alone with her. He had had trouble unbuttoning buttons, his fingers clumsy as sausages. Obsessed. He should have known—Elaine, with her caustic tongue, had told him as much—that any such sick passion would either destroy him or burn itself out, like any fever. When it did abate, as predicted, he found himself hated by his former wife, estranged from his children and living with a beautiful child-wife with whom he had little communication.

And for a Bureau man as ambitious as Halbig was, a second divorce was unthinkable. The first had been damning enough . . .

Halbig shook off the distraction, his thoughts instantly returning to the memo he had sent to Landers, flagged urgent.

This *was* hard ball. It would be interesting to see how Landers reacted.

John L. Landers was a veteran field man of the Bureau, former SAC in New York, Chicago and San Francisco. His appointment as Acting Director of the FBI by the President had been popular with agents in the field, less popular with some of the entrenched hierarchy at Headquarters—men who, like Halbig, had been bypassed when Landers was jumped over them.

So far Landers had moved slowly. Many felt that he had accepted the President's appointment reluctantly, that he would have preferred to serve out his time with the Bureau as an SAC. He had not disturbed the organizational structure at the top, which included the three Executive Assistant Directors overseeing the Bureau's eleven divisions. His predecessor, William Webster, had left the post of Associate Director, number two man in the Bureau, vacant. Webster preferred tighter control of day-to-day operations himself. "The director of the FBI should direct," he had once said. Halbig, Szymanski and James Caughey, the third Executive Assistant Director, in charge of the sensitive Intelligence and Investigation Divisions, were all carry-overs from the previous administration. But Landers had given hints that he planned to fill the Associate Director's slot with a man of his own choice.

Halbig wanted to be that man.

At the least.

But Landers obviously would not make any moves until he himself was confirmed by the Senate in forthcoming hearings. *If* he was confirmed.

Halbig held the thought—cautiously, tentatively. Landers was a blunt, outspoken man. He had already ruffled a few senatorial feathers. Among those with reservations about him was the chairman of the Senate Select Committee on Intelligence, Charles Sederholm, a man for whom Russell Halbig had been able to do a few favors in the past.

Sederholm had faced a tough, close contest in his last re-election campaign in California. Halbig had been able to provide him with some little-known information about his Democratic opponent. Nothing criminal but enough to raise doubts in the minds of voters. Sederholm had won big—so big that his easy victory had thrust him into the forefront of his party's candidates for this year's presidential nomination, thrown wide open by the President's decision not to seek a second term. If he repeated his earlier triumph in California's primary tomorrow . . .

Sederholm was a professional politician. Such men did not forget a favor.

Halbig glanced at his watch. Another minute. Landers liked people to be on time for a meeting. He didn't like them early any more than he tolerated lateness.

Landers was certain to bring up Halbig's memo about the Brea file. The missing file could have far-reaching implications for Landers personally . . . and for Halbig.

Point one: Landers had been in charge of the task force assigned to hunt down the People's Revolutionary Committee when the terrorists ran amok that summer in California. And in spite of some criticism of the violent end of that hunt, Landers had unquestionably benefited from it. It had thrust him into the national spotlight. Almost certainly it had influenced the President, a hardliner when it came to crime, in his decision to appoint Landers as Acting Director. But a belated revelation of improprieties by the FBI—acting under Landers' direction with or without his direct knowledge—would damage him. And if he had participated in a cover-up, he would be finished.

Point two: Senator Sederholm would relish inside knowledge of the Brea affair, a juicy plum to pull out during the hearings coming up in two weeks. The consideration by the Senate committee of John L. Landers' confirmation would begin with Sederholm fresh from his almost certain California victory, looking ahead to the Republican convention a month away, smelling blood as well as roses.

Point three: There was no way the file would hurt Russ Halbig, no matter what an investigation turned up. If Landers were seriously compromised, there was little doubt that Senator Sederholm would act to block his appointment. The way would be clear for someone else to become Director. On the other hand, if Landers managed to emerge unscathed, he would surely react favorably to Halbig's action in bringing the Brea file to his attention. Landers might even benefit from exposing the affair, and the result could hardly fail to enhance Halbig's position. Landers was looking for someone he could rely on as his number two, someone with administrative know-how, an Associate Director he could trust . . .

Halbig backed up, going quickly over his scenario, searching for signs of danger to himself. He found none. No matter which way the investigation went, he stood to gain.

With a chance—a real chance—to find himself on a fast horse along the rail, with all the other favorites dropping back, one by one.

He liked the image, made a mental note of it as he rose and left his office, walking along the quiet corridor toward the Director's conference room.

He didn't have to take the elevator. Halbig had already made it to the seventh floor. The Director's suite of offices was only a short walk along the corridor.

John L. Landers was a solidly built man who had always had to fight his weight to meet rigid FBI standards. Everything about him was square—including his thinking, the syndicated columnist Oliver Packard had written—from his square-jawed, heavy features to his deep, broad chest. The overall impression was of someone immovable as a big rock, and it had been suggested that this quality was the reason the President had selected him to be the Director of the FBI.

He was also said to be humorless, tough, blunt-spoken, intolerant of mistakes. Yet the agents who had served under him in three different major field offices where he had been Special-

Agent-in-Charge were, almost to a man, his most vocal admirers.

Like his predecessor, William Webster, Landers didn't think much of doing things by committee. Webster had downgraded the top echelon's twice-weekly executive conferences, which he had found unproductive, instead giving more authority to his three Executive Assistant Directors. The executive conferences were still held, but less often, chaired usually by one of the Executive Assistant Directors. Landers had adopted Webster's practice of working principally through his three key assistants. "You get fifteen people in one room, every one of them with an ax to grind, all you get is conversation," Landers had said. "With three or four people you can get down to cases."

At this morning's meeting with his three top aides Landers quickly dispensed with a number of policy matters and cases in progress. So many matters came to his desk that he had insisted on receiving only brief memos and summary teletypes, supplemented by more extensive reports only on cases of special importance. One of the latter, an ongoing investigation by the White Collar Crime Task Force unit attached to the Washington Field Office, was reported on in detail by James Caughey, quoting from a report received from the WFO. The investigation was sensitive because it involved both high-level personnel in the General Services Administration and members of Congress. Of more immediate concern was an airline hijacking currently in progress in Miami, where the Delta Airlines plane was being held on the ground.

"Who's down there?" Landers asked.

"Callahan. He has the Miami hostage unit and a SWAT team. The hijacker is a loner, about nineteen, a couple of minor arrests. Callahan already has most of the background, but he's taking it slow, letting the kid calm down."

Landers nodded in satisfaction. Callahan was the best. He had been Landers' number two man during the PRC Task Force operations, the designated chief negotiator. If only Callahan had been there in San Timoteo the day the shooting started, Landers had often thought, if he had had a chance to talk to those amateur revolutionaries, it might all have ended differently. . . .

"Good," Landers said. "The longer it goes, the better our chances. I want reports every half hour until it's over."

"Yes, sir."

When the rest of the morning's business had been discussed, Landers paused, picking up a memo from a stack on the long table in the small conference room. "This one I don't like," he said. It was the memo from Halbig concerning the missing Brea file. "According to this, Halbig, you're raising the possibility that someone stole a sensitive file—and that someone could have been an FBI man."

"It's only one possibility," Halbig said carefully.

"A lousy one," Landers growled. "Go ahead, run through it. I want the others to hear the details."

Halbig was ready for the demand. Landers liked brief, organized reports. Halbig recalled the theft of an FBI vehicle ten days before. It appeared at the time that the thief had not specifically been after FBI documents—there was a good chance that he didn't know he was stealing an FBI car. Nevertheless, he had opened one box of documents that were in the trunk of the car. That box as well as the others had been gone over minutely. All of the files had come from the San Timoteo RA's office, which had been shut down in April, two months after the death of the Resident Agent, Vernon Lippert.

"All of the files appear to be intact," Halbig said, "except one. That folder is empty. It's identified as the Brea file. Its contents are unknown."

"What about our dupes?" Caughey asked.

"There are no duplicates. That was one of the first things that caught my attention. A copy of every piece of paper generated in any investigation is supposed to come to Headquarters, of course. Whatever his motive, Lippert did not send copies to the Sacramento Field Office, so we received none." Halbig paused. "Lippert was carrying out the investigation without approval."

"There are no records at all?" Landers asked.

"We have some." Halbig had been saving this information for the meeting. "Lippert did request some lab work. Henry was very helpful in running those reports down." Halbig nodded toward Szymanski. "One of Lippert's lab reports concerned the presence of gunpowder residue on an old, rusty residential window screen. The report was positive. Another report covered voiceprint analysis of two separate tape recordings. The first recording was identified as a conversation between an agent from the San Francisco Field Office and an informant named Walter Schumaker,

dated June 10, 1980. The second tape was of an anonymous telephone call to the Sacramento office on August 27, 1981 . . . the
day before the PRC massacre in San Timoteo. Voiceprint analysis
confirmed that Schumaker made both calls. In the second one he
used the code name Brea for an FBI agent to whom he wanted to
report."

"Who was Brea?" the Director broke in sharply.

"We have no record of any agent using such a code name."

"What about the agent who was running Schumaker earlier?"

"There were two of them. Special Agents Charles Reese and
Victor Pryor. Reese is still in San Francisco, Pryor has left the
Bureau. Both have been contacted. Neither man knows anything
about the second phone call or the Brea code name."

"You'll check that."

"Of course."

There was a momentary silence. Caughey said, "It sounds like a
private code between an agent and his informant."

"That's my assumption, too," Halbig said.

"I want to hear those tapes," Landers said. "Anything else?
Your memo mentions a handwriting comparison."

"I was coming to that. Lippert asked the Handwriting Analysis
Unit for a comparison of two handwriting samples. The first was
of Walter Schumaker's known origin, a letter to the two agents
who were using him in 1979 and 1980 in Berkeley. The second
sample was on the rental deposit for the house where the PRC
were hiding out in San Timoteo. They were identical."

There was a stunned silence this time. It lasted a full ten seconds. The three Executive Assistant Directors grouped around the
long mahogany table exchanged glances. Landers scowled at them.
"What do we have?" he asked finally. "Szymanski?"

"It appears that Lippert was investigating something about the
PRC disaster. And those reports indicate that an FBI informant
was inside the group. That wasn't known before."

"No, it wasn't," Landers said tersely. He had been in command
of the task force that had spent a whole summer of frustration trying to catch the elusive band of terrorists. The possibility that an
FBI informant—and the agent to whom he was reporting—had
known all along where the People's Revolutionary Committee
were hiding brought a dark flush of anger to his stolid features.
"I'd damned well like to know why."

He glanced at Caughey. "You see it the same way, Caughey?"

"Yes, Director." Caughey was visibly disturbed by what he had heard. "What it means is, the agent who called himself Brea had inside knowledge he kept to himself. But it brings up another question: What happened to Schumaker?"

The four men exchanged glances. They were all remembering the massive explosion that brought an end to the PRC.

Landers' expression was grim. Russ Halbig found that his pulse had quickened. Now Landers had no choice, he thought. The Director's next words confirmed his judgment.

"I want that missing file found. I want Schumaker found—if he's alive. I want Brea identified." Landers' brown eyes speared Halbig. "You're assuming the man who stole the FBI vehicle also took the file?"

"No, sir."

"Why not?" Sharply.

"The nature of the file and . . . the nature of the theft. It couldn't have been premeditated. Agent Stearns's decision to stop at that particular store at that hour that night was pure happenstance—that he would have stopped at all could not have been anticipated. My assumption is that this was a random auto theft, spur-of-the-moment, amateurish. That's also the opinion of the two agents in the Stolen Vehicle Unit at the Washington Field Office who are investigating. I have copies of their initial reports if you'd like to see them. The thief's prints are all over the car but there's nothing on record in Ident. Either he has no criminal record, which corroborates the amateur theory, or any record he has was as a juvenile and his records are frozen."

"But his prints are on the Brea folder?"

"Yes, sir, on that and a number of other files. But he had no way of knowing the Brea file was important. What I cannot explain, Director, is why he would take *that particular file*."

Landers grunted, the expression noncommittal. "You have to allow for chance sometimes," he said reflectively. "The random auto theft, the file opened at random, the random witness . . ."

"Unfortunately we have none of those."

Landers didn't smile and Halbig regretted the weak attempt at humor. "Your memo recommends a special investigation with the cooperation of the OPR."

Halbig nodded. The Office of Professional Responsibility, created in the aftermath of the Watergate scandals, came under Halbig's direction as part of the Inspection and Planning Division. The OPR was charged with responsibility for investigating any accusations of misconduct or impropriety by an FBI agent or agents.

"The OPR should receive complete reports, of course. And the Attorney General's OPR should also be kept informed. But I think we should put someone in charge of the field investigation of the Brea file who is familiar with that situation and with terrorist activities generally."

"You have someone in mind?"

"The man I'm thinking of headed up Jim's Internal Security Branch before his present assignment." Halbig smiled at James Caughey, who returned a frown. "He also worked under you, Director, as part of the PRC Task Force. And he's the man who recovered those stolen files ten days ago. I'm sure you remember him"—Landers had a legendary reputation for his photographic memory of names and faces—"the SAC of the Washington Field Office, Paul Macimer."

"Do you have any other reason for suggesting Macimer?" Was there something suspicious in the question? In Landers' tone?

"Yes, sir, I do. There's a possibility that Macimer himself stole the contents of that file."

There was another shocked stillness in the room. Halbig fancied that it was reflected even in the eyes of the three men whose portraits were mounted side by side on one walnut-paneled wall— J. Edgar Hoover, Clarence M. Kelley and William H. Webster. L. Patrick Gray, who had resigned in disgrace before his appointment as Acting Director was confirmed, and William Ruchelshaus, who had served as Acting Director for only seventy-five days in 1973, were not present on the wall.

James Caughey exploded. "That's cow flop!" His circumlocutions for strong four-letter words were Bureau legend. "I know Macimer. He wouldn't do it."

"I don't say he did," Halbig answered calmly. "I merely pointed out the possibility. After all, he did have possession of those stolen files before they reached Headquarters—and no one else other than the car thief did. Moreover, he reported that he had not examined or disturbed any of the files. Yet his thumbprint was found on one edge of the Brea file—*and on no other file.*" Halbig let the significance of that finding sink in before he added,

"Macimer was also part of the PRC Task Force in California at the time Brea was there."

"So were about two hundred other agents, including myself," Landers said. "If you think there's any chance he might have taken the file, for whatever reason, why suggest putting him in charge of investigating its disappearance?"

"If he's part of a cover-up, he'll try to sabotage the investigation. If not, he's an excellent choice for getting to the bottom of this affair. Either way, we get our answer."

Landers scowled, weighing the recommendation. It was unorthodox, certainly, but Landers had been known to look with favor on unorthodox methods in the field when he was an SAC—providing they worked. Halbig had gambled that the idea would appeal to a man with a reputation as both a pragmatist and, when warranted, a gambler. And there was also the possibility that Landers might have private reasons for accepting the proposal. . . .

"All right," the Director of the FBI said. "Put Macimer on it. Make this a 'Special.' But I want it under wraps. I don't want to go public on this until we know what we have to deal with. Is that clear?"

Halbig nodded, concealing his satisfaction.

Landers' hard gaze pressed against him, as if he were trying to look inside Halbig's head to see what he might find there. He said, "And you watch Macimer."

Five minutes after the conclusion of the meeting of the Executive Assistant Directors and the Director, Paul Macimer received a short phone call from his former boss in the Investigative Division. "You're being given a special investigation," Jim Caughey said. "You'll be hearing from Russ Halbig on it anytime now, if you haven't already."

"He called earlier, said there might be something." Macimer wondered why Caughey was telling him. "Big?"

"Yeah. And it could be trouble. Watch your step."

"How so?"

"There could be more to this than meets the eye."

"Any suggestions?" Macimer didn't like the thought that Caughey might be asking him to soft-pedal an investigation.

"The same one I've always given you and every other agent.

Play it straight, right down the line. Just keep your eyes open. You don't want to be blind-sided."

Macimer smiled. "I'll try to stay awake. And thanks, Jim."

"I never talked to you."

Afterward, Macimer thought about the enigmatic implications of Caughey's comment.

Who might want to blind-side him? And why?

5

The J. Edgar Hoover FBI Building sits, massive and uncompromising, on the north side of Pennsylvania Avenue between 9th and 10th streets, occupying a large city block. The exterior of the building seems forbidding and closed, and the upper levels protrude over the floors below like a scowl. But the building, completed in 1975 at a cost of $126 million, is less massive and closed than it appears, for the interior opens onto a huge court. At ground level the courtyard is accessible from the street, and nearby office workers often bring their lunches to sit in the sun and eat within sight and sound of the fountain, looking up at the windows of Bureau offices.

Paul Macimer did not even glance at the building itself as he turned off 9th Street down the ramp to the basement garage. Even when he had been working at Headquarters he had thought little about the building's architectural appeal or lack of it. He remained impressed with its functional efficiency, the sophisticated equipment, the laboratories and data banks housed behind the thick walls.

The call from Halbig's secretary had come just as Macimer returned from an abbreviated lunch hour. "Mr. Halbig would like to see you in his office, Mr. Macimer. Would two o'clock be convenient?" The question was rhetorical.

The secretary was waiting for him when he arrived at two. She indicated that he should go right in. A handsome, leggy blonde with a face whose bones belonged on a *Vogue* cover, she reminded Macimer of Halbig's wife Erika. Careful, conservative Russ was capable of surprises.

The office was large, the carpet thick, the paneling a rich dark walnut. There was even a large window offering a view of the inner courtyard. Framed portraits of Hoover, Kelley and Webster were centered on the wall behind Halbig's huge walnut desk. John L. Landers hadn't made it yet, Macimer noted. American and FBI flags were planted in opposite corners of the wall behind the desk.

"Paul! Good to see you. You've had lunch, of course." He didn't wait for an answer. "How about some coffee? I have some fresh brewing. Let me have Helen bring us a cup." Without waiting for a response he signaled his secretary.

After the sleek young woman had brought the coffee and left, having offered a provocative display of shapely legs and swiveling hips, Halbig raised his cup as if in a toast. "Old times, eh, Paul? Those were the best."

Macimer wondered if Halbig really thought that. The Executive Assistant Director set his cup down, leaned back and smiled across the broad expanse of thick glass over polished walnut. He looked in that moment like any successful, satisfied and slightly smug business executive. His gray suit was a custom-tailored tropical worsted, his shirt white-on-white, his tie by Countess Mara. The unfinished image had been there twenty years ago, Macimer decided, waiting for this fulfillment. It seemed no accident that Halbig had served less than five years in the field before being permanently assigned to Headquarters. He had been born for the bureaucracy. A great many field agents believed that there were too many in FBI Headquarters like Halbig, men who had been so long away from the real work of the street agent that they were making decisions without hard personal knowledge of their implications.

Russell Halbig was a neat, tidy man. In spite of the volume of paper that must cross his desk each day, it was tidy. Of average height but comparatively slender, he had small, neat features, and the slim straight nose, brown eyes set close together, narrow face and ears close to the skull combined to reinforce the impression of a neat, precise and careful man.

"We have a problem, Paul," Halbig said abruptly. "The Director has made this one a 'Special.' You know what that means. It means he wants it wrapped up yesterday." From a black plastic case Halbig extracted an empty manila file folder and held it up.

Macimer stared at it, startled as he recognized the name on the tab. "Recognize this, Paul?"

"It was in that box of stolen files I brought in ten days ago, the open one. I remember the name. It was empty."

"You did examine it, then? I'd understood you reported that you hadn't touched the documents."

Macimer frowned, puzzled. "I didn't examine it. It was raining, I wanted to close the lid of the carton, and that folder was sticking up a little. I pushed it down, that's all."

"I see . . . there are water marks on the file." Halbig appeared to drop the question. "Did it occur to you to wonder what an empty file was doing in that box of documents shipped to Headquarters? I'm sure it did."

"Yes, it did," Macimer admitted.

"It bothered me, too, when it came to my attention. I've looked into it and brought what I found to the Director's notice." Briefly Halbig went over the details he had presented to Landers that morning, citing the lab reports Vernon Lippert had asked for. "The Director agrees with me that the documents missing from this Brea file must be found as an urgent priority."

"The kid who stole the car could have taken them," Macimer said thoughtfully.

"You thought that unlikely at the time of recovery," Halbig pointed out. "I still do. It's possible, of course, and that avenue should be vigorously pursued. But it seems a bit too fortuitous that a random auto thief should steal that particular file. The Brea file appears to be the only one in all four cartons of documents that was at all unusual or sensitive."

Fortuitous indeed, Macimer thought.

"I suggested to the Director that you be named to head up the investigation of the Brea file," Halbig said. "He agreed. You're one of our most experienced people in dealing with terrorist activities—and, of course, you were part of the PRC Task Force, so you're familiar with the background and circumstances Lippert was digging into." Halbig rubbed his nose pensively. "Did you know Vernon Lippert? Yes, you must have."

Macimer was still trying to absorb the implications of the missing Brea file. "Not well, but we met a few times."

"He died in a boating accident last February. I'm sure you heard. Apparently he had been conducting an unauthorized investigation of the whole PRC affair up until his death. Why he made a secret of it, and what he found, we don't know, except for the reports I've mentioned. We want to know as quickly as possible. Set up your own team—you can have anyone you want, within reason, of course. You'll have to work out of your own office, I'm afraid; you have no idea how short of space we are here. The key to this one, Paul, is resourcefulness—quality, not quantity. We can't use big manpower because we don't want this investigation to be highly visible until we know what's involved." Halbig paused, and there was a glint in his eyes that Macimer couldn't read. "Report directly to me. The Director will want to be right on top of this. I'm sure you're aware that his confirmation hearings come up before the Senate in two weeks."

For the first time Macimer had a feeling of uneasiness about his assignment. He remembered Jim Caughey's warning: *It could be trouble. Watch your step.* Circumspect as he had been, Caughey had stuck his neck out making that phone call.

Trouble for whom? Macimer wondered.

What were the contents of the Brea file? And why had Vernon Lippert concealed them?

"The Director is listening to those two tape recordings this afternoon," Russ Halbig told him. "Copies and transcripts will be on your desk in the morning. I suggest you take a look at our files on the People's Revolutionary Committee to refresh your own memory. And," he added, "to see if you can find what set Vernon Lippert off."

FBI files in the Records Management Division occupied nearly three complete floors of the FBI Building. There were more than 60 million cards in the General Index, for which the Automated Records Management System—called ARMS—provided automated index searching and name checks. The investigative files themselves numbered more than 7 million, and many of these were massive, containing thousands of forms and documents. Every piece of paper, or serial, in any Headquarters file was numbered, and there was a corresponding index card with an abstract of its contents. It was said that someone went to a file and consulted a record more than 60,000 times a day.

Not that anyone—even a Special Agent—was free to roam the seemingly endless corridors of file cabinets. Anyone doing so without specific authorization would be stopped and questioned. In the old days, Macimer remembered, messengers had been used to retrieve requested files or documents. Now there was a speedier telelift system with little plastic cars running along overhead rails, stopping at a network of 72 stations to drop off files and mail, like the dump cars of a miniature railroad set. Macimer wondered if a model-train hobbyist had designed the system.

The file on the PRC encompassed a number of folders, each several inches thick. Macimer signed for the material and left the building.

"One squad room," Macimer said. "Desks and phones for two dozen agents to start. I don't want them sitting around tomorrow waiting for a phone."

"Gotcha."

"I'll need a desk man on this, Jerry. Someone just to handle the paper work. I know we're short-handed right now, but—" Macimer thought suddenly of Harrison Stearns. The personnel report from the SRA at Dulles had gone beyond the customary "Excellent" rating to say that Stearns was dependable, good at detail, young enough to make mistakes but never the same one twice. "Is Stearns still on the nut box?"

Jerry Russell smiled faintly. "Your instructions were: 'Until further orders.'"

The nut box was an index of crank callers and doomsayers. The agent assigned to the box on night duty was stuck with answering all of the calls. The onerous duty was generally rotated among the new or first office agents. Harrison Stearns had been handling those complaint-and-crazy calls since being reassigned from the RA's office at Dulles International. "Have him here at seven in the morning," said Macimer.

"He's on the box tonight," Russell pointed out.

Macimer did not reply. Stearns would be there at seven and he had damned well better stay awake. Macimer was giving Stearns a second chance, but he wasn't going to make it easy.

"I'd like a fingerprint team out to my house in the morning," Macimer said after a moment's reflection. "I should have done that before."

Jerry Russell raised an eyebrow. "You think there might be a connection between your robbery and this missing file?"

"Let's say I'm just playing a hunch they were looking for something besides jewels."

Russell shifted uneasily in his chair. "But why would anyone think . . . ?" The question trailed off.

"Someone might have the idea that file was still intact when I took possession of those stolen cartons."

"It's that explosive? I mean, someone would think you're sitting on it? Why wouldn't they figure the auto thief grabbed it?"

"That's what we have to find out. And I think it might be a good idea to get someone Spanish-speaking in on this, just in case —preferably Cuban. Check with Personnel and see who they have in the Bank." The Bureau's computerized "skills bank" covered all active agents. If an investigation required an agent under thirty who spoke Spanish, played the guitar and was an expert skin diver, the Bank would produce his card on request. "I'd also like to talk to the team who are on that auto theft. Who do you have on it?"

"Rayburn and Wagner. But they're out and may not be back in tonight. You want me to call them in?"

"Tomorrow will do."

Russell had been making rapid notes. "Anything else?" he asked when he had caught up.

"That's enough to get us started. Send Garvey in here."

After Russell had left, Macimer picked up his phone and dialed his home. Kevin answered. "How's it going?" he asked.

"Okay."

Still not very communicative. "Is your mother there?"

When Jan came on the line Paul asked her if she had washed the sheets she removed from their bed Saturday night. "If you want the truth, they're in a plastic bag waiting to go to the Salvation Army," she said. "Unwashed."

"Don't do anything with them and don't give them away," Macimer said quickly. "And I hope you're not planning to do any vacuuming or heavy housecleaning."

"Is this a complaint, sir?"

Macimer laughed. "Hardly. But I'm sending a fingerprint team out to the house tomorrow. They'll want to do their own vacuuming."

Jan's voice instantly sobered. "Is that necessary?"

"It's a long shot," Macimer admitted, half to himself. "I'm also going to be late tonight—better not hold dinner."

"Gee, that's a change."

"I'll make it up to you when I retire."

"I can hardly wait."

Pat Garvey was standing in the open doorway when Macimer hung up. The SAC waved him in and nodded toward a chair facing his desk. Garvey's eyes looked bloodshot after a day spent poring through files and extracts. "What have you got so far?" asked Macimer.

"As of right now I have eighteen Xaviers between the ages of sixteen and twenty-five. I stretched the age parameters a little. Most of those are from the index at Internal Security. I still have a couple dozen of our own files to go through."

"When you're finished, run those names through the general index and the CCH files at NCIC. See what matches you come up with."

"I figured on that." Garvey hesitated. Busy with his own tedious assignment all day, he had been aware of the late-afternoon activity, the office talk of shuffled assignments and a "Special" under way. "Uh, I was wondering . . ."

Macimer grinned. "Don't worry, I'm not leaving you out. I've got someone else coming in to take over the search for Xavier and his pals." He paused. "You've been grousing about not getting a chance to see the sun here. How soon could you be ready to fly to California?"

Garvey's eyes lit up. "I can be through here in a couple hours." It would mean working overtime and possibly going blind, but he didn't hide his eagerness. "I could leave tonight."

"Have Willa Cunningham check on airline schedules for tomorrow afternoon. You'll be going to Sacramento. Collins will be going with you," he added, "so coordinate with him."

"Yes, sir." Garvey didn't question the obvious urgency of his new assignment. When the Director designated something as a "Special," working around the clock was not unusual. He would be smart to catch some sleep on the plane. That is, if he could get Collins to sleep. One of a score of blacks in the WFO, Collins was both a talker and an avid backgammon player.

"What are we after, sir?" the young agent asked.

"You'll be briefed in the morning. But I can tell you this much.

Vernon Lippert, the RA in San Timoteo, which comes under Sacramento's jurisdiction, was doing a free-lance investigation into the PRC blowup three years ago. Whatever he dug up, it apparently attracted some attention. The file has disappeared, and there are no duplicates on record. You and Collins will be trying to put that file back together again, following in Lippert's footsteps. I'll go over what we have before you leave."

"What happened to Lippert?"

"He died in an accident . . ." A small alarm bell rang in the back of Macimer's brain, the same kind of intuition he had foolishly ignored Saturday night as he turned into his driveway.

For the first time he wondered about the coincidence of Vernon Lippert's death and the disappearance of the Brea file.

He looked down at the stack of folders before him on his desk, the detailed record of every step of the PRC investigation. The thickness of the files was intimidating. Much of it was both routine and familiar, however, and he could skim through it. What interested him—what must have interested Lippert—were the last stages.

With a sigh he pulled the first of the files toward him, the action and his nod dismissing Garvey.

"What happened to your eyes?" Jan asked.

"Do we have any Visine?"

"I don't think that'll help, I think you need a transplant."

"I need a little sympathy, that's what I need."

He had come home late, washed down a sandwich with a glass of milk and relaxed for an hour through the eleven o'clock news, observing with relief the TV film coverage of the surrender of the hijacker at Miami to FBI Special Agent Callahan. Now he was getting ready for bed.

"What's it all about, Paul? This new case."

"You know better than that."

"Then don't ask for sympathy." She said it lightly, but there was a slight edge to the words.

He had told her about meeting Halbig at Headquarters over an assignment, and now he mentioned Halbig's casual comment about "getting together soon."

"That'll be fun." Jan Macimer and Elaine Halbig had been close. They were both young agents' wives, themselves nearly the same age, going through the same stage of their lives, having their first child only a month apart. Later, when Halbig married a blond beauty ten years younger than Elaine, less than a year after their bitter divorce, Jan had never been comfortable with the younger woman or with Halbig. "Erika and I were never exactly pals," Jan mused. "I suppose it was more my fault than hers. I couldn't forget Elaine as quickly as Russ did."

"It wasn't anyone's fault. These things happen."

"Yes . . . they do, don't they?"

"What'll I tell Halbig if he actually does set a date?"

"Oh, I don't suppose it'll come to that."

"But if it does—?"

Jan laughed. "I don't imagine you'll complain—not if I remember the way you couldn't take your eyes off Erika the last time."

"That's a gross exaggeration."

"It was gross," Jan agreed, "but no exaggeration."

Macimer glanced at her quizzically. She was standing before the dresser brushing her ash-blond hair—a color enhanced by "frosting," Jan cheerfully admitted. The color became her. So did the short, curly hairstyle. Jan had spent a lifetime having her naturally curly hair straightened by hairdressers rather than let it collapse into what she called her Orphan Annie frizz. Now fashion had caught up with nature; curly hair was in. And at forty-one Jan thought shorter hair more suited to her. She also liked not having to do much of anything to it beyond a few strokes with the hairbrush.

As she lifted her arm to tug the brush through the tangle of short curls, the pajama top she wore lifted with the motion, exposing the tight curve of her buttocks. Macimer never wore anything to bed but pajama bottoms; Jan always wore the matching tops. A practical arrangement—"Look how much we save on nightgowns," Jan had pointed out. And Paul had always thought his pajama tops more effective on her than on him. Besides, the buttons had long been a signal between them. All Jan had to do was leave the coat unbuttoned, open to his hands.

When she turned around and came toward the bed, the pajama jacket was unbuttoned.

Her response to his hands, his mouth, his body was immediate and strong. Her aggressiveness surprised and nearly overwhelmed him. The familiar pattern of their lovemaking, prolonged and slow, collapsed before this strange, almost painful urgency. It was over so suddenly that Macimer was left vaguely dissatisfied, unsure about her, confused and uneasy over her abrupt changes of mood.

He remembered something Will Rogers had said about money and women being the two most sought after and least known things we have.

Money's easy, Macimer thought.

6

When the SAC summoned him to his office at seven o'clock Tuesday morning, Special Agent Harrison Stearns cracked a shin in his haste coming around his desk. He limped on, hearing muffled laughter behind him.

Stearns had been on duty until midnight. It had been a quiet night, few crank calls, the kind of night he would ordinarily have passed reading a mystery novel. Instead he had spent the time worrying over his future, wondering if he would shortly be packing for reassignment to Butte, Montana.

He hurried into Paul Macimer's office. The SAC gestured toward a chair. Stearns stared involuntarily at a plastic bag on the chair, noting its contents. A facetious question popped into his head and he quickly repressed it.

"What is it, Stearns? What were you going to say?"

The young agent's heart sank. Macimer *knew* what he was thinking. Stearns swallowed his nervousness, hesitated, then blurted it out. "I was wondering if . . . if you brought in your laundry, sir."

Macimer laughed. "You thought that was to be your next assignment, did you? Not a bad idea, Stearns, considering what you've got us all into. I want those sheets tagged and sent over to the Laboratory. There are some semen stains on the bottom sheet, possibly on the other one." Briefly he explained the origin of the stains. Macimer wasn't sure how much could be learned from them but it was time for another miracle of the Lab. He paused,

letting   , not sure what else was coming.
"Wh   a new job for you. As of now
yo   saw the relief on Stearns's face
          re back on it before the next cou-
          got a 'Special' running, trying to put
          for us. It was among the documents in
          ringing in from the airport."

          stricken. It was worse than he had feared.
          o coordinate the paper work on this, so we
don't   own reports. Frankly, I wouldn't be using you
even as a   rk if I had anyone else. We're short-handed, so
you're it." Macimer leaned forward and spoke with heavy irony.
"All you have to do, Stearns, is see that nothing else gets lost. Do
you think you can handle that?"

"Yes, sir," Stearns mumbled.

"We'll see. Take care of those sheets, then move your stuff into
the special squad room. Russell will give you a desk. And tell him
I want to see Garvey and Collins as soon as they report in."

"Yes, sir."

It was hard to remain angry with someone so anxious to do
right, Macimer thought as the young agent went out, carefully
closing the door behind him. But good agents weren't made of
good intentions. The pressures of the coming days would tell a
great deal about Harrison Stearns.

Macimer turned his attention to the stack of files he had plowed
through the previous afternoon and evening. Next to them were
the two cassette tapes sent over from the Director's office that
morning—what time did Landers get in, anyway? Attached to the
two cassettes was a note that read: "I have listened to these carefully. They speak for themselves. I needn't tell you how important
it is to the Bureau that the truth behind them be unearthed as
quickly as possible." The note was signed "John L. Landers."

The truth. By God, that's what Landers would get!

The densely detailed investigative reports in the PRC file
had brought it all back too vividly, that long, hot, unhappy
summer. . . .

The country had seemed depressed with itself, caught in a
malaise of frustration over runaway inflation and a depressed
economy, high oil prices and low expectations. Starting in June,

the People's Revolutionary Committee struck repeatedly against the corpus of the supposedly ailing monster. The System was in its death throes, they cried. It was time for the people to rise up and overthrow the twin tyrannies of big business and big, faceless government.

They tried to do it with bombs.

California—in one view the vanguard of the new civilization of the 1980s, in another the spawning ground for the kooks and crazies—had much the worst of it. Here the PRC first appeared, claiming credit for a series of bombings and hijackings. By sending tapes to local television and radio stations, showering college campuses with their manifestos and calling for popular support in open letters to leading newspapers, the PRC became the center attraction in a media circus.

In law enforcement the prevailing opinion was that the group was an aggregation of small-time losers, a mixed bag of young white radicals, blacks and Chicanos, led by a charismatic self-styled revolutionary who called himself Ramses. His real name was Carlos Sanchez, a former teen-age gang leader from East Los Angeles with a long history of petty thievery, assault and violence.

Ramses and the PRC made the police their principal victims, banks their primary targets. The police were called Public Enemy No. 1 in a series of mocking tapes and broadsides. Small-town police—far more vulnerable than the well-trained forces in the major cities—were attacked repeatedly. By late summer every police force in northern California was jittery—and angry.

The terrorists had used small-town banks to finance their activities, sometimes even coming back to the same town and the same bank for a second robbery. More than once they lured police and the FBI into responding to a holdup alarm, then threw a bomb into the police station while it was undermanned. Once they left what looked like a stalled car on the route the police were expected to take. The stalled car was filled with explosives. When the police stopped to remove it, the car was blown up by a radio signal—a tactic refined by the IRA against British soldiers in Northern Ireland. Three men died in that explosion.

In July, in San Timoteo, a bomb planted in the parking lot of the police station went off just before two patrol cars returned after responding to a false alarm at the local branch of Bank of America. One policeman was injured by flying glass. It might have been a different story if the bomb had gone off thirty seconds later.

Macimer himself was part of the volunteer FBI task force working on the PRC case, headquartered in the Sacramento Field Office. One afternoon in late August, Macimer had received a phone call from an informant who refused to identify himself. There were a thousand false leads that summer, every one of which had to be followed up. The informant had agreed to meet the FBI agent. A rendezvous was set up at a motel outside of Fresno for five o'clock on the afternoon of August 28. Although half convinced the call was a hoax, Macimer was there in the motel room, waiting for the informant, when the core of the People's Revolutionary Committee was trapped in a house on the outskirts of San Timoteo, a hundred miles to the north. Macimer's informant never appeared.

At 4:46 P.M. the police in San Timoteo received a tip that the PRC were holed up in a house on the edge of the town, heavily armed and dug in for an all-out siege. In the initial confusion— whether deliberately or by mistake—this call was not relayed immediately to the FBI. The local RA, Vernon Lippert, was not notified until the police were already en route to the hideout. Lippert placed an urgent call for assistance to the special Task Force Center in Sacramento at 5:01 P.M. He then went directly to the address of the house the police had surrounded. He had barely arrived on the scene when the first shot was fired.

There were conflicting reports concerning who fired that first shot and under what circumstances. The official police report stated that gunfire had come from the house in response to a command over a bullhorn by Chief Harold Whittaker of the San Timoteo police, ordering the fugitives to surrender. Vernon Lippert's report, written immediately after the massacre, confirmed that the initial shot had come from the direction of the house, and that there followed a massive retaliation by the police. . . .

After listening to the tapes sent over from Headquarters, Macimer sat at his desk making notes, punctuating several of them with questions. He was still writing when Pat Garvey and Leonard Collins entered the office. Macimer waved them to the only two available chairs and continued writing. Finally he sat back and regarded the two agents critically.

Garvey was a clean-cut, solidly built man with the shoulders of an athlete or someone devoted to lifting weights. His black hair, blue eyes and jutting jaw stamped his Irish heritage. In Macimer's own class, twenty years ago, only Garvey's longer hair would have set him apart. Not so for Collins, Macimer thought. Being black was a rarity among agents in those days; so was Collins' cool, contemporary style, accented today by a superbly tailored three-piece light blue gabardine suit.

The contrast between the two agents was a reminder of how much the Bureau itself had changed in the past twenty years. White shirts and conservative suits had once been mandatory; what an agent wore now depended on his assignment, not on the need to project a standardized image. And the modern FBI was a little looser in style as well as dress. The agents themselves had changed, at least in part because 50 percent or more of each graduating class at the FBI Academy since 1979, the first year it happened, had been made up of minorities—blacks, Hispanics, Asians, women. And at the same time, with a changing perception of the challenges it faced and the priorities it should emphasize, the Bureau had become more flexible and open-minded, less rigid than it had been when Macimer first pocketed his badge.

"You're booked on a one o'clock flight to Sacramento by way of San Francisco," Macimer told the two agents. "The SAC there has been briefed, and you'll receive his full cooperation. However, he also knows that this is a low-profile 'Special,' and you'll be working independently, at least until further notice.

"Now . . . let's go over it. I presume you're both familiar with what happened in San Timoteo three years ago."

"Yes, sir," said Garvey.

"It was on TV," Collins said.

"Copies are being made of the most important abstracts and a few full reports from the PRC files. You can read those on the plane. As far as the Bureau was concerned, that case was closed. Maybe we were a little too eager to have it closed, but it did seem to be over. All the known members of the PRC were dead. Nobody survived that explosion, including the two hostages who were in the house, a young couple whose van had been commandeered to get the terrorists to San Timoteo. There didn't seem to be any reason to look beyond what was there for everyone to see, including all those millions like you, Collins, who watched the whole thing in their living rooms. Oh, there was a wrap on the investigation, tying up the loose ends, but all that really did was confirm what everyone wanted to believe—that the case was closed.

"Apparently Vernon Lippert, the RA in San Timoteo, didn't think so. My guess is the wipe-out of the PRC nagged at him. It shouldn't have happened that way. For one thing, a doctor later admitted that he had treated Ramses for a gunshot wound received during a bank robbery in Santa Rosa two weeks before the massacre. He'd kept silent because the terrorists had threatened his family. So Ramses was in no shape to lead anything. Which means the group holed up in San Timoteo to buy themselves some time. They were hurt, probably demoralized. In that state they couldn't have wanted a confrontation with the police or the FBI— not then, not there.

"If you read it that way, you have to wonder, as Lippert must have, why they picked that frame house as a hideout. It was certainly no place for a last-ditch battle.

"Then you start to wonder about that anonymous phone call to the police in San Timoteo that triggered what happened . . ."

The two younger agents had been making notes as Macimer talked. Their felt-tip pens paused as Macimer fell silent. Both men looked up at him expectantly, waiting.

"Vernon Lippert obviously wondered if there wasn't more to the story than the record showed. A lot of us who were in California that summer could never figure out why Ramses made such a blunder, unless it was a death wish. Lippert started digging into it, taking the case when it was cold and building a new investigative file of his own on it. Lippert was close to retirement, playing out his string as the RA in San Timoteo, so he didn't exactly go by the rules. He didn't ask for approval of his investigation, and he didn't make copies of what he was putting together for Sacramento or Headquarters.

"Now Lippert is dead and his file on the case is missing."

Briefly Macimer listed what had been uncovered at Headquarters during the past week, referring to his own notes and questions. One, a piece of rusty window screen sent by Lippert to the FBI Lab for examination. Residue of gunpowder was found around a tear in the screen. *Question: Where did that screen come from?* Two, Lippert requested a handwriting comparison from the Handwriting Analysis Unit. That test confirmed that

a man named Charles Smith, who rented the PRC's hideout in San
Timoteo two days before the shoot-out, was really Walter Schu-
maker. Schumaker had been developed as an informant by Special
Agents Charles Reese and Victor Pryor of the San Francisco Field
Office two years earlier. He was known to have contacts among
radical and Communist groups in the Berkeley area and on the
Berkeley campus of the University of California. Schumaker re-
ceived amounts varying from sixty dollars per month to a hundred
and fifty dollars during a period of a year ending in June 1980.
Payments were discontinued because the information Reese and
Pryor were getting from Schumaker didn't warrant keeping him on
the payroll. Schumaker then dropped out of the Berkeley area.
Question: What happened to Walter Schumaker?

Collins and Garvey exchanged glances. Collins whistled softly
through his teeth.

"Exactly," Macimer said. "A former FBI informant was with
the PRC. And that's not all of it. He wasn't just a former informant. He was being run by another agent who called himself Brea
—a code name. Apparently Schumaker didn't know him by any
other name. And there's no FBI record of such a code name being
used."

"How do we know there was such a guy?" asked Garvey.

"I'll let you hear it for yourselves," Macimer replied. He swiv-
eled his chair toward the Panasonic tape recorder on a shelf of
his bookcase behind the desk. The cassette was already in place.
"There are two tapes, both of which were sent by Lippert to the
Engineering Section of the Lab for comparison. I'll tell you about
the other tape after you hear this.

"The tape covers a recorded conversation received by Special
Agent Katherine Washington in the Sacramento Field Office at
11:02 A.M. August 27, 1981—the day before the San Timoteo disaster." Macimer punched the "start" and "play" buttons on the
recorder and sat back. Garvey and Collins both hunched forward
in their chairs to listen. Macimer said, "The woman's voice, obviously, is Agent Washington."

CALLER: I'd like to talk to Brea.
WASHINGTON: Would you please spell your name, just for our
    records?
CALLER: You don't need my name. Brea knows who I am.

WASHINGTON: I'm not sure I understand. Who is Brea?

CALLER: Hey, don't play games with me, lady. I don't have much time. This phone number he gave me to call if there was an emergency doesn't answer, and I've got an emergency.

WASHINGTON: What kind of emergency?

CALLER: I've got to talk to Brea.

WASHINGTON: If you'll give me your name, and tell me who Brea is—

CALLER: He's the one I been reporting to. Listen, okay, if he's not there, just give him the message. Tell him the situation isn't what I told him. It's changed.

WASHINGTON: Can you be a little more specific?

CALLER: On the telephone? Are you kidding?

WASHINGTON: Sir, there is no Agent Brea in this office. Are you sure you have the right name?

CALLER: Sure I'm sure! Listen, I know it isn't his real name. It's —what do you call it?—his code name. Okay. You get him the message, and I mean fast! I got to know if the plan is still on, you know? He's got to give me time to get out, and I'll need some bread.

WASHINGTON: Where can he reach you?

CALLER (laughter): You think I'm stupid? He knows where I am. I'm with the Egyptian.

WASHINGTON: The Egyptian? What—?

Macimer punched off the recorder. "That's where he hung up." For a long moment there was silence in the small, crowded office as the two young agents digested what they had heard. Garvey appeared puzzled. Collins, Macimer thought, was quicker. He pursed his lips, the whistle this time silent.

"The Egyptian," Garvey said suddenly. "Ramses?"

"Maybe. Remember, at the time this call was received, it was just one of some two hundred calls that came into the Task Force Center at Sacramento during a forty-eight-hour period, nearly half of them claiming to have information about the PRC. So at the time nobody paid much attention to the call for Brea. No one had ever heard of Brea, as a real name or an agent's code name."

"And after the big blowup, the call didn't seem important. It got lost in the shuffle," Collins suggested.

"That's right."

"What's on the other tape?" Collins sounded as if he had already made a guess. Collins had a good cop's instincts, Macimer thought. Sometimes that was more important than experience or intelligence . . . and Collins was also intelligent.

"It's a recording of a conversation early in 1980 between Special Agent Reese and Walter Schumaker, the informant we know rented the PRC's hideout. According to a voiceprint comparison in the Lab, the voice of the man who talked to Agent Washington on August 27, 1981, is the same as the voice of the informant on the second tape. The man who made that call to Brea was Walter Schumaker."

Garvey was beginning to grasp the implications. A look of consternation appeared in his eyes.

"Two hundred agents were looking for the PRC," Macimer said slowly. "And one of them had an informant planted inside the group, we don't know for how long. But at the time of the shootout, that agent, the one who called himself Brea, either knew or could have known exactly where the terrorists were."

"And he didn't report it?" Garvey was incredulous.

"Neither then nor afterwards."

Garvey broke a somber silence. "What about Schumaker?"

"We don't know." Macimer glanced down at one of the reports he had removed from the master PRC file. "Interviews with neighbors of the house on Dover Street indicate that no one was seen leaving there on the twenty-eighth. Schumaker apparently left the house the day before, probably to buy groceries and whatever else the group needed. He could go out safely because he wasn't on any wanted list—and he used that time to call Brea. That's speculation," Macimer added, "but it would seem to be a good guess that he was inside with the others on the twenty-eighth.

"The FBI Disaster Squad went in after the explosion," the SAC went on quietly. "They were able to find parts of seven or eight bodies. Two of those were identified as the hostages. Their van was found abandoned in the next town, by the way, ten miles away. Fingerprints of at least two of the victims were never found for verification. Schumaker's prints are in the criminal file. I think it's a reasonable assumption that one of the unidentified bodies was his."

"That means Brea knew . . ."

"Don't get ahead of yourself, Collins. Let's see what the facts say when they're all in. What I want you two to do is go to San Timoteo and find out what else Vernon Lippert learned. Find out who he talked to and what they told him. Talk to the neighbors, the police. Check with Pacific Telephone and see if you can find out where that phone call to Sacramento came from on the twenty-seventh. My guess is it was long-distance from San Timoteo. Find out where Lippert got hold of that window screen. I want to know everything that Lippert dug up, everything that was in the Brea file."

He paused, staring at the two agents as they scribbled on their pads, actually two-by-four-inch cards small enough to hold in the palm of your hand as you wrote. He waited until both men had finished writing before he said, "We're going to finish what Vernon Lippert started. Find out who Brea was."

7

Late that Tuesday afternoon the two agents who had been assigned to the case of the stolen FBI vehicle reported to Macimer's office.

Jack Wagner was in his thirties, one of the famous class known in the Bureau as the "Berrigan 1000." These were an extra thousand agents authorized by Congress in 1970 at the urging of J. Edgar Hoover, after the Director testified about the "plot" of the Berrigans to kidnap prominent government leaders and blow up government buildings. Wagner had a degree in economics from Columbia on top of three years in Vietnam. He was blond, broad-shouldered and athletic, with a perennial boyishness about his handsome features. Only his eyes were old. Calvin Rayburn, his partner, was thin and stoop-shouldered, five years younger, with black curly hair, heavy black eyebrows and eyes so deep-set that he seemed to wear a perpetual scowl. Where Wagner was outgoing and deceptively casual, Rayburn was silent, as sober in demeanor as his gray flannel suit.

Hell, Macimer thought, what happened to that FBI stereotype you always read about?

The two men worked well as a team in the Criminal Section. The file containing their daily reports of the ten-day Interstate Transport of Stolen Vehicle investigation was, however, disappointingly thin. Macimer thumbed through the reports and sat back in his chair, swiveling gently for a moment. Finally he said,

"Stearns doesn't remember anything about the people in the Fedco parking lot who helped him up after he fell?"

"Only that there was an older couple and a younger man. The man might be interesting, but Stearns doesn't remember much. Only that he was young, thin, on the tall side. He may just have looked tall because he was helping Stearns up off the ground." Wagner grinned. "He must've done that with one hand while he was pocketing the car keys with the other."

Macimer didn't smile. "According to your latest report, you found a gas station in Paris where he stopped for gas. How solid is that?"

"It was him," Rayburn said.

"Yeah," Wagner agreed. "It's one of those self-service stations, and usually those guys don't notice much. It was a rainy night, and the attendant never left his booth. The only reason he noticed anything at all was that he saw this young guy get out of his car, a blue Ford sedan, and go around and open the trunk. It stuck in his mind because all the guy did was look inside the trunk and then slam the lid shut. By then the attendant in the booth was watching him—they get a feel for anything unusual because of hold-ups—and he thought the kid was agitated. He stopped pumping gas at an odd number. Most people round off to a dollar or some even number, unless it's a fill-up, but this was something like two dollars and thirty-seven cents, which is why the attendant remembered. The kid came straight over to the booth and paid cash. No credit card."

There was a moment's silence before Rayburn said, "He back-tracked."

Macimer glanced at him. "I noticed that. He came back to Highway 17. Why? Because of what he saw in the trunk of the car?"

Rayburn shrugged. "Could be."

Macimer glanced at the file once more. The two agents had found footprints in the meadow leading away from the scene where the car had been abandoned after going off the road. Softened by a month of rains, the ground had yielded good castings of the footprints. Their pattern turned out to be that of a popular brand of jogging shoe that sold in the millions.

"The fingerprints and shoeprints are a dead end," Macimer

mused aloud. "But that kid didn't walk back to Washington. He must have hitched a ride, if he came back at all."

"We're working on that," Wagner said cheerfully, his expression at odds with the tediousness of this phase of the investigation. "I figure we can make a career out of it."

This time Macimer returned a smile. "You'll have to make it faster than that. As of now you're part of a special squad. This assignment comes straight from the Director. One of the files that was in the trunk of that stolen car is missing. Maybe the kid took it, maybe not. He's the only one who can tell us." Macimer paused. "There'll be a general briefing of the squad in the morning. Meanwhile, if you don't have anything better to do, go back to Fedco. What was that kid doing there? Shopping? Getting off work? He didn't have his own transportation. Does he live near there?"

"Gotcha," Wagner said enthusiastically.

Macimer grinned at him. "Have fun."

Macimer glanced at the clock on his desk after the agents left. Nearly five o'clock. He was wondering if he might snatch one normal evening at home and a good night's sleep—it might be the last for some time—when his secretary buzzed him on the intercom. Willa Cunningham was a good-humored, efficient, self-reliant woman who had returned to office work after her agent husband died of a heart attack at forty-nine. Besides her formidable abilities at taking dictation, typing, answering the phone, organizing paper work and sifting gossip, Willa even made good coffee—without complaining that it wasn't part of her job.

"There's a reporter waiting on line three," Willa said. "Name of Gerella. Do you want to talk to him?"

"Did he say what it was about?"

"He wouldn't say. But there is a Gerella who works for Oliver Packard. And you know how Packard has been exploiting Senator Sederholm's Intelligence Committee hearings."

Macimer frowned. Oliver Packard, syndicated columnist, skeleton rattler, confidant of senators and Presidents, was one of the most powerful men in Washington. In the post-Watergate decade Packard had learned the lessons of no-holds-barred investigative journalism even better than his colleagues. He was for the 1980s what Jack Anderson had been in the 1970s and Drew Pearson before him.

Macimer had a grudging respect for Oliver Packard's skill at digging into events. The man was a fine investigator with superb instincts for finding where the bones were buried. What Macimer didn't like was Packard's apparent willingness, when hard evidence was lacking, to attack by innuendo and suggestion.

Senator Charles Sederholm was in some ways Capitol Hill's counterpart to Oliver Packard. An imposing man of immense power and influence, he had used the latest round of inquiries into the government's various intelligence agencies to polish his image in preparation for his run at the presidency.

Macimer realized suddenly that California's primary election had been held today—the polls would still be open out on the coast. That was Sederholm's home state, and he would almost certainly lock up its delegates for the coming Republican convention before this day was over.

"I'll talk to him," Macimer told Willa Cunningham. "While I'm at it, see what your private grapevine says about Gerella."

The reporter proved less openly aggressive than Macimer had braced himself for. After a few preliminaries Gerella suggested a meeting with Macimer away from his office.

"What is it you want to see me about, Mr. Gerella?"

"I'd prefer to go into that face to face. Let's just say that . . . I've been looking into some recent FBI history. I hear you might be able to help me."

The casual comment could be a routine ploy, Macimer thought. It seemed to suggest something without actually saying anything. "I don't see how I can help you," he said. "Does this have something to do with Senator Sederholm's hearings?"

There was a short pause before Gerella said, "What I'm looking into, Sederholm doesn't know about . . . yet."

There it was again. The hint, the oblique but unmistakable intimation of . . . what? A threat?

"Would you care to be more specific?"

"I can't do that over the phone—and I don't think you'd want me to, Mr. Macimer."

"I don't know what that's supposed to mean."

"I'd really like to talk to you, sir," Gerella said, adopting a more respectful tack. "Maybe I've been listening to somebody's fantasies. You know how rumors are in this town." He paused a moment, as if willing to give Macimer time to evaluate the implied suggestion that what Gerella was looking into was based on substance, not the fanciful spinnings of Washington's rumor mill. "We could make it some out-of-the-way place where we won't be seen."

Macimer laughed. "You don't want to be seen talking to an FBI agent?"

"I was thinking of you," Gerella said.

The words confirmed the decision Macimer had already reached. He would meet the reporter. It wasn't so much that it was important for him to know what story Gerella was digging into or what rumors he had heard. Macimer wanted to know why Gerella had called *him*.

"Whereabouts?" Macimer asked.

"I was thinking of Georgetown."

"Why Georgetown?"

"I like to eat there. You want to buy me dinner?"

"This isn't a social get-together," Macimer said dryly.

"Okay. Then I know a bar where we won't be noticed."

They agreed on the time and place and the reporter hung up. Macimer regarded the silent phone thoughtfully for a moment. Then he sighed and dialed his home phone number. Every FBI agent, and especially any Special-Agent-in-Charge of an office, ought to have a prerecorded message, he thought, telling his wife he wouldn't be home for dinner.

Macimer parked on a side street off Wisconsin Avenue. He walked back along the tree-shaded street past rows of Victorian and Federal period row houses, narrow brick buildings with tall narrow windows, extruding short flights of steps. The careful detailing over windows and doors spoke of a bygone craftsmanship that was now too expensive to duplicate.

Although it was still early for the dinner hour, Wisconsin was crowded. Throngs waited to get into the small, fashionable French restaurants, and young people crowded the occasional singles bars. Macimer turned right on M Street. A half block beyond the Café de Paris he found the entrance to the arcade Gerella had described over the phone. On impulse he walked past it and continued along the street to the next corner. He crossed over and started back along the sidewalk the way he had come. No one crossed the street behind him.

Macimer turned the corner onto Wisconsin and stepped quickly into the entry of a small shop whose windows displayed a collection of old prints. The shop was closed.

He stood patiently in the sheltered entry for some minutes, watching the traffic at the intersection of Wisconsin and M Street. Waiting, Macimer felt a familiar and pleasurable tension. He had spent too much time behind a desk in recent years. He missed being in the field.

At the same time he wondered about his caution. He had no reason to fear being seen talking to Oliver Packard's reporter. But he continued to have the feeling of being watched—he had had it that night of the robbery when he spotted a brown Chevrolet several times.

Yet why would anyone be following him? Because someone believed that he had the Brea file intact? That, like Vernon Lippert, he had sat on it, hiding its contents even from his superiors?

Macimer shook himself impatiently. If what he guessed about the file was true, he understood why it was so important. What he didn't know was to whom.

After five minutes, satisfied that on this occasion he had not been followed, Macimer retraced his steps along M Street to the brick-faced arcade. A dark tunnel led from the street to a broad inner courtyard faced with fashionable shops on two levels. Most of them were closed. Two young women with lank straight hair parted in the middle glanced out hopefully from a boutique as Macimer walked by.

On the far side of the arcade another narrow passageway tunneled through to the alley. The land here tilted downward toward the river. Standing in the gathering dusk, Macimer felt the warm, soft air of a Washington evening in June against his face. There was a smell of rain. From somewhere up the alley came the sounds of muted jazz from a small nightclub.

No one had followed Macimer through the nearly deserted arcade.

Across the alley was the rear entrance to a bar that fronted on the next street. Macimer entered through the back door. He stood for a moment near the doorway, letting his eyes adjust to the gloom.

The bar was long and narrow. There was just enough room for an old mahogany bar with a polished brass rail and a dozen or so tall stools, a narrow aisle and a row of wooden booths upholstered in cracked red vinyl. A couple of the booths and several stools were occupied.

Joseph Gerella had chosen the last booth, nearest the alley. He was sitting with his back to the room. Macimer sensed that the reporter had been watching him for a number of seconds before the FBI man spotted him.

Macimer stopped beside the booth. "Gerella?"

"Check. Sit down, Mr. Macimer. You want a beer?"

"Just coffee."

Macimer sat opposite Gerella, conscious of a feeling of caution and a trace of hostility. The man on the other side of the table was not reassuring. Joseph Gerella wore a poor-fitting polyester suit made to resemble gray flannel. His shirt collar was unbuttoned, his tie tugged loose and to one side. There was a dark stain on the tie. His black hair came almost to his shoulders in a straight Prince Valiant cut that needed pruning. Macimer was not misled by the careless appearance. Gerella might look less like Prince Valiant than one of the Three Stooges, but there was nothing careless about his silent appraisal. According to Willa Cunningham, Gerella had a reputation as a tough, even ruthless investigative reporter. He had to be that to work for Oliver Packard. Over the years Macimer had done his own share of interrogating, and he recognized the attempted intimidation in Gerella's stare.

A waitress wearing a tiny fluted black skirt and black mesh stockings over heavy thighs came to the booth. Gerella ordered coffee for Macimer and another beer for himself. Neither man spoke until the waitress had left them alone. Then Gerella said, "From what I hear, Mr. Macimer, you're one of the Bureau's straight ones."

"I don't know what that's supposed to mean."

"No offense—all I meant was, you haven't got into anything sticky. Nobody's suing you for violating their civil rights, and you're not one of the appointed apologists."

"The FBI doesn't need any apologists," Macimer said sharply.

Gerella smiled. It was a wolfish display of teeth that reminded Macimer of the actor Jack Nicholson; the smile did not touch his eyes. "You really believe that? Come on, Macimer—what about all those agents who were disciplined for black-bag jobs? What about Felt and Miller and the Weather Underground break-ins? What about the whole COINTELPRO? Are you defending all that?"

Macimer sighed. COINTELPRO—the FBI's Counterintelligence Program launched in the mid-1950s and officially halted on J. Edgar Hoover's orders in March 1971—was not one of his favorite subjects. COINTELPRO was a "covert action program," borrowing techniques more commonly used by foreign intelligence agencies. Few law enforcement people could be found who would disagree with the program's goals. It had approved actions designed to discredit, expose or embarrass advocates of dangerous causes who could sometimes not be reached by the law. Sanctioned actions had involved harassment of extremist groups of the Right as well as the Left, from the Ku Klux Klan and the American Nazi Party to the Black Panthers and the Weathermen. Methods had included leaking details of Klan identities and activities to the media, provoking disputes among rival factions of target groups, even, according to some stories, false accusations. Maybe the CIA had to engage in dirty tricks—Macimer's mind was open on that question—but the FBI and its reputation had suffered when it used such tactics.

"You're lumping a lot of things together," he said. "I'm not here to defend any of them to you, but I will tell you what I think —off the record." He waited for Gerella's reluctant nod. "I think, on balance, COINTELPRO was a mistake on the Bureau's part, even though a lot of what the program accomplished was positive. The thing you people seem to forget is that it's possible to do some wrong while trying to do good. And sometimes what you see as good and necessary for the country comes at the expense of someone else's good. That kind of balance isn't as simplistic as some people like to make it. As for those black-bag jobs and break-ins, I think the people involved were acting in what they believed to be the best interests of the United States—and without the clear guidelines we have now. We were fighting fire with fire, even if that sometimes meant technical violations."

"You call civil rights a technicality?"

Macimer shook his head. "You're using catchwords, Gerella. The FBI isn't in the business of violating civil rights. It's in the business of catching criminals and protecting innocent people— including their civil rights."

"Like you protected Martin Luther King?" Gerella said quickly.

"If you're going to bring up that Mark Lane hysteria, you know better—if you're any kind of reporter."

The two men fell silent as the waitress checked their booth and was waved away. Macimer became more aware of the murmurs of sound around them, the heavy beat of music from a jukebox, the competing voice of an overhead TV set at the far end of the bar. He was glad of the confusion of sounds. Gerella had succeeded in provoking him into talking too much, and he suspected that to the reporter his words only sounded self-serving.

"You always wanted to be a hero?" Gerella asked, surprising him. "Join the FBI and save the world?"

"Something like that."

There was amusement in Macimer's answer, but Gerella wasn't really far off the mark. As a boy growing up in southeast Detroit, his had been a neighborhood of heroes. Some of them in uniform, limping along the sidewalk, their war over for them, the scars permanent. Others in the darkness of the old Jefferson Theater on Saturday afternoon. He could still remember watching the G-men catch up with Dillinger on screen as the famous robber emerged from another theater in another town on another hot Saturday afternoon—the Biograph on the north side of Chicago in 1934. Long before television's smaller-scaled heroics there had been Jimmy Cagney and Lloyd Nolan and Jimmy Stewart and others equally dedicated and determined, FBI men all. There had been few doubts then, no second-guessing about the rights of criminals. Maybe something had been gained, Macimer thought; something also had been lost.

"There are no heroes," Gerella said.

"Maybe you're not really looking for them," Macimer responded quietly. "You can usually find what you're looking for."

Gerella wagged his head, his expression suggesting awed incredulity. He lit a cigarette and waved the pack at Macimer, who shook his head. "Save me from true believers. Don't you know people are scared of cops, Macimer? Haven't you seen it in their eyes? And when you're not kept on a goddamned tight rein, when the law runs wild, you scare the hell out of me."

Macimer wanted to say that innocent people had nothing to fear from the FBI, but he suddenly thought of the two hostages who had died with the People's Revolutionary Committee in the terrorists' hideout. He stared at Gerella, weighing the coincidence of his search for the Brea file and the reporter's phone call. "What do you want, Gerella? You didn't call me up and act mysterious just so we could get together and debate the history and policies of the FBI."

Gerella leaned forward abruptly. "Okay, how's this? I hear you ran into something interesting out on Highway 17 a couple weeks ago."

Macimer took his time responding. Gerella had tried to stampede him with the sudden question, which might mean that he didn't really know anything. "Where did you hear that?"

Gerella shrugged. "I'm supposed to hear things. That's *my* business. I hear there were FBI men crawling all over the hillside. You were there. Want to tell me what it was about?"

How did Gerella know he had been there? The reporter had to have an inside source at the Bureau. What source? And how much did he know?

"The public doesn't need to know what I'm working on."

"Maybe the public has a right to know about this case."

Macimer's expression betrayed nothing, but he felt his internal defenses clanging into place like bars. Could Gerella know about the missing Brea file? Or was he simply casting blindly? The intensive FBI search for the youth who had stolen and abandoned an FBI vehicle would not have gone unnoticed in the Virginia countryside. There were also a number of people who might have talked about the incident—the state trooper, the truck driver, the salesman from Georgia, others who happened along that road that night. Their knowledge, however, was limited. Only the trooper knew about the documents found in the trunk of the car, and he knew no more than that.

"I have nothing for you, Gerella. And I don't know why you wanted to talk to me."

"I think you do."

"What gives you that idea?"

"You're here, Mr. Macimer."

The FBI man smiled. "It's not that easy, Gerella."

The reporter was undismayed. "Can't blame me for trying. Okay, Mr. Macimer—what do they call you around the Bureau, Mac? Yeah, it would be Mac, wouldn't it? I'll level with you if you'll level with me. The way I hear it, there were some documents stolen. I hear you're sitting on something hot—maybe too hot for you to handle." He offered a friendly open grin for the first time. "If you're as straight as they say, Mac, I'm offering you a way to get the facts out in the open. And no one has to know it was you I talked to."

Resenting the deceptive grin, Macimer was also jolted by the cynical proposal. He stared at the reporter in silence, thinking of the damage to the Bureau that might come if his own suspicions about the Brea file were true.

Misreading his silence, Gerella said, "Whatever it is, I can get it, Macimer." At least he had dropped the friendly "Mac," quick to perceive that it had been a mistake. "Under the law you're going to have to release it, sooner or later."

Macimer did not point out that no law sanctioned blind fishing expeditions through the Bureau's files. "I don't know who gave you a bad tip, Gerella, but I don't have anything for you. It's true that an FBI vehicle was stolen while transporting classified documents. You probably already know the car was recovered when it was abandoned on Highway 17 after an accident. The boxes of documents were in the trunk of the car and they were recovered. There's nothing in the story Oliver Packard would give a paragraph to." Careful truth, Macimer thought, quickly became a lie.

Gerella stubbed out a cigarette and immediately lit another, using a Cricket lighter. His fingers were stained the color of old mustard. His hands surprised Macimer. They were stubby and callused, nicked and scarred, the hands of a laborer rather than someone who made a living pounding a typewriter. "Nothing in it, huh?"

"That's right."

"You wouldn't know about any quick trip to the shredder with one of those files."

Macimer felt his neck reddening. He hoped Gerella would attribute the reaction to anger rather than guilt. He hadn't used a shredder, but somewhere along the line there *had* been a cover-up. He pressed anger into his voice, giving his reaction a label. "I don't know anything about any shredding, Gerella, and you don't know what the hell you're talking about. If you're interested in anything in the FBI files you can request it under the Freedom of Information Act like anyone else. But you're not using me to find

out whatever it is you want to know. You sound like you're string-
ing for the *National Enquirer,* not Oliver Packard. And you've
come to the wrong source. Do your own dirty work."

"Methinks you protest too much."

"I don't give a damn what you think." Macimer dug into his
pocket for a couple of quarters and dropped them onto the table
as he rose. "Thanks for the coffee."

He was turning away when Gerella said, "The car theft isn't the
story, Macimer."

"Then why play games?" the FBI man snapped. "Say what's on
your mind."

"I'm interested in the PRC affair."

Macimer felt a chill slice along his spine like the cut of a sur-
geon's knife. It was a moment before he answered, his voice controlled and even. "You're a little late, Gerella. Senator Sederholm's committee requested everything we had on the People's
Revolutionary Committee. You can read all about it in the *Congressional Record.*"

He walked out, not looking back, angry and shaken.

*How much did Gerella know about the Brea file? And how did
he know?*

From the alley Gerella watched the FBI agent walk quickly
through the empty arcade. Macimer had the build and moves of
an ex-jock, Gerella thought. Like Staubach five years or so after
retirement. At the far end of the arcade Macimer hesitated for a
moment before he disappeared around the corner onto M Street.

Gerella wondered why Macimer had made a quick reconnoiter
of the street before leaving the arcade. Did he think he was being
watched?

Macimer knew something. Gerella could feel it. And the FBI
man had lied about recovering all the documents from the stolen
Bureau car. Gerella knew he had lied because folded in the inside
pocket of his suit coat was a copy of one of those documents. It
had come to the reporter anonymously in an envelope with a
Washington postmark. With a promise of more where that came
from.

Gerella didn't know who the anonymous contributor was or
what he wanted. Money, probably. Either that or he was someone
with a grudge against the FBI. The brief printed note attached to

the single photocopied document had revealed little: "This is just a sample. If you're interested there's more."

The document itself was enigmatic. It was one page of an obviously longer list of assignments of agents who had been part of the PRC Task Force in the summer of 1981. What interested Gerella was the date at the top of that list: August 28.

The day the terrorists' hideout was blown sky high.

Gerella hadn't made up his mind before meeting Macimer whether or not to show him the document, of which he had made additional copies. He had wanted to play it by ear, sounding out the FBI man. In the end he had decided to withhold it. Gerella trusted his reporter's instincts, and they told him he was onto something big. And Paul Macimer was part of it.

8

After Paul Macimer called to say he wouldn't be home for dinner, Jan found herself unexpectedly at loose ends. Linda was staying over at a girlfriend's house. Chip had baseball practice, and Kevin begged an advance on his allowance to see a rerun of *Star Wars IV* at the local theater. Jan's class was having its final exam tomorrow night, which meant no lecture to prepare. The examination pages had already been photocopied.

On impulse she reached for the phone again and tapped out Carole Baumgartner's number. Carole answered on the first ring, which Jan suggested must violate some unwritten rule.

"On a Tuesday night as beautiful as this one, and at this hour," Carole retorted, "there are no rules."

"Well, if you don't want to wait for a better offer, how about dinner?"

"Where's the honcho tonight?"

"Paul had something come up. He'll be home late." Jan was used to Carole's slightly scornful references to husbands—anyone's husband.

"I can be ready in a half hour," Carole said.

On the drive over to pick Carole up at her elegant little Williamsburg-style condominium, Jan's thoughts turned toward the end of the semester and her teaching project. It would be nice to have those Monday and Wednesday evenings free all summer, not to mention the time taken up in preparing lectures and grading papers. All the same, she realized she was going to miss the classes. The students, especially.

She had started out with a class of twenty-six. If someone didn't get cold feet at the last minute, there should be twenty-two students taking the final exam. That was an exceptional survival rate for any adult education class, according to the other teachers Jan had talked to. She was inordinately pleased that four out of five male students had stuck it out. The other eighteen survivors were all women, mostly young, a few in their thirties or forties.

Hoping that the school administration was pleased with the class and her work, Jan found herself anticipating what she might do differently—better—if she taught a similar class again in the fall term. There were other possibilities as well. Workplace English, after all, shouldn't be shunted off to an adult education program exclusively.

But there was time enough to think of that. A summertime of ease. Of restless ease? Jan smiled, deciding not to give Carole Baumgartner a shot at that errant thought.

Carole was slower than promised in getting ready, but an hour later the two women were having a drink in the cocktail lounge at Adam's, an out-of-the-way but trendy small restaurant in McLean that was one of Carole's latest discoveries. There was a thirty-minute wait for a table.

As Jan glanced around, a man at a neighboring table caught her eye and smiled, lifting a glass filled with ice and amber liquid. He was tanned, thirtyish, wearing an expensively tailored light gray suit with the sheen of silk, black Bally shoes, shirt open at the throat, the predictable gold chain. Jan wondered if he could guess how many years his senior she was. She looked away.

"I'll take the older one," Carole murmured, indicating the tanned young man's stockier companion, who had a very large mustache salted with gray. "He looks like he's been around long enough to know how, at least."

Jan smiled. She knew that Carole was far more particular about her dates than she pretended.

At the piano in a corner of the lounge a young man with long, sun-bleached blond hair began to play and sing. He had a plaintive, high-pitched voice that suited the whine of the melancholy lyrics. Watching him, Carole said, "How are things with you and Paul?"

"Fine. Why shouldn't they be?"

"I mean . . . *really*, Jan. Be forthcoming, as they say. Are you two having trouble?"

"Why do you keep asking that? I've told you . . . everything's fine."

"I ask because I know what I see and hear."

"You see and hear what you want to."

"That's not true!" Carole protested. "I don't wish trouble on you. You know me better than that."

"You simply think it's inevitable, right?"

"Well . . ." Carole offered an impish smile. "Isn't it? Oh, I know, we all had those once-upon-a-time, fairy-tale dreams. Love and cherish, forever and ever, into the golden sunset at last, hand in hand. It was lovely, but it was never true."

"Never?" Jan said softly. "I don't believe that."

"People change," Carole said seriously. "That *is* inevitable. And the funny thing is that women change more than men do. Most men are still happy as clams as long as they can go to the football games or slam a racquetball and make believe they're still the same old muscle-bound sophomores. They *want* to stay that way. Women don't."

"I don't see—"

"Of course you do! I've watched you two, don't forget, over the last couple years. Everything I've seen of Paul tells me he's the same gung ho FBI believer he was when he joined up twenty years ago. But you don't buy all of it anymore, Jan. And all those fairy-tale promises can't make it otherwise."

Jan sat back, examining her reaction. She had been feeling restless tonight, uneasy. Had she wanted Carole to confirm those feelings? Or to help her understand them? "You're talking slogans, Carole," she said quietly. "Of course people change in different ways. Paul and I are no exception, but that doesn't mean we're in trouble, even if we don't always see eye to eye about what the Bureau does. What's that line from the poem? 'Love is not love which alters when it alteration finds.' Shakespeare, right? You see, my education wasn't all wasted."

"Ever the romantic," Carole said with a sigh. "I suppose I ought to envy you."

As Carole spoke she glanced toward the two men at the adjoining table. They were both rising. Carole kicked Jan under the table, not too gently. Jan glanced up, startled, to find the stranger in the gray suit standing beside her. "Jan?" he said.

"I'm sorry . . ."

"I know, we've never met." His smile was boyish, engaging. "I heard your friend call you Jan. Look, we've just been called for our table. Why don't you two ladies join us for dinner? Save you a long wait, and save us from being bored with each other."

"I think you've made a mistake."

"You're sure? No strings—why don't you ask your friend? Let's let her decide."

Jan stiffened. She could be the Ice Lady if necessary. "I can decide for myself," she said coolly. "And you'd better hurry if you don't want to lose your table."

Her tone and manner dismissed him. When the two men had left the lounge, Carole said, "I said I ought to envy you your illusions, but I don't know. That one could be from Central Casting."

Jan laughed quickly. "He shares your flattering opinion of him. Even if I were available, that was a little too smug."

"So? That comes with the blue ribbon."

The incident had sobered Jan Macimer. After a moment of pensive silence she said, "You're right about my having things on my mind. But it isn't Paul I'm worried about—it's Linda."

Carole's interest immediately quickened. She reminded Jan of a bird pecking sharply at new tidbits—an exotic, self-absorbed bird with glossy plumage. "Don't tell me she's fallen in love. Let *me* talk to her."

"Just the opposite. She hasn't got over the way she was manhandled by that young thug during the robbery. All of a sudden she's picking up on all the anti-male propaganda you're always dumping on me. It's everywhere, you know. You don't have to hand out literature on your own. It's like a new religion. I wouldn't be surprised if some of the sisters came around to the door on Sunday mornings giving a little spiel and handing out the latest tract."

"Hey, I thought you were simpatico!"

"Don't get me wrong. I can get my adrenaline flowing when I listen to the beautiful Gloria Steinem or read about the latest atrocity in the boardroom. But Linda's too young to get it all in perspective. Overnight she's started sounding like those teen-agers who go around announcing they'll never get married or have children or take part in supporting a patriarchy."

"So she's learning early," Carole said approvingly. "You shouldn't be worrying, you should be lighting a candle."

"It's easy for you to find it all amusing. She's not your daughter."

Jan regretted the words instantly. As Carole turned away Jan reached out impulsively. "Carole, I didn't mean . . ."

"I know you didn't."

"It's just that . . . Carole, she doesn't *know*. That kid Xavier holding a knife at her throat and pawing her the way he did has distorted everything. Linda's almost a grown woman, and he made her afraid of being a woman. I don't want her locking herself off, closing doors that should stay open."

"Those creeps didn't really do anything to her—?"

"To her it *feels* as if they did."

Carole's eyes met Jan's, her own private grief concealed. "You're both overreacting," she said. "Believe me, Jan, she'll get over this. Just don't try to force her. Let her take her time. She's got plenty of time, God knows. And she has a good example to follow right at home. I'm going to tell her so when we have our girl-to-girl talk."

Jan's smile was rueful. "Do I sound that overanxious?"

"You sound like you need a little moral support, that's all. Now how about another drink?"

Before the waitress's eye was caught again their dinner call came. Over another glass of Chablis and filet of sole Jan found herself feeling unaccountably better. Just talking about her concern had seemed to put it into better perspective, making it less frightening, more ordinary. It occurred to her that such reassurances usually came from talking with Paul. Those talks had broken down lately. Too often, lying beside her, he was somewhere else.

With someone else?

She shook off the speculation impatiently. That wasn't the problem eating at him. She was sure of it. An SAC, she thought with a trace of amusement, didn't have the time.

Leaving the restaurant after dinner, feeling the caress of the balmy June breeze through open car windows, Jan felt more in control of her emotions than she had for days. Sometimes it was restorative just to sit in comfortable surroundings and be waited on and fussed over, even if the fussing was in anticipation of a generous tip. And Carole, bless her, had worked hard through the meal at being bright and amusing.

Then she noticed that Carole was peering back through the rear window, her expression decidedly not amused. "What is it?" Jan asked.

"I'm not sure . . ." Suddenly Carole laughed. "I'm not sure I'd want you along on single's night, Jan, dear. You get too much attention. Who wants to be the ugly girl sitting with the beautiful one?"

"That'll be the day when you believe that," Jan retorted amiably. "Who are you talking about—Gray Suit?"

"Him for one. But he wasn't the only one." Carole twisted in her seat to glance back again. She gave a small impatient shrug. "I guess I was wrong."

"About what? Stop acting mysterious, Carole." Jan glanced into the rearview mirror. A pair of headlights swerved abruptly as a car swung into a side street. Behind it the road was clear. "Did you think we were being followed? By those two would-be swingers?"

"Not them. Did you notice the man over in the dark corner by the front windows when we first came in? No, I guess you didn't. But he saw *you,* I'd swear to that. Either it was love at first sight or he was scared of you seeing him, I don't know which."

"You never mentioned that one."

"I was going to, but when I looked for him after we sat down he was gone."

"What did he look like?" Jan asked curiously.

"Well . . . it was dark off in that corner, especially when we first came in from outside. All I can tell you is he was solid, square—you know, an FBI type. All wrong for the beautiful blonde he was with."

"Beautiful blonde? Oh, for heaven's sake, Carole—"

"But he *did* just about lose his teeth when he saw you," Carole insisted. "The blonde was one of the things that made me notice his reaction—no offense, dear, but she made Miss America look tacky. So why did he have a roving eye?"

Jan smiled. "Maybe you were the one who caught his eye, not me."

"I don't think so." Carole was silent for a few moments, then said reflectively, "He looked familiar, you know? Like somebody I should have known. Maybe that's it, maybe he's someone notable. Anyway, he sure got out of there in a hurry. But . . ."

Jan had a sudden intuition that caused her to look again into the mirror at the road behind them. "Did you think *he* was following us?"

Carole gave a quick little laugh. "Okay, so I'm being paranoid, but I did think the same guy was watching us from a car in the parking lot when we left. And he pulled out right behind us."

Without knowing exactly why, Jan felt a chill at the nape of her neck. "There's no one there now."

"I know, I know. I guess it was my imagination." After a moment's consideration Carole shrugged, a self-deprecatory gesture. "He was probably one of the shy ones. God save us from the ones who hide behind trees!"

Jan dropped Carole Baumgartner off at her condo, declined an invitation to come in for coffee and drove on home. Alone with her thoughts, she found herself wondering about the man in the bar who had left so hastily.

Once again Jan felt an unmistakable chill. As she turned off the highway onto Long Valley Road, she glanced into the rearview mirror, saw no one following her and suddenly remembered Paul doing the same thing the night of the robbery.

9

By seven o'clock Wednesday morning, when the first agents began to arrive, the special squad room had been set up for the task force assigned to the Brea investigation. Desks had been borrowed or requisitioned from other units and even from an office of the GSA which was in the same building.

The file that would rapidly grow to a thick volume on the Brea investigation was thin that first morning. There was one new item of interest: a Nitel from Agents Collins and Garvey. The two men had been routed to Sacramento by way of San Francisco, where according to the night teletype report, they had been met by Agent Charles Reese of the San Francisco Field Office. They had talked at length to Reese about Walter Schumaker, whom Reese had originally recruited as an informant. Reese's former partner, Victor Pryor, who was now working in private security for a Bay Area electronics firm, was presently attending a security conference in Chicago, staying at the Chicago Hilton.

Reese had added little that was not already known. Vernon Lippert had requested a copy of the tape recording of Walter Schumaker's voice back in January. That was the first Reese had learned of what had been an extensive search by Lippert into the records of informants—always kept in special indices—run out of the San Francisco office. Reese had been curious about Lippert's inquiries, but not enough to sustain his interest after Lippert's death. He knew of no reason for Lippert to be interested in Schumaker, who had dropped out of sight about three years ago after being dropped from the FBI's payroll. "He didn't give us anything worth paying for," Reese had said.

Macimer called Harrison Stearns into his office. The young agent would be copying, filing and forwarding the field reports as they came in. "I want to know where Collins and Garvey are staying as soon as we hear," Macimer said. "And inform them I want telephonic reports of anything important in addition to the teletypes. Give them my home phone number. With the time difference, they might have to reach me there at night."

"Yes, sir."

"And send Rodriguez in here."

William Rodriguez had been pulled from an undercover assignment in New York—the kind of work J. Edgar Hoover had disapproved of for his agents, but which in recent years had proven to be indispensable for investigations into white collar and organized crime, government corruption and terrorist activities. Rodriguez was stocky, round-faced, with thick glossy black hair that came almost to his shoulders and a bandido mustache that drooped on either side of his mouth. He had not slept, arriving from New York on an early-morning flight, and he still wore his street clothes from the Puerto Rican barrio—jeans and a T-shirt that carried a printed message: "I'm Gonna Be a Poppa."

"Is that true?" Macimer asked with a grin.

"I hope not," Rodriguez said. "I'm not married."

He spoke without an accent. Rodriguez was American-born of Mexican parents, his father having been an illegal alien who found work in Texas. The agent spoke fluent Spanish, but he also had a good ear and was adept at accents, enabling him to blend easily into different Latin communities. He could pass for a Chicano in Los Angeles, a Puerto Rican in New York or a Cuban in Miami.

Macimer told him about the robbery at his house and described the three Hispanics who had taken part. "Your job is to find them. You'll have a partner. Have you worked with Jo Singleton before?"

Rodriguez shrugged. "She's okay." White teeth flashed in a grin. "She's got a lousy accent, that's all."

"Then you'll have to cover for her."

"You got any drawings of those robbers?"

Macimer removed some photocopies from a folder. Rodriguez studied them briefly, then slipped them into his own vinyl briefcase. "Anything from the lab yet on those sheets you sent over?"

"Not yet—I'll let you know as soon as we have anything."

Rodriguez was brash, cocky, but Macimer wasn't ready to complain if the cockiness was deserved. That remained to be seen. For now, Rodriguez could follow up on Garvey's name search. It wasn't much to hang an investigation on, Macimer thought as the agent left, but there wasn't much else.

He wondered if Collins and Garvey were in San Timoteo and what they were learning. If anything were to be discovered that would fill in the missing pieces of Vernon Lippert's mysterious file, it would probably be found in Lippert's own territory.

"Yes, sir!" Harold Whittaker said enthusiastically. "Vern Lippert used to come in here regular as clockwork. Used to sit right there in that chair you're sitting in, Mr. Collins, sir. We worked fine together—none of that stuff you hear about where the police and the FBI are stepping on each other's corns, you know? You'll find we're happy to cooperate with you folks."

Collins refrained from reminding the San Timoteo police chief that, at the big moment of his law enforcement life, he had failed to call the resident FBI agent when he went out with his men to surround the People's Revolutionary Committee in their hideout. Apparently close cooperation had its limits. "I'm glad to hear that, Chief Whittaker. What we're most interested in right now is why Lippert was digging into that disaster after all this time. Did he talk to you about it?"

The police chief shifted his bulk in his chair. He was in his shirt sleeves. The office in a yellow brick building on Main Street in downtown San Timoteo was cooled by one of those big wooden ceiling fans that reminded Collins of an old Sidney Greenstreet–Peter Lorre movie. Outside, at nine-thirty in the morning, it was already hot. Collins didn't mind heat when he was working. He found that it tended to distress the people he was dealing with more than it did him.

"Vern had a bug up his . . . in his ear," Whittaker amended. "No getting away from that. If you want my opinion, Mr. Collins, sir, I think it was, you know, kind of an obsession with him, what happened to the PRC that day. He was there, you know."

The comment was condescending but Collins gave no sign. It had taken the burly police chief a while to get over the shock of having a black FBI agent walk into his office, Collins thought. He said, "You were there, too, weren't you, Chief?"

"That's right! Yes, sir, that's true. You'd have seen that in your reports, I reckon. Mr. Collins, that affair was over and done with a long time ago. It was investigated every which way, but Vern couldn't let go of it, like a dog worrying a bone."

"You don't think he had learned anything new about what happened?"

"What was there to learn? Hell, Mr. Collins—beggin' your pardon, sir—thirty million people seen the whole thing on the TV. If there was anything left to be dug up that we didn't find, or the FBI didn't find, you can be sure those reporters would've dug it up. We had reporters upstairs and downstairs here, sir, hundreds of 'em, for weeks after the dust settled. Seemed like we had a reporter for every single citizen of San Timoteo. I doubt there's anybody in this town wasn't interviewed about what he had for breakfast that day, much less what he might have seen."

"But Lippert had been asking some of those questions again, hadn't he? Recently, I mean—just before he died?"

"Well . . . yes, sir, I believe he was."

"Like who fired the first shot that triggered what happened?"

Harold Whittaker scowled. It was a question he had been asked too many times. Collins watched the chief struggle to control his exasperation. "That shot come from the house, Mr. Collins, sir. My men didn't shoot until they were shot at. They had their orders, and they knew I'd of had any man's badge that fired his weapon without provocation. You'll excuse me, sir, but I've been asked that question a thousand times and the answer's still the same. We didn't go in there like it was the O.K. Corral. We surrounded that house and I ordered those terrorists to come out. The answer was a gunshot, and that's the way it happened."

"A rifle shot, Chief Whittaker?"

The police chief looked startled. "Well . . . yes, sir, I'd say it was a rifle shot. Can't swear to that now, after so long, but you get to know the difference without thinking about it. Rifle gives you a kind of slam instead of the pop you get with a handgun."

Collins nodded, making brief notes as Whittaker watched. "Thanks a lot, Chief. You don't mind if I talk to some of the officers who were there, the ones Vernon Lippert questioned? I want to know what Lippert was looking for exactly."

Whittaker had another struggle with himself. Collins regarded him impassively. San Timoteo's burly police chief had been visibly surprised when Collins entered his office, but Whittaker possessed the small-town lawman's respect for—even awe of—the Federal Bureau of Investigation. After covering his initial reaction, Whittaker had been "sir-ing" Collins to an embarrassing degree. Once again, that respect won out.

"You go right ahead, Mr. Collins, sir. Like I said, we've always cooperated fully with your people. We were sorry to have the local FBI office shut down here after Mr. Lippert passed away, and that's a fact. People hereabouts liked knowing there was a government agent just down the street, someone they knew. You talk to my men, Mr. Collins, but it won't change anything in the record."

"It's routine, Chief Whittaker. We're simply trying to find out what Agent Lippert was digging into those last few months before he died." Collins paused. "Were you particularly surprised by his accident?"

Whittaker frowned. He swung around in his chair to stare through the window toward the tiny park across the street. In the still, hot air two old men sat motionless on a green bench, and an old VW without a lid over its exposed rear engine drove by with a deep-throated growl.

"Surprised? Now that's an interesting question, Mr. Collins, sir. Yes, sir, that's one question nobody asked me before. Fact is, I *was* surprised. I been fishin' with Vern Lippert up at Lake Hieronimo. He knew that lake, he knew how to handle a boat and he could swim. But the coroner's report up there made it plain. Vern drowned, that's all."

"No bruises, nothing unexplained?"

"Only one thing," Harold Whittaker said. "How a man like Vernon Lippert could have let it happen."

Late that afternoon, after losing a flip of a coin with Collins, Pat Garvey drove the forty miles from San Timoteo to the FBI's field office in Sacramento. There he visited the secure cable room and telexed copies of the two agents' reports for their first day of work on the Brea case.

When he got back to the motel on the outskirts of San Timoteo he and Collins went out to dinner. They ate at a Sambo's Restaurant. "This okay with you?" Garvey asked.

"As long as they got pancakes," said Collins.

They slid into a booth, ordered hamburgers instead of pancakes and looked out the windows at the quiet main street. "Lively little town," Collins observed. "Looks like Sambo's is one of the real night spots."

Garvey glanced around the restaurant. The booths were crowded with young people in jeans and T-shirts and shaggy hair, older families with children, a few elderly couples. One baby was banging on its special high chair with a spoon. "It's a nice town," Garvey said. "Decent people, not much crime. I can understand why Vernon Lippert never wanted to leave here."

Collins stared at him. "It still has its one claim to fame. It blew up the whole People's Revolutionary Committee."

Garvey shrugged. "Those nuts didn't belong here. They came from outside."

"They had to be born somewhere." Collins regarded his partner speculatively. He had not worked with Garvey before, although they had both been with the WFC the past two years. Although two years younger, Garvey was actually the senior agent of the two, having been with the Bureau a year longer than Collins. Collins hadn't especially looked forward to the pairing. Not that there was anything wrong with Garvey—or maybe that was the problem in itself. He sometimes seemed a little too good to be true. A little too wide-eyed, Collins thought. Maybe that was it. He envied Garvey his innocence. He said, "You really like this place? You'd like to end up in an RA's office someplace like this? In Sleepy Town?"

"Yes," Garvey said, nodding at first tentatively, then more emphatically. "Wouldn't you?"

Collins thought of the scene in the park outside the police station that morning, the two old men sitting on the bench, dazed in the sun, the desultory traffic along the main street, the lone fly buzzing against Chief Whittaker's window. "I like a little more action," Collins said.

They walked back to their motel after dinner. They carried cold soft-drink cans from a dispensing machine to their room, where they relaxed in wood-and-leather Mexican chairs more comfortable than they appeared. Collins described his interview with

Chief Harold Whittaker and several members of the San Timoteo police department. "One of them, Forbes—he's a sergeant—was in charge of the detail behind the house on Dover Street that night. He insists none of his men fired the first shot. And everyone seems to agree that it didn't come from out front." Collins reviewed the ground he had covered during the day. "You could say they're all covering for themselves, but I don't think so. Forbes swears the shot never came from any of his men behind the house. He heard it, but couldn't say where it came from."

"And that's what Lippert kept asking?"

"The same questions, nothing new. How about you? You come up with anything?"

Garvey shook his head. "I hit every house in the 1200 block and the 1300 block, where the hideout was. I've got a half-dozen places to go back to where nobody was home or there's someone else who was there back in '81. The best witness is the one we already knew about, Mrs. Torgeson. She lives right across the street from where the PRC hideout was. She saw the whole thing from an upstairs window."

"The nosy woman?"

Garvey nodded. "There's one on every street. The kind who knows when everyone comes and goes. The one who's always looking out from behind a curtain. Mrs. Torgeson had her eye on that house especially because of all the young people who'd moved in." Garvey smiled. "She thought there were some funny goings-on, all those young people in one house, and she didn't approve. She figured maybe it was one of those communes she'd read about. She has arthritis—she has one of those metal hip sockets that enables her to walk, but she doesn't get around well. So she spends a lot of time at her window, looking out."

"She saw Schumaker leave the house on the twenty-seventh?"

"She saw a man go out that morning, and the description fits Schumaker. He came back with groceries about noon." Garvey shook his head. "You won't change that woman's story. It made a celebrity out of her, she was interviewed so many times, even on television. But the story holds up."

"She's absolutely sure no one left the house all day on the twenty-eighth? How can she be so sure?"

"She says she was home all that day, and my guess is she spent the whole time close to that window. That neighborhood is far enough away from any shops that a stranger couldn't have walked far without being noticed. If anyone had gone in or out, they'd have used a car . . . and no one did."

Collins looked at him steadily. "You know what that means, don't you?"

Garvey wore his intent, serious expression, the blue eyes curious under heavy black eyebrows. "I'm not sure . . ."

Collins asked himself, not for the first time, how he had got teamed up with this All-American. He said, "It means that when Schumaker was out getting groceries on the twenty-seventh he made that call to Brea in Sacramento asking for help. And if he didn't leave the house the next day, it means he couldn't have made the call to the police, the one that tipped them off and sent them charging out to the house on Dover Street."

Garvey was silent, staring at his partner.

"Brea," Collins said softly. "He was the only one on the outside who knew the PRC was holed up in that house. So he's the only one who could have tipped off the fuzz."

"For God's sake, why?"

"He wanted it to happen," Collins answered quietly. "He made it happen."

The time was three hours later in Washington, D.C., than in San Timoteo, California, and in a gracious southern colonial house in Chevy Chase, Maryland, Erika Halbig warmed a Waterford brandy glass between her hands. She was reclining on the cut-velvet gold chaise in the big upstairs bedroom, wearing an almost transparent nightgown that clung softly to her full breasts and long, smooth thighs. When Russell Halbig entered the room he glanced at the glass in her hands but made no comment. Erika watched with detached interest as he undressed, retired to the bathroom, where she could hear the Waterpik growling, then reappeared. The brandy—her third of the evening—had its usual effect of making her less tense, enabling her to feel a little detached.

Halbig had come home late, then spent much of the evening in his study. During one period he had talked for a long time to a United States senator. Not that he had told her of the call. Erika knew because the maid, Alma, had answered the phone in the hall and, after Halbig took it in his study, whispered the name of the caller to Erika.

"Anything interesting happen today?" Erika asked him now,

watching as he did his exercises beside his bed. They had had twin beds since the first year.

"The usual," Halbig said, grunting as he did sit-ups with his feet hooked under the bed frame.

The usual, she repeated to herself. What was usual? How was she supposed to know when he never talked to her of the usual or the unusual? "What did Senator Sederholm want with you?"

Halbig halted in the middle of a sit-up exercise, his hands locked behind his head. His head really was too small for him, she thought. "Alma told you?"

"Yes, wasn't she supposed to?"

Halbig did not reply to that. Instead he said, "The senator just won a big primary election in California yesterday. I congratulated him."

Erika nodded, as if he had answered her question. She wondered when she had first begun to accept his responses as if they were real answers. "Will you be inviting him to the house?"

Halbig finished his exercises. He was not breathing hard. He didn't even breathe hard after sex, she reminded herself. As if it were just another form of exercise. Climbing into bed and turning off the light on the nightstand beside it, leaving her in a pool of light on her side of the room, Halbig said, "I don't know about that, but I did invite some guests for this Saturday night."

"Who?"

"The Macimers—you remember Paul and Jan. And Gordon and Mary Ruhle."

Erika Halbig felt an odd fluttering of her heart, a moment's breathlessness. She put down her empty brandy glass on the small fruitwood table beside the chaise. She did it very carefully, pleased that her hand was steady. "Whatever for?" she asked. "What made you invite them?"

Halbig turned over in his bed, settling himself with his back toward her and the light. "I have my reasons," he said, in a tone that made it quite plain she was not to ask what they were. "Besides," he added, "they're old friends."

"I really don't understand this sudden interest in old friends," Jan Macimer said.

"Gordon, Russ and I haven't been in the same place very often in recent years. I guess Halbig thought we ought to make a stab at old acquaintance."

"Mmmm." Jan skimmed through another of the examinations she had brought home with her from the final class of the semester. She would read thoroughly and grade them later. For now she wanted first impressions, a sense of how much had been learned, how much was still to be done. Idly she asked, "How long has Gordon been at Quantico?"

"A couple of weeks, it turns out. He came in as a special instructor for the Anti-Terrorist Task Force. A volunteer," Paul Macimer added. "You know how gung ho Gordon always was."

"Yes," Jan said dryly. "Have you talked to him?"

Paul shook his head. "I'll see him tomorrow and surprise the old bastard." He would also be seeing Timothy Callahan, but Macimer did not mention this. In a late-afternoon call Russ Halbig had suggested that Macimer drive down to Quantico in the morning. "Why Callahan?" Macimer had asked curiously. "Have you forgotten, Paul? He was Landers' number two on the PRC Task Force. He knows that case as well as anyone alive. The Director thought you should talk to him. Callahan also knew Lippert well—was once quite close to him. They worked together, I believe."

Halbig knew perfectly well, Macimer thought, exactly when and for how long Callahan and Lippert had worked together.

Jan put her students' exam papers aside, satisfied with the first run-through. Better than she had feared, not quite as good overall as she had hoped. But some of the gains in the class, she felt, were intangible, such as increased self-confidence and improved self-images, benefits that wouldn't necessarily show up in a written test.

"Was tonight the last class?" Paul asked suddenly.

Jan looked up with a smile. "It was. You get a B-plus for remembering. A little late, maybe, but . . ."

"I meant to ask you earlier," he said lamely. "I hadn't really forgotten." There was a moment's awkwardness, a silence that left room for Jan's unspoken thought that he did not regard her class as very important. He said, as if reading her thought, "You're wrong, I do care. How did it go? How do the exams look?"

"Pretty good. I'll know better tomorrow."

They went upstairs together. While they were undressing, Jan said, "Paul . . . I'm worried about Linda."

"What's wrong with Linda?"

"You know perfectly well. You haven't been *that* remote from your family these past few weeks, though it seems like it."

"I know she was upset over the robbery—"

"Upset! Paul, she isn't only upset. It goes a lot deeper than that. I think she should talk to someone."

"Like who? You mean a doctor?"

"I mean an analyst."

"A shrink? Are you kidding?"

"There's nothing funny about it."

Macimer frowned. He had a reflex reaction against the notion of his daughter seeing a psychiatrist. He knew it was an old-fashioned response—hell, he was quick enough to call on the insights of a criminal psychologist when a case called for it. But that was different. . . .

"Do you really think it's that serious?"

"I think *you* ought to have a talk with her for a start. Maybe that would help."

"All right, I will."

He went to the window and stood in his pajama bottoms staring out at the soft rain, which created a mist like fog around streetlights and muffled the sounds of distant traffic. In that distance an ambulance wailed, the cry bodiless and remote like the anguish of a lost soul. Behind him, from the bed, Jan said, "There's something else. Paul . . . is there any reason someone from the Bureau would follow me? Or why anyone else would, for that matter?"

Macimer turned to stare at her. "What makes you ask that?"

"Carole thought a man followed us from the restaurant last night." She gave a brief account of the evening, concluding with Carole's description of the stranger who had reacted so sharply to Jan's entrance and had later followed them when they left the restaurant.

"Sounds to me as if you picked up an admirer."

"I didn't pick him up and he apparently didn't want to have anything to do with me," she said dryly. She had not mentioned the man in the gray suit. "Would you tell me if you knew why someone might follow me?"

He hesitated a moment too long. "Of course. Unless it was better for you not to know."

"And I don't get to decide what's best for me, right?"

"Jan, honey, I didn't say that. I don't know anything about anyone following you. There's no reason for it."

"Well, *something* odd is going on. Our house is invaded, our daughter is terrorized, I'm followed by a stranger—"

"We don't know you were even followed. That's Carole's vivid imagination."

"She didn't make him up!" Jan snapped.

"How can you be sure?"

"How can I be sure of anything? Paul—is this family in some kind of danger? What about the children?"

"No."

"How can I believe that? I'm not sure you'd tell me."

"Why should you believe me? Nobody believes the FBI anymore, right?"

"You said it, not me. Anyway, I'm not talking about the FBI. I'm talking about you and me and our children."

"*And* the FBI."

"If you say so."

As always when they argued, the tension in the room was palpable, so charged you would expect it to expode if either of them struck a match. But Macimer sensed something different about this sudden clash. Jan was further from him. They were not simply a man and a woman suddenly lashing out. They were shouting across a chasm wider than he had known was there.

Crawling into bed and turning off the lights, Macimer told himself something he had been reluctant to accept for a long time: the problem between them went deeper than momentary angers.

He could feel the warmth of her body beside him, smell the familiar scent. As if aware of his response, she turned away slightly, a small but meaningful gesture. "I had a letter from Mom today," she said quietly. "They want to know if we're coming out to Arizona. We said we might come as soon as the school year was out."

"I won't be able to get away just now." Paul thought of the man in the restaurant and of Carole Baumgartner's acute perceptions, which he took more seriously than he had let on. Jan's parents had moved to Sun City outside of Phoenix after her father retired. It was a long way from Washington. Sunny and safe. "Maybe you and the kids should go."

"You mean it might be a good idea if we were separated for a while?"

"I didn't mean that at all. And I don't think it."

"I do," Jan said. "I think it might be a good idea for both of us."

10

By Wednesday morning the skies had cleared. The air was hot and humid as only Washington can be in June. After a review of general cases under investigation by the WFO, which Macimer had turned over to Jerry Russell, the ASAC, and a quick glance at the first reports in from the agents in California on the Brea case, Macimer left the Washington Field Office and drove across the Rochambeau Bridge. He had a glimpse of the Thomas Jefferson Memorial off to his right, serene and white and classical. Then he swung onto the Washington Memorial Parkway heading south.

As Macimer left Alexandria behind and drove on through the rolling Virginia countryside, his thoughts soon drifted far from the current tangle of WFO cases and came to rest on another hot and humid morning, in the Blue Goose Cafe in downtown Omaha, when Gordon Ruhle told him that he was volunteering for transfer to the newly created field office in Jackson, Mississippi.

Omaha had been Macimer's first office assignment after graduation from the FBI Academy. After two months of tedious file searches and employee background checks, Macimer had been assigned to the Resident Agent's office in York, where Gordon Ruhle was the Senior Agent.

It was the kind of town where, in the perspective of each year, the county fair stood out as an exciting event. Everyone in town knew the FBI men and respected them. There was an easy camaraderie with the local sheriff and his deputies—every Friday morning they held an informal "law enforcement breakfast" at the Pancake House, ostensibly to discuss mutual problems but actually to socialize.

Most of the cases involved auto thieves, parole violators, deserters or Selective Service defaulters. Macimer reported to a criminal squad in the Omaha Field Office. An RA was, in fact, simply an extension of the parent field office, and supposedly Macimer's assignments were those that came from the parent squad through his field supervisor in Omaha. In practice, Gordon Ruhle, as the Senior Resident Agent, operated a very loose ship in the York office. Everyone worked on any case that came up. Even though most of them were routine and unexciting, it was an ideal way for a first office agent to break in. In a larger office, as Macimer would later learn, he might have spent most of his first year or more doing nothing but humdrum applicant work—interviewing neighbors and friends, checking school and credit records, running name checks through the Bureau's criminal and security files. The kind of work older agents near retirement were often glad enough to settle into, since it involved no risks of rocking the boat or in any way jeopardizing what they had worked a whole career for.

Eventually, during a flap over suspected sabotage at the home of the Strategic Air Command outside Omaha, both Gordon Ruhle and Macimer were called back into the Omaha office. They were both working on the espionage squad in Omaha when the call came from FBI Headquarters for volunteers to go to Mississippi, in the summer of 1964.

That morning in the Blue Goose Cafe in Omaha when Ruhle made his announcement, there was never a moment's doubt in Paul Macimer's mind that he would also volunteer for the Jackson assignment.

Puzzled that Gordon Ruhle would be eager to protect civil rights workers drawn to the South by the Movement, Macimer soon understood that Gordon's views had not changed. Ruhle had little sympathy for liberal activists, but he was an FBI man through and through. He had sworn to uphold and enforce the laws of the land. If that meant protecting long-haired northern radicals in jeans and T-shirts from the hatred and violence of southern rednecks and Klan terrorists—for whom Ruhle had no more use than he did for New York Jewish liberals, Communists or militant blacks—then he would protect them. Or find their murderers.

When Macimer expressed surprise that Russ Halbig would volunteer for dangerous duty in Mississippi, Gordon Ruhle shook his head. "No surprise," he said with a cynical grin. "The Old Man is gonna be watching what we do down there. Halbig knows that. He could work ten years in Omaha without ever being noticed."

In the hue and cry following the murder of three civil rights activists earlier that summer, J. Edgar Hoover gave a veteran agent, Roy K. Moore, five days to have a new field office open for business in Jackson, to serve as headquarters for the Bureau's greatly expanded effort to find the killers and to prevent further violence. Moore was not exactly your typical SAC, although he had Hoover's confidence. He was flamboyant, action-oriented, a man who got things done and would overlook departures from the FBI Manual if they brought results. Gordon Ruhle loved him.

Moore set up the Jackson office in July of 1964 at the height of that summer's voter registration drives and in an atmosphere of hostility and threatened violence. Macimer, Ruhle and Halbig arrived in August. Two nights later Macimer was crouching behind a hedge bordering the dirt lot of a Negro church when a shotgun blast neatly decapitated the hedge. It was his first real taste of being under fire.

The agents had plenty of action over the next two years, shepherding youthful activists from the North and trying to protect those blacks who were bold enough to provide the outsiders shelter, sympathy and a reason for being there. Jackson itself was not what the agents called hazardous duty. The Mississippi power structure kept things under control in the larger and more prosperous cities. Danger waited back in the woods, on the remote farms and in the small rural towns. Macimer and Ruhle spent nights in a mosquito-ridden swamp on a stakeout, crawled under a grocery store to defuse a ticking bomb, had the tires of their moving car shot up. From Ruhle, Macimer learned how to ferret out and use informants, who generally acted less from altruism or moral conviction than the need of money. Russ Halbig, true to form, became useful to the beleaguered Moore as a liaison between the SAC and the hundreds of reporters who were underfoot, for the Jackson office had become the information center for the civil rights struggle in Mississippi.

In the summer of 1966 a young man named Ira Rothleder came to Mississippi from New York, where he had worked in a settlement house. He was accompanied by his wife Maureen, a pretty, sunny-natured Irish girl who had a special way with children. The young couple opened a child-care center and library, stocked with books they had brought with them in cardboard boxes in their overladen VW bus. Maureen began luring children and their mothers to the center while Ira joined other activists in that summer's voter registration drive.

On a hot evening late in July, the Rothleders and a seventeen-year-old black girl from Hattiesburg who was helping out at the center were busy unpacking boxes of newly arrived used books. Without warning fire bombs crashed through two front windows and exploded. In panic the three young people tried to escape through the back door of the small frame building. Another bomb turned the narrow back hallway into an inferno. There was no way out of the burning building except the front door.

Outside, parked in the street with the motor of their pickup truck running, four men waited, at least three of them armed with rifles or shotguns. Rothleder, the first one through the door, was struck down by two rifle bullets in the chest. He died almost instantly. A shotgun blast nearly cut the slim young black girl, Cynthia Watson, in half. The last rifle shot, as the pickup roared away, struck Maureen Rothleder in the jaw. She would survive the fire, the rain of gunfire and a series of operations over the next six months to rebuild her shattered face.

Paul Macimer and Gordon Ruhle were among nearly a hundred agents who worked on the case over the next six weeks. The pickup truck was found two days later parked on a street in Greenville. It had been stolen in Jackson twenty-four hours before. Although a score of FBI lab technicians sifted the cab and bed of the truck for every hair, fiber and smear of dirt from a muddy boot, no evidence was found that would identify the four men who had waited outside the Rothleders' child-care center for the flames to drive their victims toward them.

What seemed a promising lead developed through one of Macimer's informants, who claimed to know the identity of the driver of the pickup truck involved in the killings. The driver was a nineteen-year-old who had been present that night to prove his worth as a new member of the local klavern of the Ku Klux Klan. According to his story, he had not been armed. Because he was the only one involved who hadn't fired one of the murder weapons, he was not trusted by the other three attackers. He was afraid for his life.

After a series of aborted meetings, Macimer finally came face to face with Leroy Parrish in a remote, abandoned farmhouse. Parrish was not a prepossessing youngster—skinny, chicken-necked, his face blotched with acne, he wore the hangdog air of a born loser. The kind, Macimer thought, who would say anything to get attention—or a reward.

But something about Leroy Parrish rang true: his fear.

That first meeting the youth refused to admit that he had driven the pickup truck to the scene of the bombing. He would not reveal the names of the other three men. He demanded assurances of protection if he talked—and enough money to get a long way from Mississippi.

The SAC of the Jackson Field Office was skeptical. There were dozens of more solid leads to track down. Agents were meeting would-be informants on every street corner and behind every barn. Nevertheless, after wary negotiations over the next two weeks, an agreement was made to protect and relocate the young man, and to pay him $10,000 for his testimony—providing that he could produce evidence leading to the identity of the three bomber-slayers.

The deal was conditional. It was one of many being made, all of them contingent on some proof that the informant was telling the truth. No one gave Leroy Parrish's story much credence—except Macimer.

Abruptly the youth vanished. For two frustrating weeks there was no word. Either Parrish's story had been a hoax, a con game designed to get him some money for nothing, or he had been murdered. Then, late one Saturday afternoon in September, Macimer received a phone call. He recognized Leroy Parrish's voice immediately. The deal was on.

Leroy agreed to meet the FBI agent at the farmhouse where they had first met. But the youth insisted that he would deal only with Macimer himself. If the agent didn't come alone, there would be no meeting. Parrish trusted no one else. When Macimer was dubious, Leroy offered an irresistible inducement: he would take the agent to the place where the murder weapons had been buried.

It was a hot September day and the office was quiet. Even most of the hordes of reporters had escaped to their motel rooms and cold six-packs. The SAC could not be reached, and the few agents on hand had their own assignments.

Russ Halbig came on duty at four o'clock; he would be in the office until midnight. Macimer told him what he was doing. Then he tracked down Gordon Ruhle. The older agent was skeptical of Leroy Parrish's story, and he didn't approve of Macimer meeting the youth alone in an isolated place. But he finally agreed to trail behind Macimer with two other agents in a backup car, staying well out of sight.

Macimer drove alone to the farmhouse. He waited there with Leroy Parrish until dark. They drove north in the FBI man's car for a half hour. Then, at Parrish's insistence, Macimer let the youth take the wheel as they turned along back roads away from the main highway. Parrish drove with surprising speed and skill, turning frequently onto side roads. Macimer realized that the backup car had probably been lost far behind. He wondered if Parrish had known or guessed that they were being followed.

The last dirt road led them onto a desolate farm, dark and empty, bordered by an almost impenetrable swamp.

Macimer was knee deep in mud at the edge of the swamp, bathed in sweat as he dug by the light of a full moon, when Leroy's scream alerted him. A car's headlights slashed the dirt road leading across the farm toward the marshy bottomland.

"You tricked me! I tol' you no one else was to know!"

Macimer stared at the headlights racing toward them. "Those aren't FBI."

"Oh my God!" Parrish moaned. "Then it's them! They been watchin' me."

Macimer floundered out of the swamp. The mud sucked one shoe from his foot. "Get down!" he warned. "Behind the car."

The whine of the approaching car's engine cut off abruptly. An instant later the headlights vanished. In the sudden darkness a rifle crashed. The bullet smacked through a side window of Macimer's automobile. Macimer fired at the muzzle flash with his Smith & Wesson. Someone cried out.

Macimer felt a surge of adrenaline. But even if he had scored a lucky hit with his first shot, he thought, it wasn't going to be much of a fire fight. Not if the remaining attackers carried rifles to overpower his handgun.

He crawled over to the car door on the driver's side. Ruhle and

the others in the backup car might have been left behind, but they
would be searching, somewhere not far off. If he could send a
radio message for help . . .

When he had first taken possession of his assigned vehicle Macimer had taken the precaution of taping over the button on the
door frame that turned on the car's interior light when the door
opened. He reached cautiously for the door handle.

Either the tape had come loose or the connection had not been
securely broken. As Macimer opened the door, the light came on.

Two rapid shots drove him away from the car door. The shots
had come from a second rifle, this one off to his left.

Then another bullet ricocheted off the rear bumper.

"Back off!" Macimer ordered Parrish. "We're going to have to
get wet."

"No! I can't—"

"If they hit that gas tank," Macimer said grimly, "you won't
spend any of that reward money."

He dragged the shivering youth into the swamp. The thick
marsh grass and stunted trees would hide them.

As if in response to his thought a searchlight sprang on. From
its height and steadiness Macimer guessed it was attached to the
terrorists' vehicle. The bright beam began to track across the edge
of the swamp. Macimer took careful aim and fired. The light exploded.

With the return of darkness the attackers began to fire at Macimer's car, a fusillade of high-powered rifle shots seeking out the
gas tank. When a bullet finally found the target, the concentrated
force of a half tank of gasoline exploded with the fury of two hundred sticks of dynamite. Forty yards away in the swamp, Macimer
was flattened by the concussion.

He came up spluttering, found Leroy Parrish underwater and
pulled the youth's head up. Sensing the boy would scream in his
terror, Macimer clamped a hand over his mouth.

Crouching in the swamp, up to his waist in the muddy water,
Macimer wondered if the attackers had been able to see him and
Parrish in the searing light of the explosion. There was a good
chance they hadn't. The terrorists themselves had been close
enough to the ear-shattering explosion to have been knocked flat,
or even hit by flying shrapnel if they hadn't had the sense to fire
from cover.

He retreated deeper into the swamp. Young Parrish resisted, moaning and shivering. Macimer warned him angrily. "If they find us before help gets here—if it gets here at all—they'll gut us and fill our bellies with rocks and dump us so deep into this mudhole we'll never be found. So make up your mind whether you want to keep sending them messages."

"It . . . it's not just them," Parrish sobbed. "It's . . . the snakes! I can't stand snakes."

Macimer felt his own blood run cold. He had forgotten that these swamps teemed with water moccasins.

Fifty yards into the swamp Macimer found a patch of relatively solid ground. There he huddled with Parrish in the tangled grass. One thing was now certain, he thought wryly: Leroy Parrish had told the truth. And his fear had been justified.

A half hour dragged by. With each passing moment Macimer's hope that Ruhle and the other agents in the backup car might have seen the glare of the explosion and fire became dimmer, dwindling like the glow from the burning car. He could hear the terrorists prowling about along the edge of the swamp. They, too, were reluctant to enter it in the darkness. Occasionally they called out to each other. Two voices. That meant that one of the attackers had been dealt out of the game by Macimer's first shot.

Silence closed over the swamp, whose surface was now bathed in an oily sheen of moonlight. The only sounds were an infrequent small splash from something moving in the water and the buzzing of mosquitoes zeroing in on their tempting targets. Macimer began to wonder if the mosquitoes would leave enough of him to care about. He fought off the urge to slap at them. His only protection was to slip into the muddy, foul-smelling water, leaving only his head exposed. Once he dipped his head underwater to wash off the persistent mosquitoes. When he broke the surface again something flicked past his cheek. Macimer shook the water from his eyes and stared. A four-foot snake glided across the moonlit surface of the swamp, its speed astonishing. The moccasin's tail had stroked Macimer's face as it passed. The agent crouched in the swamp, shuddering as Leroy Parrish had shaken in his fear.

A rifle shot shattered the long silence of the night. Startled, Leroy Parrish gave an anguished cry. Macimer reached for him to silence him, but his attention was diverted. He stared at the point where he had seen the muzzle flash. The direction of the flash had been skyward. As if the rifleman were shooting at stars.

A faint hope grew as Macimer waited. Then a cool voice floated over the swamp. "You out there, Paul?"

He grinned in delicious relief. "Me and the snakes."

"You got your pigeon with you, too?"

"He's here, all in one piece."

"Well, you can come out and dry off," Gordon Ruhle said. "These old boys won't be giving us any more trouble."

Ruhle himself had jumped the man who had fired his rifle skyward in a reflex jerk of the trigger. Two other agents had overpowered a second terrorist. The third, wounded in the arm, had been found lying beside the attackers' vehicle. Offering no resistance, he had even told the agents where to look for the Rothleder murder weapons buried at the edge of the swamp.

A long time ago, Paul Macimer thought, as he drove south from Washington toward Quantico. Looking back, it seemed like a different world. The lines of choice, so clear just a few years earlier, had already begun to blur a little in the mid-sixties. But there had been nothing uncertain or unclear about the satisfaction Macimer had felt when he labored out of that muddy bottom and found the three redneck terrorists subdued and handcuffed.

His reminiscent smile faded as he thought of Russ Halbig. Did Halbig also remember that night in Mississippi? On night duty at the Jackson Field Office, he had taken Macimer's call. He had warned against the agents talking to any reporters. The three prisoners were to be brought quietly to Jackson while Macimer took Leroy Parrish into hiding.

Then, Macimer later learned, Halbig thoughtfully placed a call to Washington, D.C. By the time the agents reached Jackson with their prisoners early the next morning, J. Edgar Hoover, alerted by Halbig's call, had personally released the announcement of their capture, thus scooping the hundreds of reporters who were in Mississippi that day.

For Paul Macimer, the Rothleder case was the high point of his tour of duty in Mississippi. Six months later he was transferred to northern California, where violent student anti-war protests were causing concern. Russell Halbig was rewarded for his role that night in Jackson by being assigned to the Administrative Division of the Bureau in FBI Headquarters. Gordon Ruhle stayed on in

Mississippi for another four years. He had been particularly successful in developing a network of informants in the Klan. Ruhle became part of the FBI's expanding operation in the South designed to disrupt and discredit the KKK, a program called COINTELPRO. . . .

A long time ago, Paul Macimer thought again. Although their paths had sometimes crossed, that summer in Mississippi was the last time Ruhle, Halbig and Macimer had worked together. Now, at least for one night of nostalgia, Halbig was bringing them all together. Macimer wondered why.

Russ Halbig was not a sentimental man.

11

Some forty minutes after he left the Washington Field Office, Paul Macimer turned off Highway 95 as he spotted the first green sign announcing the presence of the big Marine base at Quantico. He followed the signs westward. About a half mile from the main highway a large brown bug splattered against Macimer's windshield. Soon the collisions became frequent. One of the bugs landed in the trough for the windshield wipers. Only stunned, it clung there as Macimer drove on.

Suddenly the ugly brown bugs were everywhere. Neatly lettered green signs directed Macimer through portions of the Quantico Marine Base until he saw the sandstone towers of the twin seven-story dormitories of the FBI Academy. Sheltered in the air-conditioned silence of his car, the windows rolled up, Macimer drove through a dancing cloud of the bugs. Only when he stopped on the broad, hot parking area in front of the Administration Building and opened his door did the full assault of the locusts strike him.

The din was a solid canopy of sound. The shrill singing enclosed him and the brick-and-glass buildings and the surrounding woods like a dome over a stadium. Macimer hurried through the swarming cicadas, grimacing once in distaste when one of the bugs in flight struck him in the mouth. Close to the front of the building the swarm thinned out. Macimer plunged through the glass doors with a sharp feeling of relief.

In the wide lobby he brushed a couple of locusts from his jacket. Then he paused to catch his breath, staring back across the broad, sun-baked parking area and its unwanted carpet of brown. He had forgotten about the locusts. There was always concern, each time they reappeared in their periodic cycle, that they would overtake and destroy the quiet country towns in their path. The FBI Academy seemed impervious to this attack.

Macimer had been present when the new Academy, one of J. Edgar Hoover's longtime dreams, was formally dedicated back in 1972. He remembered learning then how effectively isolated the agents and other Academy students were from the outside world. The new agents in training, and the other law enforcement officers selected for one of the eleven-week Academy training programs, were aware of neither the crying of locusts nor the humid June heat. The entire facility, including the administration buildings and classrooms, recreational and physical training facilities, and the tall dormitory buildings, was enclosed. Each building was connected to the others by way of glass-walled corridors. Except for visits to the outdoor firing ranges and specialized training sites, students at the Academy never had to set foot outside.

At the main desk in the lobby Macimer identified himself and asked where he could find Timothy Callahan. The clerk behind the counter checked a schedule on a clipboard. Callahan was giving a demonstration talk over at the Big Bird at eleven o'clock. The "Bird" was a grounded aircraft used in mock hijacking field exercises. It was located near the wooden tower used to demonstrate SWAT tactics in sniper situations.

"I can have a driver take you over there, Mr. Macimer. Mr. Callahan is going to describe the Florida hijacking, the one that happened Monday."

Macimer glanced at the clock on the wall behind the desk. Almost a half hour, but that probably wasn't time enough to catch Callahan, a talkative man, before his demonstration exercise. On the other hand, it gave him a few minutes to touch bases with Gordon Ruhle, his second reason for driving down to Quantico. He asked where Ruhle was lecturing.

There were two dozen small classrooms and a number of larger, seminar-sized conference rooms in the Academy, in addition to the thousand-seat main auditorium, the library, gymnasiums and conditioning rooms, cafeteria and coffee shop, lounges and dormitory facilities. Macimer found the seminar room number the clerk had given him and peered through the window set into the door.

The room was a miniature amphitheater, the rows of desks in ascending tiers looking down at the lecturer's podium with its sophisticated modern teaching aids, which ranged from a series of retractable blackboards and graphics display boards to a television console and a small computer console with its keyboard and cathode ray tube display panel. A man stood before a blackboard, his back toward Macimer. There was no mistaking those wide shoulders, the forward thrust of the neck, the thick black hair turning iron gray. Macimer opened the door at the back of the room and slipped into a seat just as Gordon Ruhle turned around.

The older agent's glare caught Macimer instantly, held him, then moved on without a change of expression. Macimer grinned. It was always one thing at a time with Ruhle, and duty came first. "I could make it short and sweet, what I think you should do about terrorists," Gordon Ruhle said to the attentive group of agents. "You should line them all up against a wall and have your own Valentine's Day garage sale." He waited out the small explosion of laughter with its startled undercurrent. "But that isn't the way we do it at the Bureau, of course. We have a manual and charter to go by. I'll fill you in on what the Manual says, and maybe a few other things you should know about that aren't in the book, as we go on.

"You've heard the old saw, if you want to catch a thief you have to think like a thief. Well, that applies to terrorists in spades. If you're going to get anywhere dealing with them, whether you're negotiating for the release of a hostage, bargaining, stalling for time, trying to convince them the game isn't worth the candle, or whatever, you have to know the people you're dealing with. You've got to know how they *think*."

Gordon Ruhle paused. The room was in total silence, the creak of a desk coming like a shriek when one listener moved. Gordon still had that presence, Macimer thought. The agents in the room, all volunteers for the Anti-Terrorist Task Force, knew that this speaker was not going to give them academic theories. He would say what he thought—and what he thought was the product of hard-earned experience in the field. The knowledge he spoke of that went beyond the FBI Manual was not printed anywhere; it was inside the heads of agents who had personally fought the battles against bank robbers and wartime spies, auto thieves and embezzlers, organized mobsters and corrupt public officials—and terrorists.

"The first thing you have to know," Ruhle said, "and maybe it's the last thing, too, and everything in between, is this—and don't you ever forget it: *The terrorist doesn't accept any of your rules.* He doesn't believe in your moral or legal restrictions. He doesn't recognize your laws. The only law he recognizes is his own. The only justice he believes in is what he creates for himself. There isn't anything else. So he isn't hamstrung by any nice ideas of right and wrong, of what can or cannot be done, of honor or duty or any of the other things that impose restraints on the actions of democratic governments."

As Ruhle talked he prowled the miniature stage, flicking angry glares upward at the rows of agents. He didn't have to raise his voice. No one had any trouble hearing him.

"It was Marx who said that revolutionary action has to be reckless," Ruhle continued. "What he meant was, a revolutionary can't be afraid of the results. He doesn't care who gets hurt. The IRA doesn't give a damn if some school kids or the parish priest gets blown up by a bomb along with the British soldier it's intended for. The PLO doesn't give a damn if a bunch of old women or nice old men are blown to bits by a bomb left in a market. The true terrorist doesn't even care if *he* is the one who is wiped out along with his enemy. All he cares about are the results he wants, not the side effects. Hell, he'll fill the playground swing with plastic explosive if that will get the results he wants. And he won't lose any sleep over those kids."

Gordon Ruhle stalked back to the lectern, glanced at the wall clock, which now read ten minutes before the hour. "That's the message for today," he growled. "We'll start getting into specific tactics as we go along. Right now you've just about got time to jet over to the hijack demonstration and hear what Agent Callahan has to say. When it comes to terrorists, especially hijackers, he could write the book."

"You didn't even blink," Macimer said, bracing Ruhle near the doorway as his class of agent-students spilled along the wide, brown-carpeted corridor outside the classroom. "How did you know I'd show up for your sermon?"

"Halbig mentioned it. Did you let him put something over on

you?" Ruhle asked with a laugh. "I thought I taught you better than that."

"I should have guessed he'd tip you off. And if I were to make another guess, it would be that he's asked you out to his place Saturday."

"Yeah, you've got it. You and Jan gonna be there?"

"Yes. Is Mary here with you?"

"She's coming in tomorrow for a weekend visit. When I tell her about Saturday being Homecoming Night, she'll wet her pants."

Macimer grinned. "It's good to see you, even if you're as ornery as ever. Did Halbig also tell you why I wanted to see you, besides friendship?"

Ruhle's dark eyes sobered. "He told me about some file you're looking for, has to do with the People's Revolutionary Committee business back in '81, right?"

"That's it. The Director has made this a 'Special.' That's why I'd like you in on it with me." The compliment was indirect but unmistakable, and Macimer saw something flicker in Ruhle's eyes.

"I don't know," the older agent said thoughtfully. "Hell, Paul, you know ordinarily I'd jump at a chance to get in on something like that, but . . . this ATTF program is a volunteer thing, too. And it's important."

"I know it is. Look, let's talk it over at lunch." He checked his watch. "I have to see Callahan first—maybe I can catch him after his press conference."

Both men grinned. Callahan's relish for the media was well known, though it did not detract from his reputation as the chief of the FBI section dealing with hostage-holding terrorists. "I imagine there's at least a couple of reporters here today for the big story," Ruhle said.

"Are you coming over?"

"You know me and speeches. I wasn't even planning on showing up for Landers' show for the grads next week." Ruhle shrugged his heavy shoulders. "Yeah, why not? I've heard the Irishman before, but it might impress the kids in my seminar if I show up. Besides, it'll give us time to swap our own war stories."

They drove over to the demonstration area in Macimer's car. Macimer did not turn on the air conditioning for the short ride, and he quickly felt his shirt clinging to his back as the sweat built up under his suit jacket. He remembered a hundred other times the two men had ridden together, sharing a moment of triumph or frustration, a quiet council of war, the revelation that a case was about to break or a new child was on the way. They had been more than working partners, and sliding into the old, comfortable relationship was as easy as slipping on a pair of worn moccasins, shaped to the foot.

Macimer parked by the side of the road, looking down on an open field and the faded silver shell of a venerable C-54, acquired from the U.S. Air Force ten years ago. A crowd stood on the far side of the plane, their faces tilted upward. Macimer heard the metallic sound of an amplified voice. He could not see Timothy Callahan from the roadway, but the sea of faces in the crowd was turned toward the plane's forward doorway.

Macimer and Ruhle slid down the incline from the road and started around the tail of the Big Bird, as agents had nicknamed the plane. The voice of the white-haired Irishman speaking into a microphone came to them clearly. "It's all ego," Callahan was saying. "If the police are in on a situation, you've got their ego to deal with. And the hostage taker's ego, that most of all. And your own ego and even the government's ego. What you have to do is get past all that and play up to the hostage taker's ego. He wouldn't be where he is if it wasn't important to him to be taken seriously." Coming around the tail of the plane Macimer could see Callahan far forward near the pilot's cabin, framed in the doorway to the plane. He followed Gordon Ruhle, circling behind the crowd for a better view. Callahan said, "So you don't attack his ego. You stroke him. That's the way it was with this youngster down in Miami on Monday. I had to get him calmed down, and then get him focusing on ordinary things, like did he want us to send in some sandwiches for himself and the hostages he was holding . . ."

Macimer could not later recall the exact sequence of events. One moment he was at the back of the crowd facing Callahan, turning his head as Gordon Ruhle started to mutter an aside to him. Then Macimer found himself on his back in the grass with dust and debris in the air all around him, shouts and screams coming very thinly through his clogged ears, and there was a sense of chaos, of sky showing where there shouldn't have been sky, of the C-54's tail on the ground and a gaping section of her forward fuselage ripped open like a tin can, of people lying flat or crumpled or kneeling, of others staggering around in seemingly aimless confusion.

Gordon Ruhle bent over him as Macimer struggled to his hands and knees. There was a smear of dirt on Ruhle's cheek, a small cut bleeding slightly on his forehead where he had been struck by a piece of flying debris. "It's Callahan!" Ruhle said hoarsely, his eyes burning in the blackened face.

"My God, what happened?"

"It was a bomb," Ruhle said, his mouth a tight, grim line. "There isn't enough of him left for the locusts to feed on."

12

In Burbank, California, it was eighty-eight degrees at five o'clock Thursday afternoon, three hours earlier than it was in the nation's capital. The day had been smoggy, and Mary Ruhle's eyes were stinging as she spoke into the phone. "You're sure you're all right?" Her tone was anxious, as if she feared that he was hiding something from her.

"I'm fine," Gordon Ruhle insisted. "A couple of scratches, that's all. Paul and I were way at the back of the crowd, far enough for most of the flak to miss us."

"You could have been up front."

"We could have been but we weren't, so stop worrying about what didn't happen. Listen, Mary, maybe you shouldn't come just now. I'm gonna be tied up with this investigation—"

"I'm coming!" she insisted. "You can't stop me."

"Is it worth it for just a few days? Maybe you should wait—"

"I don't care if I have to turn around and fly home the next day. You know how I've been counting on this, Gordon. I never get away from the house . . ." She seemed to become aware that the words sounded like a complaint, and she amended them. "I don't often get to go anywhere. It'll be a treat for me, no matter how brief a time it is. Don't take it away from me."

There was a brief silence, the line humming with other conversations only dimly heard, like a conclave of ghosts. Then Gordon Ruhle growled, "I may not be able to meet you at Dulles. You'll have to use a rental car. I'll make the arrangements so it's waiting for you."

"Oh, dear, don't you already have a rental? We don't need two cars—"

"For God's sake, I can turn mine in!" He often spoke to her in a tone that was brusque, sounding half angry, half exasperated, as if he were impatient with her. He was not, and she knew it. Others, unfortunately, were not so understanding, including their two children. She knew that Gordon's tone and manner had frequently been a source of some of the friction between Gordon and their son and daughter.

"Is the seminar going well?" she asked.

"Yeah, sure. What the Academy needed was another old has-been spouting about how we did it in the good old days."

She smiled. It was a gentle, tired smile. Mary Ruhle, though she was only fifty-three, sometimes seemed to be ten years older, her hair completely gray, her expression resigned, the joy prematurely squeezed out of her. "You're not a has-been." She was not cajoling him. There was pride in the words. She had always been proud of what he was.

At 8:05 P.M., in the modern offices of Oliver Packard, located in a converted town house on M Street in Washington NW, the night receptionist answered a call. There was someone on duty at the switchboard twenty-four hours a day, although Packard himself had long since departed for his luxurious Watergate Towers apartment overlooking the Potomac. As the columnist had often said, "The news doesn't punch a time clock. Anything can happen, anytime, anywhere. I don't want to hear about it next morning."

The caller, who refused to identify himself, wanted to speak to Joseph Gerella. "I'm sorry, sir," Toni Grissom, the night receptionist, said, "but Mr. Gerella is out of the office on an assignment. Would you like to leave your phone number?"

"I don't have a phone—this is, you know, a pay phone."

"Would you care to leave a message, Mr. . . . ?"

"No, no message. Wait a minute! Yeah. Listen, you tell Gerella I sent him something, but I haven't seen anything in the papers yet."

"You sent him something?"

"Listen, he knows. It's about the FBI. You tell him I'll send him, like, one more sample, that's all, just so's he'll know there's more where that came from."

"How can he reach you?" She tried again to encourage him to give his name, again without success.

"He can't. I'll call him again, okay? What I've got ought to be worth plenty. But if he isn't interested, there's other reporters."

"Wait—!"

When he hung up Toni Grissom hesitated only a second before looking up Joseph Gerella's home phone number. There were other reporters and investigators on Oliver Packard's staff on call that evening, but the caller had specifically asked for Gerella.

"Gerella," he snapped into the phone.

"Hi, this is Toni at the office. You just had a call, Mr. Gerella—he wouldn't leave his name. Do you want his message now or can it wait until morning?"

"You tell me. I guess it's important or you wouldn't be calling."

"You sound grumpy." She repeated the words of the anonymous caller. The tired rasp instantly vanished from Gerella's voice.

"That's all he said? Listen, Toni, this is important. Did you get it all on tape?"

"Yes, it's all there. I turned the recorder on as soon as he asked for you."

"Good girl. I'll be down to pick up that tape."

"Tonight?"

"You know what our boss says," Gerella answered, sounding positively cheerful now. "The news doesn't punch a time clock, and neither do we."

"What happened?" the FBI Director demanded. There was outrage in his voice, his strong features, his thick square body. He rose to lean over the curving edge of the conference table, planting his palms down flat against its surface, his manner almost threatening. "Damn it, I want to know! The President wants to know! The whole country wants to know!"

No one in the conference room, or watching and listening in secure communications rooms in all sixty FBI field offices across the country, answered him.

This full-fledged summit conference, involving the three Executive Assistant Directors, the Assistant Directors in charge of the eleven Bureau divisions, and representatives from all of the field offices, was the first such broad-scaled meeting to be called since John Landers' appointment as Acting Director of the FBI. All of the top echelon from FBI Headquarters were physically present. Another sixty men—fifty-three Special-Agents-in-Charge and seven ASACs sitting in for their immediate superiors—simultaneously heard Landers' words and saw the anger in his eyes, but they were participants in the summit conference by way of the Bureau's own satellite communications system. Within the past two hours every available SAC had been summoned to his office if not already there. At that moment, 9:02 P.M. Washington time, two of a network of satellites were in position for line-of-sight communication both with each other and with all sixty field offices, able to receive and relay signals to and from the conference room in FBI Headquarters.

Carrying on a tradition begun under J. Edgar Hoover, the full complement of Special-Agents-in-Charge had been called together on rare occasions involving cases seen as crises for the Bureau, highly publicized cases such as the Patricia Hearst kidnapping or far more ominous ones which had to deal with nuclear bomb threats that were never known to the public. With the advent of closed-circuit satellite television communications systems, the Bureau had followed the example of many major U.S. corporations in installing facilities for electronic super-conferences. In a special room adjoining the seventh-floor operations room in the FBI Building, and only steps from the Director's office, an elaborate television console filled one wall, housing a bank of twelve small and two large monitor screens. In separate housings were two video cameras. The smaller screens of the console were arranged in two rows, six screens on each side of center. At each end of the console was a larger screen, on which one of the pictures displayed on the small monitors could be shown. The twin of this larger screen at the opposite end of the console was a monitor on which the Director's square, heavy features were now on view. They were also visible on the screens in all sixty field offices. The pictures on the smaller screens changed every twelve seconds, rotating among the sixty offices so that each man present in his communications room at every field office came on screen for twelve seconds of each minute. The rotation was changed when one of the men spoke and appeared on the large screen.

It was notable that, of the fifteen persons gathered in the Headquarters conference room, and the sixty present in the various field offices, not one was a woman.

The men in the field had heard only the most meager details of what had occurred at Quantico that morning. Landers called on Paul Macimer, who was in the WFO's communications room, to describe what happened. "As most of you know," Landers said, "Special Agent Macimer was present this morning when the bomb went off near the FBI Academy."

Like many other SACs, Macimer had been reached at home and called back to his office for the conference. He felt oddly conspicuous as he stared at the single camera's eye, sensing that all those other eyes were studying him in field offices all across the country. Briefly he told of the explosion, his own stunned reaction, the confusion that followed, the emergency measures that were taken. As he spoke he watched the screen before him, which displayed a view of the conference room at FBI Headquarters. Halbig, Macimer noticed, was sitting to Landers' right at the conference table. He wondered if that was intended to be noticed by the SACs, all of whom were sensitive to the nuances of power politics at the seat of government.

"There was no warning," Macimer concluded. "No message was received threatening the Bureau or claiming credit for the bomb, either before or after it exploded. As far as we know right now, no one was seen near the plane who didn't have reason to be there."

"How could any outsider get at it?" one of the SACs demanded.

In the Headquarters conference room a camera focused on Henry Szymanski, whose area of authority as an Executive Assistant Director covered not only the lab and Identification Division but also the Training Division and its facilities. Szymanski cleared his throat. "The outside training areas—that is, those that are outside the actual FBI Academy buildings—are not under round-the-clock surveillance. As you know, they are accessible to public roads. There's nothing we can do about that. The Academy itself is secure, of course."

"Maybe," someone muttered.

The FBI Director picked up on the comment at once. "If you have something to say, Magnuson," he snapped, "let's all hear it."

Frank Magnuson was the Special-Agent-in-Charge of the New York Field Office, the only office in the Bureau whose chief was also ranked as an Assistant Director of the FBI. "We'd better not be too sure of our security," he said. On the monitor screen he looked not unlike Landers himself, a heavyset man with a large, fleshy nose and jaws like two small blocks of granite. He and Landers were old friends who had worked together in the past, but in that moment Magnuson was aware for the first time that the FBI Director had changed. Either that or it was the aura of the office itself that Magnuson felt, the power and prestige and authority J. Edgar Hoover had vested in the FBI Director's office. "What I mean is, we better be prepared to face more of the same. I'm not even surprised. The surprise is that we haven't been targeted before. They're taking it to us, that's what it looks like to me."

"They meaning whom?"

"Terrorists," Magnuson answered bluntly. "We've all known it was going to come here, sooner rather than later. There's no reason for us to go on thinking this country is off limits to the world's terrorists. And if we're going to be hit, then the FBI would have to be a high-priority target."

Other men agreed with Magnuson as Landers allowed the discussion to open up, encouraging reactions. "They didn't use to hit us," commented the ASAC of the St. Louis Field Office. He was the only black among the sixty men whose faces kept appearing on the monitor screens. "But I guess we can all remember when that punk walked in off the street in El Centro and wiped out our agents, and then it happened in Denver. And to Agent McWilliams right there in Washington. How long ago was that? Twenty months? This is just the next phase."

Landers allowed the speculation to continue only long enough to perceive that it was leading nowhere. "Is it the general feeling, then," he asked, "that this bombing was directed at the FBI?"

There was a general murmur of agreement from the men around the horseshoe-shaped conference table that faced the television console like a giant magnet. Waves of assent lapped over the first reaction as the key men of the Bureau reacted in the isolation of their communications rooms from Maine to California. No one seemed surprised. The day when the FBI would become a target for terrorism had long been expected. John L. Landers, observing the unanimity of agreement, the collective anger on the rotating televised faces, wondered if there might not be an aspect of collective paranoia involved. All through much of the 1970s the FBI had felt besieged, attacked by citizens and congressmen. None of those who were now top-level Bureau officials had forgotten.

At that moment Russ Halbig, sitting next to the Director, said quietly, "I'm not sure that assumption is justified by today's event. We can't be sure that Callahan himself was not the specific target of that bomb."

There was a moment of startled silence. Then James Caughey spoke sharply. "Who the hell would want to hit Callahan? Hell, every one of those damned hijackers ends up thinking Callahan is his uncle. Was," Caughey corrected himself.

Halbig regarded him calmly. He was the only man in the conference room or in any of the field offices who had not shown emotional outrage, John Landers thought. The only one who seemed to regard the bombing at Quantico as just another problem to be solved. "It's certainly possible that that bomb was intended as a blow directed against the FBI itself, not Callahan in particular. But I don't think that is by any means certain. In fact, my own view is that Callahan himself was the real target. I can't offer any direct evidence at this time, but there's no evidence the other way either. What we do know is that Callahan was killed, no one else."

There were voices of agreement and disagreement, the beginnings of a fruitless debate, before John Landers intervened once more. "Let's get back to specifics," he said. "Szymanski, does the lab have anything yet on that bomb?"

Szymanski, like Richard Nixon, showed at his worst in close-up on the television screen, his cheeks blue with a day's growth of beard, his eyes a little watery and anxious, a nervous tongue probing his lower lip as if searching for a crack. "We have a preliminary report that indicates the explosive was U.S. Army plastic T-4. Unfortunately, a very common type."

"Commonly obtainable?" Landers said with irony.

"I'm afraid so, Director."

"How was it detonated?"

"We don't know that yet. The trouble is, there was enough of that plastic to obliterate everything close to the point of detonation. We're going over the plane and the ground, inch by inch. If there's anything to be found, we'll find it."

"Any guesses on the method of detonation?"

Szymanski hesitated, the tip of his tongue searching for the elusive crack. "We don't make guesses, Director."

Landers' face darkened, but before he could respond James Caughey spoke up. Caughey, the Executive Assistant Director in charge of investigations for the Bureau, was to provide overall direction of the massive investigation into the Quantico bombing. "It was almost certainly a remotely activated device," he suggested. "A timer would have been too uncertain of success."

"Why?" Landers demanded. "Everyone knew Callahan would be there giving his spiel at eleven o'clock with a whole class from the Academy there to hear him. The bomb, according to several witnesses, went off at exactly 11:03 A.M. That allows a three-minute margin if the killer or killers figured Callahan would start his demonstration at eleven o'clock."

Caughey didn't back down. "No one could be sure how Callahan would set up his exercise. He might have started out explaining the Miami situation from ground level. On the other hand," Caughey added grimly, "he might have had twenty or thirty people inside that plane right from the start."

"I might point out," Russ Halbig cut in, "that whoever planted that bomb was familiar with the way in which Callahan conducted his exercises."

There was a shocked moment of total silence in the conference room, a shock reflected in the silent parade of faces succeeding each other in orderly rotation on the screens of the video console.

"What the hell!" Frank Magnuson said. "You're implying that someone on the inside planted that bomb—someone in the FBI!"

One of the conference room cameras caught Halbig's face in close-up on the large right-hand screen. His expression was imperturbable. A cold fish, John Landers thought, watching Halbig closely. "I am merely citing a possibility that must be considered," Halbig said calmly. "Along with many others, of course."

"That's one hell of a suggestion," Magnuson retorted.

The meeting continued for another fifteen minutes. At the end Caughey outlined the procedures already being put into action to investigate the bombing. Unlike the Brea file investigation, which was not discussed during the summit conference and was deliberately being carried out with low visibility and a minimum commitment of manpower, the Quantico bombing was to be a classic demonstration of the Bureau's capability for swiftly organizing and carrying out an investigation on a massive scale, with hundreds of agents already committed and hundreds more to be thrown into the hunt as the scope of the investigation expanded. Everyone present at the time of the bombing, either near the plane or in the vicinity, was being interviewed. A search of the terrain had begun in the early afternoon and would continue through the next day in a widening circle, seeking to turn up anything unusual, anything out of place, any evidence of loitering. The area surrounding the plane had been sealed off and, as Szymanski had indicated, was being minutely combed by experts from the FBI Laboratory, specialists in unearthing and preserving the tiniest speck of physical evidence. The Internal Security Section of the Criminal Investigative Division was tracing and questioning known terrorists. The Anti-Terrorist Task Force, which had already assembled at the FBI Academy for specialized seminars and training at the time of the bombing, would be coordinating its intelligence on terrorist activities with the efforts of the Internal Security Section. Until some specific lead turned up, the main thrust of the investigation would be on developing links to individual terrorists and groups, especially those who had made threats against the FBI or the government.

When Caughey sat down, John L. Landers addressed the men under his command. "You will all assign agents on standby to assist in this investigation if, as and when called upon. I am also ordering that priority security measures be in place within the hour in all FBI field offices. There will be no exceptions. At the moment we don't know if this was a single, isolated incident, perhaps directed specifically at Agent Callahan, as Mr. Halbig has suggested, or the first shot in an attack against the Federal Bureau of Investigation itself. In any event, we must be prepared for anything—including an attack against any of our field offices." Landers paused, allowing the physical force of his personality and rocklike image to dominate the thoughts of the listening men. Then he concluded, "This much I want you all to know: We are going to hunt down Callahan's murderers and bring them to justice. And if the FBI is to be the target for new attacks, we shall be ready to meet them—and, gentlemen, to defeat them!"

In the FBI Director's office, where Russell Halbig had followed Landers at the close of the summit conference, the burly chief of the Bureau sat heavily in his high-backed chair and waved Halbig toward a seat on the other side of the big desk. Landers appeared suddenly tired, his heavy features hanging in folds, as if he had let down after being so prominently on display for the past hour. Observing him, Halbig realized how intensely emotional an event the summit meeting had been for Landers. It was the first time he had directly faced the key men of FBI Headquarters and all sixty field offices at one time, acting as their Director in the midst of a crisis. He knew the men he had summoned for the conference had questions about him and would have been judging him by his performance tonight. Now, almost certainly, he was wondering how he had done—what the judgments had been.

But when Landers finally spoke he said, "You had your reasons for sending Paul Macimer down to Quantico this morning, I'm sure."

"Yes, Director. He was to talk to Callahan about Brea."

Landers grunted noncommittally. He washed his cheeks with a broad palm, as if trying to massage life back into his features. The gesture also had the effect, Halbig noted, of covering any reaction. "What makes you think Callahan could tell him anything new?"

"It just seemed like a good idea. After all, Callahan was your number two that summer—the operations man, if I'm not mistaken."

"You know damned well you're not mistaken." Landers frowned, then muttered as if to himself, "Maybe Callahan's murderers didn't want him to talk to Macimer." He came to his next question with ponderous care, like a bear sniffing out a trap. "Do you still suspect Macimer of stealing or covering up the file Vern Lippert put together? From the reports coming in, I don't see any foot dragging on Macimer's part."

"I didn't say I believed Macimer guilty—only that it was a possibility."

"You made a good case for it. Are you still planning on having Macimer and his old partner—Gordon Ruhle, is it?—out to your house Saturday?"

"I see no reason not to. As a matter of fact, it gives me an opportunity to observe Macimer under . . . relaxed circumstances."

"Ummm." The expression might have been approving or skeptical. Landers pushed up from his desk and prowled his office, an angry bear. He said, "I want detailed reports from Caughey on the Quantico investigation, not summaries. Also on the Brea case. That one stays quiet, but arrange press briefings on the bombing investigation." He turned to glare at Halbig. "Is the bombing connected to the Brea file? Is that why you think Callahan was the target? Your personal opinion, Halbig."

Halbig was slow to answer. When he did his words were chosen with caution. "I'd like to reserve final judgment on that, Director. But I think a distinct possibility does exist that Callahan was murdered because of what he knew—or might have known—about the Brea file."

"Sticking your neck out, are you, Halbig?"

"You asked me for my personal opinion, sir."

Landers nodded slowly. "So I did."

After Halbig left, Landers continued to stare after him, his eyes fixed on some point beyond the heavy paneling of the door. Halbig *was* a cold fish, Landers thought. Cautious and correct, looking under every stone, not letting his personal feelings get in the way. Still, it was hard to feel quite comfortable with anyone that emotionless, that cold.

Not the kind of man John L. Landers would feel comfortable with as his second in command.

Later that evening, at 10:30 P.M., the telephone rang in Paul Macimer's study at home. The phone there was on a separate line from the other instruments in the house, the number unlisted. The caller was Pat Garvey. He was following Macimer's instructions that anything important in the Brea investigation should not wait for teletype communications from Sacramento to the Washington Field Office.

"We heard about the bombing at Quantico," Garvey said soberly. "This is a black day for the FBI."

Macimer did not smile at the melodramatic comment. "I was there," he said.

"Why would anyone want to get Callahan?" Garvey demanded

angrily. "Because he was working against hijackers and terrorists, is that it?"

"It's possible. Or the bomb might have been a message for the FBI, not for Callahan personally. Right now that's guesswork. But whatever the motive, and whoever did it, we'll find them. Now, what about our own investigation? What have you and Collins come up with? I take it you have something that couldn't wait overnight."

"Yes, sir." Garvey became crisply businesslike in response to Macimer's abrupt change of subject. "Collins is over in Sacramento sending in the full reports. We've found where that screen came from, the one Agent Lippert sent in for a lab report. And it ties in."

Garvey had continued to canvass the neighborhood surrounding the 1310 Dover Street address. By late Thursday afternoon he had worked his way around to the houses on the adjoining street—Sussex Street—which backed up to the Dover Street site. By luck Garvey had struck pay dirt almost immediately—in the house directly behind the former PRC hideout, now an empty lot.

"The man's name is Lazzeri. He's lived there eighteen years, so he was living there at the time of the People's Revolutionary Committee blowup. He wasn't home when it happened, though—he and his family were visiting relatives back in Minneapolis. They saw the whole thing on television. Lazzeri couldn't believe what he was watching."

"Not many people could," Macimer said. "Are you saying Lazzeri's house was empty that day?"

"That's right, sir. And that's what's interesting. Lazzeri never noticed anything wrong, but I found out that Vernon Lippert canvassed the whole neighborhood this past winter. He learned that Lazzeri was away during the PRC period. He asked if he could look through the house, Lazzeri said, and when he came to one of the back bedrooms on the second floor, Lippert got very excited. The window in that room looks out directly over the lot where the PRC hideout was. Lippert asked to borrow the old rusty screen from that window. It had been there for years, Lazzeri says. Lippert promised to get Lazzeri a new screen but apparently he never got around to it. That happened back in February. Lazzeri can't give an exact date, but the time frame corresponds to the date of Lippert's lab request."

"The screen had a hole in it," Macimer said. It was not a question.

"Yes, sir. Lazzeri thought it was just a tear—but Agent Lippert guessed otherwise. And according to the lab's analysis, he was right. There was gunpowder residue around that hole. It looks like Mr. Lippert figured someone was inside the Lazzeri house that day and fired a shot from the upstairs window."

"The shot that triggered the blowup."

"Yes, sir."

Macimer was silent. Garvey's discovery was no surprise, but it was important. It offered solid evidence to prove what Macimer had already surmised. He said, "Good work, Garvey. Tell Collins I said so. What else do you have?"

"The telephone call the day before the blowup. Collins checked that out with Pacific Telephone Company records. They show a phone call coming from the pay phone at Sambo's Restaurant—it's inside, near the rest rooms—to the Sacramento number assigned to the FBI Task Force. The call was placed at 11:02 A.M. That's the exact time the call for Brea was logged in Sacramento on August 27."

"So what do you make of all this?"

"Well . . ." Possibly disconcerted by the sudden question, Garvey hesitated.

"Walter Schumaker left the hideout that morning and made the call to Brea," Macimer said. "According to your Wednesday reports, especially the interview with the Torgeson woman, Schumaker didn't leave the house on the twenty-eighth. No one did."

"Yes, sir," Garvey said quietly. "So he was inside that house when the shooting started—and his agent knew he was there." There was a thread of controlled anger and disgust in the young agent's tone.

"Which leaves us with the big question. Who fired the shot from the Lazzeri house?"

Pat Garvey didn't answer. An answer was not really necessary, Paul Macimer thought. The pattern and focus of Vernon Lippert's investigation were becoming clearer.

After Garvey said good night, Macimer sat for a long time in the quiet of his den, the door closed, the sound of a television game show reaching him dimly from the family room, like those voices faintly heard on the long-distance telephone line.

Blowup. That was the word Garvey kept using about the PRC affair. An explosion. Like the blowup of the C-54 used by the FBI for training exercises at Quantico.

Macimer shook his head, almost violently. What he was thinking couldn't be true—it wasn't possible.

But his heart kept beating heavily, loudly.

You didn't ignore a pattern in a series of crimes, even if the apparent pattern might prove to be nothing more than coincidence. On the contrary, you always looked for a pattern. Criminals tended to repeat themselves. Someone who would use a bomb to blow up the People's Revolutionary Committee's hideout might also use a bomb to get rid of someone dangerous to him.

Like Callahan.

And like Carey McWilliams, the former SAC of the Washington Field Office, blown to bits by a bomb explosion in his office at the WFO over eighteen months ago.

Bombs in themselves were not rarities anymore. Ten or more bombs, on the average, exploded somewhere in the United States every day of the year. There was no reason normally to connect a bombing in California with another in Washington, D.C., and a third in Quantico, Virginia, occurring at eighteen-month intervals or more.

Except that there was a connection, however tenuous. Timothy Callahan and Carey McWilliams had been John L. Landers' number two and number one men in the FBI Task Force assembled in the summer of 1981 to hunt down the People's Revolutionary Committee.

And now, of the three men who had directed that hunt and had had total knowledge of its operations from top to bottom, only one survived.

And he was the Director of the FBI.

The call to Chuey Gutiérrez came shortly before midnight at the motel in Silver Spring where he was staying with Xavier and Rosalba. When he recognized the deep voice on the other end of the line he motioned quickly to the girl to turn down the sound on the television set. Rosalba continued to watch the movie—an old musical—without sound.

"You did well," the man said without preamble. "I've just listened to the first of the tapes. Everything is working perfectly."

"*Bueno.*"

"You may be able to be of service to me again in this matter. It isn't over."

"To you and to our country," Gutiérrez said. Xavier, who was listening, smirked, and Chuey glared at him until the young man's smile faded.

"I'll be in touch. I may also want you to retrieve any future tapes."

"I will be waiting, Maestro."

Chuey half expected the other man to hang up but there was a pause, the line remaining open. Chuey waited patiently, guessing that the FBI man had something else on his mind.

His name was Raúl Jesús Gutiérrez y González, but he was called Chuey, the nickname for Jesús. He had grown up in and around Miami. His father, a policeman in Cuba during the Batista regime, had fled to the United States when Castro came down from his mountain. Ramón Gutiérrez had died on the beach at the Bay of Pigs, the year his son Jesús turned thirteen years of age, ceased to be a child, and became a patriot.

Chuey Gutiérrez had never blamed his adopted country or the men who had encouraged and ultimately abandoned the quixotic invasion of Cuba. He had heard and seen many of these men with his father—tough, hard-bitten, cold-eyed men who shared a soldier's uncompromising code, even though many of them dressed in expensive suits instead of uniforms. The boy admired them. They were men like his father. Battles were won and lost, often for reasons beyond comprehension, but one did not cease to believe.

Even as a teen-ager Chuey had run errands for a man vaguely identified with "the Company." Through him he had come to the attention of a man with another government agency, the FBI, a man he would always think of as his benefactor, the man he called "Maestro." Through him Chuey Gutiérrez had been able to strike back at the enemies of his father, pro-Castro agents and sympathizers, and also at other enemies of his adopted country.

When the FBI man had summoned him to Washington on a matter of "grave importance to the Bureau and to the United States," Chuey had neither hesitated nor questioned his role. Acting on the FBI man's instructions, he had recruited Xavier and Rosalba and brought them with him to Washington. For nearly three weeks, except for one night's action, they had been holed up in the motel in Silver Spring. Chuey welcomed the hint that their mission was not yet over. The two young ones were becoming restive, more difficult to control.

The FBI man broke the silence. "The boy is a hothead. Is he to be relied on?"

"I will see to it," Chuey answered, glancing across the room at Xavier, who was watching him.

"What about the girl?"

Chuey smiled. "She is also reliable. The body is hot but the head is cool, you understand? She is . . . *muy dura.*" He had almost said *más dura,* tougher than the boy.

"I may have use for both of them. Keep them out of sight and out of trouble. Do *you* understand?"

"I understand perfectly, Maestro."

"Bueno."

The connection was broken. For a moment Chuey sat on the edge of the bed, staring across the room at the silent television screen, holding the receiver in his hand. He thought of the FBI man's opening words—"You did well"—and he felt a surge of pride.

13

Rock Creek Park winds along the spine of the northwest section of Washington, D.C., extending beyond the District past Chevy Chase and Bethesda all the way to the outer reaches of the city. Along the way there are dense wooded areas, picnic groves, a golf course, nature center and zoo, bike paths and jogging trails. It was along one of these, early Friday morning, that a gaggle of reporters and photographers, their attitudes mirroring amusement or incredulity or mock horror, trotted in the lumbering wake of Senator Charles Sederholm.

Washington is a city of joggers, and there is nothing unusual about runners clad in shorts or designer jogging suits trotting through the parks or even along the main boulevards in the morning mists. But Sederholm was not cut from the mold of a Senator Proxmire, long a familiar figure jogging along Connecticut Avenue toward his office, trim and vigorous, looking as briskly efficient as he did on the Senate floor. Sederholm, wearing a dark blue sweat suit with white piping and a matching pair of Adidas, reminded one reporter of Laird Cregar, an actor of large girth and dominating presence who was prominent in the 1940s. The senator was about the same size as the late movie actor, well over six feet tall and weighing at least two hundred and fifty pounds. Older than Cregar in his prime, Sederholm wore a flowing mane of silver hair, but he had the robust actor's air of extravagant appetites and joyous self-indulgence that belied his sixty years.

Within a quarter mile, wheezing and huffing, his face already a deep red, Sederholm slowed to a walk, wavered from the path and plopped onto a bench, which sagged alarmingly under his weight. Almost immediately the reporters caught up and swarmed around him. "When did you take up jogging, Senator?" one of them called out. "Is this because of the convention?"

"Do you know how many people in this country run?" Sederholm countered. "Half the population! This is the age of self-flagellation in public, gentlemen. Running and dieting, giving up smoking and drinking, treating our bodies like temples."

"That's quite a temple, Senator!"

Sederholm joined in the laughter. "Ironic, isn't it?" Sederholm asked rhetorically. "Considering our abandonment of all restraints over the past two decades, now that we have made ourselves free to do anything we want, it has become fashionable to deny ourselves everything."

"Won't this jogging ruin your image, Senator?"

"I'm doing it for you, gentlemen," Sederholm said with a magnanimous wave in the direction of several portable television cameras. "A man of my girth, a United States senator, jogging through the park in Washington at the risk of being mugged or having a heart attack, that's as good as a squirrel on skis."

Cutting through the laughter, a local TV political reporter said, "Does this mean you're definitely running for President, Senator?"

Laughing uproariously (Laird Cregar in *Blood and Sand,* the reporter from the New York *Times* thought), Sederholm said, "It's a little early to be looking at the finish line. I will say this, gentlemen"—he paused to let the TV cameras zoom in for an important statement—"no one has this convention locked up. Which means . . . yes, I'm still in the running."

A babble of questions spilled over the senator's last words, the reporters drowning each other out. Sederholm waved off the questions. He turned resolutely toward the jogging path that snaked through a stand of birch trees. From the back of the jostling circle of reporters someone shouted loud enough to be heard, "What about this bombing at Quantico, Senator? Do you have a statement on that?"

Charles Sederholm swung about with surprising nimbleness. The opportunity was too good to miss. "I do, indeed. The FBI is one of our finest institutions. It has known some difficult times, as the country itself has, but it has emerged from the fire with an unsullied reputation as the finest law enforcement organization in the world. I consider yesterday's bombing a blow struck not only against the FBI but against the very heart and fabric of this government and its institutions. It was also an act of the most outrageous and cowardly terrorism. I knew Special Agent Callahan personally as a fine public servant and a man of generous mind and spirit. His murder is a loss to all of us."

"Have you talked to Director Landers since it happened?"

"Yes, of course."

"Will this have any effect on Landers' confirmation as Director?"

Sederholm pushed back his thick, flowing hair from his forehead, the gesture revealing a large patch of sweat under his arm. "I see no reason it should have any effect. The committee, as you know, has not completed its own evaluation, but John Landers can hardly be blamed for this vicious act. It's a symptom of what has become increasingly a lawless society."

"Isn't the FBI partly to blame for that?"

Sederholm ignored the thrust, choosing instead to answer another reporter, who asked, "Have there been any new developments in the bombing investigation? Any message from the bombers?"

"I understand there have been a number of communications received by the FBI, all of which are being analyzed and will be investigated. But none appears to be genuinely related to the bombing."

"What about the Florida hijacking?"

"No connection that the Bureau is aware of." Sederholm turned again along the path through the woods, which was narrow enough to force the reporters into a column behind him.

"Just one more question, Senator," a stocky reporter said close to him. He had somehow pushed ahead of the others to join Sederholm on the pathway. "What do you know of the FBI's Brea file?"

Sederholm halted abruptly. His eyes, peering out from under deceptively sleepy lids like small hoods, recognized the stocky young man as one of Oliver Packard's reporters. "I don't know what you're talking about," he said. "If it involves the FBI, I suggest you ask your questions there."

He turned and lumbered off through the woods, not looking back.

Within the hour, from the private baths in the basement below the Senate chambers, Charles Sederholm placed a call to Russell Halbig at FBI Headquarters. "You've got a leak, Russ," Sederholm told him. He mentioned Oliver Packard's reporter and the question about the Brea file. "You told me you had a tight lid on that."

"We do, Senator," Halbig said.

"I don't want any surprises sprung on me," Sederholm said, and there was nothing of the familiar jovial bombast in his tone. "I don't want egg on my face. The confirmation hearings on the Director come up a week from Monday. Just remember, I'm the star of that little show. I'm supposed to get all the best lines."

"You will, Senator," Halbig said quickly. "I think I'll have something for you before then. And if anything does break, you'll know it first."

There was a moment's silence. Then Sederholm chuckled. "Before the Director, Russ?"

More recruits for the special squad working on the Brea case had arrived during the night. After briefing the squad, Macimer called Harrison Stearns to his office to review the reports that had come in late Thursday and by overnight teletype from California and Chicago. The written reports from Garvey and Collins confirmed in more detail what Macimer had learned by phone from Garvey. An agent from the Chicago office had sent in a 302 of his interview with former agent Victor Pryor, who had been found at a security conference in the Windy City. Pryor knew nothing of Walter Schumaker's activities during the past three years. He had provided names of former acquaintances of Schumaker; these would be followed up by agents in the Oakland RA's office, the largest resident agency in the country.

Another thick sheaf of reports detailed the activities of agents Wagner and Rayburn in trying to locate the youth who had stolen the FBI vehicle—and, Macimer believed, the Brea file. Macimer decided to assign some of the squad's new arrivals to the search for the missing auto thief. Wagner and Rayburn would continue to concentrate on the Fedco department store and its environs. Other teams would direct more attention to the area of the youth's escape after ditching the stolen car.

Macimer turned to the preliminary lab report received that morning from FBI Headquarters. It described the findings yielded by analysis of the stains on the sheets Macimer had sent over to the FBI Lab. In addition to tests of the semen stains, the sheets had also been examined by the Latent Fingerprint Analysis Unit, using laser equipment in an attempt to bring out fingerprints that were otherwise undetectable. Predictably, the fingerprint examination had been unproductive; Xavier *did* wear his gloves in bed. The lab's analysis of the stains, however, was another story, and Macimer studied the report with quickening hope.

Macimer called in agents Rodriguez and Singleton, the two Spanish-speaking agents he had recruited from the New York office. He handed them the lab report and waited in silence while both agents scanned it. Singleton, he remembered, had majored in biology at the University of Cincinnati before deciding that she would rather employ her flair for languages and a relish for challenges in an unexpected direction: an FBI career. She was among the large numbers of female agents recruited during Director William Webster's tenure.

"Well, where does that report get us?" Macimer asked finally.

Rodriguez shrugged. "Maybe you should ask my partner," he suggested.

Singleton regarded him coolly before she said, "El chauvinist thinks I'm going to turn pale using the word 'semen.' The truth is, he's not sure what the report proves."

"Hey—!" Rodriguez protested.

"What it comes down to is this," Singleton went on. "There are over three hundred genetic markers on human red blood cells. A few of these are present as soluble substances in body fluids, such as semen. That means you can perform tests on semen stains, even old ones, that enable you to identify the blood type of the person responsible." She glanced down at the FBI Lab report, which she was still holding. "The lab used two different enzyme tests, both the commonly used acid phosphatase test and the LAP color reaction test, to verify that the stains found on the sheets were human semen. Then they used the agglutinin inhibition test to determine the blood type of the individual." She paused as she glanced again

FEDERAL BUREAU OF IDENTIFICATION
LABORATORY REPORT

File No. 431

SUBJECT: Identification of stains on Exhibit A.

DATE: June 7, 1984

Tests were conducted on sheets (Exhibit A) of polycotton material.
Ultraviolet light was used to locate stained areas. Greenish coloration
indicated probability of semen. Microscopic examination for detection
of spermatozoa was positive but not conclusive because no spermatozoa
were found intact. The follow tests were then performed:

(A) Walker acid phosphatase test. Male ejaculate produces a high
acid phosphatase activity as compared with other body fluids such as
saliva, urine, etc. Test result was positive.

(B) The LAP test. This is a qualitative color reaction test based
on a histochemical technique for demonstrating the presence of
leucine aminopeptidase (LAP), which is more abundant in human semen
than in any other body fluid or animal semen. Test result positive.

(C) Precipitin test was performed to verify that the semen stain
was derived from a human source. Test result positive.

(D) Precipitin test was performed using known reagents and control
to determine blood group of the person from whom the seminal stain
was derived. Tests were conducted of unstained material (from
Exhibit A), known group O blood sample, and the subject stains.
This test is based on the fact that group-specific substances in
blood are able to neutralize their corresponding agglutinin in a
serum. Test results shown in table.

TABLE 1. RESULTS OF INHIBITION TEST TO DETERMINE BLOOD GROUP

Add	A_1 cells	A_1 cells	A_2 cells	A_2 cells	B cells	B cells	O cells	O cells
Serum	Anti-A	Anti-A	Anti-A	Anti-A	Anti-B	Anti-B	Anti-H	Anti-H
Tube	1	2	3	4	5	6	7	8
	Stain	Unstained	Stain	Unstained	Stain	Unstained	Stain	Unstained
Control		+		+		+		
Group O	+	+	+	+	+	+	−	+
Unknown*	−	+	−	+	−	+	−	+

(+) indicates agglutination   (−) indicates no agglutination = inhibition

* Test demonstrates both A_1 and B group-specific substances present in sample.

at the report. "That's where we got lucky. Our subject has a rare blood type, A_1B."

"How rare?" Macimer asked quickly.

"About three percent of the population. That applies to both Europoids and those of African descent. I imagine the same percentage would hold true for Cubans and other Hispanics, but we can verify that."

Rodriguez was staring at his partner with new respect. Macimer repressed a smile and said, "So . . . we have a young man, probably Cuban, certainly not American-born, about seventeen years of age, with a rare blood type. Any ideas on how we find him?"

Rodriguez shifted nervously in his chair—anxious, Macimer guessed, to recover some lost face. He pursed his lips so that his bandido mustache drooped even more. "Suppose he was one of the boat people who came over in 1980, the ones Castro wanted to get rid of, a lot of them troublemakers. He'd have been through one of the camps. We have complete records on all those people. That ought to include blood types." There had been the suspicion at the time that Castro might have planted agents of his own among the refugees. All had been closely scrutinized by the FBI. And there would be medical records, Macimer thought.

"That's a long shot," he said.

"Maybe not so long." Jo Singleton shot a glance of approval at her partner. "We haven't exactly had what you'd call a regular immigration quota from Cuba since the Bay of Pigs, which happened before this Xavier was born. So if he's Cuban, and he wasn't born in this country, there's a good chance the only way he could have got here was with the boat people, given his age. He would have been thirteen, fourteen at the time if he's seventeen or eighteen now. There shouldn't be too many in all those records that meet all the criteria of the profile you just gave us."

"There were thousands of those boat people—"

"But only a small number were young children," Singleton said. "Eliminate all the adults and younger children, and all the females, and you're probably down to only a few hundred possibilities. And with a blood type that rare, there shouldn't be more than a handful that fit the profile."

"If Xavier was one of the boat people," said Macimer.

"It's worth a try. And if we do find him, that report gives us a

positive identification. He won't be able to claim he didn't use
your sheets."

Macimer smiled. "Why not?"

"Those stains. Identification of special antigens in the stain
means you can match them up with red blood cell antigens. Take
a blood sample from Xavier, and if the antigens match, the
chances of identification are something like two million to one, if I
remember my lessons."

"You seem to be doing pretty well," Macimer said. "Okay, go
to it. Find Xavier for me."

In San Timoteo, California, Pat Garvey and Lenny Collins met
by prearrangement at one o'clock that Friday afternoon at the
Burger King out on the highway to Sacramento. California seemed
to be distinguished more by the number of fast-food outlets than
by surviving palm trees. It was another hot, dry day, the temperature in the mid-eighties.

Over hamburgers and french fries and chocolate milk shakes
the two agents reviewed their three days in San Timoteo. Both
thought they had accomplished as much as they could in the town.
Lippert's investigation must have taken him further afield, Garvey
suggested. To find out where, they would have to follow him elsewhere. "I'd say we start digging into the records of the PRC Task
Force. There's a copy of that file in Sacramento. That was the
office of origin for that investigation."

"There's also a copy at FBI Headquarters."

"But we might see something that anyone who hasn't been dog-
ging Lippert's footsteps would miss."

"You're probably right, but . . . there's one thing I'd like to do
first, if we're all wrapped up here." Collins had reached the bottom of his milk shake and made sucking noises with his straw as
he tried to get the last drops. "I'd like to have a look at Lake
Hieronimo. Have you thought any about Vernon Lippert drowning when he did?"

"You mean when he was just about ready to retire. Yeah . . .
it's ironic. You work your ass off all your life, and just when
you're about to reach the point where all you have to do is go
fishing, your boat springs a leak or the wind comes up and you're
wiped out."

"That isn't what I meant. I meant . . . how many FBI agents

do you suppose there are who drown alone in the middle of a little fishing lake? What do you suppose the statistics are on that?"

Garvey stared at him. "I doubt there are any," he said after a moment.

"Right." Collins drawled out the word. "I'd kind of like to wander up there, maybe talk to a few people, the coroner, people who live there year-round. There must be a few."

"You think there's something fishy about that lake besides the fishing?"

Collins gave up trying to extract any more chocolate from the bottom of the shake cup. "Could be. I looked up Lake Hieronimo on the map. It's maybe an hour's drive up into the mountains. Probably cooler up there. We could make it this afternoon, then let the boss decide what comes next. That is, if you'd like a break from all the excitement around here."

"Why not?" Garvey was playing it cool but Collins caught the sharp interest in his eyes.

"You ever do any fishing?" Collins asked.

"Are you kidding? I grew up in a boat." Garvey laughed at Collins' transparent surprise. "What did you think, that I grew up playing backgammon in a private school? Or polo?"

Collins grinned to cover the surprise of his perception that there might be more to his partner than the All-American façade suggested. "Polo crossed my mind," he said.

14

wet... Friday night...

After going off duty, Harrison Stearns spent that Friday evening in
and around the Fedco department store. He knew his SAC was
convinced that the thief who had taken Stearns's vehicle three
weeks ago was not a stray in the area. He either lived or worked
nearby; otherwise, what had he been doing there on a rainy night
without transportation of his own? "If you have to go any distance
to go shopping without a car," Macimer had said, "you don't pick
a rainy Friday night."

But Agents Rayburn and Wagner had already checked out all
Fedco employees, paying close attention to any who had recently
been fired or quit. None of them fitted the description of the auto
thief.

He lives near here, Stearns told himself. Or he works somewhere else close by. And gets off work late.

That speculation narrowed the scope of the search. But there
were no offices or small businesses in the area that let employees
out around eight or nine at night. The kid might be a busboy at a
McDonald's or a supermarket, or—

Or a thief.

Stearns, who at that moment was in the television and stereo
sales area of the big discount store, watching the crowds, withdrew
into a corner with his new idea. He began to get excited. Suppose
it was no accident that the kid was in the parking lot that night?
Suppose he wasn't really an auto thief but a small-time scavenger,
one who worked the parking lots, the cars that were left unlocked?

Would he feel safe enough, after three weeks, to come back here again?

Stearns reacted gloomily. Putting himself in the thief's shoes, he could not see himself returning so soon to the scene of this particular crime.

But there were other crowded parking lots not far away. A group of stores nested around that intersection to the west, less than a half mile from Fedco. A restaurant on another corner, even closer. It had valet parking, but the kids chasing the cars didn't have time to pay attention to loiterers—not discreet ones. And a parking-lot thief, usually bent only on stealing loose packages or car stereo units, was small-time enough to panic if he actually stole a car and belatedly discovered that it was a police car. Even worse, an FBI vehicle.

Leaving Fedco, Stearns located his own car and drove a half mile down the street to the next traffic light. There he turned into the parking lot serving a group of stores clustered around a Walgreen's and a supermarket. When he got back to the office, he thought, he would check out any reports of parking-lot thefts. Might have to ask for police reports covering thefts in this vicinity; reports of petty thievery might not get past the first basket.

From a back corner of the lot, hunched down in the passenger seat of his unmarked car—anyone checking a parked car to see if it was occupied instinctively looked at the driver's seat—Stearns began his own private surveillance.

Back at Fedco, Jack Wagner and Cal Rayburn bought a cheese and pepperoni pizza in the cafeteria and carried it to one of the undersized Formica-topped tables. While Rayburn carefully wiped debris left by the previous occupant from the table, Wagner folded a wedge carefully and brought it to his mouth. Through a mouthful of pizza he said, "What do you suppose Stearns was doing here? Free-lancing?"

"Could be," said the taciturn Rayburn. "But he isn't the only one around."

"What do you mean?" Wagner grabbed a napkin and wiped some juice from his chin.

"I've seen another one a couple times. Don't know his name, but I know his face."

"You're sure he's an agent?"

"Uh-huh." Cal Rayburn glanced sleepily around the busy cafeteria. The place was about ready to close. Which made it close to the time of night the FBI vehicle was stolen from the parking lot. He attacked his wedge of pizza, chewing it methodically. "Maybe our boss isn't telling us everything. Maybe he's got a backup team assigned to give us competition."

Jack Wagner grinned. "Hell of a waste," he said.

Paul Macimer left the office in the late afternoon. Jan's car was not in the drive or garage when he arrived home. He found Kevin alone in the family room. "How's it going, Kev?"

The boy ducked his head and mumbled something. He picked up his baseball glove from the couch beside him, stuck his left hand into the glove and slapped a fist into the oiled pocket.

"Do you know where your mother is?"

"She had to go to the store."

"When are you going to get over being mad at me?"

Kevin studied the spotless floor. "I'm not mad."

"Disappointed?"

The boy hesitated, stuck his fist again into the glove's pocket and shook his head.

"Still think I should have gone against those robbers with guns blazing? Have you thought about what that might have meant? The risks involved?"

"I know. It's just that . . . I don't know what I thought."

"I think I do," Macimer said gently. "I was more than a little bit disappointed myself, if you want the truth. Maybe I can do better the next time. Or make sure there isn't a next time. But sometimes, Kevin, the thing you'd like to do isn't the right thing." Hearing his own words, he wondered if they sounded as hypocritical to the boy as they suddenly did to him.

Kevin pounded his glove, avoiding his father's gaze. "I bet you could take those guys!"

Macimer was silent a moment, studying the boy, resisting the strong desire to take him in his arms. He didn't want to embarrass Kevin any more than the boy already was. "Just remember this, Kevin. I wouldn't have stood by while anything happened to you or your sister or your mother. No matter what."

Kevin looked up at him, his manner suddenly sheepish, his eyes suspiciously moist. "I know *that*."

Macimer grinned. "Good. Were you planning on using that
glove, or were you only improving the pocket?"

"Davey and I were gonna play catch."

"Okay, go ahead. Don't be late for dinner." As Kevin bolted
toward the sliding patio doors Macimer called after him, "Is anyone else home?"

"Just Linda!"

Macimer watched the boy race across the yard, heading for the
home of Davey Kramer. Kevin had been eager to escape, but his
step seemed lighter, more buoyant after the brief exchange.

I wouldn't let anything happen to you. Confident promises, Macimer thought. He was remembering again Jan's fears that not
only she but also the children might be being followed. And
watched.

He found Linda in her room. The door was open but Macimer
tapped lightly with his knuckles. "Okay if I come in?"

She was lying on the bed, propped up against the headboard
with a copy of *People* magazine in her lap. Her extension phone
was on the pillow beside her but the instrument was in its cradle.
"Sure," she said, without expression.

"Mom had to run out?"

"Yes. She went so fast she didn't even ask if I wanted anything."

Macimer found a place to sit on a chair crowded with cushions
in the shapes of stuffed ladybugs, frogs and other comical crea-
tures. It was his afternoon for trying to mend fences within his
family. He knew why Jan had gone out so suddenly, probably
soon after his telephone call saying he was leaving the office early.
She hadn't given Linda a chance to go with her. She had created
an opportunity for Macimer to have his talk with Linda.

"Mom tells me you're having trouble with what happened that
night with the robbers. That you haven't been able to forget it—to
put it behind you."

"What did you expect?" The question was sharp. Linda's eyes
were cool, alarmingly adult, strikingly like her mother's when Jan
was feeling hostile.

"I don't know. It happened to you in a different way than it
happened to me." Macimer, trying to prepare for this moment,
had found no magic words, few that seemed any good at all.

"What can I tell you? There are people like that. They have all kinds of things pushing them, all kinds of motives. Sometimes nothing more than anger."

"Don't try to make me feel sorry for *them!*" Linda cried. "Those creeps! I don't need to understand them. They made me feel like I was some kind of bug they could squash anytime they wanted. Only first they'd have some fun, you know, like pulling off the wings and the legs."

"That's one of the hardest things to learn," said Macimer. "That there are some people to whom you don't matter at all. Even your life means nothing to them. Nobody ever found that easy to accept."

"You know what it was mostly?" Linda demanded. "The macho thing. Strutting around this house, those two apes telling each other and trying to show the girl what big men they were. I'm beginning to think all men are the same. Some just have nicer manners."

"We're not all the same," Macimer protested. He smiled. "What about your brothers? Look at Chip. Can you imagine him hurting anyone deliberately, especially a girl? You, for instance?"

"Lots of brothers rape their sisters."

The comment chilled him. He reminded himself that he was talking not only to his daughter but to a young woman who had been hurt. "A great many people find an infinite number of ways to hurt each other. But that isn't *us,* Linda. You know that. You didn't answer my question about Chip just now because you know the answer, and it doesn't fit with what you want to believe right now. That's my point. All men aren't like those two creeps. You know that from your own experience. Don't take my word for it. Lean on what you know yourself."

"What else would you say?" Linda answered with dignity.

"Because I'm a man? Because I'm a chauvinist myself, an exploiter of women?"

She was silent for a moment, staring at him, troubled. Then she said, "I don't know. I'm not sure."

As Macimer stared at his daughter in silence, baffled and worried, wondering if perhaps Jan wasn't right and the girl needed outside professional help, someone she could accept as objective and wise and supportive (fathers had once been supposed to be wise and supportive), another voice called out. "Yoo-hoo! Any-one there?"

Macimer and Linda exchanged glances. He offered an exaggerated grimace that brought a faint smile to her lips. They both recognized the voice, and there was an evident relaxing of the tension between them. "To the rescue, Daddy."

"Once more unto the breach. . . . You see, we aren't all bad."

"Yoo-hoo? Paul? It's Aileen . . ."

Linda looked unconvinced but willing to let their confrontation be set aside for the moment. Macimer went down the stairs to the family room. Aileen Hebert, a neighbor, stood just inside the open patio doors. Her face lit up with relief.

"Thank heaven you're home! I saw your car, and I was hoping you'd be here. The door was open. . . ."

"What's happened, Aileen? Lock yourself out again?" Divorced and living alone—one child was married, the other away at school —Aileen was forever losing her car keys or locking herself out of the house.

"It's not my fault this time, Paul. I *know* I had the house keys when I went out, I just can't find them."

"Everything's locked? Have you tried all the windows?"

"Well, I think so. I put the keys in my purse as I was leaving, I remember that distinctly. I only went over to the mall to do some shopping."

Macimer walked her back toward her house, which was two doors down the street, while they talked. She was a graying, still attractive woman in her forties whose vague manner, hair that seemed to have been used for nest building, and a tendency to dress uncertainly, as if she wanted to be ready for both a dinner party and a picnic, caused observers to overlook well-composed features and a fine figure. Macimer wondered if the vagueness, the haphazard dress and the lost keys were not all a consequence of the divorce, a cry for attention. But what particularly puzzled him about Aileen Hebert was how she could function efficiently— as she apparently did—as a secretary in one of Washington's prestigious law firms.

"You ought to have a house key with your car keys," he sugested.

"Well, I don't know, Paul . . . I mean, you know I often forget my car keys, or leave them in the car. And if there was a house key with them and someone found them, well, they could just walk into the house, couldn't they?"

Macimer had no answer for that.

Aileen Hebert followed him around her house, chattering as he checked the doors and windows. At the back of the house he found a bathroom window open about six inches. There was a "burglar-proof" stopper for the double-hung window, but it had been carelessly opened out to allow the window to be pushed up. Macimer found a narrow putty knife in the garage and used its blade to pry loose the catch on the screen. Then he opened the window, climbed inside, rehooked the screen, set the window stopper to the safe position and walked through the house to the front door, where he let Aileen Hebert in. Her house keys were in a tray on a table in the foyer.

"I don't know how that happened," she said in bewilderment. "I know I put them in my purse. I must have been thinking of something else on my way out and put them down there, do you suppose?"

Macimer grinned. "Aileen, you and keys aren't compatible, that's all."

"Not only me and *keys,*" she murmured ambiguously. "Would you like some coffee, Paul? It won't take a minute. Or a drink?"

"No, thanks, I—"

"I've been meaning to talk to Jan. The funniest thing happened the other day. Was it Monday? No, I think it was Tuesday. Are you sure you won't have a beer?"

"Thanks just the same, Aileen."

"I was listening to the radio—I always keep it on FM, you know, I like to listen to the music. The house is so empty if I don't have the radio on. Anyway, I was changing to another station. All of a sudden, as clearly as if she were standing right there in the room with me, I heard Jan's voice!"

Macimer paused in the doorway. "Jan's voice? Are you sure?"

"Yes! She was talking to someone on the phone. I didn't mean to listen but, you know, I was so *startled.* She made a date—it was with another woman, Paul," Aileen added archly, suppressing a giggle. "They were going out to dinner."

"Tuesday night," Macimer said slowly.

"Yes, I'm sure it must have been Tuesday. That is . . ."

"I think I will have that beer," he said. "Then I'd like you to tell me exactly what happened."

Macimer had come home early but his working day was not over. He spent the evening in his den, waiting for telephonic reports from Taliaferro, the case agent monitoring the surveillance of the suspect Molter from the Energy Research and Development Administration. The phone rang shortly after eight o'clock and Macimer snatched it up.

"He's on his way!" Taliaferro said, excitement in his voice.

"How many cars on him?" Macimer asked.

"Three on him and six more in reserve. We've got a close tail, a backup and one out front." The bracketing technique enabled the cars in a moving surveillance to keep contact with the subject even if he made an abrupt turn or darted down a parkway off ramp at the last second in a maneuver designed to expose a tail. The surveillance vehicles could also change positions so that the subject did not always see the same car behind him.

The number of men and vehicles being deployed would not have been necessary if agents had been able to plant a beeper on Molter's car, a sleek Toyota Celica coupe. But it was parked each night in a locked garage at Molter's security apartment complex, and during the day it was left in the ERDA garage in a section that happened to be within sight of the security guards at the entrance. Macimer had been unwilling to risk drawing Molter's attention by breaking into the apartment garage or involving the security guards. It was up to the surveillance team not to let Molter get away this time.

"Where is he heading?" Macimer asked.

"Looks like Arlington Memorial Bridge. Which means he's going down the Washington Parkway again if he sticks to his pattern."

"Keep me posted."

Macimer went to the kitchen to pour himself another cup of coffee and retreated to his den. While he waited his thoughts turned once more to Aileen Hebert and her chance revelation.

Macimer was not an expert in electronic surveillance, but he had had basic FBI training in the use and detection of bugs. In many cases clandestine surveillance was the only practical investigative approach available to law enforcement. The method of accidental reception over a neighbor's FM radio suggested a wireless bug. Most of them had a short range, from a few feet to perhaps a half mile. One of the simplest ways to pick up a signal from such a bug was on an ordinary FM receiver, tuned to an empty space in the commercial FM band. All you had to do was tune the transmitter to that frequency, set your radio to the same frequency and listen in—either directly, the eavesdropper in a car parked nearby, or by means of a voice-actuated tape recorder hidden within range.

The method was simple and effective, but it had a clear risk that made it unappealing to most professionals: *anyone* could receive the same signal if an FM receiver happened to be tuned to the right frequency.

Immediately after leaving Aileen Hebert, Macimer had made a quick search of his house, checking each phone, the wall boxes where the telephone lines entered a room, picture frames, lamps, chair seats and other obvious places to plant a bug. He discovered the first one inside the wall thermostat in the upstairs hallway. It was mounted just outside the master bedroom, the transmitter drawing its power from the wires serving the thermostat. Its tiny microphone would have been able to pick up anything said in the bedroom. A hole no larger than a pinprick penetrated the bedroom wall. A wire antenna about fifteen inches long dangled inside the wall between the studs.

A second listening device was hidden inside the telephone in the master bedroom. Macimer recognized it as a series bug, emplaced by cutting the phone wire and inserting the tap—about the size of a square sugar cube—in the line. It was the type of eavesdropping device that was hard to detect if not spotted in a physical search. Because it worked only when the phone was in use, there was no loading of the line at other times.

Aside from his anger over the intrusion into his private life represented by concealed microphones and transmitters, Paul Macimer was bothered by the method of their accidental discovery. Whoever had ordered them put into his home had accepted such a risk. Perhaps Macimer had even been expected to be alert enough to find the devices on his own.

Too easy. It was an old technique, the mark of the professional. Those two bugs had been meant to be found, lulling Macimer into a false sense of his own cleverness.

Which meant that other listening devices, harder to detect, remained in place.

Why? Because someone believed he had the missing Brea file? Or because someone hoped, by monitoring his calls, to learn details of the investigation? If the private line in Macimer's study had been tapped, for instance, then someone knew everything Pat Garvey had said during his call from San Timoteo.

Macimer tried to recall every word of that conversation. Enough had been said to let the clandestine listener know that the agents in San Timoteo were digging into the events Vernon Lippert had documented in the missing Brea file.

Macimer jostled his mug, spilling coffee. *Wrong!* How could the listener have known Macimer would even be involved in the Brea investigation? The bugs had almost certainly been planted by the three Latinos who had invaded his house, ostensibly carrying out a foolish robbery. No other strangers had had access to the house for the necessary period of time. But that meant the bugs had been put in place *before* Macimer was assigned to this "Special" by the Director.

Macimer didn't like the direction his speculations were taking. He was no more comfortable with the realization that his family, a sheltered part of his life during his years with the Bureau, was no longer immune . . .

A terse report from Taliaferro brought Macimer up to date on the surveillance. Molter, as he had on other nights, had doubled back along his route and changed direction several times to throw off or expose any possible pursuit. The first FBI teams had been replaced by others along the way. From the Columbia Pike, Molter had timed a changing light onto Glebe Road, making a left turn just as the traffic signal went from yellow to red.

"We were ready for that one," Taliaferro said. "We had a car ahead of him on Glebe. He won't give us the slip tonight!"

Molter was now heading south on the Jefferson Davis Highway toward Alexandria. "He's not going to the airport" was all Macimer said.

The last call came thirty minutes later. Molter had left his Toyota on a side street in downtown Alexandria. Agents had followed him on foot. One of them was walking parallel to the suspect along Washington Street when Molter went down a short flight of steps and entered a small print shop. Another agent strolled past the shop while Molter was engaged in a discussion with a clerk behind a glass counter. "They do framing and stuff like that," Taliaferro reported to Macimer. "Looks like Molter is going to have something framed."

"A neat cover for a drop."

"Do we move in?" Taliaferro asked. He *wanted* Molter.

"Not yet," Macimer said. "This shop might lead us to a lot more than Molter. Besides, we'll need cooperation from the Alexandria office now. Get your report in to Headquarters and ask for surveillance of that shop."

"They won't take the case away from me?" Taliaferro sounded worried.

"It's still your case, but I want that shop placed under surveillance and that's Alexandria's job. We're in their territory."

"What about Molter?" Taliaferro asked after a moment. "There can't be any more doubt that he's selling out."

"No, but we need proof. And we want to know who else is involved." Macimer knew the frustration his agent was feeling. "Don't worry, Alexandria will have to send you everything they get. We're still the office of origin, and you're the case agent."

"And Molter's mine," Taliaferro said grimly. Like most FBI agents, he felt a special antipathy toward traitors, those who would sell out their country's safety and security for whatever distorted motive—or price.

"Molter's still yours. If he follows the pattern, he may still catch tonight's shuttle to New York. Have you got someone from the New York office standing by at La Guardia?"

"Yeah," Taliaferro said glumly. "If he goes there he'll be spotted and followed."

"Good. Whoever he sees in New York may have no connection with the sellout—that may just be where he goes to spend the extra money he's making. But let's find out." As he paused Macimer could hear the crackle of other voices over the line, agents reporting in to Taliaferro that Molter was now returning to his car. "That's probably it for tonight," Macimer said, "but stay with him. No matter how you feel, Joe, it's been a good night. Remember that."

He hung up and wondered if, at precisely that moment, a voice-actuated tape recorder mounted on a nearby telephone pole had stopped hissing.

15

Early Saturday morning, while the mountain air held a breathless stillness, Lenny Collins and Pat Garvey slipped gently away from the shoreline of Lake Hieronimo in the Sierras and glided across the unruffled surface of the lake. In the soft, pre-dawn light the water was blue-black and surprisingly cold. Not a big lake, Pat Garvey thought, but deep. He let the oars bite deep and gave a long, strong pull.

In the center of the lake he shipped the oars and sat motionless, enjoying the stillness, the smells of water and piney woods, of oil and fish and weathered boat. That sturdy old rowboat had belonged to Vernon Lippert. Al Boulanger, owner of the boat rental and bait shop at the west end of the lake, had had it in dry dock since the sheriff left it with him back in February. "I expect Vern Lippert's widow woman will come for it eventually," Boulanger had surmised. "But she ain't been up to the lake since Vern's accident. And the sheriff, he just said not to do anything with the boat. I mean, it was state's evidence or something like that."

Boulanger had not seen what happened to Lippert out on the lake that February morning. No one had. The FBI man had gone out early in his own boat, probably before dawn. Around eight o'clock two hikers had spotted the boat adrift in the lake with no one aboard. Boulanger had motored out to bring in the empty rowboat.

"Did you notice anything about it unusual?" Collins asked. "Anything at all?"

"There was nothing. It was just an empty boat." Boulanger shrugged. The questions were not new. He had told the sheriff everything he knew, which wasn't much. Lippert often went out on the lake early in the morning when he was staying at his place. He often came there alone. There hadn't been a storm that morning, not even much of a wind, although it didn't take much to whip up the waves on a lake the size of Hieronimo. "Only one thing," he added as an afterthought, prompted by the fact that he had to hunt up oars when the two FBI men asked to take Lippert's boat out on the lake. "There was an oar missing."

"An oar?" Collins' question was sharp.

"That's right. When that boat was brought in, there was only one oar."

Drifting over the smooth surface of the lake, Collins and Garvey watched the sky lighten, the tips of the pines along the eastern rim of hills begin to burn. "Satisfied?" Garvey finally asked.

"Not very."

"What's bothering you?"

"Two things. One is what Boulanger said about the weather. No real wind that morning—not enough to make you afraid to take a flat-bottomed boat out. And then . . . there's that missing oar."

"What about it? If Lippert fell overboard, which he obviously did, he could've grabbed an oar."

"Sure he could. But they float." Collins' eyes had a keen expression Garvey hadn't seen in them before, like the eyes of a hunter who has spotted sign of a deer's passage. "They don't just disappear at the bottom of the lake. And that oar never showed up anywhere."

Following his partner's line of thought intently, Garvey shook his head. "I know what you're thinking, but the coroner's report found no evidence of violence. A bruise on Lippert's temple, but he could've got that if his head hit the side of the boat."

"Then what happened to that oar?" Collins paused, his gaze circling the lake, seeing the last gray of the water melt into blue as the sun stained the horizon. FBI agents had combed the shoreline routinely, corroborating the sheriff's report that no oar had been found. "It's not that big a lake. I can think of reasons why an oar had to disappear—and I don't like any of them."

At six o'clock Saturday evening, Paul Macimer turned off Connecticut Avenue onto a side street near the Chevy Chase Country Club. A moment later he drove between open wrought-iron gates and followed a circular drive that arched between fragrant clouds of dogwood and forsythia. The house, which brought a murmur of admiration from Jan, was white brick with ivy almost covering its two-story front. In front of the house, at the edge of the circular drive, an antique iron figure of a black jockey waited to take the reins of an arriving horse. Macimer pulled up near the hitching post. Another car was parked a short distance away on the drive. It bore Virginia license plates and a car rental sticker.

Held up by an accident ahead of them in heavy Saturday traffic, they were later than Paul had intended. Gordon and Mary Ruhle had arrived earlier, and the Macimers found Gordon sitting on the end of a diving board above the Olympic-size pool. He wore tight black swim trunks and his chest and shoulders were deeply tanned. The fresh white bandage on his forehead stood out against his sunburned face like a badge. Ruhle looked remarkably fit for a man in his mid-fifties, the chest deep and solidly muscled under its mat of curly black hair, his belly flat and hard. He waved to Paul from his perch and grinned at Jan. "Come on in—how often do us peons get to use the boss's pool?"

Jan shook her head, laughing. "I didn't bring a suit."

"So what? Erika can fix you up. Hell, seeing you in a bikini is the main reason I'm here. You look great, Jan."

"I'm afraid you'll have to settle for Erika today."

Jan glanced sidelong at Erika Halbig as the younger woman climbed up an aluminum ladder at the side of the pool and emerged into the late-afternoon sun as if onto the apron of a stage. Tall and slender, she seemed unconsciously sensuous as she removed her cap, shook out her short, white-blond hair and padded toward the newly arrived guests, her bare feet toeing in slightly. Jan restrained the impulse to look at Paul. The appraising approval she saw in Gordon Ruhle's unabashed gaze was, she suspected, an adequate mirror.

"Jan—and Paul! How marvelous you could come!"

Her swimsuit was not a bikini but a maillot, a variation on the skintight suits popularized by Olympic swimmers in the seventies. Erika's suit was a vivid cyclamen pink. She smiled slowly and with apparently genuine warmth, completely unselfconscious as she kissed Jan's cheek and Paul's in turn, the kind of social kiss in which lips seemingly missed their general target. "It's been *much* too long!"

"Yes, it has," Paul said.

"I don't know where the time has gone," Jan said politely.

"I think I know—you have those three children!" Erika spoke with frequent breathless exclamations. "How *are* they?"

"Fine, just fine." The question caused Jan to warm slightly.

"You should have brought them. Didn't Russ tell you—?"

"Hey, what's happening to the party?" Gordon Ruhle demanded from the diving board. "Come on, Paul. Get your feet wet."

Macimer waved him off. "I wish I'd thought of it and we'd have got here earlier. I didn't even expect to see the sun today."

He accepted a drink from Russ Halbig at the bar near one end on the pool terrace. Strolling over to the water's edge, he watched Gordon launch into a flat dive. Ruhle burst out of the water close enough for spray to catch Paul Macimer's shoes and slacks before he jumped back. Gordon hadn't changed, he thought with a grin. He still had to be the youngest, hardest, toughest—younger, harder and tougher than any agent he served with, regardless of age.

After swimming two fast lengths of the pool, Gordon Ruhle climbed out and walked over to the bar, where he claimed a Bourbon on the rocks. Jan and Erika had disappeared into the house. "Son of a bitch, it's good to see us all together again," Gordon said carelessly. "And Jan—she does look great, Paul."

"That she does."

Their eyes met on a level. Macimer had always thought of Ruhle as taller, though they were about the same height. The illusion came from Ruhle's broader, more heavily muscled build. Macimer wondered if Gordon still prided himself on jerking over three hundred pounds.

He grinned again. Gordon Ruhle had always challenged him.

"If I hadn't showed up at Quantico, I don't suppose you'd ever have got in touch," Gordon said.

"I haven't been in hiding," Macimer retorted. "All your messages must have got lost."

"Gordon's been on the road a lot the last couple of years," Russ Halbig said.

"Oh? Selling brushes?"

"That comes later," Ruhle said with a scowl. Then, with a shrug of his heavy shoulders, he added, "Somebody's got to chase down the crazies. I've been on the fugitive squad. Working mostly out West."

There was a sudden commotion as three women emerged from the house. Leading the way was a small, earnest woman with unexpectedly white hair. "Paul!" Mary Ruhle cried. "Paul Macimer!"

She flew across the terrace while Macimer tried to cover his slight shock over the way she had aged in a short time. She darted past his outstretched hands to embrace him. For a moment she clung to him tightly. Then she stepped back, her eyes moist. "It's so . . . so . . . oh God, I'm going to be a mess. I just went through this with Jan and I thought I was over it."

Macimer's lingering question about the purpose of this get-together melted away in that moment. Mary Ruhle's unguarded sentiment made his wariness seem mean, even foolish. Old friends didn't put up guards. They didn't need to.

The initial strains quickly eased in the familiar babble of reminiscences, family gossip, barbed humor and casual shoptalk about the Bureau. After an hour of talk and drinks on the terrace, Russ Halbig broiled steaks over an open barbecue pit. He played the role of genial host like an actor, Macimer thought. If Halbig's engineering of this occasion had been a surprise, his evident enjoyment was even more unexpected. He cheerfully refilled glasses, watched the fire and the steaks, gave orders to Alma, the quiet black woman in crisp white uniform who emerged from the house without apparent signal to set up a table and to bring heaping bowls of salads, relishes and casseroles, far more food than six people could eat.

Macimer was glad enough when the food came. He realized that he had overstepped his usual limit of three drinks. He had lost count, in fact, but he thought he was up to five.

He was also glad when Erika Halbig went into the house and changed out of her skintight bathing suit.

It was a busy Saturday night at Farrantino's Restaurant in Arlington, across the Potomac southwest of the nation's capital. Three young black men handled the valet parking, and they were kept on the run all evening. When the clean-cut young man tried to stop Allen Brown to ask a question, Brown cut him off. "Hey, man, I got no time, you know?"

He jumped into a Seville after handing its owner a claim check and wheeled off into the darkness with a squeal of rubber. But when Brown came back to the restaurant's entry he found the same sandy-haired dude waiting for him. This time the dude flashed a gold badge. Brown took a second look and choked off a smart remark. What the hell—he hadn't sniffed any grass for over a week. And he wasn't dealing. What could the FBI want with him? "What is it, man?" he asked suspiciously.

"Just a couple of questions," the FBI man said. "Have you had any problems with theft out of the cars at night? Somebody stealing things, or even taking stereos and hubcaps?"

"Hey, you jiving me? We get hit that way two, three times a week! Hey, where were you last night? We had one Mercedes cleaned out while the dude was inside eating. You should've heard him scream! But listen, we got a sign right there, you dig it? 'We Are Not Responsible for Personal Articles Left in Vehicles.' Hey, we can't guard 'em, you know? We just park 'em."

Harrison Stearns grabbed the young man's arm in his eagerness. "I want to know everything you remember about that Mercedes. What time did it come in? How long was it parked?"

"Hey, man, we're busy! This is Saturday night." The young black attendant pulled against Stearns's tight grip. "You costin' me money."

Stearns caught himself, eased his hold on the youth's arm but did not release him. "You must take a break sometime. When?"

"Yeah, yeah . . . maybe about ten o'clock. It eases off."

"I'll be waiting," the FBI man said firmly.

Darkness. The smell of charcoal and seared meat still hung in the air. The plates with their leftovers had been whisked away by the silent, efficient Alma. The evening air held a soft blue haze like smoke from a thousand barbecue fires.

From a group of chaises near one corner of the pool came the murmur of women's voices. The artificial blue glow of the backlit water reflected from the women's hair like a blue rinse.

Macimer sat in a corner of the terrace with Gordon Ruhle and Russ Halbig. Ruhle lit a large, fat-bowled briar pipe and puffed the tobacco mixture into a red glow. He still smoked the same cherry blend he had used twenty years ago, Macimer noted with amusement. Gordon the Traditionalist.

"Hell, you could almost think nothing had changed," Ruhle said, staring off into the darkness. "Is Ike still President?"

Macimer said, "He's gone but some things don't change. Family, friends . . ."

Ruhle blew out an angry cloud of smoke. "Bull. Don't kid yourself. It looks the same on a night like this, but that's a whole different world out there from what it was when we all started out. A whole different world."

"Everything may not be all right with the world," Macimer said lightly, "but God's still in His heaven, and we're still the Good Guys."

"I'm not so sure about either of those things anymore." Ruhle glowered at Macimer through cherry-scented smoke.

"You always did have a tendency to exaggerate things, Gordie," Halbig said, chuckling diplomatically. Ruhle had always hated being called Gordie. "I seem to remember your insisting the Commies would have swallowed us up by 1980. It hasn't happened."

"You think it won't?"

There was a momentary silence. Macimer heard the lilt of Erika Halbig's laughter floating toward them from poolside. Erika seemed to be laughing a lot. He saw her face catch the light from the pool as she turned toward him, as if she were staring directly at him. Jan's face was in shadow.

Gordon Ruhle's words took him back twenty years. Gordon's suspicion and hatred of Communists had not seemed exaggerated then. The Cold War was a reality to be dealt with, not a policy to be questioned. Even John Kennedy had reflected prevailing attitudes in his early confrontations with the Russians, who had done little to ease the tensions between the two great powers. As a new agent fresh out of law school, Macimer had quickly learned the importance J. Edgar Hoover placed on the Communist conspiracy, and he had been eager to do his part. He had had no reason to doubt Hoover's estimate of the danger to the country posed by an aggressive Communist foe. And he had not questioned the polarized convictions of the tough, seasoned agent who had befriended him. . . .

"Your kids giving you any trouble, Paul?" Ruhle's question jolted Macimer back to the present.

He laughed. "Only the usual. My youngest boy wasn't speaking to me for a while." He gave a brief account of the robbery and its aftermath. "I'm afraid I didn't come off like Superman."

"I think you handled it very well," Russ Halbig said.

Ruhle's pipe had gone out. He tamped the tobacco down with a nailhead and struck another match. When he stopped puffing he said, "That's exactly what I mean. Now we've got the punks invading our own houses, for Christ's sake. And what happens if we catch 'em? They go off laughing."

"What about your two? Ann and Gordon, Jr.?" Halbig asked Ruhle.

"My kids . . ." Ruhle fell into a long, prickly silence. Finally he shrugged. "Why not? You might as well know." For a moment longer he was silent. "When I was a kid nobody talked about cancer. If you had it in the family, you just didn't talk about it out loud. In whispers, maybe, not looking anyone in the eye. Now . . . now it's drugs and our kids. Yeah, both of mine are into that scene. Hell, they're all into it. Why should my kids be any different?"

The revelation was painful for Ruhle and it made Macimer uncomfortable. He suspected Chip had tried marijuana, at least. Given Chip's age and the prevalence of grass in the high schools, it would have been surprising if he hadn't. All-American jocks were not exactly shunning drugs. All-Pros were being picked up at airports with their pockets full of coke or heroin. And it was not only a drug scene. It was a fast-buck scene as well. That bothered Macimer more than the hunch that Chip and his pals used pot the way Paul and his friends had discovered booze a thousand years ago.

"My kids are no better than the rest," Ruhle was saying. "They didn't have the guts to stand up for themselves and say no. Pot, speed, coke, PCP—you name it, they're into it. And you can't talk them out of it. You can't tell them anything. If you try, they just clam up on you, or they look at you as if you're coming at them out of the Middle Ages. Ask *them* if God's still in His heaven, Paul—they don't believe in anything but themselves. That's what Mary and I raised—a couple of charter members of the Me generation." Ruhle paused, suddenly reaching out to empty the ashes from his pipe into a glass ashtray, viciously banging the hot briar. The clatter caused the voices of the three women near the pool to fall silent, three faces to turn toward the men at the other end of the terrace. "Believe it or not," Ruhle muttered in a lower voice, "I found out Gordon was dealing in uppers and downers at his school. When I learned that, I kicked him the hell out of the house. Then I found out Ann wasn't living in her dormitory at college like she'd been telling us, she'd been sleeping with this fag teacher ten years older than she is. I haven't talked to either of them since."

On the drive home Macimer told Jan that he had asked Gordon and Mary Ruhle over for dinner on Sunday. If she was surprised, Jan did not say so. Instead she began to supply him with more pieces of information about their old friends.

"Did Gordon tell you about their kids? Gordon, Jr., and Ann?"

"Yes. I gather he won't even talk to them—doesn't see them at all. That's like Gordon, of course. How's Mary taking it?"

"Not very well. You know how she is—she's very Catholic, very family-oriented. She does see them, of course, but she has to do it behind Gordon's back, when he isn't home. Which is a lot of the time, I gather."

"He's on the road a lot," Paul Macimer said. "He's been on a national fugitive squad."

After a moment's silence Jan said, "Erika drinks."

"What do you mean?"

"You know what I mean. She never stopped. I don't know how she held it all without falling down. You didn't notice?"

"No . . . she seemed sober enough to me."

"It's about the only thing about her you didn't notice," Jan said. "My God, that bathing suit, why did she even bother?"

"The young have different standards these days. Fewer hang-ups, I guess they'd say."

"Thanks for reminding me," Jan said, a little too sweetly. Macimer regretted his words, which seemed to say more than he had intended about Erika Halbig's comparative youth. "Her standards seemed to appeal to you and Gordon. Talk about treating women as sex objects!"

Macimer said nothing. The problem was not that they had treated women as sex objects, he thought ruefully. The trouble

was they had reacted specifically to Erika Halbig as a sex object.
An attention she hadn't exactly resented.

"She liked it, all right," Jan said, as if reading his mind. "I
wonder if that's part of the trouble."

"What trouble?"

She glanced at him in surprise. "Between her and Russ, of
course. Honestly, Paul, for someone who's supposed to be a
trained observer you certainly can avoid seeing what you don't
want to notice."

"Obviously," Macimer said, "I didn't catch all the nuances you
did."

"In all fairness, most of the little hints came during our girl
talk, not when you men were around. Are you really surprised?"

"I guess I'm not," he said thoughtfully. "I remember I was
stunned when he and Elaine broke up, but this time . . ." He
shook his head. "Funny I didn't catch any signs of trouble. I guess
my mind was on . . . other things."

Jan looked at him directly for a moment. "These days," she
said, "it usually is."

Gordon Ruhle turned his rented Ford compact south on Connecticut Avenue and drove toward town. A moment later a battered vintage Volkswagen emerged from the same street onto Connecticut. Its lights came on only after it reached the main street.

The VW lagged behind the Ford but kept it in sight through the
center of the District and again as Gordon Ruhle crossed the
Fourteenth Street Bridge and swung south on the parkway toward
Alexandria. Though traffic was moderate, there was enough to
screen the Volkswagen until the two cars passed Washington National Airport. As traffic thinned out south of the airport, the
tailing car dropped further behind.

Joseph Gerella abandoned his pursuit when the Ford swung
into the parking lot of a Ramada Inn in Alexandria. He turned
back toward town. He was not troubled by the possibility that the
FBI agent in the rented car might have spotted him. Even if he
had, Gerella reasoned, the agent could not have known who was
following him.

On his way home Gerella stopped off at a fast-food restaurant
for a hamburger, fries and chocolate shake. He carried his tray to
a booth by the window. As he ate he pondered the seemingly in-

nocuous Saturday-night reunion he had witnessed at a distance. Paul Macimer had done nothing unusual in the week Gerella had been maintaining a discreet watch on the agent's movements. Nor had the reporter learned anything significant from Jackie Macauley, an eager young female assistant on Senator Sederholm's staff. Very eager. But the morning's mail had brought another page from the missing FBI file, sent by the anonymous informant who had called Oliver Packard's office asking for Gerella. By itself the page—containing a list of names, times, places in what looked to be a schedule of assignments—meant no more to Gerella than the original page he had received in the mail.

But Macimer's name was on that second page.

Gerella lived in an apartment in an old building east of the Capitol, not far from Robert F. Kennedy Memorial Stadium. It was an integrated neighborhood, but it was one he felt at home in. His only complaint was finding street parking for the Volkswagen; he had had to rent a garage two blocks from his building. By the time he had parked and locked the garage, it was after one o'clock in the morning. Walking along the deserted street, he told himself the night's work might not have been fruitless. Perhaps there was some connection among the three agents that was worth exploring.

Gerella had a habit of walking with his head down, absorbed in his thoughts. He did not notice anyone on the street until he was almost in front of his building. Then three figures materialized from the shadows. One stepped from behind a parked car. The other two emerged from behind the steps leading up to his apartment entrance.

One of the men was a chunky figure about Gerella's own size. The other two were youthfully slim, almost frail. Gerella was not deceived. He knew instantly he was in trouble.

"Let's cool it, huh?" he said quickly. "I've only got ten bucks on me—"

The stocky man wasted no words. He moved in fast, feinting with something held in his right hand. A gun? Gerella wasn't sure. He was angry now, and scared. A mugging to top off his Saturday night was just what he didn't need. He tried to block an expected blow from the stocky man's right hand. One of the other figures snaked behind him.

Gerella broke for the steps to his building. He made it only as far as the bottom step.

A foot jabbed between his legs, tripping him. As he fell forward he felt a glancing blow off a shoulder blade. The impact chilled his brain.

He rolled and came up fighting. Gerella had had more than his share of street fights as a youngster. He hadn't forgotten how to give as much punishment as he received. There were no rules for this kind of fight. He caught one of the slender attackers in the groin with a savage kick. The youth doubled over with a soft moan. Gerella had a disconcerting impression the victim was not a boy but a girl.

With a guttural cry—Gerella heard only the word *Dios!*—the second of the smaller figures charged. Gerella heard the sharp click of a knife blade jumping from its sheath. He was moving even before his brain consciously identified the sound. The blade tugged at his jacket. Gerella threw a right-hand punch. He felt a leap of excitement as his fist landed. Bone and cartilage yielded under the blow. Two down!

The satisfaction was short-lived. As the chunky attacker moved in, Gerella aimed a kick at his kneecap. He wasn't quick enough. The first solid blow from the object in the stocky man's hand caught Gerella on the biceps. It numbed his entire arm and shoulder. A shocking pain stabbed through his whole body.

Demoralized by that blow, the reporter tried to ward off another with his one good arm. He knew that no fist could strike with such terrible force. He wanted to run but his feet were suddenly clumsy. He remembered how his father tried to walk after his stroke, how he would be on the sides of his feet without knowing it.

Hands plucked at Gerella's arms from behind. For an instant only he was caught and held. It was enough. He was helpless when a fourteen-inch length of lead pipe crushed his jaw. His mouth was suddenly filled with blood and fragments of teeth. He screamed, but he was not sure there was any sound. Maybe the scream was only inside his head.

The entire attack had taken place in deadly, purposeful silence, broken only by that one muttered Spanish oath, by the slap and scuff of shoe leather, grunts and exploding breaths, the smack of bone on flesh—until that deceptively silent impact against the side of Gerella's face. There had been no cries to alert anyone in the apartment building. No one appeared at any of the windows. No one was in the street. No one could help him.

Gerella sagged to the sidewalk. His body involuntarily curled into a protective ball. Other blows and kicks punished him as he lay on the sidewalk at the foot of the steps. He was hardly aware of them. The pain of his broken jaw was all-enveloping. He wanted to scream at them. Why? Why do this for a lousy ten bucks?

Just before the last blow from the pipe battered him unconscious, Gerella knew that this was not just another Saturday-night mugging. It wasn't for ten bucks. It was an attack far more callous and dangerous.

He sank toward blackness, as if the sidewalk were melting beneath him. One of the attackers' faces loomed over him. It seemed bloated, as if distorted by the curve of a camera lens. Beneath the smeared nose the youth's mouth moved. Gerella heard a single contemptuous word, harsh and clear: *"Traidor!"* His mind seized upon the word, puzzled over it, tried to understand what it meant.

Traitor. Betrayer.

The sense of it slipped away, and there was only darkness and pain.

At about the same moment Joseph Gerella lost consciousness, in their suburban home on the other side of Washington, Paul and Jan Macimer were climbing into bed. To his surprise Jan did not seem sleepy. She wanted to talk.

"It's not the same," she said, after turning out the light and settling in beside him. "Nothing is anymore."

"That sounds very significant," he murmured. He had to force his eyelids open.

"It wasn't the same tonight. Oh, I enjoyed seeing them all again, especially Mary. And I'm glad you asked her and Gordon over. She's stuck in that motel while he's down at the Academy." Jan paused. "You can't go back. Even we can't go back."

"That sounds gloomy."

"I was a bobby-soxer once, remember? I went on fraternity weekends and wondered about kissing on our first date. I wore your pin. I never made love to anyone else."

"I wouldn't want it any other way."

"Don't be glib." Jan sighed. "Tonight it seemed such a long

time ago, those early years. Me and Mary and Elaine, all three of us with babies at about the same time, all of us learning how to cook hamburger a hundred ways, sharing our spaghetti recipes, wondering when you or Gordon or Russ, or all three of you, would be home again."

"It *was* a long time ago."

"Everything's changed. Gordon hasn't," she corrected herself with a short laugh. "But everything else has. I was thinking tonight, listening to Mary, that we've done it all, all the cliché things. Painted the Easter eggs, stayed up all night waiting for the doctor, wrapped the Christmas presents, sewed on the buttons, joined the PTA, watched the ball games. And scrubbed a thousand floors and cleaned up the vomit and trained the dog to go outside. And sometimes, a lot of times, I was so damned *alone*. I didn't like that part of it, Paul, I never did. And I don't like it now."

"Jan—"

"Maybe what I'm saying is, I need more of you. Or . . ." She couldn't bring herself to finish the thought, either because she was afraid of the ending or was not yet sure what it was.

"Are you wondering if it was all worth it?"

"No! That's not it at all! It was right for me then, for both of us. You've no *right* to say that."

"I'm sorry."

"To hell with you!"

Reaching for her impulsively, he discovered to his surprise that the pajama top was unbuttoned. His hand closed over the soft mound of her breast. He kept it there. She did not push him away.

After a moment her breathing had quickened. Still caressing one breast, he kissed the other. When she did not resist he let his hand flow down over the smooth, familiar curves of hip and belly. After a brief exploration his fingers stopped, as if surprised by what they found.

"Don't ask *me!*" she said fiercely. "I don't know why. Don't ask —just don't talk."

He was left to wonder at the mystery of her moods. His own response to her was immediate as always. She clutched him almost cruelly, rose to engulf him. In the moment they were joined he thought that he had to send her away, that once again she would be alone.

16

From the Macimers' patio off the family room, sheltered from the all-day Sunday rain, Gordon Ruhle watched a sudden squall drive the branches of a willow tree toward the ground, as if they had gone limp. The air was as warm and humid as a greenhouse. "Is it always like this?" he growled.

Macimer, standing behind him, laughed. "It stopped for Halbig's party."

"I suppose it had to."

Macimer recalled Gordon's old remark about Halbig's ability to dodge the raindrops. It seemed to have held true throughout Halbig's career, in spite of periods of turmoil within the agency. And now? When the Brea investigation was closed, would Halbig, as usual, be in the clear?

Would John Landers be untouched?

The two men turned back inside the house as a gust of wind blew rain across the patio. The family room was empty, Jan having taken Mary Ruhle with her on an unnecessary trip to the store —a maneuver Macimer had prearranged with her, postponing an explanation. Macimer had told her only that he wanted to talk to Gordon alone about FBI business. The three children had been treated to an after-dinner movie at the local theater.

Gordon Ruhle followed Macimer across the family room to the den. Near the doorway he stopped to inspect a number of framed photographs and other family memorabilia on the paneled wall next to the door. Gordon's eye had been caught by the photo of

Macimer in a handshake with J. Edgar Hoover. The picture had been fitted with new non-glare glass to replace the original glass maliciously broken by one of the three Latin intruders. Then Ruhle peered at a smaller photograph, a snapshot showing Macimer and Ruhle together, standing in front of the old post office building in Omaha—two men nearly twenty years younger, looking tough and efficient with their close-cropped hair, conservative suits, white shirts and ties. "What happened to those guys?" Ruhle asked.

"They let their hair grow," Macimer said. "That's all."

"Yeah." Ruhle grinned at him. "Okay, what about these bugs of yours?"

"Did you bring your toolbox?"

"Yeah. You want to tell me what it's all about?"

Briefly Macimer described the discovery of clandestine listening devices in the hall thermostat and master bedroom. "I can't be sure, but my guess is there might be others. I figured you're more of an electronics expert than I am, you might be able to find them." Macimer did not try to tell Ruhle why he was being asked to find any other devices, rather than someone from the WFO. He wanted to find out what he was dealing with without having someone from the Washington Field Office involved—and without having a report go to FBI Headquarters.

Even admitting that much to himself left him unhappier than he could remember being in his twenty years with the Bureau.

"You think your three Latinos planted them?" Gordon asked.

"I don't know who else."

"This place isn't Fort Knox. It wouldn't be so hard to break into. It could've been done without your knowing."

"But I know about those three. The logical assumption is they did it."

"Why?"

Macimer shrugged. "I wish I could be sure. . . ."

The answer was not completely frank. But there was no point in going into the Brea investigation with Ruhle, who had removed himself from involvement in it by his own choice. "Any other time, you know I'd jump at the chance to work with you, Paul," he had said at Quantico after the bombing. "But I can't walk away from this. Hell, I've been lecturing these kids about terrorism. Now we can all see what we're talking about."

Macimer unlocked a desk drawer and removed the two bugs he had found on Friday. Gordon Ruhle immediately identified the first as a simple wireless transmitter. It was this bug's signal Aileen Hebert had overheard, since it worked by radio transmission in the FM frequency range. The second device, which had been attached to the telephone in the bedroom, was confirmed as a type that worked only when the phone was in use.

Gordon Ruhle had brought in from his car a small black leather case. He removed a portable instrument from the case, identifying it as an electronic field strength meter. "Your ever popular sniffer," he said. "If there are any other radio transmitters in the house, this will sniff them out."

He went through the house methodically, room by room. As he worked he began to sing in a rich baritone, watching the meter on the electronic sniffer, which he tuned continuously across the range of possible frequencies.

"Is that raucous moaning necessary?" asked Macimer.

Ruhle grinned. "If there's a radio bug here, it'll pick up my golden tones, naturally. This little meter will let out a howl when I hit the right frequency."

The sniffer remained silent.

Macimer felt some relief when they returned to his den. But the search was not over. There was still the possibility of another kind of wiretap, a device intruded into the telephone lines or one of the instruments. From his leather case Ruhle removed another testing instrument, about the size and shape of a cigar box. "A telephone analyzer," he said when Macimer raised an eyebrow. "It's got a built-in VOM that reads the resistance in the telephone line."

Ruhle disconnected the telephone line in Macimer's den at the wall outlet and connected the line to the analyzer. After taking a reading, he plugged the telephone into the other side of the analyzer. After a moment he offered an unreadable grunt.

"Well?"

"The normal reading is just under a million ohms. That's without your telephone in line. Look at it now." Macimer peered at the dial. The reading was a little over half a million ohms. "That means you've got more trouble."

Using the same test instrument, Ruhle then examined Macimer's telephone, checking the voltage reading. A high reading with the phone off the hook would indicate a series bug like the one Macimer had found upstairs. The reading, however, was normal.

When Ruhle took another measurement with the phone in its cradle, he gave a low whistle.

"You mind cutting the melodrama, Gordon?"

"First it's my singing you don't like, now it's my whistling." Ruhle's tone was unruffled but his eyes were serious. "The reading is too low. My guess is you've got some kind of parallel device in there. I'll have to check it out. Is there a public telephone anywhere close?"

"There's one at the gas station on the corner."

"Okay. You stay here. Make some noise—I don't care what it is. Sing or whistle or use the typewriter. Wait about five minutes until I get to that phone, then go into your act."

It was a long five minutes. Outside, the rain was still coming down steadily, drenching everything, not a downpour but a soaking rain. Gordon Ruhle seemed not to notice it as he ran out to his car. A few minutes after he drove off Macimer checked his watch. He began to whistle, feeling foolish.

"All right, Gordon, damn it, stop showing off," he said after a moment. "And where did you become such an expert, anyway?" He broke off, searching for something else to say. It was surprising how difficult it was to talk aloud without an audience. Feeling increasingly foolish, he began to sing "From the Halls of Montezuma . . ." That ought to be right up Gordon's alley.

The telephone rang. Macimer snatched it up. "Gordon?"

"Yeah. To answer your question, the FBI taught me everything I know. As for your singing, I think you better confine it to the shower."

Macimer stiffened. "You could hear me?"

"Loud and clear. You've got an Infinity Transmitter in place. It's tone-activated, which means the listener can activate the transmitter by calling in from outside, using a specific tone to turn on the tap. What that does is prevent the phone from ringing at the time, and it turns the phone itself into a combination microphone and transmitter. Your eavesdropper just dials in and he might as well be in the room."

"How did you turn it on?"

"My handy-dandy little wiretap finder can produce all the possible tones. I just ran up the scale until your IT was triggered."

Three minutes later Gordon Ruhle was back at the house. He took the telephone apart carefully, inspecting everything. Macimer had done the same without finding anything that did not appear to be a normal component of the instrument, but Ruhle finally held out the circular mouthpiece in the palm of his hand. "That's the culprit."

"It looks like an ordinary mouthpiece to me."

"It's supposed to." He glanced questioningly at Macimer. "You want to leave it where it was, or replace it?"

"Why would I leave it there?"

"If we remove it, whoever planted the device will know you found it."

Macimer took the bug and rolled it thoughtfully between his fingers. At last he said, "I want him to know."

Before Gordon could answer voices came from the adjoining family room. Gordon made a face, but there was tolerant acceptance in his eyes as they heard Mary Ruhle call out, "Gordon? Are you two still in there? Can't the FBI wait till Sunday's over?"

"Well, it's your baby," Gordon murmured. "I wish I could help some more, but . . ."

"You've helped a lot. Thanks, Gordon."

"You want this just between us, right?" Gordon's question was shrewd and to the point.

"For now," said Macimer. "What about the other phones? You didn't test them with your box."

"That's easy," Gordon Ruhle said. "Get new ones."

The Ruhles left late, Mary obviously reluctant to have the evening end. She was flying back to the coast Monday night, and this was the last chance for these old friends to indulge in nostalgic reminiscence and family news and recycled gossip. When the two visitors finally left, the house seemed unnaturally quiet and empty. Kevin had long been asleep, Linda closeted in her own room. Chip, as usual, had gone out again after returning from the movie.

Macimer was heading for his den when Jan stopped him. "Let's talk a little, Paul."

She made some instant coffee and they sat in the family room, walled in by darkness and rain. "I always liked Gordon," Jan said after a moment. "I don't think I could take very much of him now."

"Because he hasn't changed like the rest of us?"

"I knew you'd defend him."

"I'm not defending him, honey. I didn't know he needed defending." He knew, of course, what had set Jan off. Gordon's remark about "bleeding-heart judges" had started it. "They're out to clip our wings and let the Commies take over," Gordon had said.

"Oh, really, Gordon," Jan had said impatiently. "Maybe you people need to have your wings clipped. Especially if you still believe there are Communists hiding under every bed."

Ruhle had stared at her in disbelief. "You think there aren't any Reds in our government? Or even on the Atomic Energy Commission? Hell, Jan, just last year Ivan was kicked out of Norway, Sweden, Canada, Switzerland, France and West Germany for spying. You think he's not *here*? That we don't have our own Ivans right inside the government and our defense industries, calling themselves good old Joe or Brian or Jack Armstrong? What kind of Alice-in-Wonderland thinking is that?" Ruhle's glare had switched suddenly from Jan to Paul. "What are you grinning at?"

"I was afraid you might have gone liberal on me."

Fat chance, Macimer thought.

Jan peered at him over the edge of her coffee mug. It was an ancient mug, now chipped and stained, he had got in a gas station years ago as a giveaway premium. Talk about songs of yesterday . . .

"What were you two up to?" Jan asked quietly. "You had a special reason for wanting Gordon over—and the house to yourselves."

"It was our last chance to see both of them. With Mary going back so soon—"

"Stop stalling, Paul. If something is going on that affects us, I want to know what it is."

Sooner or later she had to be told about the bugs. Even if Macimer hadn't wanted to tell her, Aileen Hebert was certain to say something to Jan. And Jan had been an FBI wife long enough to know what that overheard conversation might mean.

Jan rose abruptly, interpreting his silence as a refusal to talk. Without another word she carried her battered mug up to the kitchen, left it on the counter and went up the stairs. Macimer winced as the bedroom door slammed.

He sat unmoving in the troubled silence. From somewhere nearby a dog barked in protest at being left outside in the rain. Another bark answered him. He remembered something Jan had once said about people who left their dogs out in the rain. If they wanted something to decorate the yard, why not plant a tree?

It was the coincidence of Carey McWilliams and Timothy Callahan both being killed by bombs, and their link to the PRC affair three years ago, that bothered him.

And the way the threads kept leading back to John L. Landers . . .

Macimer shook off the troubling speculations. Don't borrow trouble, he reminded himself.

He routinely checked the door locks, left a light on for Chip and started up the stairs. The phone rang.

Wondering who could be calling at this hour on a Sunday—it was improbable that Collins or Garvey would be phoning him tonight—Macimer went back down the stairs and detoured to his den. At least he knew his private phone was now clean.

"Macimer?" The voice was clipped, arrogant, unfamiliar.

"Yes, who is this?"

"You son of a bitch," the answer came like a warning rattle. "If you think you can get away with what your goons did last night, you don't know Oliver Packard!"

Macimer came alert like an animal sensing danger, his weariness dropping away. Not only was Oliver Packard a name to be reckoned with in Washington; he was also Joseph Gerella's boss. "I don't know what you're talking about, Mr. Packard. Maybe you should calm down—"

"You put one of my people in the hospital! I'm going to crucify you for that!"

"You'll have to be a little clearer, Mr. Packard. Who are you talking about?"

"You know damned well," Packard snapped. "Joe Gerella was attacked last night outside his apartment. He's in intensive care in Georgetown. He has a broken jaw, fractured ribs and God knows what manner of internal injuries. It was an expert working over, Macimer. Very professional."

"I'm not sure what that's supposed to suggest," Macimer replied evenly. "I'm sorry about Gerella, but what makes you so certain he wasn't simply mugged? It happens every day."

"Not this time. I'll tell you what makes me so certain, Macimer. Joe won't be doing any talking for a long time—someone made sure of that. But before he passed out in the ambulance after he was picked up he managed to write something down. The paramedics had to pry the sheet of notepaper from his fist. It had only one word on it." The columnist paused significantly. "Your name, Macimer. Just your name."

Macimer held the phone away from his ear as if the instrument itself were to blame for the shock generated by Packard's disclosure. What had Gerella been trying to say? Had he simply had Macimer's name on a piece of paper in his pocket? If not, why, in the last seconds before slipping into unconsciousness, write down Macimer's name?

"You still there, Macimer?"

"I'm listening, Mr. Packard. But I have no idea why Gerella would have been holding such a note. I did talk to him recently— he thought I might have a story for him. I told him he was wrong."

"I don't believe you," Packard said tersely. "And if I can prove you had anything to do with what happened to Gerella, believe me, I'll make you and the FBI think Nikita Khrushchev was Santa Claus. I'll bury you, Macimer!"

"You have the shovel for it!" Macimer lashed back angrily, suddenly fed up with Oliver Packard's arrogant assumptions. "You seem to make a career out of shoveling dirt. I can't stop you printing whatever you want, but this time you'd better be damned sure you can back up your dirt with facts!"

There was a moment of silence. When Packard spoke again his tone was unexpectedly mild. "I think that's the first time you've sounded like a man who's innocent."

"I don't really care what you think. It's late, Packard. I'm sorry about Gerella, but if that's all you wanted to talk about—"

"Take it easy, Macimer. Maybe you *are* innocent, but that still doesn't explain why Gerella was holding that note with your name on it. Gerella may be able to tell us by tomorrow. Do you want to make any guesses about what he'll say?"

"No, I don't make guesses about what might or might not be in someone else's mind."

Packard let that go. He said, "I think we should get together for a talk."

"I don't see why—"

"I think you will, Macimer. You see, there's another reason I don't believe this was a routine mugging. I happen to know from our records—I insist on my people keeping detailed records of things like mail received—that Gerella had received a couple of communications by mail from an anonymous informant, material that had something to do with the FBI. Whatever that information involved, Gerella either had it on his person or in his apartment, not in his desk at the office. And after he was attacked, Macimer, his keys were taken and his apartment was ransacked. Those communications are gone, Macimer. They were stolen!"

When Packard hung up, Macimer heard a small sound and turned quickly. Jan stood in the doorway of the den, staring at him. "You raised your voice," she said. "What was that all about?"

Macimer was tired of keeping things from her, even if his job sometimes made that silence mandatory. He gave her a brief account of the telephone conversation, leaving out only the final revelation about Gerella's apartment being searched.

Jan leaned against the doorframe, studying him closely. "Why would that man—Gerella—write down your name at such a time? He must have been desperate."

"I don't know."

"Oliver Packard seems to think you do. He's a powerful man, Paul."

"I'm well aware of that."

Her silent scrutiny evaluated his answers. She knew when he was holding something back, he thought. But when Bureau business was involved, even when she disagreed with him or with the FBI's activities, as she had made clear during the 1970s when a history of black-bag jobs and dirty tricks had been revealed, she had never tried to interfere. "Is there anything else you want to tell me?" she asked finally.

"You were right about my having a particular reason for having Gordon over today."

"I knew that."

He told her about Aileen Hebert's strange experience and his discovery of listening devices in the hall and their bedroom tele-

phone. Gordon Ruhle, he said, had also found a device called an
Infinity Transmitter in the phone in Paul's den.

"What's an Infinity Transmitter?"

"It's a device that can be activated from outside the house just
by dialing our number."

"And there was one of those things *in our bedroom?*"

"Not the same kind, but . . . there was one in our phone and
one hidden inside the wall."

"Someone listening in could hear . . . anything?"

Paul Macimer nodded.

"That's obscene!"

"Whoever it is isn't interested in our sex life, if that's what
you're thinking."

"Then what? Who put those things there?"

"I can make a good guess."

"Those three robbers!" For the first time she linked the intruders to the presence of the bugs.

"They had the time and opportunity. Kevin and Linda had no
way of knowing what they were up to."

"Why? For God's sake, why?"

"I can't say for sure until I know who wanted them there. Our
Latino friends didn't do it on their own."

"You know more than you're telling me. Paul, what's going on?
Why are you worried about being followed? Why am I being spied
on? Why was that reporter beaten up?"

"I can't tell you. Jan, it isn't that I don't want to tell you, or
even that I can't because it's FBI business. I just don't have all the
answers." He paused, weighing what he would say carefully.
When he made the decision in his own mind he felt an immediate
relief. "I want you to leave here for a while, Jan. You and the
kids. Take that trip to Arizona we planned—your parents will be
happy to have you."

"You want us . . . out of harm's way?"

The old Navy term summed it up as well as any. Paul Macimer
reached out and pulled Jan to him, feeling the tension in her body
before she relaxed against him. "Not that there's any real risk," he
murmured, "but I'll just feel . . . easier."

17

After his Saturday-night attack Joseph Gerella had been rushed to D.C. General Hospital by ambulance. On Sunday he was transferred to the Georgetown University Hospital's Shock Trauma Unit, where he was still under heavy sedation. Hanging up the phone after calling the hospital Monday morning, Macimer wondered if patients were ever sedated in any other way.

The police in the District had treated both the attack and the burglary of Gerella's apartment as routine incidents until they heard from Oliver Packard. Now they were waiting to talk to Gerella himself when he was able. Macimer assigned two agents to check out the police reports and to go through the apartment. Other agents were to fan out over the neighborhood to see if anyone had witnessed either the mugging or the break-in. Macimer expected little of these efforts, but they had to be tried.

He was more hopeful about the search for Xavier, even though the lists of potential Xaviers from the FBI's internal security files had proved disappointing. Agents William Rodriguez and Jo Singleton were now concentrating on the search for a Cuban youth of the proper age, background and blood phenotype to match Xavier's profile. They had flown to Atlanta to examine National Health Service records of the Cuban boat people who had fled the island for America in 1980, as well as the FBI's own files. "We're pulling a name list and a blood type list," Rodriguez reported to Macimer by phone from the Atlanta Field Office. "Then we'll see what matches up. If it's a long list, which we don't expect, we could use some help—those kids are scattered all over the country by now."

"Just bring your lists back here. We'll get you more help if you need it."

That extra help might mean making the Brea investigation more visible, Macimer thought. And that brought him back to the question that was beginning to disturb him more than he cared to admit. Why had the Director wanted the Brea case kept as quiet as possible? Why keep a lid on it? Because it might mean bad publicity for the Bureau? Or was it because John L. Landers would go before Senator Sederholm's committee for confirmation as FBI Director exactly one week from today?

From the noonday heat of K Street, Macimer passed through the glass doors of the Prime Rib into the cool, dim elegance of the narrow reception room. The reservations man reacted with alacrity when Macimer mentioned Oliver Packard's name.

Packard was in a black leather booth in a corner of one of the intimate dining rooms. The booth was both secluded and strategic, commanding a view over the room. Behind the syndicated columnist, framed by one of the brass-rimmed black wall panels, was a Louis Icart print. Packard seemed perfectly at ease in the elegant Art Deco setting. He wore a beautifully tailored light blue jacket that appeared to have the approximate weight of a handkerchief. His pink shirt had a ruffled front, and he wore a blue bow tie with white polka dots. The bow ties, which he wore for almost any occasion, were a trademark. His hair flowed luxuriantly over the collar of his jacket. Macimer placed his age at well over fifty, and there seemed no reason for Packard's hair to be that blond.

"So you're Macimer." Oliver Packard clucked in mysterious disapproval. "Pity. You're all letting your hair grow. And colored shirts! It's getting so you can't tell *who* is a G-man anymore." The columnist smiled coldly, showing a thin edge of nicotine-stained teeth. His coal-black eyes, Macimer thought, would have done credit to a Borgia. He said, "You'll have lunch, of course."

"Some other time," Macimer replied. "Suppose we get down to what you called me about. Do you know what was in those papers Gerella supposedly received from an informant?"

"Precious little," Packard admitted. "But there's nothing supposed about them—he *did* receive some FBI documents. They were samples, according to the informant." He paused, staring at Macimer with his medieval eyes. "They must be important for your goons to bloody their butchers' hands on my best reporter. Or are you prepared to deny that?"

"I don't think even you believe it."

"No? Do you know where Joe Gerella was Saturday night?"

"How would I know that?"

"You must have known he was following you."

Macimer stared back at the columnist in obvious surprise. "No, I didn't know. I talked to Gerella last week, Mr. Packard. I told him then I had no story for him. And I don't know anything about the attack on him. I didn't know about this informant until you told me. Gerella never spoke of having received FBI documents." He paused. "When exactly was he attacked?"

"Around one o'clock in the morning."

"That's a good time for a mugging. And if Gerella was following me, that explains why he had a slip of paper with my name on it."

Oliver Packard shook his head. He took his time fitting a filter cigarette into a mother-of-pearl holder and lighting it. "I think it means more than that, Macimer. I don't put much stock in coincidence—not in this town. In any event, we'll find out. Gerella's going to survive, Macimer. I'm going to see to it that he does." The pronouncement was Godlike. "He can't talk—his jaw is all wired. He can't move because of his ribs. He can't walk because he has a broken ankle. But as soon as his head is clear enough he'll be able to do one thing: he can still *write!*" Packard leaned forward, his bow tie bunching under the fleshy folds of his neck, the cigarette in its holder jutting upward in a way that called to mind pictures of Franklin Roosevelt. "I give my people their heads if they're good—and make no mistake, Macimer, Gerella is good. He was working on his own time, and he wouldn't have been doing it without good reason. He wouldn't have spent a dull Saturday night checking out a dull gathering of old cronies in the Bureau without a *very* good reason. Do you want me to learn what it was from him or do you want to tell me?"

"Let him tell you himself," Macimer answered shortly. "I can't. But I want to be there as soon as he can communicate. I want to know what FBI documents came into his possession and why he didn't inform the Bureau."

Packard leaned back in the booth and gazed past Macimer. The Prime Rib at lunchtime was always busy. Macimer noted, however, that the booths on either side of Packard's corner location were empty. In the District, Oliver Packard could have just about any accommodation he wanted, including privacy.

The columnist tapped another cigarette out of a brightly colored box. The cigarette was wrapped in pink paper. It was long, handmade and expensive. Macimer wondered if Packard had them in colors to match his shirts. The speculation was deprecatory and he told himself to back off. Packard was a poseur but he was also wickedly smart. And dangerous.

Packard lit the second cigarette from the glowing ash of the half-smoked one. He blew a cloud of smoke in Macimer's direction and said, "Gerella calls you Mr. Clean—it was in some of the notes in his desk at the office. Unfortunately he didn't say much else."

"I'm no cleaner than average, but this time Gerella jumped to the wrong conclusion—just as you did—if he thought that I or the FBI had anything to do with what happened to him."

"Perhaps." Packard's tone was deceptively mild, almost indifferent. The abrupt change made Macimer wary. "But he could be wrong and right at the same time, I suppose. Perhaps you didn't have a hand in his being mugged by those Latinos. But he could be right about the story he's after."

"Latinos?"

"That's right, didn't I mention that? Gerella is still groggy this morning, but he managed to scrawl that much during one of his periods of coherence. He thinks the three goons might have been Cubans. Of course, Cubans are more the CIA's touch, aren't they? Don't tell them too much, convince them it's for a patriotic cause, and send them out to do the dirty work." Packard fixed Macimer with his malevolent stare. "They called Gerella something. It's the only thing he remembers them saying. *Traidor!* Traitor. Care to make any guesses why, Macimer?"

Macimer shook his head slowly. Cubans, he thought. Three of them. He wondered if, in the darkness and confusion of his attack, Gerella would have known if one of the attackers was a girl.

As for accusing Gerella of treason, betrayal, Oliver Packard's sarcastic reference to the CIA suddenly made sense. If the muggers had been led to believe that Gerella was working on a story that might damage the FBI . . .

"If you're telling the truth," Packard said, "maybe you are clean, Macimer. And maybe it's time to tell the rest of the truth. Come clean all the way. I think Gerella is onto something, Macimer—he has to be or there wouldn't have been an urgent need to shut him up and steal those documents. I won't let this story go now. The truth *will* come out."

"I can only tell you what I told Gerella. I don't have a story for you."

"You don't have to worry about the repercussions, I can assure you. A man of your background, you don't have to stay with the Bureau. And you can be taken care of."

"Are you offering me a bribe, Packard?"

The columnist showed a thin ridge of small yellow teeth. "It would be exceedingly foolish of me to offer a bribe to a G-man, wouldn't it? Especially these days, with all your sting operations, your hidden cameras and the like."

The repetition of the archaic term for an FBI agent was mocking, intended to keep Macimer off balance. He ignored it. "I have nothing more to talk to you about, Mr. Packard. There's no story." He slid out of the booth, pausing at the end of the table to stare down at the columnist. Packard delicately put out his cigarette in a crystal ashtray. Half smoked, the butt lay there like a pink worm next to three other dead worms. "But I'm going to find out who attacked Gerella and why. I can promise you that."

"So am I, Macimer. So am I."

Oliver Packard raised a soft, long-fingered hand in an elegantly casual gesture as the FBI man turned away. Instantly an attentive waiter hurried forward. "I think I'll have another, Francis," Packard murmured as Macimer walked away. "Very, *very* dry this time."

Only when he was on the sidewalk outside the restaurant did Macimer allow his anger to surface, the anger he had not permitted Oliver Packard to see.

18

A man named Antonelli had telephoned twice while Macimer was out. He had left a number where he could be reached. Macimer checked first with Willa Cunningham. "He has something to do with the Senate Committee on Intelligence," she said.

"What does that mean?"

"I think he's an investigator."

Macimer returned the call. The phone was answered on the second ring. "I have to talk to you, Inspector," Antonelli said.

"I'm not an inspector, Mr. Antonelli, but go ahead."

"Not on the phone."

"Just who are you, Mr. Antonelli?" The voice seemed muffled, as if the man had a cold. The accent was vaguely New Yorker.

After a moment's hesitation the guarded answer came. "I'm a PI from New York. For the last two months I've been doing some work for Senator Sederholm's committee. I guess you know what about, Mr. Macimer."

"No, I don't. Suppose you tell me."

Antonelli chuckled uneasily. "The senator don't know about this—why I'm calling, I mean. Nobody does."

"What do you want, Antonelli?"

"I think we should talk, Mr. Macimer."

Macimer felt his pulse quicken. First Gerella, now a private eye, both hinting at dark secrets. Gerella was covering the Senate hearings, Antonelli worked for the committee. He said, "All right, when can we meet?"

"Yeah, well . . ." Antonelli seemed to weigh the problem, although he must have chosen a place in advance. "Tonight. Nine o'clock."

After dark, Macimer thought. "Where?"

"I'll get in touch. You like seafood, Mr. Macimer?"

"Well enough."

"Be at Hogate's at seven. I'll call you. In the bar."

"I thought you didn't trust telephones, Mr. Antonelli."

The private eye chuckled. "I'll trust that one."

As soon as he had hung up Macimer asked Willa Cunningham to dig up an index on private investigators. She had it on his desk in five minutes. John Antonelli was listed in the Manhattan directory as a private investigator and security consultant. He had an office on Third Avenue.

Macimer decided to place a long-distance call. After the fourth ring it was answered by a woman with a bored manner. Mr. Antonelli was not available.

"Is this his answering service?"

"That's right."

"When can I reach him?"

"I'm sorry, we are unable to divulge that information," the woman said in a singsong voice, as if she had said it a thousand times before. "If you'd care to leave your name and phone number, your call will be returned as soon as possible."

"That won't be necessary."

Not if Antonelli was in Washington.

As Macimer thought about their meeting, he wondered why someone who was planning to talk to him face to face would bother to disguise his voice over the phone.

When Macimer had first come to Washington back in the early 1960s, Hogate's was a small, unpretentious waterfront fish restaurant. He had found its warmth and friendliness appealing, not to mention the heaping quantities of fresh seafood offered at prices suitable to a new agent's income.

The modern Hogate's is a warehouse of restaurants, embracing the brown waters of Washington Channel with wide glass wings. There were several tour buses stacked out front when Macimer arrived. He found a parking place on the street a short distance away and walked back to the restaurant in a fine soft drizzle.

There he mingled with tourists debarking from the buses and the downtown evening crowd of diners.

The bar was a low-ceilinged cavern off to the right side of the main entrance and the oversized lobby. In spite of its size, the lounge was crowded and noisy. There was a small bandstand, empty at this hour, but recorded music pounded from multiple speakers. The decor was predictably nautical, with heavy beams, grayed woods, ship's artifacts scattered about and the inevitable red vinyl upholstery.

Macimer found a stool where he could look out through the wide windows at the channel. Under a gray sky the water was still and flat as pavement. Raindrops pattered over its hard brown surface. There was no activity in the channel or across the way on the greenbelt that was East Potomac Park. Surrounded by noisy confusion, Macimer gazed out upon a drizzly scene as peaceful and soothing as the memory of childhood summers at a rented cottage on a lake in Michigan. Something of the stillness of the water, unruffled by the soft drizzle, seemed to enter the spirit.

"So this is where the FBI disappears when the sun goes down," said a voice behind him.

Macimer turned. "Erika! For heaven's sake . . . where's Russ? Isn't he with you?"

"Don't get up." She placed a restraining hand on his shoulder and slipped onto a stool beside his. "I like sitting close to the bottles, don't you? Oh, don't look for Russ, he isn't here. He's married to the Bureau, didn't you know? But of course you do. You're one of the bridesmaids, right?"

Macimer grinned. She was well on the way, he judged, remembering Jan's comments about Erika's heavy drinking. "I guess you could say that."

"I just did."

"Is Russ meeting you here later?"

"Maybe he is and maybe he isn't. The question is, do I have a need to know?" Erika peered at him with exaggerated suspicion. "Are you on duty?"

"As a matter of fact, I'm waiting for a phone call."

She leaned toward him and whispered in a conspiratorial tone. "Is Hogate's under investigation? I've always thought there was something fishy about this place."

He laughed, and Erika Halbig smiled crookedly in acknowledgment. Macimer was aware of her scent without identifying it. She wore a dress of a soft, clinging fabric in a turquoise color that glowed in the artificial light like a jewel. The skirt was slit along one side almost to the hip, exposing a smooth expanse of brown thigh. Macimer wondered how many bars Erika frequented alone on the evenings Halbig worked late. There was uncomfortable truth in her slightly bitter comment about Halbig's relationship with the Bureau. As an Executive Assistant Director there might be many such evenings when he would not leave Headquarters until very late. Young, childless, bored and beautiful, Erika Halbig was one of a vast legion of those American women who begin drinking to fill a void.

They talked idly for several minutes, Macimer listening with one ear for the message from the bartender that he had a phone call. Seven o'clock passed. Searching for something to say, he felt the nudge of her bare knee against his. The pressure might have been accidental. He told her how much he had liked Hogate's years ago when so many things were smaller and more personal.

"If you don't like it so much anymore," Erika commented as her empty glass was replaced with another Beefeater on the rocks, "why do you still come here? For your phone calls?"

"I don't dislike it. Besides," he added with a smile, "the mixed seafood platter is still one of the best bargains in town." He shifted slightly on his stool to break the persistent pressure of her thigh. "What about you?"

Erika shrugged indifferently. She rattled the ice cubes in her glass and sipped the smooth dry gin.

"Do you come here often?"

She nodded. Her profile was virtually flawless, Macimer decided. So was the smoothly modeled elegance of neck and shoulder.

"You must like something about it." The noisy crowds, perhaps. They offered company and anonymity at the same time.

"I don't like it much." Then Erika added, by way of explanation, "It's not such a good idea to drink often in places you like."

There was an awkward pause. She smiled crookedly at Macimer's discomfiture. "Don't tell me you didn't know the lady was a lush? I'll bet Jan noticed."

Macimer did not reply to that. Jan had noticed, and Erika knew it. "Aren't you being a little hard on yourself?"

"Who should know better? What's the matter, Paul, do I embarrass you?"

"No. But you do concern me."

"That's sweet." She placed a hand impulsively over his. The touch lingered, as if she were reluctant to break the contact. "That's very nice."

"Erika . . . my business may not take very long. Why don't you get something to eat here? I'll meet you as soon as I can and see you home."

Her hand withdrew. "I'm not smashed, Paul. I'm not helpless. And you don't have to worry about my picking up a stranger at the bar." Her wryly bitter smile reappeared. "You're not a stranger, Paul. And you're not just anybody."

The words seemed to have reverberations which echoed beyond their surface meaning. Before the exchange could move onto even more disturbing ground, the bartender signaled. "Mr. Macimer? Your call. Do you want to take it here?"

"I'll take it down at the end."

"Have fun!" Erika Halbig called after him.

The babble of music and conversation around him made it difficult for Macimer to hear the muffled voice on the phone. "You alone, Macimer?"

"As alone as you can be in a place like this." He glanced toward the other end of the bar. Erika Halbig was raising her glass to her lips, tilting her head back as if to display the long graceful line of her neck.

"Good. Listen, we'd better meet a little later, like I said. You know the Roosevelt Memorial? Out on the island?"

"Yes, of course."

"Meet you there around nine. It'll be getting dark then."

"Why there?"

"One good reason. There won't be anyone else there. They close it up as soon as the sun goes down. There's a gate at the land-side end of the pedestrian bridge. It'll be locked but it won't keep you out."

"Isn't there a security patrol?"

Antonelli chuckled. "What's there to steal?"

"Wait a minute, Antonelli. Give me a reason why I should meet you after dark on a deserted island. Why shouldn't I just call Senator Sederholm and ask him what kind of work you're doing for him?"

"Because you know he wouldn't tell you. You want a good reason, Macimer? I'll give you one. I know about the Brea file."

Before Macimer could answer he heard the click of the receiver. Antonelli had hung up.

In another corner of the lounge a three-piece group of musicians began tuning up their instruments, one man plucking at an electronic guitar, another fingering a bass fiddle. A burst of laughter enveloped some new arrivals. Macimer stood motionless, still holding the phone, as the questions boiled up. Was Antonelli a free lance in this affair? Had he stumbled onto the same information Gerella had? Did he know who Gerella's informant was? Was the thief sending samples from the file to Sederholm's committee as well as to Gerella? And what was in those samples?

Macimer wished that he had talked to Gerella, but the latest word from the Georgetown hospital had the reporter still under sedation, though resting comfortably. He could probably answer questions for a brief period in the morning.

Without more information from Gerella, Antonelli was even more of a mystery. Why did he want a secret meeting? Was he selling information—or his silence?

Macimer moved slowly back along the length of the bar, pushing his way through the good-natured crowd, sorting out his questions but finding few answers. Erika was sitting where he had left her. There was a question in her eyes and he answered it immediately. "It looks like I have some time, after all. And we could both use some supper. How about it?"

"Lead on, chief. Us troops will follow you anywhere." She was joking, smiling crookedly, but he thought afterward that she had seemed relieved.

For the dozenth time Raymond Shoup nervously examined the contents of his unlovely rented room. It was spartanly furnished—an unmade twin bed without a frame, resting on the floor in one corner; a beige vinyl chair with a cigarette burn on the seat; an old black-and-white television set on a roll-about stand; a couple of scarred tables holding battered lamps, overflowing ashtrays, a pile of old *Playbody* and *Hustler* magazines. One wall contained a combination stove-refrigerator-sink unit. The sink was full of unwashed dishes.

Unlovely. Undisturbed. Nothing missing.

But someone had been here.

Raymond wasn't even sure how he knew. Maybe it was the magazines. They were where he had left them on the table next to the beige chair, but . . . not exactly as he had left them. He was not an orderly person—"I don't know where you get it," his mother used to complain. "Your father was so orderly, so neat about everything. You should have seen the polish on his boots. And the crease on his trousers—you could cut your fingers . . ." Raymond had never seen the knife-edge pants or the gleaming boots except in the photograph on the dresser, the uniform crisp and clean, the cap precisely cocked over one eye. And the ears sticking out, the Marine haircut leaving the temples scalped. Jack Shoup had been killed in Vietnam; he had never seen the son who was born three months after he shipped out.

The magazines had been carelessly stacked, he saw as he stared at them. But *stacked*. He threw one down when he was done with it, speared another randomly from the pile when he was in the mood. He didn't stack them.

The bed was unmade but he was certain the mattress had been moved. It was never exactly in place over the worn box-spring unit. It was now.

The room had been searched. He *knew* it.

His thoughts jerked back, like a twitch of panic, to what Alice Volker, who ran the boardinghouse for its wealthy absentee owners, had said. "There was someone asking about you. Are you in any trouble, Raymond?"

"Who was it? Did he say who he was?"

"He said it was insurance, but . . ." Alice Volker had a nose for cops. The burly man asking about Raymond Shoup had been polite, soft-spoken, but he hadn't been sure of the name. An insurance investigator verifying the address of a witness to an accident would have known his name, wouldn't he?

"What did he want? What did you tell him?"

But Alice Volker had told the investigator little. That Raymond Shoup lived in 211. That he was respectable—she ran a respectable boardinghouse. That Raymond lived alone and was presently unemployed. That she didn't know when he would be back that afternoon.

"You didn't let him in?" There was anxiety in Raymond's question.

"Of course not!" she snapped. "Are you in trouble with the police, Raymond? I don't want any trouble here."

He had reassured her, but he was far from being reassured himself. Who had been asking about him? The police? The FBI— because of the stolen car and its missing file? But how could they possibly know his identity? How could they have found him? Was it the reporter, Gerella?

"Raymond?" Alice Volker was at the door, looking peevish as she generally did when she had to walk up the stairs. "You have a phone call."

"A phone call? Me?" A weight of dread lay cold and heavy in his stomach.

The telephone was in the hallway at the bottom of the stairs. Alice Volker lingered in the doorway of the manager's apartment, but Raymond waited her out, staring at her until she sniffed and turned back into the apartment, closing the door. Then Raymond picked up the phone. "Hello, Gerella?"

"Yeah!"

Raymond Shoup leaned against the wall. His hands shook and his knees went soft in the wash of relief. Not the police! Not the FBI!

He missed something the reporter said. Then he stammered out a question: "How did you find me?"

"Do you think there's much that Oliver Packard can't find out in this city?"

Raymond laughed weakly. In his relief he did not pursue the question of how Oliver Packard or his reporter could have tracked him down when he had given no name, no address, no phone number in his communications with Gerella.

"We want the file, Raymond. The whole thing. What's your price?"

Raymond had thought about it, and the figure he had settled on surfaced without hesitation, in his mind a bold grab for as much as he thought he could get. After all, there was nothing in the file that seemed important. "Five thousand dollars!" he blurted.

After a slight hesitation his caller responded. "You've got it,

Raymond. But we want the file tonight. Have you got it with you?"

Shoup grimaced. He knew instantly that he had set his sights too low, that he could have got more. "I can put my hands on it," he said. Not where you could find it, he thought, not in my room. And suddenly he was angry, realizing that the reporter had tried to steal the file, to get away without paying off. In that moment Raymond made the decision to hold out for more. Five thousand wasn't enough, it was peanuts to Oliver Packard. There had to be something important in the FBI file that Raymond hadn't recognized.

"Raymond, we'll have to meet somewhere we won't be seen together."

"Why?" Raymond demanded, immediately suspicious.

"Hey, Raymond, use your head. Don't you know there are laws against stealing FBI classified documents?"

"What about publishing them?"

"Let us worry about that. But we don't reveal our sources, so you're in the clear as long as we're not seen together. If we were, the file might be traced back to you once the fat hits the fire, and you could be charged. Neither of us wants that."

Raymond Shoup's habitual suspicion faded. He didn't want to be on the FBI's list. That part of it had frightened him from the moment he opened the box in the trunk of the stolen car and saw that it contained FBI documents. "Okay," he agreed. "Where do we meet?"

"You know how to get to Roosevelt Island?"

"Hey, man, no way, I don't have any wheels!"

"So much the better. Cars can be traced. For God's sake, don't steal one. Look, you can pick up the Metro blue line. Take it across the river and get off at Rosslyn. You can walk from there to the island in ten minutes. Go over the footbridge to the island. I'll meet you there by the monument."

"Why can't you pick me up in Rosslyn? No one would see us."

"Don't ever underestimate the FBI, kid. They're combing this town for that stolen file. Don't forget . . . I found you."

Raymond Shoup shivered in spite of the close muggy heat in the dim hallway. He glanced toward Alice Volker's doorway. The door, which had been firmly closed, was open a crack. The bitch! She was listening!

"Okay, okay," he said. "What time?"

"Eight o'clock sharp. If you've got to pick up that file somewhere, Raymond, you'd better get started."

"Don't try to follow me!"

"Now why would I do that, Raymond? How many times do I have to tell you we can't be seen together? It isn't us you have to worry about. Do you think we want you blowing the whistle on us, telling everyone we bought stolen FBI documents? The way this is going to come out, Raymond, it's going to look like someone leaked them to us. Nobody will ever know who or how. That's the way it's got to be."

"Okay, man, okay," Raymond said, his last objections dissipating. "You bring the money." *It'll buy you something,* he thought, the roller coaster of his emotions rising to angry resentment once more, *but not what you think, not the whole file. That's gonna cost you!*

"Eight o'clock. Don't be late, Raymond. This is one boat you don't want to miss!"

"What shall we talk about, then?" Erika Halbig asked, the tone of voice sardonic rather than amused. "Is it going to rain again tomorrow, do you think?"

"Probably."

"Ah, the careful Bureau-cratic response, right? Don't commit yourself, never reveal too much."

Paul Macimer wondered if having Erika join him for dinner was not a mistake, after all. She had left most of her huge seafood platter untouched after picking at her salad. And she continued to drink, switching from gin to the white wine she had asked for to go with the fish.

"Don't mind me, Paul. Sometimes I get this way. Doesn't Jan ever complain? About the late nights and the sudden trips? And the silences? Especially those silences! Or is she a good sport about it all, like poor Mary Ruhle?"

"Poor Mary?"

"Poor Mary, poor Jan, poor Erika . . . we're all in the same boat, aren't we?" Erika leaned forward suddenly, spilling a little white wine onto the tablecloth. "Or do you actually talk to Jan sometimes? I wonder . . ."

"Russ has a very important job, Erika. There probably isn't a hell of a lot he *can* talk about."

"Will you tell Jan about tonight, Paul? About having dinner with me?"

Macimer smiled. "I don't see why not."

"I do," Erika said softly, her eyes suddenly sober. "And I think you do, too, Paul . . ."

Theodore Roosevelt Island is in the middle of the Potomac. The river runs north to south at that point. Across the eastern fork of the river are the Foggy Bottom district and the Watergate complex. Along the west bank is a greenbelt interlaced with the parkway system. It is from this bank that a wooden pedestrian bridge spans the river to reach the island.

Raymond Shoup paused at the foot of the bridge and glanced back over his shoulder, his shoulders hunched against the light rain. From nearby came the steady hiss of traffic along the wet pavement of the parkway, but it seemed oddly remote. Otherwise the night was silent, and Raymond felt a stirring of uneasiness.

His right hand touched the papers tucked under his belt, protected from the rain by the lightweight jacket he wore. Five thousand dollars, he reminded himself. And more where that came from. He had stopped at the Greyhound Bus Terminal on New York Avenue at 11th Street before catching the Metro's blue line to Rosslyn. He had taken only about a third of the documents in the file he kept in a baggage locker there. Then, on impulse, he had mailed the locker key to himself. Not that he didn't trust Gerella, he told himself with a grin, but you never knew . . .

A double metal gate barred access to the bridge. The gate was padlocked, but it was low at the center and easily vaulted. Raymond Shoup landed lightly on the wooden planks beyond the gate. He started across the bridge.

In the open it was still reasonably light, but the island ahead of him was dark. Trees grew down to the water's edge, their branches leaning out over the muddy river. At the end of the bridge was a small clearing. It was empty.

After a moment's hesitation Raymond stepped off the bridge and was instantly adrift in the featureless gloom of the woods. He was conscious of the silence around him, accentuated by the soft dripping of rainwater from leaf and branch.

The path twisted and began to climb. Raymond Shoup walked gingerly over the uneven footing, a treacherous stew of mud and scattered gravel. His nervousness increased as he plunged deeper into the interior of the island.

Suddenly the silence was shattered by a jumbo jet crashing through the black night almost directly overhead, on its swift climb from the runway at Washington National.

Raymond giggled nervously.

After a few minutes the wall of darkness ahead of him thinned out and began to break up. He saw patches of gray sky, the sharp black silhouette of a branch stabbing the gray. In a moment Raymond Shoup stood at the edge of the clearing. A broad platform, paved and pebbled, glistened in the rain. It extended across the open space in front of him. On each side of this raised platform shone the dark crescents of reflecting pools. From a dais at the far end of the platform Theodore Roosevelt shook his fist in a characteristically aggressive pose. Orderly rows of trees flanked the twin ornamental pools, bringing a note of formality at odds with the natural wilderness covering the rest of the island.

Another jet roared into the sky from Washington National two miles away and climbed over Roosevelt Island, crushing the deep silence. As soon as it was gone the silence closed in again, all light and sound muted and softened by the fine mist of rain.

"Gerella?" In spite of himself Raymond's voice quavered.

The man had been standing on the dark side of the monument, at Roosevelt's feet. Raymond Shoup did not see him until he stepped forward. He resembled the statue towering above him, a figure burly and powerful, except that he stood at quiet ease, hands shoved into the side pockets of a black gabardine raincoat. "Right on time, Raymond," he said. "Did you bring the file?"

Raymond Shoup stepped nervously into the open, staring at the man who advanced across the paved platform to meet him. Raymond had never seen Gerella in person—to him the reporter was only a name culled from a newspaper story about the Senate Committee on Intelligence, the name of a reporter who worked for Oliver Packard—but he was surprised by the impression that the man before him was older than he had expected.

"Let's see what you have."

"Let me see some money first!" Raymond replied, summoning up a moment of bravado.

"You're a careful man, Raymond. So am I—I want to be sure I'm getting what I pay for." He paused, then asked sharply, "You didn't by any chance make a copy of the file, did you, Raymond?"

He was quite close to Raymond then, peering at him intently. Apparently satisfied as Raymond shook his head, he reached under his coat to pull out a bulky white envelope. It was thick enough so that it had been sealed with tape to make it secure. Shoup seized it eagerly as he handed over the manila envelope he had brought with him. "You can count that while I'm making sure you delivered the real goods, Raymond." He had the manila envelope open before Raymond could tear open his own prize.

In the darkness Raymond could see only that his envelope contained a thick sheaf of bills. He hunched over to protect the money from the rain as his cold fingers plucked at it, his heart racing with excitement. Suddenly he felt an iron grip on his biceps, fingers tightening so viciously that Raymond winced in pain. "What is this, Raymond? This isn't the whole file—what have you brought me?"

Raymond shoved the money envelope into his jacket pocket, as if he feared that it might be snatched back. "The whole file is worth more than five thousand," he said, trying to sound confident and unafraid when in truth he was neither. "You know it is! That's a good sampling. The rest will cost you more!"

The burly man stared at him, visibly struggling for control. "Where's the rest of it, Raymond? Have you got it locked away somewhere? That's it, isn't it? You were just smart enough not to keep it in your room—"

"You tried to steal it!" Raymond Shoup cried hotly, anger breaking through his fear. "Now it's gonna cost you more! And if you don't want it, Gerella, I'm sure there are others who will!"

"You're a very foolish boy, Raymond, but if you picked up these papers on your way, you must have had them in a locker someplace. Do you have the key, Raymond?"

"No, I don't," Raymond said, delighted with his cleverness.

"You're lying, Raymond."

"No—I thought you might try to take it. Why not? You tried to steal the file. But why should I give you the whole thing for peanuts?" Raymond started to back away, made uneasy by the older man's relentless gaze. He wanted suddenly to be off this island, away from this big, quiet, determined man who looked as if he would roll right over you like a steamroller if you got in his way. "You know where to find me—"

Raymond Shoup was so startled at the man's sudden move that he slipped on the wet paving as he turned to run. He was caught by the arm. The rest happened with unbelievable swiftness. Raymond's arm was twisted up and around, then brought downward in a quick, chopping movement. The wrist snapped like a flimsy matchstick, and Shoup screamed.

At that instant another of the big aircraft from Washington National boomed overhead. Its roar punctuated Raymond's scream, coming at the moment of his convulsive spasm of pain and terror. For an instant the grip was loosened, and Raymond broke free.

The man lunged after him. Ducking away, Raymond Shoup plunged off the platform toward the nearest path. He ran wildly, out of control. He crashed headlong into a tree. With a sob he bounced off the tree and lurched on blindly. Tree branches tore at him. One struck his arm, wrenching another shriek from his lips. He saw the fork of the path directly ahead of him. There, barely discernible, the big man blocked his way.

Raymond Shoup stopped, hugging his broken wrist against his body, sucking in great gulps of air as his panic made it hard to breathe. "You . . . you're not Gerella!" he cried.

"That's right, kid."

"Oh my God, who . . . who are you?"

"Just someone who has to have that file, Raymond. You should have played straight with me."

Raymond looked wildly about him, but the dense woods at night were like solid walls on both sides of the path. Something in him broke. With a scream he threw himself directly at the burly man in his way.

It was the one thing his assailant had not expected. Raymond's headlong rush threw the man backward and into the brush. Raymond raced down the path, crying and raging, half blinded by his tears but somehow keeping his feet. He could hear the other man behind him, crashing through the undergrowth like a powerful animal smashing his way through a jungle.

Fear gave Raymond Shoup the strength and will to keep going in spite of his pain. When he saw the clearing that opened out at the edge of the river, hope was a new kind of anguish, stabbing deep into his chest.

Steps from the footbridge, on the brink of escape, Raymond Shoup slipped. His right foot missed a patch of gravel and skated over saturated earth. He flipped into the air like a comic figure, a clown stepping on a banana peel.

He landed hard on his back. Before he could recover the breath jolted from his body, his pursuer loomed over him. Raymond Shoup knew that he had lost, just as he had always lost.

He made a last desperate effort to drag himself toward the bridge. He made it only to the swampy ooze at the river's edge before powerful hands caught him.

The stranger held him as if he were a child. "Did an FBI man get the rest of that file? Damn it, tell me!"

"Yes!" Raymond screamed, seizing on the question as a way out. "Yes, that's it—I don't have any more!"

"You shouldn't have tried to hustle me, Raymond," the big man said.

Before Raymond Shoup could retract his desperate lie his head was thrust underwater. His nose and mouth and throat filled with muddy water. He thrashed around futilely for a short while, feet and hands kicking and pushing at the water like a child trying to learn to swim. But the strong hands at his neck and spine did not support him, as the father he had never known might have lifted him up and made him safe. These hands held him under, until the convulsive struggling ceased and he was still.

Paul Macimer put Erika Halbig into a cab at eight-thirty, a little surprised that she offered no protest.

Low gray clouds and the continuing light drizzle had made the summer evening prematurely dark. He drove along the road that swung west past the Thomas Jefferson Memorial and onto the George Mason Bridge. From there, after crossing the river, he exited onto the Washington Memorial Parkway and drove slowly along the waterfront.

The parking area across the way from Roosevelt Island was empty. As Macimer left his car and walked toward the pedestrian bridge, the drizzly evening which had seemed so quiet and tranquil when viewed through the windows of Hogate's Restaurant appeared far less peaceful in the gloom over the river and the black island. Macimer wondered if Antonelli was already on the island, waiting, and if so where he had left his car.

The FBI man crossed the bridge quickly. The thick growth of trees and shrubbery seemed impenetrable until his flashlight picked out a footpath. As he entered this tunnel the beam of light was quickly scattered and lost in the dark wilderness on either side.

Following his darting light, he saw fresh scars in the muddy earth, as if someone had slipped and fallen. He felt a momentary uneasiness, aware that he had agreed a bit recklessly to this rendezvous with someone he did not know on a deserted island. He shrugged off the feeling with impatience. He was already committed.

Ahead of him the pathway forked, and a moment later he reached the clearing and saw the figure of Teddy Roosevelt on the far side, looking down on a broad platform flanked by twin reflecting pools.

The body lay face down, floating in the pool to the right of the platform.

Macimer waded into the pool. Even before he reached the floating body Macimer knew the man was dead. And even then he had an intuition about the identity of the dead man, someone thin and, to judge by his clothes and the long hair floating about his head, a young man.

When Macimer pulled the body out of the water and turned him over and saw the youthful, sharp-featured face, he knew that he had found the thief of the Brea file.

19

That Tuesday morning the executive conference involving the FBI Director and his three top-level assistants was stormy. Five days had passed since the explosion at Quantico in which the popular Timothy Callahan had been killed. The press was clamoring for answers. Two separate committees of Congress—including the Senate Committee on Intelligence that would have to confirm Landers' appointment as Director—were planning their own investigations. The President had publicly and privately expressed his concern. And in spite of a massive commitment of manpower and expertise, involving hundreds of the FBI's finest agents, the killer or killers were still at large, their identities a mystery.

As the man in charge of the investigation, James Caughey was first on the carpet. It did no good to remind the Director that the bombing was only one of an enormous load of cases that came under the wing of the Executive Assistant Director in charge of the sensitive Intelligence and Investigative Divisions. One of Caughey's predecessors, the feisty William Sullivan, had once written that he was responsible at one time for eighty to ninety thousand criminal and security cases. Caughey knew that the figure was only slightly exaggerated. But John L. Landers was fully aware of Caughey's other responsibilities. It made no difference. The Callahan case was an embarrassment to the Bureau. Landers wanted the bombers found.

Then it was Henry Szymanski's turn. The deficient security at Quantico had not been explained to the Director's satisfaction.

And the failure of scores of FBI Lab technicians to find evidence that would lead to the identification and apprehension of the bombers was the subject of withering interrogation by the Director.

The FBI Lab, in spite of its favorable reputation with the general public, had sometimes been criticized—most notably, again, by Bill Sullivan—for being long on paper work and short on science. The lab's purchase of a million-dollar high-resolution electron microscope had drawn the scornful observation that the lab's scientists did not know how to use the supervoltage microscope after it was installed. The criticism, coming during the 1970s when the Bureau itself was the object of intensive media scrutiny, was not entirely fair; the truth was that the scientific community in general was slow to learn how to make effective use of these remarkable instruments. By 1984, however, as Szymanski's report made clear, the FBI Lab was employing the electron miscroscope routinely for viewing single atoms, making information available on their organic and inorganic material structure to identify materials and their sources. The tests completed during the past five days, involving microscopic examination of minute fragments and scrapings from the scene of the bombing, had identified the specific Army plastic explosive used and the estimated quantity required to produce the resulting material stresses. It had been learned that the plastic substance had been implanted in the sill and frame of the doorway to the aircraft, concealed as rubberized sealant. The explosion had then been triggered by an acoustic activator rather than a mechanical, chemical or incendiary time-delay fuse.

"Acoustical!" Landers interjected.

"Callahan set it off himself," Szymanski explained. "My people tell me the activator could have been set to respond to Callahan's voice alone, to specific predictable words he might use or to a specific decibel level." He paused a moment before adding, "That means, of course, that the bomb could have been planted at any time over a period of days prior to the actual explosion."

The discovery proved that the criminals had access to and knowledge of sophisticated bomb activators, but it offered no further clue to the identity of those whom Szymanski termed "the perpetrators."

When John L. Landers turned his attention to Russell Halbig, his mood was no more jovial. He questioned Halbig sharply about

the identification of a young man murdered on Roosevelt Island
Monday night as the thief who had stolen an FBI vehicle carrying
classified documents, including the missing Brea file. "Has he been
positively identified?"

"Yes, Director. His fingerprints are the same as those found in
the stolen vehicle."

"And Macimer discovered the body."

There was a prolonged, heavy silence.

"What about this Antonelli?" Landers finally asked. "The private investigator who arranged by phone to meet Macimer on the
island."

"There is a PI named Antonelli in New York," Halbig said,
"but he was on a case in upstate New York yesterday. He never
heard of Macimer, and he wasn't in Washington. Those statements, of course, are being verified."

"So someone else telephoned Macimer," the Director said.

"A call from Antonelli—or someone using that name—was
logged at the Washington Field Office. It has also been confirmed
that Macimer received another call while at Hogate's Restaurant.
That call came at about seven o'clock. Macimer didn't leave Hogate's until around eighty-thirty, after eating dinner there."

The Director studied Halbig curiously. Halbig had displayed no
emotion over the revelation that his wife had had dinner with Paul
Macimer at Hogate's. Perhaps there was no reason for him to be
disturbed. It was a chance meeting, Halbig had said. He had been
working at FBI Headquarters until eight o'clock himself. He had
hoped to meet his wife for dinner earlier but had phoned her in
the afternoon to say that he would be unable to break away. Erika
Halbig had then gone to Hogate's on her own. Halbig had not
known she was going there and had driven home alone, arriving
shortly before his wife returned home in a taxi.

A cold fish, the Director was reminded.

"When can we expect the coroner's report on the cause and
time of Raymond Shoup's death?" Landers asked.

Szymanski volunteered the answer. "The FBI Lab has already
examined the preliminary police reports. They indicate death by
drowning, but there are indications of violence. Shoup's left wrist
was broken. Time of death has tentatively been placed at between
seven and ten o'clock last evening. We'll know more definitely
when the full autopsy report is completed."

James Caughey said, "He could've broken his wrist when he fell."

"That is a possibility," Halbig admitted.

None of the four men in the conference room thought it was. Study of the footprints along the muddy path through the woods on the island confirmed the presence on the island of someone other than Macimer and Raymond Shoup. Castings had been made of those footprints. Additional tests would be made of the material under Shoup's fingernails, and of his clothing, in the search for identifiable hair, skin, fibers and other substances. In spite of this, Macimer's involvement had raised disturbing questions. No one seemed prepared to suggest that the Special-Agent-in-Charge of the Washington Field Office might have been responsible for Raymond Shoup's death, acting alone or with someone else, but the possibility hovered behind the other questions being asked. Macimer had recovered the boxes of stolen documents from the vehicle Raymond Shoup had stolen. The Brea file was missing, presumably taken by Shoup. Now Macimer had found Shoup dead, and the file was still missing.

"I know what you're all thinking," James Caughey said, "and I don't buy any of it."

"No one is being accused of anything—yet," John Landers said sharply. "Not without proof." He glared at his three executive assistants, none of whom spoke. Finally his angry gaze settled once more on Russell Halbig. "Have the Office of Professional Responsibility briefed on the entire case to date. I will talk to the Attorney General myself. The integrity of the Bureau is involved in this case. One way or another, I want it cleared up—and I want it before Monday!"

Landers did not have to remind the other men of another unspoken question hovering over the meeting: How would Senator Sederholm's committee react to an FBI scandal on the eve of hearings to confirm Landers' appointment as Director of the FBI?

"How the hell did someone else get to Shoup before we did? How was he found?" Paul Macimer demanded. No one in the Washington Field Office had ever seen him angrier. "What the hell were we doing out there?"

Jack Wagner and Calvin Rayburn did not look at each other. They sat stiffly and uncomfortably in the two chairs across from

Macimer's desk, reluctant to draw personal attention by any movement. Wagner, for once, was unable to think of any humorous remark, and would not have made it if he did.

Finally Rayburn said, "We didn't cut spoor, it's as simple as that. Sometimes you have to get lucky."

"I'd like to think we rely on something besides luck," the SAC said sarcastically. He had picked up a pencil and was tapping it back and forth, reversing the ends. Watching him, Wagner thought of Johnny Carson, who used a pencil that way as an unconscious prop on his late-night television show. Wagner winced as Macimer abruptly snapped the pencil in half between his fingers. "Damn it, he didn't live six blocks from Fedco—he was right under your noses all the time!"

After another awkward moment of silence, Wagner said, "What about the other guys? I guess they didn't stumble on anything either." He realized as he spoke that attempting to divert the heat to another target probably wasn't going to work.

"What other guys?" Macimer snapped.

This time Wagner exchanged glances with Rayburn. He cleared his throat. "We weren't the only ones assigned out there," he said cautiously.

"You were the only ones from the Special squad—or from this office." Macimer paused, suddenly alert. "Who did you see?"

"Well . . . I don't know who he was, but I'd swear this one guy was Bureau. I spotted him Friday night at Fedco. I've seen him before, I know that."

"What did he look like?"

Wagner shifted uneasily. He had the feeling he was walking through a minefield. "I didn't get a real good look at him . . ."

"Just good enough to be sure you'd seen him before." Macimer's tone was dangerously soft.

"Yes, sir. But he was on surveillance, I'm sure of that. You get so you have a feeling for it."

"Did you see him, too, Rayburn?"

Rayburn shook his head. He seemed relieved to be clear of that particular line of fire.

Macimer stared at Wagner. He too felt a prickle of warning over the suggestion that another agent had been looking for Raymond Shoup. Who was he? And who had assigned him to a case already being covered by the Special squad?

"You're sure he wasn't MPD?" Macimer asked abruptly.

Wagner broke off a shrug, seizing on the question as a possible way to safer ground. "Could be he was a city cop, someone I've met before. Maybe he was working another case altogether." Wagner paused a moment before venturing to add, "But I was sure you'd put the kid out there . . ." His voice trailed off uncertainly.

"What kid?"

"Why . . . Stearns, of course. Agent Stearns."

Macimer didn't bother with the intercom to call Stearns to his office. His summons rattled some glass partitions. Stearns entered hesitantly as Wagner and Rayburn hurried out, glad to escape. The young agent's eyes were miserable, haunted by dark circles. Defeated, Macimer thought. He felt his anger drain away.

He allowed Harrison Stearns to sit in silence for a moment, pulling himself together, before he said, "Okay, let's have it, Stearns. What were you doing at Fedco?"

In a dull, empty voice, bereft of hope for himself, Stearns recounted his attempt to trace the thief who had stolen his FBI vehicle, a theft Stearns held himself personally responsible for. The SAC's expression remained impassive as the young agent described his after-hours vigils over the weekend. On Sunday night Stearns had thought he was onto something. He had followed a youth whom he had spotted loitering near the parking lot of Farrantino's Restaurant, where there had been a number of recent thefts from parked cars. "I wondered if maybe our thief might not have a record because he wasn't into stealing cars so much as stealing *from* them. Stealing my car might have been a freak thing because the keys just fell into his hand. This kid was acting suspicious, all right, but that's all I had. I couldn't be sure he was the right one. I followed him to this boardinghouse where he lived and I found out who he was. I figured that was all I could do then."

Stearns had intended to pursue his investigation further when he finished his desk assignment Monday. As it happened, he didn't get away from the WFO until after seven o'clock. He returned to the boardinghouse where he had tracked the suspect. He parked a short distance away and staked out the place from his car, but the youth never appeared. After two hours or so Stearns gave up for the night. By then, he now knew, Raymond Shoup was dead.

"Why didn't you put your suspicions on report?" Macimer asked quietly.

"At that point I thought it was just a shot in the dark. I couldn't be sure it was him." There was a dogged truthfulness in the words rather than an attempt to justify himself. "I only saw him at a distance Sunday night, and it was dark. And I never got much of a look at the one I bumped into the night I lost the car."

"If you'd made a report, we could have checked him out yesterday. Instead . . . someone else did."

"But how did anyone else find him? How could anyone else know who he was?"

Macimer regarded the young agent with what was, under the circumstances, a surprising amount of sympathy. The fact was that, rather than making a second major blunder within a month's time, Stearns had done a commendable piece of investigation on his own initiative. He had just missed breaking the case—arriving at the boardinghouse within minutes of the time Shoup left. Understandably, that was not the way Stearns saw it at the moment. It might not be the way Headquarters saw it.

"There's only one way anyone else could have found Raymond Shoup," Macimer said. There was no way to soften the blow. "He followed you, Stearns. He guessed that you might be on the right track, and he followed you."

Harrison Stearns's face was ashen in the seconds following Macimer's quiet statement. "Oh my God!" he whispered.

On the way to the hospital in Georgetown, Macimer stopped at the boardinghouse where Raymond Shoup had been staying and spoke briefly with the manager. Alice Volker had "just happened" to hear portions of a telephone conversation Shoup had had just before hurriedly leaving his room shortly after seven o'clock Monday evening. What the woman had heard was not helpful, but Macimer left his office and home phone numbers with her. She might remember something else, he suggested. Alice Volker seemed eager to cooperate. "Such a nice young man, he was," she said, and Macimer guessed that she would repeat those words before television news cameras, if she hadn't already done so. "Who could have done such a thing to him?"

Macimer drove on to Georgetown. Raymond Shoup had not been such a nice young man, but he hadn't deserved his fate. Such

ends were not neatly doled out; the punishment didn't always fit
the crime. Shoup had died because he knew too much—or asked
for too much. Or simply because he had the file.

And was the Brea file now in the hands of his murderer?

Macimer found a space in the crowded visitors' parking lot at
Georgetown University Hospital and sat for a moment in the car,
ignoring the heat that quickly gathered under the roof on this hot,
bright morning. He thought of the way he had been manipulated
by the man who called himself Antonelli—a man almost certainly
involved in Raymond Shoup's death. The youth's murder had
been cold-bloodedly planned. And Macimer had been meant to
find him.

But why Macimer? What had been gained by that?

Macimer stepped out of the car into the morning glare. He did
not notice the two men who had parked their gray Fairmont sedan
so that the morning sun reflected off the windshield, rendering
them almost invisible. They watched him enter the hospital before
the man in the passenger's seat spoke briefly into the car radio.

Joseph Gerella had been removed from the critical list of the
Shock Trauma Unit at Georgetown University Hospital. Macimer
found him in a semi-private room on the third floor. The adjoining
bed was empty.

For several moments Macimer stood motionless in the quiet
room, thinking that Gerella was asleep. Over the years Macimer
had seen many people beaten, brutalized, shot, overdosed on
drugs, drowned, stabbed, hacked and mauled—the endless march
of society's victims. His stomach no longer automatically heaved
at the sight of violence or death. Nevertheless, the condition of
Joseph Gerella sickened him. The reporter's face was swollen and
distorted under his heavy layer of bandages. His chest was simi-
larly wrapped, his right arm in a cast. His breathing was a labored
wheeze. His jaw had been wired shut, leaving an opening only
large enough for a glass straw, forcing him to breathe through his
nose.

Only one eye was visible. It was open, staring at Macimer.

That single eye followed him as he drew closer to the bed.
Without a framework of facial expression to define it, Gerella's
stare was impossible to read. Impaled by that one eye, Macimer
felt compelled to say, "You're wrong if you think the Bureau had
anything to do with this."

Gerella fumbled with his free hand for the tray at the side of the bed. Macimer saw a 5x7-inch pad of white notepaper and a felt-tip pen. He handed them to Gerella. The reporter printed his reply with his left hand while balancing the pad awkwardly on his stomach. The letters were childish in construction: Gerella was right-handed. His message, blocked out in capital letters, read: WHAT HAPPENED TO THE PRC?

Straight for the jugular. Staring at the note in silence, Macimer felt an ungrudging admiration. Gerella wouldn't quit.

"What do you know?" he asked. "The people who attacked you searched your apartment. What were they after, Gerella?"

The eye was not surprised. Packard would have discussed the search with his reporter, trying to learn what might be missing.

"I know you received some communications from an informant," the FBI man said. "Pages from a missing FBI file concerning the PRC case." He leaned closer. Two eyes were better for glaring than one. "This is important, Gerella. *What was in those pages?*"

Gerella attempted to print a response. The note pad slipped from his stomach and he grabbed for it with his free hand. His eye snapped shut and his body quivered with pain from the sudden movement.

Macimer retrieved the pad. He held it firmly in place while Gerella completed his awkward message. The reporter sank back as if exhausted, his eye closing.

After reading the message quickly, Macimer went back over it, frowning. NAMES & ASSIGNMENTS. FBI. AUG 28 – 81. PRC.

He waited for Gerella to look at him again. The single lid rose slowly, the eye staring. "That's all? An assignment roster, something like that?" When Gerella blinked slowly in the affirmative, Macimer asked, "In and out times? Destinations?"

His mind raced ahead of the reporter's confirmation. Assignment and activity listings were routine. Signing out was mandatory in most situations. What could be important about these records? Important enough to kill for?

Or was there, buried somewhere in those routine postings, proof that could be linked with other documentation to show that someone was not where he was supposed to be that day?

All it needed was someone—Vernon Lippert—to start looking!

Controlled excitement. Not so overriding that Macimer lost sight of something different in Gerella's expression, a hostility that expressed itself even with most of the reporter's face masked in bandages. Gerella fumbled for the note pad once more. Laboriously he printed out a terse note. Reading it, Macimer understood Gerella's silent accusation. YOUR NAME — ON LIST!

For another moment Macimer met the probing stare of that single baleful eye. The fact that a roster of assignments for the People's Revolutionary Committee FBI Task Force on August 28, 1981, should contain his name and assignment neither concerned nor surprised him. He had been chasing a phony tip that day that took him to Fresno, well away from the action. . . .

He felt a prickling sensation. He was remembering the unknown informant who had not shown up at the motel in Fresno where Macimer waited.

"You shouldn't have withheld those records from the FBI," he said. "If you'd come to us in the first place, your informant might still be alive."

He saw the shock in Gerella's visible eye. There had been nothing in the information released to the media about the Roosevelt Island murder to allow Gerella to make the connection to his informant.

"He was murdered last night," Macimer said bluntly. "And the rest of the file is gone." Watching Gerella's eye close tightly, the lid squeezing, Macimer felt the other man's pain. His own anger eased. "You were wrong in withholding evidence, Gerella, but you were right about something else—something you said that first night we talked. About how important it is to keep the law on a tight rein. We need rules to go by, just like everyone else. What happened to you was a taste of the anarchy that takes over when any man can make his own rules."

Macimer saw the puzzled speculation in Gerella's eye. It was still there when the FBI man walked out.

From the hospital lobby Macimer called the WFO. He instructed Harrison Stearns to try to locate Agents Collins and Garvey in California and have them stand by. The order was urgent. Macimer would be in the office in twenty minutes.

"Should I get the Sacramento office in on it? I mean, let them know it's urgent?"

"No," said Macimer. "Just find Collins and Garvey yourself. I don't want anyone else involved."

20

The temperature that afternoon was in the low eighties and humid. Chip Macimer had disappeared with some friends and an ice-cold six-pack. Kevin had gone to the community pool. Alone in the house, Linda Macimer answered the phone when it rang. She recognized Carole Baumgartner's voice. When Linda said her mother was out, Carole surprised her. How would Linda herself like to get out of the house and play some tennis?

Twenty minutes later, happily relaxing in the comfortable passenger seat of Carole's white BMW coupe, Linda said, "This is neat! Am I ever glad to get out of that house."

"I thought you were all one big happy family there."

"Mom and Dad love it. You know, we've always bounced around from one place to another, so we never had a real house of our own."

"But you don't like it?"

"I did . . . but not now." Linda shivered, her bare arms prickling with gooseflesh in spite of the rush of warm air through the open window. "I hate being there alone."

"You should have a boyfriend stay with you."

Linda glanced at her quickly, her enthusiasm cooling. "Did Mom ask you to talk to me?"

"I told her I wanted to," Carole Baumgartner admitted frankly. "But no . . . she doesn't know about today. In fact, when I called this afternoon I knew Jan was going to be at the travel agency—

she told me last night." Carole laughed lightly. "Jan is afraid I might try to win you over to my side."

"What side is that?"

"You don't know?" Carole laughed again, a warm and throaty laughter. She was, Linda thought, a very beautiful woman. And so cool, so smart, so . . . sure of herself. "I'm supposed to be an extremist of the women's movement. Hard core, you know, up the bastards. My side is . . ." Her expression became gentle, sympathetic, infinitely wise. ". . . the woman's side. And make no mistake, Linda. That means your side."

The Horizon Hills Country Club looked invitingly plush with its unnaturally green lawns and the dun-colored modern architecture of its buildings. Linda was wearing her tennis shorts and a T-shirt. Carole Baumgartner changed into a smart tennis outfit in the locker room. Her arms and legs were smoothly muscled and evenly tanned. She looked no more than thirty, Linda thought. It was hard to believe she had a teen-age daughter of her own.

There were a half-dozen tennis courts, all of them busy. The still, warm air was filled with the steady plop of ball against strings, sunlight glinting off aluminum and steel and carbon tennis rackets, the busy courts showcases of expensive and fashionable outfits, expensive and less spectacular skills.

Carole Baumgartner had reserved a court, and in a few minutes she and Linda were out on the hard surface, quickly falling into a ritualistic pattern of serve-and-volley, serve-and-volley. Linda had been playing regularly for two years and could more than hold her own with most of the girls in her high school class. She liked to play deep, relying on her ability to return shots steadily from the back of the court until her opponent made a mistake. Carole played aggressively, constantly forcing, attacking the net. She kept the younger girl running. In spite of her seventeen-year-old legs, Linda had to beg for a breather after the second set.

They settled at a table on a wide flagstone terrace overlooking the tennis courts and, off to the right, the sixteenth tee of the golf course. Linda regarded Carole admiringly as the older woman ordered a drink for herself and, after an inquiring glance, a 7-Up for the girl. Carole wasn't even breathing hard after two sets of tennis.

"I think we've had enough exercise for one day," said Carole. "You could be very good, you know, if you worked at it."

"You *are* good."

Over a tall Collins that was mostly shaved ice and gin, Carole Baumgartner talked amusingly about the club and its members and the current popularity of tennis. She assured Linda that at least a half-dozen members could beat her in straight sets. "It's become a mid-life goal," Carole said with a smile.

"I bet they don't look as good doing it," Linda burst out. The gushy sound of the words caused her to flush.

"Do you think a woman's looks are terribly important? How she looks to a man, for instance?"

"That isn't what I meant," Linda said, her flush darkening.

"I know you didn't. And I don't want you to think I don't like being told how good I look. I work very, very hard at it, believe me—but I don't do it for anyone else. I do it for *me*. I think that's what I want you to understand."

The girl watched and listened intently as Carole talked. She thought she was beginning to understand better why her mother and Carole were such good friends. And yet, in spite of what they shared, the two women were so different.

"Your mother told me how you've felt since that night those brave warriors with their brains between their legs roughed you up. No, don't be upset with me, Linda—listen to me. Your mother and I are very good friends but we don't always see eye to eye. She's just as much a champion of women's rights as I am, but your mother's problem is that she tries to be *reasonable*. She thinks it's important to be reasonable. I don't think so at all. What's important is not to let yourself be *used*, whether it's the way those bastards used you or any of a thousand other ways. Believe me, there are lots of others just as bad, and it doesn't hurt to know that. Let's face it, the girl who was with them was being exploited and abused, too." Carole paused. "Do you mind if I tell you a story?"

Linda hesitated, for the older woman's swift darts of thought made her feel awkward and ignorant and unsure, but yes, she *did* want to listen. She felt that Carole was sincerely trying to tell her something important, and that it was not the conventional reassurances she had heard from others until she wanted to scream. They had not felt Xavier's knife at their throats. They hadn't felt his arm crushing their breasts. "Please . . . go on."

"It's about my mother," Carole said. "I felt about her the way you must feel about Jan. She was very beautiful. An intelligent, vivacious, lively woman. She had half the young men in Charlotte chasing her, so, as the old joke has it, she caught my father. He was a good catch, everyone said. Scion of an old family, a doctor, handsome, formidable sportsman, huntsman—Daddy was all the things men were supposed to be in those days." Carole's eyes seemed to darken. When she went on, pensively, she seemed to be talking as much to herself as for Linda's benefit. "I was fifteen when she killed herself. The funny thing is, now that I have women friends—now that I have *time* for them, can get to know them, women like your mother—I've learned that my mother's case wasn't all that unusual. Oh, they didn't all commit suicide. Some of them started in on the Southern Comfort and graduated. Others became . . . strange. My mother had so much *energy!* So much to offer! But her life bottled it all up, it had no way to come out, it wasn't even considered quite *proper,* like a good woman enjoying sex. She did everything she was supposed to do, played her pretty role to perfection. Everyone thought how marvelously happy she must be, what a perfect couple she and Daddy were. No one knew what was happening to her, not even Daddy. Least of all Daddy! No one could understand . . ." Carole broke off, gulped an inch of her Collins. Her gaze, birdlike, pecked around the terrace, quickly appraising the sleek women and a scattering of leathery men there on a lazy summer afternoon at the club. The gaze darted back to Linda, measuring her. "Do you know what I'm saying, Linda?"

"Yes, I . . . I think so."

"We have choices now. We don't have to be shortchanged. We don't have to be . . . used."

Linda nodded eagerly. She was flattered by the interest in her shown by this older, wiser, so much cleverer woman, and she was excited by the knowledge that Carole Baumgartner was, undeniably, encouraging and supporting the rebellious thoughts and emotions Linda had been nurturing since the night of the robbery. Carole had not talked to her like her school friends, who had been more stimulated than alarmed by her tale of being held at knife's point by a very macho young Latin criminal. Nor like her mother, anxious and concerned but unable to escape an authoritarian role, unable to conceal that tone of knowing best. Carole had spoken to her like a real friend, an adult—another woman. Carole's interest, her concern, even the story about her mother added substance to

Linda's confused emotional state. She was not simply reacting out of fear and revulsion. She was beginning to see and understand some harsh realities. Doors were opening in her mind that she hadn't even known were there.

Carole Baumgartner ordered a second drink. Pouring a little of it into Linda's glass, she laughed lightly and said, "Don't worry about me—I didn't let myself get trapped in Mother's cage, with or without a bottle."

Carole Baumgartner drove her BMW effortlessly, using the five-speed gearbox with casual skill. The road wound downward out of the hills until it came to a long straight grade that leveled out on the lowlands where, in the distance, a river glinted here and there in its winding course.

A little more careless than usual perhaps, her senses dulled just a little by sun and gin and hard exercise, Carole did not notice the battered blue pickup on the road behind them until they were coming down the long grade. By then the truck was close behind the white car.

"Look at that son of a bitch!" Carole cried in exasperation.

The pickup swung out. Carole slowed a little to give it plenty of room to pass. Quickly the truck drew level with the smaller vehicle. Carole glanced up at it, an expression of hostility on her face, a caustic comment on her lips. But the side of the truck was splashed with mud that completely covered the side window. She couldn't see the driver.

For several seconds she waited for the pickup to draw ahead. With a prickly feeling of surprise she finally realized that it was staying even with her, matching her speed. She felt a tug of anxiety. Glancing down the long two-lane grade, she muttered, "Games!"

As if accepting a challenge, Carole's foot tromped down on the accelerator. The BMW jumped a few feet ahead of the truck. The gain was short-lived. Within seconds the bigger vehicle surged alongside of the car once more.

In the passenger seat beside Carole, Linda Macimer felt the first strong beat of fear. She glanced sidelong at the speedometer. They were racing downhill at over seventy miles an hour. The rasp of the BMW's engine grew louder as their speed increased even further. Linda looked ahead anxiously. The road remained clear.

"Oh my God!" Carole cried. In the same instant Linda felt a jarring impact. There was a crunching of metal as the truck lurched into the side of the small white car.

Carole Baumgartner fought to hold the car on the road. The pickup swung away from them for an instant. It was a scene Linda had seen a hundred times on television, a staple of the low-budget thriller. It couldn't really be happening.

The truck swerved back suddenly, smashing into the side of the car.

Linda had a last glimpse of the rear of the pickup as it sailed down the road. The white BMW was airborne for an instant as it shot off the side of the road. Then it bounced over slippery gravel. The front wheels nudged a shallow ditch and the car rolled. With an odd clarity Linda remembered Carole's insistence that she buckle up her seat belt when she got into the car. She felt grateful.

Her head struck something hard and she knew nothing else.

21

Paul Macimer paced the hospital corridor slowly. He had left Linda's room a few minutes before. The silent vigil with Jan in the narrow hospital room, while his mind churned with questions raised by Linda's "accident," had become too much for him. He felt as if he were going to explode.

Jan could always sense his moods. When he had slipped from the room, saying he would be just outside the door if Linda woke, Jan had glanced at him searchingly.

He stared at the paintings lining the corridor. They were an attempt to relieve the stark white walls and blank sheets of glass with splashes of bright color. They were a desperate distraction. They kept him from thinking about what might have happened to Linda and Carole this afternoon. And why it had happened.

A check with the FBI's SMV file had so far failed to turn up a stolen pickup matching the description of the one which had forced Carole's car off the road. Scrapings of blue paint from the left front fender of the BMW had been sent to the Bureau's Instrumental Analysis Unit, which specialized in hit-and-run investigations. If it was the original paint, it would identify the make, model and year of the vehicle.

Macimer expected little from these investigations. The truck would be found abandoned somewhere in Washington, probably close to a subway terminal. It would be identified as stolen. There would be a routine examination of mud from the accelerator and brake pedals, clothing fibers or human hairs found on the seats of the truck, fingerprints from the steering wheel, shift knob and door handles. If the driver of the truck at the time of the accident were found, such evidence would be damning enough. First he would have to be found. Macimer suspected that might prove a lot more difficult than tracking down the blue pickup.

The case had begun with another car theft, Macimer thought. And another accident. He tried to find some parallel between the two incidents but it eluded him.

An urgent whisper caught his attention. "Paul!" Jan was at the door to Linda's room, beckoning him. The girl was awake.

Linda stared up at her father, whose face was like stone. On the other side of the bed her mother appeared drawn, and her eye makeup was smudged. Linda tried to smile encouragingly, as if it were her parents who needed moral support. She felt bruised from head to foot. "How do I look?" she asked.

"Beautiful," said her father. "Remember that TV show a few years back? *The Munsters?* You'd fit right in."

"Oh, thanks a lot!"

"You're going to be fine," Jan Macimer said.

Jan had not asked what Linda was doing in the speeding car with Carole. No lectures, no recriminations. Linda felt tears threaten.

"How . . . how is Carole?"

"You were luckier than she was. She has a broken leg, but she's going to be all right. You were both lucky, really."

"Linda . . ." Her father seemed different to her. After a moment she realized it was his eyes. She had never realized how soft was his normal expression when he looked at her. Now his gaze was hard, probing intently. "I don't want to press you, but . . . I'd like to ask you about that pickup truck. Just a couple of questions."

"He ran us off the road!" she wailed, a cry that mingled pain with remembered fear and anger. "He did it on purpose!"

"Did you get a look at him?"

She shook her head.

"What about the license plate? Could you make out anything at all? Even one or two numbers?"

"I saw the truck when it went by after it hit us, but you couldn't see the license plate. There was mud all over it."

She thought something shifted in her father's eyes, but he nodded without comment. "Okay. Carole told us it was dark blue, maybe a '75 or '76 Chevrolet. That sound about right?"

"I think so . . . I don't know. It was just an old pickup."

He didn't ask any more questions. Soon afterward Linda began to feel sleepy again—they must have given her something to make her sleep—and her parents drifted toward the door of her room. She heard her mother ask, "Who'd do such a thing? What kind of man would do such a thing?"

"We have a good description of the truck. If we find it, we'll know more."

As Linda floated toward unconsciousness she remembered Carole Baumgartner's muttered word: "Games!" But it hadn't been a game, Linda thought. Whatever it was, it wasn't a game.

Carole Baumgartner was in a great deal of pain. She hoped it would go away soon. She didn't like pain at all; she wasn't very good at enduring.

The door to her room opened after a gentle knock. She stared past the monstrous encumbrance of her right leg, which was raised in traction, at Jan Macimer.

"We're leaving," Jan said. "I'll look in on you tomorrow."

"I won't be going anywhere."

"Stop being brave."

"You know me better than that. Jan—"

"You don't have to say it."

"Yes, I do. I wasn't trying to undermine you or anything. You know how I am. I get fired up, and I thought maybe I could help."

"You care."

"Yeah." Carole studied her friend anxiously. There wasn't much else she could say. She had gone behind Jan's back in a sense, arranging to have her "little talk" with Linda while she knew Jan was elsewhere. "You're sure Linda's going to be okay? If anything serious had happened to her because of me . . ."

"You couldn't help what happened." Jan didn't sound completely convincing. But what did Carole expect? Hosannas for nearly killing Jan's daughter?

"You know what I can't figure out?" asked Carole after a moment. "Why did he do it? Do you suppose he was getting even for women's lib? Do you think some lady truck driver took his job? Or maybe his wife told him to get lost last night?"

"He doesn't like women drivers," Jan murmured.

"Or German cars."

"People who belong to country clubs." When you thought about it, the actions of the man in the pickup were too bizarre for any easy explanation. How else explain him except with macabre jokes?

Paul Macimer entered the room briefly. He asked Carole for the second time about the mud-spattered license plate and side window of the truck, looked thoughtful when she answered and urged her to take it easy. She wanted to know how she could do anything else in her position.

The Macimers left and she was again alone in the room. There was another bed but it was unoccupied. Carole was glad of that. Her own pain was bad enough without having to listen to someone else's.

She stared up at the paraphernalia assembled to keep her going. There was a needle in her arm with a long thin tube attached that led upward to an IV bottle. She was receiving antibiotics with the IV, Nurse Jane had told her.

Nurse Jane was Filipino. All the nurses seemed to be either black or from the Philippines. Carole couldn't understand most of what the latter said. They giggled a lot when they talked among themselves in their own language, which had a ridiculous name. What was it? Tagalong? Not quite it. Taga-something.

Why were all the hospitals being forced to recruit nurses from the Philippines, even from Canada? American women were deserting the profession in droves. Even RN's were finding better things to do. It wasn't that the job was beneath them, Carole thought defensively. The medical world was simply a microcosm of the whole system, a chronically male-dominated world in which men were Daddy and women cleaned up the bedpans. The doctors (male) drove Cadillacs, played golf on Wednesday and wintered in Bermuda. The nurses (female) barely received a subsistence wage, fought their way home on the night shift through the rapists in the parking lot and became the butt of jokes about their morals.

No wonder they had to go out of the country or far into the boondocks to find women still willing to put up with that, or innocent of it.

Satisfied with her analysis, Carole drifted off to sleep.

When she woke she was sweating and trembling and her leg hurt like hell. The fragments of a frightening dream eluded her as she tried to remember them.

The room was very quiet. The hospital was quiet. Drapes were drawn over the window of Carole's room, but she could see enough through them to know that it was dark outside.

Her room was dimly lit. Someone must have come in to push the buttons that turned off all the lights with the exception of one recessed into the ceiling above the doorway. It spotlighted that area but left the rest of the room in twilight.

Carole watched the slow drip of the clear liquid from the IV bottle into the tube. The tube was like an umbilical cord, carrying food and medication into her bloodstream. The room was so quiet that she found herself listening for the soft "plop" of each drop of liquid from the bottle. But there was no audible sound at all, of course. Except . . .

She could hear someone breathing.

Carole turned her head quickly on the pillow. Seeing the white jacket, she relaxed a little, though her heart was beating rapidly. "Hey, don't you ever knock, Doc, when you come into a lady's room?" To her own ears her humor sounded forced.

"You were asleep. You didn't hear me." Great voice, she thought, for a bedside manner. Like having Orson Welles doing the honors.

He had been standing behind the rack of survival gear near the head of her bed, lost in shadows. He stepped closer when she spoke to him, but she still could not see his face clearly.

"How'm I doing?" she murmured.

"Very well, it appears. There is a possibility of internal injuries, but nothing serious."

"Who cares if a woman bleeds a little inside? We're supposed to, aren't we? It's true, you know, the way God worked things out. He had to be a male."

"Don't you believe in God?"

"You don't have to get mad about it. What are you, a doctor or the hospital chaplain?" She peered up at him, puzzled. He had leaned closer when he spoke to her sharply, and she had a quick glimpse of his features. He looked familiar. She couldn't see him very clearly, but there was something about him . . .

Her eyelids were heavy. Not sexy, Doc, just tired. Don't get any ideas.

She was aware of feeling weak and helpless, lying there with her leg caught in its complicated trap, unable to move, while a white-jacketed man, a stranger, stood beside her bed and gazed down at her with hostile eyes.

She stared at the IV bottle and its assembly of control valves as if she might find a message there. The fluid continued to drip slowly into the long tube that led to her arm. The doctor fiddled with one of the small appendages protruding from the tube near the top assembly.

"What are you doing?"

"We're going to add something to your diet," he said with a smile. "To make you rest comfortably."

Maybe I don't want to rest comfortably, she thought. Aloud she said, "What do you call those things sticking out there? Side-somethings, right?"

"Those?" He appeared to examine one of them thoughtfully, even though he was apparently in the act of inserting the needle of a big syringe into the end of it. "Side valves, that's all."

Carole frowned. That didn't sound right. She stared at him in alarm. He regarded her impassively. Strong silent type. He looked very . . . strong. Carole shivered. "Who . . . who are you?" she whispered. "Don't I know you from somewhere?"

"Do you?"

"No . . . no." It seemed important to deny her knowledge. Because she did recognize him now.

"I'm sorry it has to be this way," he said, in that deep, calm, soothing voice. Then his hand moved, his thumb driving the plunger of the big syringe forward. Too late she saw that what the syringe held was not another liquid so pale as to be invisible to the eye. It held . . . nothing! Air!

"But you did see me," he said. "No—don't try to scream."

She tried, but it was already too late. She began to pant and struggle for breath. Only seconds had passed and already she was sweating, sucking noisily for air, her heart hammering. Her bulging eyes stared past the broad hand now holding her down, past a hairy wrist with a gold watch, past a white-sleeved arm, directly into his eyes. *My God—why? Why me? I've got a daughter—*

The first massive blow struck her in the chest. The pain was unbearable. Her heart stopped.

It required all of his considerable strength to hold her when her body convulsed. She rose off the bed, heaving upward. The violent movement tore the tube loose from the IV bottle. The clear fluid from the bottle continued to drip slowly.

Only when she had been still for a full minute did he release her. The bulging eyes no longer saw him.

At the door he turned off the single overhead light, plunging the room into total darkness. Cracking the door open, he peered along the corridor. The nurses' station was some distance away. The duty nurse was not in sight.

He stepped quickly into the corridor and walked to his right, away from the nurses' station and toward a stairway exit.

22

Jan Macimer, who hated pills, had reluctantly accepted the need for a sedative. She fell into an exhausted sleep around midnight. Paul Macimer was in his den, talking on his private line to a night desk clerk at FBI Headquarters about the blue pickup. Tests by the FBI Lab had already identified the vehicle from paint scrapings as a 1976 Chevrolet. The truck had not been found, however, or identified as being on the stolen vehicles list.

Chip Macimer was in the family room watching Johnny Carson on the *Tonight* show when the extension phone rang. He called his father out of his den. "It's the hospital," Chip said awkwardly, feeling clumsy with his anxiety. "Someone named Sims. He wouldn't say what it was—says he has to talk to you."

Macimer grabbed the phone. Darrell Sims was the assistant night security supervisor at the emergency hospital where Linda and Carole had been taken. Macimer had talked to him briefly that evening. "What is it, Sergeant?"

"I'm afraid I have some bad news, Mr. Macimer. It looks like a fluke thing. I mean, she was alone in her room—"

"For God's sake, who? Who are you talking about?"

"What . . . oh Jesus, I'm sorry, Mr. Macimer, it's not your daughter. It's the other lady, Ms. Baumgartner."

"What happened?" Macimer's heart continued to pound from the massive shot of adrenaline, and the wash of relief left him shaken.

"It's like her heart just stopped."

"She's *dead?*"

"Yes, sir. And the thing is, I heard the night resident, that's Dr. Lansberg, a real bright young fellow"—there was a hint of disapproval in Sims's tone, as if a doctor had no business being bright and young—"worrying out loud about maybe there was an accident with the IV feeder. I thought you'd want to know, seeing as how you were looking into that auto accident, and the lady was a friend of yours. Kinda funny," Sims added. "I mean, you know, two accidents in one day to the same person."

Macimer felt as if he had been clubbed with a two-by-four. "Do you have any reason to think what happened tonight wasn't an accident?"

"Well, no, sir. You understand, Mr. Macimer, there could be a question of liability here, and I'm not qualified to say any more than I have. Wouldn't have said this much if it weren't . . . well, you know, special circumstances." Sims was letting him know that he was doing the FBI man a favor, sticking his own neck out. "If there's anything else you want me to do, Mr. Macimer . . ."

"I appreciate your calling me, Sergeant. How late are you on duty?"

"Well, fact is, I just got off at midnight."

"Would it be possible for you to wait there a little longer? I'll be there as soon as I can."

"Sure, I can do that," Sims agreed with alacrity. "You think that—"

"I don't think anything, Sergeant. I'd just like to go over what happened with you. Will Dr. Lansberg be on duty?"

"He's here until morning."

"Good. Maybe you could let him know I'd like to talk to him."

"You've got it," the security man said.

When Macimer hung up he knew that he had to answer the anxious question in Chip's eyes. "Linda's fine," he said. "But there were complications with Carole. Her heart . . ."

"Geez," Chip muttered in disbelief. At nineteen, Macimer thought, death was hard to believe.

And it never got easier.

Mitchell Lansberg was thirty, athletic, curly-haired, with dark brown eyes set close to the bridge of a prominent nose. His appraisal of Paul Macimer held the skepticism of his generation's liberal intellectuals toward America's intelligence establishment, but he was willing enough to talk about Carole Baumgartner. The case interested him, Macimer thought.

"She had a heart attack," Lansberg said. "Technically, that's what killed her."

"Technically?"

Lansberg hesitated. "Is this official in some way, Mr. Macimer?"

"It could be important."

"I don't see how," the young resident said slowly. "There's a possibility—it's only a theory of mine—that she could have been the victim of a freak accident—an air embolism. That air somehow got into the IV tube."

"That would kill her?"

"If it was a big enough bubble."

It turned out that Lansberg was specializing in kidney work. When patients were treated using a kidney dialysis unit, where the blood was actually circulated outside the body, the risk of an air embolism was even more life-threatening than would normally be the case. Rarely—very rarely, he said—an accident occurred. Lansberg had been involved in one such incident himself, and it was one he would not soon forget.

"The Nazis did all the early research on air embolisms," the resident explained, warming to his subject. "Before World War II we didn't know anything about them. They were simply isolated accidents, without explanation. But the Nazis ran elaborate series of tests, working out just how much air per body weight could be injected into the bloodstream before fatality would occur." Lansberg paused. "They were human experiments, of course."

"Does that kind of thing happen often with the IV equipment?"

The resident shook his head emphatically. "It's a thousand to one. Hell, even less than that."

"What makes you think it might have happened here?"

Lansberg hesitated. "It's only a hunch. Her heart stopped suddenly, we know that. The reaction was violent enough for her to tear the IV tube loose. And she was sweating profusely, which is one of the symptoms."

"If an air embolism did kill her, how long would it take?"

"Seconds," Lansberg said tersely. "Two or three minutes before there was irreversible brain damage. It's very, very fast, Mr. Macimer."

"Would an autopsy show that's what happened?"

"It could," the doctor said. "But normally it wouldn't. I mean, if it was a standard autopsy, you'd be working in the open and you'd never know if there was air trapped in there. The only way you'd know would be if the autopsy was conducted underwater. Then you'd literally see any air bubble escape when you cut into the heart. But that's only done under special circumstances." He studied Macimer curiously.

"There would be an autopsy in any event?"

Lansberg nodded. "She died unattended. That calls for an autopsy."

"But it wouldn't be an underwater examination?"

"Are you asking for one, Mr. Macimer?"

Macimer understood what Lansberg would not say openly. The hospital would not go out of its way to find evidence for which questions of liability might be raised, not unless there was a compelling reason.

"I am," Macimer said.

Macimer questioned Darrell Sims about security procedures at the hospital on the night shift. All exits were locked after visiting hours except for the main emergency area and fire doors. The latter could only be opened from the inside. Anyone entering the hospital through the emergency section had to pass a security officer in order to reach elevators or stairways. Sims was confident that no unauthorized person or persons had entered the hospital.

Macimer saw little point in asking if any hospital personnel ever used the fire exits to step outside for a smoke, or propped a door open for convenience that should have stayed locked. It happened all too often. And someone who had gained access to the hospital during visiting hours wouldn't have needed a clandestine entry. He could easily have found a place to hide.

Macimer thanked Sims for staying on after his shift was over. He said nothing to relieve the security man's curiosity, instead asking him to say nothing about the night's events to anyone other than his own superiors.

On his way home, driving slowly, Macimer was struck by the strange emptiness of early morning in the suburbs. The surface streets were as deserted as those in a science-fiction movie depicting the world after the Big Bang, silent and empty and unreal.

It was a time of the morning for confronting unanswered questions. Who was Brea? Was he someone Macimer knew? Was he acting on his own, or was he part of a larger conspiracy?

Carole's murder had answered one question. She had been the intended victim of the accident created by the driver of the blue pickup truck, not Linda. But why had it been necessary to silence Carole? What could she possibly have known or seen? Macimer thought of the incident Jan had described, the stranger Carole had noticed in Adam's Restaurant. But even if the man in the restaurant had been Brea, why would he feel threatened by Carole seeing him there?

Macimer admitted one possible answer, reluctantly: the man in the restaurant had a public face. And Carole had seen him under circumstances that, for reasons Macimer could not yet divine, might somehow be compromising.

Macimer's restless thoughts turned to his late-afternoon briefing of Collins and Garvey. Acting on the lead provided by Joseph Gerella, Macimer had instructed the two agents to begin digging into the records of agent assignments on the day of the PRC disaster. Checking all those records meant tedious interviews, backtracking along trails now three years old, sifting and sorting, comparing and corroborating. It was a task that would have proceeded much more swiftly if Macimer had requested massive support from the Sacramento office. Given enough time and manpower, such an investigation would surely unearth whatever it was that Vernon Lippert had stumbled onto, the clue to Brea's identity. But Macimer's uncertainty over the ramifications of the Brea cover-up within the Bureau made him more than ever reluctant to ask for the additional help. Collins and Garvey would have to do it on their own, he had told them emphatically when he outlined the new focus of the investigation, stressing that they should report *only to him directly.*

Reason told him his instructions had been valid and correct, but his uneasiness persisted. Limiting the investigative effort carried its own risks, underscored by Carole Baumgartner's death. There might not be enough time. The murders of Raymond Shoup and Carole on successive nights suggested to Macimer something more than a desperate need on Brea's part to remove any risk, however remote. They suggested that some final shackle of restraint had broken. If Raymond Shoup's murder had been coldly calculated, Carole Baumgartner's had been recklessly dangerous, the act of someone out of control.

It was as if something which had long been carefully caged had broken loose and was running wild, something savage and bloody-fanged, beyond law, beyond moral restraints, beyond reason.

Jan was waiting for him in the kitchen when he entered the house from the garage. "I called the hospital," she said. "When I woke up and found you gone, I was afraid . . ."

Her eyes were puffy from crying, but in them there was also an unhappy guilt. Macimer guessed what she was feeling. When she put her frantic call through to the hospital, her fear was for Linda, not Carole. Her sorrow over Carole's death was tainted by the se-cret knowledge that she had been relieved to learn Linda was all right. Macimer himself had felt the same guilty relief.

"Does Linda know about Carole?" Jan asked anxiously.

"No. I told them under no circumstances should she be told anything, even if she asks about Carole. She'll find out soon enough."

"I want to be there." Jan stared at him thoughtfully, measuring his fatigue. "Would you like something to drink?"

"Do we still have some of that Christmas brandy?"

"I think so."

They carried the fat crystal glasses into the family room and sat at the dining table. Macimer thought if he sank into the sofa he would tip instantly into sleep.

"Why didn't you wake me, Paul?"

"You needed the rest."

"So did you." She paused, staring into the amber pool of liquid at the bottom of her glass. "What happened?"

"They don't know for sure. Her heart stopped." After a mo-ment's hesitation he told her of the resident's theory about an air embolism, a bubble that entered the bloodstream and went straight to the heart. "It would have killed her instantly."

Jan turned away from him. For a moment she had to hide her anguish. Carole had been her friend, not Paul's. When she faced him again she was in control. "I'm going to cancel that flight to Phoenix. I can't go now."

"I don't want you to cancel it."

"But it's impossible! There'll be Carole's funeral—and Linda won't be ready for a cross-country flight so soon."

"I'll see that Linda is put on a plane as soon as possible."

"You mean I'm to go without her?" Jan stared at him for a long time in silence. "There's something you're not telling me."

"I can't explain."

"You damned well *have* to explain." When he did not answer she asked, "Does it have something to do with a case?"

"Yes."

It was a very tough equation. In recent weeks Jan's home had been invaded, her bedroom bugged, her activities spied on. This afternoon her daughter's life had been threatened. Tonight her good friend—perhaps her best friend—had died. She deserved to know why.

That was on the one side. On the other Paul couldn't discuss a confidential FBI investigation with anyone outside the Bureau, even her. And it was also true that she couldn't afford to know even as much as he did.

Carey McWilliams. Vernon Lippert. Timothy Callahan. Raymond Shoup. Carole Baumgartner. Each of them had known or seen something he or she shouldn't, something that might be dangerous to someone.

To Brea.

Macimer had the sensation of being on the very edge of revelation. He was that far away from having it all laid out, the entire scheme visible, the odd-shaped pieces falling into place in the odd-shaped holes.

But it stayed just out of reach.

"I'll tell you this much," he said. "We know that what happened this afternoon wasn't an accident."

"The truck . . ."

"That truck deliberately forced Carole off the road. But it didn't end there." He watched the horror of what he was saying reach her eyes, flood them, scream a silent protest. "I think Carole was murdered tonight. Linda wasn't the target of that accident this afternoon, Carole was. But the driver didn't care if Linda was hurt. She was in the way, that's all. Tonight he finished the job." Macimer paused. "I don't want any of you in the way any longer.

I want you, Chip, Kevin, Linda—all of you—as far from here as possible. As soon as possible."

"You're telling me to run."

"I'm asking you," he said.

It was the fact that he had asked, he thought later, that finally won her over.

23

American Airlines flight 115, nonstop to Phoenix, left Dulles International Thursday afternoon. Chip and Kevin were eagerly looking forward to the trip but Jan was unusually quiet. While the two boys were getting reading material from a newsstand, Paul and Jan had a few moments alone in the vast waiting area.

"I still don't like leaving without Linda," Jan said.

"As soon as she's released, I'll put her on the first available flight. Meanwhile I won't have to worry about the rest of you."

"You're serious about that, aren't you?"

"Carole was murdered, Jan." The underwater autopsy had confirmed the presence of an air embolism. Even though it could not be proven that the deadly air bubble had been deliberately caused, Macimer had no doubt.

"We've never been threatened before, not that I know of. Not once in twenty years."

"Twenty years ago you didn't have underground newspapers printing the names and addresses of agents, making us targets." It was a plausible evasion, he thought.

"Maybe it's time for you to get out," Jan said quietly.

"You know better than that, Jan. Besides, I couldn't leave in the middle of a case. Especially this case. I have to see it through."

"Without me." Jan was silent for a long moment, staring at him. Over her shoulder Paul saw Chip hurrying toward them. Kevin trailed behind, leafing through a magazine as he walked.

Jan said, "Maybe you're right, Paul. And maybe I'm the one who doesn't belong here anymore."

The words echoed in Macimer's mind as he watched the shuttle bus taking Jan, Chip and Kevin away from the terminal. He could not even guess how final Jan's words had been, or whether the gulf between them could still be breached.

The plane, a 707, waited out on an apron near the runways, which undulated in the heat like cheap mirrors. Unlike most major U.S. airports, Dulles International did not have separate terminals for each airline. From the single huge terminal, serving all carriers, a fleet of cumbersome-looking but surprisingly efficient shuttles loaded passengers for departure and brought new arrivals in from the landing strips.

Macimer continued to stare across the hot apron as the passenger cab of the shuttle rose slowly from ground level to the height of the 707's passenger door. Then there was the pantomime of the shuttle cab's silent descent and crabbed retreat. The faces at the windows of the plane were small and unrecognizable.

When the aircraft trundled out toward its takeoff, Macimer turned away, depressed.

On the way to his car he took the wrong aisle in the parking lot and caught a glimpse of the two men sitting in a gray Ford sedan. Macimer paid them no notice.

Traffic was relatively light on the wide, divided highway heading east from the airport toward Washington. Otherwise the unobtrusive gray sedan would easily have gone unnoticed, since it lagged far behind him. It stayed visible in his rearview mirror all the way into downtown Washington, and he was not sure it had broken away until he was within a few blocks of the Washington Field Office.

By then, Macimer reflected, there was no need to keep him under direct surveillance.

At the WFO Macimer reviewed the teletypes received that morning from Collins and Garvey. He read the reports by the agents who had combed Gerella's apartment; the search had been unproductive. He also read summary reports from Rodriguez and Singleton on the search for the three missing Cubans; attached was a list of three youths—two were named Xavier—on whom the search was being concentrated because they matched all or most of the subject's profile. Next were the FBI Lab's reports on the detailed examination of evidence found on Roosevelt Island, along with Raymond Shoup's autopsy report. Water in Shoup's lungs had come not from the pool where he was found but from the river, indicating that the body had been moved after Shoup was drowned. Footprints found with Shoup's in the soft earth near the shore of the island and along the footpath had been made by a heavyset man wearing rubbers over his shoes. Which meant no identifiable footprints, Macimer noted, unless the rubbers themselves, which had a distinctive ribbed sole pattern, were found. They wouldn't be, he knew. Brea had worn them deliberately, and he would quickly have disposed of them.

The Special squad's accumulation of records covering the Brea investigation now filled most of a four-drawer file cabinet. But Brea was still out of reach.

Just before five o'clock Joe Taliaferro returned to the office, and Macimer briefly reviewed with Taliaferro and the ASAC, Jerry Russell, their plans for another Friday night surveillance of the suspect from the Energy Research and Development Administration. The Alexandria office, Russell reported, was maintaining photographic surveillance of everyone who visited the print shop suspected of being the suspect Molter's drop. A registered clerk from the Soviet Embassy in Washington had been identified as one of those visitors.

Macimer left the office shortly after this briefing—an early hour for him. He instructed Harrison Stearns to call him the minute anything important came in on the Brea case. Then Macimer drove through heavy traffic to the suburban hospital near the Meadows where Linda had been kept for observation.

Linda seemed improved—more alert, less remote. Macimer was encouraged. To occupy the girl's mind he had her make a list of what she wanted to take to Arizona with her. He would do her packing and have everything ready.

He wanted her away from Washington.

On the drive from the hospital he looked for the gray Ford Fairmont sedan but was unable to spot it. He arrived home shortly after six-thirty.

To cover any attempt to reach him at home during his absence from the empty house he had hooked up the answering device to his private telephone. He disliked using the tape-recorded system, though it was sometimes useful. There were three messages clocked on the recorder. He rewound the tape and switched the instrument to playback.

The first caller had hung up without speaking, rousing Macimer from his slumped position in his chair. He shrugged off his curiosity; a great many people disliked dealing with the tape-recorded message system and automatically hung up.

The second call was from Jan, who had arrived in Phoenix on schedule. Macimer turned off the answer-phone and dialed the number of Jan's parents' home in Sun City. Jan was asleep, her mother told him, tired from her flight. Macimer gave her the flight number and time of Linda's scheduled arrival in Phoenix on Friday. If there was any change, he added, he would telephone again.

When he hung up he wondered if Jan had really been asleep.

Several minutes passed before he remembered that there had been a third message on his recorder. He switched on the instrument once more.

This last call was the least expected and most puzzling. It was from Erika Halbig.

Special Agents Lenny Collins and Pat Garvey dined that evening at the Nut Tree, a popular restaurant in Vacaville, an easy drive from Sacramento. It was crowded and they had to wait for a table. They were finally seated next to an interior garden which had been enclosed as an aviary. Bright-plumed birds flitted among the greenery and vivid splashes of hanging fuchsias. After watching the spectacle for several minutes, ordering a dinner of curried chicken breast and sipping an icy margarita, Collins said, "This beats Sambo's."

Garvey managed only a forced grin. The day had been tiring and frustrating, a dogged attempt to reconstruct the movements of some two hundred agents who had been part of the People's Revolutionary Committee Task Force, cross-referencing assignment sheets against daily reports for the date of August 28, 1981, and verifying these by personal interviews. Most of those agents were easily eliminated from suspicion of involvement in the Brea affair; they had worked in pairs or squads on the fateful day. That information did more than provide corroboration of their activities. "We're looking for someone who was alone that day, acting on his own," Paul Macimer had said. "We're looking for Brea himself."

Twenty-three agents listed as part of the Task Force had been on individual assignments in the field that day. So far Collins and Garvey had managed to account for only eleven of them. One of the things that was bothering Garvey was the knowledge that a commitment of more manpower would have made the review much swifter, much more certain of success. Yet Macimer's orders had been explicit: Collins and Garvey were handling this part of the investigation on their own.

Garvey didn't like investigating other FBI agents, even though he knew that Brea had to be identified and exposed. He didn't like working in the dark, and he sensed that his boss, Macimer, knew more than the agents did. And he liked least of all the fact that, sometime on Friday, he and Collins would be working their way down to Fresno—investigating Macimer himself. And like it or not, Macimer was not above suspicion.

Garvey picked at a steak while Collins devoured the curried breast of chicken and a heaping platter of fruits, nuts and condiments. Finally, over coffee, Garvey brought up the possibility which Collins, only half jokingly, had suggested. "I can't believe Macimer is involved."

"Then why are you so worried?" Collins asked cheerfully.

"It doesn't make sense they'd put him in charge of the special investigation if he was under suspicion."

"Maybe the people who put him in charge were also in on it. We don't know that Brea acted on his own that day. Don't forget, Macimer worked at the seat of government himself for a while. He also got nice fat promotions ahead of older agents. He's got friends where it counts. Maybe he's holding some IOUs."

"I don't think even you believe that."

Collins shrugged. "I'll tell you one thing, if Macimer was so eager to get at the bottom of this thing, we wouldn't be out here on our lonesome. There'd be a few dozen other agents digging into these assignment checks looking for Brea. Hell, that's one of the things the Bureau does best, throwing in the big manpower when that's what's needed to break a case open. And I'll tell you something else. No matter what we find tonight or tomorrow or the next day, if there's anything that points a finger at one of the big boys, Macimer or anyone else, and we send in our report, it'll just disappear. That's the last you'll ever hear of it. Unless . . ."

Collins paused, cocking his head to listen to the song of a bird
with bright yellow on its wings. Collins wondered what it was; he
had never had time in his life for birdwatching, any more than he
had made space in his thinking for taking people on faith alone,
trusting in the goodness of mankind. Garvey, he thought, was up-
setting that. . . .

"Unless what?" Garvey prodded.

"Unless we turn something up that we feel we should take
straight to Headquarters."

Garvey stiffened. His skin felt cold, as if the air conditioning
had been turned up too high. "Disobey Macimer's instructions?"

"Why not?" Collins demanded. He had been stirring another
spoonful of sugar into his coffee, and he pointed the spoon at Garvey as if in accusation. "Why should we keep quiet, if those orders
are part of the whole stinking cover-up?"

"I don't believe it," Garvey said flatly.

"You don't want to. Hell, neither do I. I like Macimer. But the
world doesn't surprise me as much as it does you, Garvey." He
paused, then grinned broadly. "Besides, you're forgetting there's
one other big name on that list. You know who it is."

Garvey knew. It was the name of the man who had been in
charge of the task force hunting the PRC in the summer of 1981:
John L. Landers, now Acting Director of the FBI.

At nine o'clock that Thursday evening, while Collins and Garvey were sitting down to dinner, Paul Macimer turned off the Beltway at Exit 19 and swung south toward Bethesda. He had not
seen the gray Ford following him, but almost certainly it—or another car—was close behind.

After a short drive he spotted the brightly lit façade of the Marriott Hotel, which Erika had mentioned as an easy-to-find land-
mark. He turned up the hill past the Marriott and found a parking
space in front of the sprawling hilltop complex of the Linden Hill
Hotel.

Macimer had once attended a law enforcement conference at
the hotel. Quickly reviewing his memory of the layout, he headed
away from the main entrance toward a separate large building off
to the left, housing a private tennis club, open to hotel guests and
members only.

Inside the entrance Macimer was stopped by a deeply tanned

fugitive from a seaside lifeguard station. He stopped flexing his muscles when he stared at Macimer's credentials.

"Nothing to worry about," Macimer said. "I'm meeting someone here. If anyone asks for me, I'll be in the locker room."

"Yes, sir," the disconcerted young man said.

Macimer walked quickly through the locker room, emerged at the far side of the courts area and immediately spotted what he was looking for: a fire exit with panic hardware, opening only from the inside.

He glanced back across the huge open floor, past the busy courts with their scurrying, white-clad figures in shorts, toward the entrance. No one in street clothes was visible. The attendant was out of sight.

Macimer stepped outside and moved immediately into the cover of a grove of trees behind the building.

Five minutes later, certain that he had not been spotted, he walked past the pool area behind the Pook's Hill Lodge and used a back entrance to reach the lobby. Through the front windows he could see the upper floors of the Linden Hill Hotel, only a quarter mile away.

The Pook's Hill Lodge was large, expensive, more an apartment hotel than an overnight stop, catering to those with large expense accounts. As Macimer crossed the lobby toward the elevators he could feel the sweat on his face and body drying from the air-conditioned chill. He wondered if he would have been sweating anyway, even without his brief run through the woods, on his way to an unexpected meeting with a beautiful woman.

"Paul! Thank God!" Erika had cried when he telephoned the number she had left on answer-phone's tape. "I was afraid I'd missed you—or you wouldn't call back."

"I just got home. What is it, Erika?"

"I have to see you."

To his dismay there had been a small leap of excitement. "This isn't a very good time, Erika—"

"Paul, I *must* talk to you!" The anxiety in her voice reached him clearly. This was no casual phone call. He remembered that she had been in the lounge at Hogate's the night he waited for the man who called himself Antonelli. Coincidence, surely. Or perhaps he didn't want to believe otherwise.

"What's it about, Erika?"

"You know . . . you must know. Paul, it has to be tonight."

There was something definitely wrong with her voice. Anxiety, yes. Or had she simply been drinking the evening away? He was unsure of her and of himself, suspicious of his own swift marshaling of arguments for responding to her plea. Because he did want to.

"Where are you, Erika? This isn't your home number."

"In Bethesda. It's called the Pook's Hill Lodge. Just over the hill from the Linden Hill Hotel. You can come right up, Paul, number 1115. I'll be waiting . . ."

You must know.

What did he know?

The elevator enveloped his overheated body in cold, as if he had stepped into a refrigerator. The day had been one of the hottest of the year but he had hardly noticed the heat most of the time; he was conscious of it now by contrast. The elevator hummed upward in soft cool silence, stopping gently at the eleventh floor. The doors opened with a barely audible hiss.

Wide, softly illuminated corridor, carpeting about two inches deep, Van Luit papers on the walls, a hush like that of an old church. He found 1115 and knocked. There was a tiny peephole in the door at eye level. He sensed rather than saw an eye peering out at him, then heard a bolt shoot back. The door flew open.

"Paul!" It was an exclamation, as if she had not quite believed he would come. "Come in, come in . . ."

The living room was large, with floor-to-ceiling windows at the far end opening onto a private balcony and a view of city lights. The thick white carpeting, casement draperies, modern furnishings were all quietly but insistently expensive, chosen by a decorator for effect rather than because someone liked them.

"One of the perks of living at the top," Erika Halbig said, following the direction of his gaze toward the long windows. She answered a question in his eyes before he spoke. "It belongs to a friend of mine. She's in the country for the summer—everyone who is *anyone* leaves this city for the summer. She asked me to look in once in a while." Erika laughed lightly, nervously. "So you see, we're quite alone."

Macimer looked full at her, catching the nervousness in her eyes as well as her voice. Why was *she* nervous?

"What is it, Erika? You said it was important."

She laughed again, and the tip of her tongue flicked over her lips, moistening them. "Yes, I did, didn't I? You're really not making it easy, Paul. Would you like a drink?" The question might have been a sudden inspiration. "I'm one or two ahead of you. What is it—Bourbon on ice?"

"That'll be fine."

She was more than one or two ahead. The smell of gin mingled with a tantalizing fragrance as she brushed past him toward a wet bar. Watching her splash whiskey over ice cubes, then spill Beefeater's gin over the ice in her own empty glass without measuring, he asked himself if she was acting like someone bringing him an important message, someone putting a friendly, civilized face on an ugly secret.

Quite suddenly he knew that she was not. Her manner was almost coquettish. Her dress—a plum-colored chemise with a miniskirt, the soft, flowing, silklike fabric clinging to her body as if charged with static electricity—was calculatingly provocative.

Carrying her drink over to a white sofa, she curled her legs under her as she sat in a corner. "Don't look so surprised, Paul, you must have known. And for heaven's sake, sit down!"

He smiled as he dropped into a chair facing her, a chrome-and-glass cocktail table between them. "What must I have known, Erika?"

"Why I asked you here, of course." The nervousness was still evident, but there was vulnerability as well, nervousness become anxiety. He found it astonishing in so flawlessly perfect a creature that she could feel vulnerable, unsure of herself. "How long has it been, Paul?"

"How long?"

"Since you first knew you wanted me."

He stared at her, startled but at the same time oddly relieved that they would not have to play any complicated games. And he didn't have to worry tonight about the Brea file.

"If the truth be known," he murmured.

"Yes, the truth," she said brightly. "By all means, the truth."

"It must be the same for every man you meet," he said.

"I'm not asking every man. I'm asking you."

"You're a very desirable woman, Erika, and I'm not made of stone. But . . ." He glanced away from her, taking a deep breath, letting the new tension which had replaced his own earlier nervousness have its way. Then he thought with sudden force of Jan.

He scooped his drink from the table in front of him and took a deep swallow, ice clicking against his teeth.

"What's wrong?"

"The usual." His smile was rueful, almost apologetic. "We both have . . . other obligations."

"Oh, Paul. Dear, dear Paul." She placed her glass on the table and stood very carefully, as if she weren't quite certain how steady she was. Then she walked slowly over to him. "No one believes in that one man–one woman thing anymore. Surely you don't think Jan does!"

"If she doesn't, she puts on a good act." Macimer smiled. "I suppose it sounds as if we came here from another planet."

"I think it's kind of nice . . . but not very practical. I mean . . . nothing lasts. Not like that." Her fingers toyed with the deep scoop of her neckline, drawing his gaze. The silken fabric defined the precise shape of her nipples. "Do you wonder why the lady keeps herself slightly sozzled with dependable old Beefeater's?"

"Last time we met, I got the idea that Russ leaves you alone too much."

"He leaves me alone even when he's with me. I'm not important enough for him even to find out who I am or what I think. I'm not an empty-headed porcelain doll, Paul, something you put on a shelf and dust off when company's coming. And I'm not proper old Elaine, either, the charming hostess who always said the proper thing and evidently never sweated." Erika's hip was pressing against Macimer's shoulder. Her hand came to rest lightly at the base of his neck. "You're sweating, Paul. I like that."

Staring up at her, feeling the heavy beat of his pulse, the small burning spot where her hip leaned against him, the feathery tips of her fingers teasing the back of his neck, he thought how lame and even ridiculous his protest about marital obligations had sounded. What Erika said was true. Fidelity was now a subject of humor, seriously discussed by a public television panel as a naïve twentieth-century American invention, like the motorcar.

"You're here, Paul—and I'm here. Jan isn't. This has nothing to do with her. She'll never even know."

"I will." He wondered how she knew that Jan was away. Russ Halbig did. Agents had been following him wherever he went.

"Is that so terrible?" Erika laughed, and he heard again the nervousness beneath the throaty promise of her laugh. "This could be a night to remember."

"Erika, that's a line from a bad play."

Suddenly she sank to her knees before him. "Paul, *look at me!* Am I so easy to reject? Forget about Jan, forget about Russ! Forget about being that damned gentlemanly, soft-spoken, shoes-shined FBI man for once." She reached behind her back and did something to the chemise. It slipped from her shoulders and drifted downward slowly, as if reluctant to release the flawless breasts. When it was around her waist Erika lifted her face toward his. He was startled to see tears in her eyes. "What do I have to do, Paul? Beg? I will, you know, if that's what you want."

The impulse came from a tangle of desire and embarrassment and the need to comfort her, to reassure her that she was indeed beautiful and important. He reached for her as he stumbled awkwardly to his feet, pulling her up with him. Her dress collapsed around her feet. He was not surprised to find that she wore nothing else. As his arms embraced her she pressed feverishly against him, warm delicious curves and parted lips and sleek skin of youth, as eager as a girl in an adolescent's fantasy, breathlessly murmuring in his ear, "Say it, Paul! You want me, too. I know you do. I've always known."

Too eager, he thought. Too sudden. Too timely.

He pushed her away in a spasm of self-disgust. How predictable he had been! How eager to come running when Erika beckoned!

His words were harsh. For a moment he had wanted to strike her. "Did Russ put you up to this? Was I supposed to talk to you afterward or what? How much did he tell you about the file?"

He saw the answer in the leap of fear in her eyes. Panic had no reason to be there unless his guess was accurate. "What . . . what are you talking about, Paul?" she faltered. "What's wrong? What did I do?"

"I think that's obvious." He reached down for the dress on the floor. It weighed about as much as a sigh. "Here, it's cold in this place. You'd better put this back on. Tell him you did your best."

At the door, feeling like a man who has just reached the far side of a minefield, he said, "You don't have to tell him this, but your best is damned good. You didn't make it easy for me either." He smiled grimly. "There'll be times when I'll probably kick myself, but I'll survive. I guess we both will."

Her stricken, naked image pursued him along the silent corridor.

24

Linda was released from the hospital at eleven o'clock Friday morning, less than two hours before the scheduled departure of United flight 27 for Phoenix by way of Dallas. Macimer drove directly from the hospital to Dulles International. "I've packed everything on your list," he told his daughter on the way. "And anything else I could think of that you might need."

She nodded indifferently.

"If I've forgotten anything, you'll just have to go shopping in Phoenix," he said lightly.

"Just like that?"

"Just like that."

Instead of responding she gazed out the car window. He was disturbed by the lack of response, the dull eyes, the absence of normal excitement over a cross-country flight.

In spite of its size the Dulles terminal was crowded and noisy. When they got through the baggage check and reached the waiting area, they were a half hour early. Macimer sat with his daughter and tried to talk to her. Her responses continued to be limited to monosyllables and shrugs.

In desperation Macimer said, "I know it makes everything seem senseless, what happened to Carole. I don't think there's anything that's harder to accept than the idea that none of us really counts for anything, you or Carole or anyone else. So there are a couple things I want you to think about. Maybe they won't help, but think about them. One is that you do matter—to me, to your mother, to Kevin and Chip, to your friends, your grandparents, a great many other people. Especially to us, your own family. The other thing is that what happened with that truck wasn't a senseless, meaningless accident. The driver of that truck deliberately forced you off the road."

"I know!" Linda whispered fiercely. To his relief the veil fell away from her eyes. Her face was angry, but alive. *Stay angry,* he thought. "Why did he do it? That's what I don't understand!"

"I think I know," Macimer said quietly. "I can't go into details, but it's very probable that the driver of that truck was someone involved in an FBI investigation—someone Carole had seen."

Linda's eyes grew round. "That's weird!" She took a moment to digest this revelation before asking, "What's it all about? Is he some kind of terrorist the FBI is after?"

"Yes." It was a good word for Brea, Macimer thought. "I wish I could tell you more, Linda. I can't, not right now. But what I want you to try to understand is that what happened wasn't blind chance."

"Carole is still dead." The girl winced at the word. "Nothing changes that."

"No . . . nothing changes that."

Before any more could be said an announcement over the public address system caught their attention. "United flight 27, for Dallas and Phoenix, now boarding at Gate 3. Please have your boarding passes ready."

The shuttle vehicle that ferried passengers from the terminal to the waiting 727 aircraft was standing by. There was the usual flurry of activity at the departure gate, the usual crowding, the usual hasty goodbyes. "Have your mother call me as soon as you arrive," Macimer said.

"Hey, I'll get there. You're not trying to make me afraid of flying, are you?"

Macimer smiled. At least he had succeeded in breaking her silence. "I just want to talk to her. She was asleep when I called last night to say when you were coming. I only talked to your grandmother."

The line was thinning out at the gate as the bulk of the passengers found seats on the shuttle bus. Macimer was telling Linda again to let him know if there was anything else she might need in

Arizona when she interrupted him. "Daddy, that's you they're calling!"

"What?"

"On the loudspeaker. Listen!"

When the announcement was repeated Macimer heard it clearly. "Telephone for Mr. Paul Macimer. Please report to the information desk on the lower level."

Macimer frowned. The WFO knew where he was. Had something come up? An emergency that couldn't wait?

"Go ahead, Daddy, I'm okay. Maybe it's important."

"Whatever it is, it can wait until you're aboard."

"Hey, I'm getting on in a minute. Maybe it's Mom. Isn't she the only one who knows this is where to find you right this minute?"

Macimer grinned affectionately. "You should be the detective. Okay, wait as long as you can before you get on the shuttle. I'll try to get back before you leave."

"It's all right, it really is."

He kissed her quickly, before she had a chance to turn away, catching her by surprise. "Okay. Take care, punkin."

"I will if you promise not to call me that." For the first time that morning she was smiling.

She was going to be all right, he told himself.

Macimer hurried across the wide floor of the terminal, dodging a spill of passengers arriving through another gate. Before stepping onto the escalator that led to the lower level he glanced back. Linda was at the tag end of a dwindling line before her departure gate.

He ran down the moving steps. At the information desk he identified himself and was directed toward a nearby telephone booth. He snatched up the instrument. "This is Macimer."

"Paul Macimer?" The man's voice was muffled, vaguely familiar.

"That's right. Who is this?"

"There's something for you at the Hertz counter."

"What? What's this all about?"

The line went dead.

Macimer felt a puzzled apprehension. He knew when he had last heard that voice.

The auto rental counters were bunched to one side of the escalators. They were brightly lit and sleekly plastic, with girls to match behind the counters. There were two pretty young women behind the Hertz counter. One was a blonde, a slightly plumper version of Erika Halbig.

"Yes, sir, may I help you?" Her teeth were so white and even they looked like caps.

"There's supposed to be a message or something for me. Macimer. Paul Macimer."

The girl's mouth formed a small, soundless *O*. She peered under the counter, her smooth forehead wrinkling in a frown of concentration. The wrinkles smoothed out abruptly. "Here we are, Mr. Macimer!"

It was a gray envelope, about six by nine inches in size. His name had been printed on the front with a felt-tip marker in large, bold letters. Macimer thanked the Hertz girl and left the counter. He paused in a quiet corner to one side of the escalators. As he felt the thickness of the envelope, an instinctive caution prompted him to probe gently with his fingertips, searching for any unnatural bulges or the presence of wires. There were none. A letter bomb delivered in such a fashion seemed wildly improbable, but no more melodramatic than Timothy Callahan's death.

Inside the envelope were a half-dozen glossy photographs. The focus had not been perfect and the images were grainy, but they were clear enough for their purpose.

More than clear enough, Macimer thought with chagrin. From the top photo Erika Halbig stared at him. The expression on her face was eager.

This picture had been taken from an angle looking over Macimer's shoulder, revealing his back and Erika's head and shoulders. She appeared to be looking directly into the camera's lens. Two other photographs had been taken from the same camera position. In one of them Macimer had turned slightly toward the side. Erika's arms were reaching around his neck, and her nude figure was plainly visible, pressing against him.

The remaining three pictures had been shot by another camera, apparently positioned high on the wall behind the white sofa in the Pook's Hill apartment. In each of these there was a full view of the naked woman in the arms of the fully clothed man.

No problem identifying either of the principals, Macimer thought. And he certainly didn't appear to be fighting her off, even if he did still have his clothes on.

He slid the photographs back into the gray envelope, feeling the heat in his face. Anger was rising, dominating the confused tumult of guilt and disgust and dismay.

He had been set up for blackmail by one of the oldest ruses of all, modern only in the sophisticated deployment of at least two sequence cameras—there were time lapses of an undetermined number of seconds between pictures—in the living room of the borrowed apartment. Other cameras, no doubt, had been positioned in the bedroom, carefully focused on the bed.

Macimer shook himself. The shock of the photographs had momentarily blotted out everything else. Even Linda.

He ran up the steps, bypassing the crowded escalator, taking the steps two and three at a time. Hurrying across the main level of the terminal, he saw that the crowd in the United waiting area for the Dallas–Phoenix flight had dispersed completely. The area was empty except for a single male flight attendant at the reception desk.

Macimer sought him out. He was young and handsome, his sculptured features those of a male model in a men's fashion advertisement. "My daughter was boarding your flight 27 for Phoenix."

"Yes, sir, those passengers are boarding the plane now."

From the nearby expanse of windows Macimer stared across the hot tarmac. The last of the passengers from the shuttle bus were disappearing into the plane. He squinted against the glare. A slim young woman stepped from the bus into the plane. Not Linda. Macimer himself had picked out the gray slacks Linda was wearing. The woman he saw wore a skirt.

He went back to the counter in the waiting area. This time the attendant was less patient. He had folded up his clipboard and closed down the station. Macimer reached into his right-hand coat pocket with his left hand and produced the wallet containing his FBI badge and credentials. "I want to make sure my daughter is on that plane," he said firmly. "Her name is Linda Macimer."

"Yes, sir." Flustered, the young man checked the flight sheet. "She checked in."

"Are all the passengers aboard?"

"There's only one missing, a Mr. Samuelson for Dallas. All the others are accounted for."

Satisfied, Macimer thanked him and went back to the windows

facing the runways. He waited until the plane eventually taxied slowly toward its assigned ramp. Five minutes later, as United flight 27 climbed steeply and began to bank in a wide turn toward the southwest, Macimer headed for his car in the parking lot. It was brutally hot inside the car and he thought of the men who had him under surveillance, wondering if they had waited in the hot sun as they had the day before, not risking a quick departure on his part that would leave them stranded.

Driving back toward Washington, he watched the road behind him. The divided highway was almost completely flat for long stretches. Traffic was heavier than on Friday, and he was unable to spot a tail.

At the Washington Field Office, Macimer once again reviewed the plans for that night's surveillance of the suspect Molter, glanced at the summary reports Jerry Russell had prepared for him on the general case load and went over the Brea case reports with Harrison Stearns. Nothing from Headquarters, he noted. No new directives, no summons to appear, not even a query about developments from the Director.

As soon as possible Macimer isolated himself in his office, told Willa Cunningham to hold any but the most urgent calls, and slowly read the summary report he had asked Agent Stearns to compile covering all known developments in the Brea affair. There was nothing in the review to surprise him; he had not expected any fresh revelations. What he was looking for was an overall perspective on the case, the appearance of a pattern, a way to reconcile elements that refused to go together. There was madness in Brea's actions. How could that madness be part of the cool calculations of a widespread conspiracy of silence and suppression of evidence?

Macimer had never believed in the national post-Watergate paranoia about the government and everyone in it, a galloping cynicism that judged all politicians as venal or incompetent, and viewed agencies such as the CIA and the FBI as monster legions. What disturbed him more than anything else about the Brea file was that it reinforced all that distrust. No matter that the case was an aberration. There were over eight thousand FBI agents, men and women, and Macimer knew you would have a hard time finding even a handful among them who thought their FBI shields gave them a license to trample over the rights and lives of ordinary citizens. And Macimer had been stunned to discover there was even one who would commit murder to cover up his own betrayal of trust. Excesses of zeal there had been, disastrous errors of judgment for which the Bureau had justifiably taken its lumps, even the dirty tricks of COINTELPRO—but all of it together didn't add up to a single murder, much less Brea's record of carnage and betrayal.

The thought of dirty tricks reminded Macimer of the envelope delivered to him at the airport. Those photographs might be all that was needed to destroy an already shaky marriage. Macimer believed that Jan was close to leaving him. One glimpse of those pictures might force that decision, shattering the bonds forged over twenty years. Especially if Jan were to learn that the rendezvous documented so vividly in the photographs had taken place the very day Macimer had talked her, against her will, into leaving for Phoenix.

Macimer was a little surprised to discover that he felt no animosity toward Erika. He felt sorry for her. Like himself, she had been used. She had acted willingly enough, perhaps, but the idea had not been hers. It was Russ Halbig who inspired Macimer's contempt. Who else could have used Erika in a crude blackmail scheme?

But if Halbig had tried to set Macimer up for blackmail to keep him silent, how could a conspiracy theory be avoided?

Trying to understand Halbig's role in the Brea affair, Macimer could only conclude that Halbig had become a participant in the cover-up after the fact, in order to further his own ambitions. Certainly Halbig had not been directly involved in the destruction of the People's Revolutionary Committee. For one thing, he had been in Washington at the time. For another, the PRC massacre was not his kind of operation. It had been dangerously tricky, its ramifications unpredictable, its success by no means certain, its potential for disastrous exposure too great. Halbig might be capable of putting the Bureau above the truth and even above the law. He might willingly exploit his wife's beauty and desirability to gain his ends. But he was not a risk taker. That role was out of character. *Halbig will always find a way to dodge the raindrops.*

Was Halbig then acting on Brea's behalf, part of a conspiracy that went so high in the Bureau that its resources—including agents to keep Macimer under surveillance—could be manipulated to serve Brea's purposes?

There was only one man who ranked over Halbig, one man who commanded total loyalty, one man whose favor would advance or protect Halbig's career enough to justify the apparent risks he was now taking.

But Macimer found the suspicion that John Landers was Brea— or had directed the Brea operation against the PRC—unbelievable. It did violence to everything he had known of Landers' character and career.

Frustrated, Macimer stared at the mottled-glass panel in his office door. The answers he sought were as murky as the details of the outer office beyond that glass. He remained baffled by incongruities. Struck once more by the fact that, although Brea had used others in peripheral actions, such as the three Cubans who had terrorized Macimer's family and brutally beaten Joseph Gerella, in each of those moments in which Brea's own lethal hand was visible, he had acted alone.

Not a band of conspirators, Macimer thought. One man out of control. A trained killer.

And what was he planning next? If he believed that Macimer was holding documents that incriminated him, and if he was prepared to try blackmail to get them, why hadn't he made his demands? What was he waiting for? And what other pressures would he try to bring to bear?

He would stop at nothing, Macimer knew. The cage door could not be closed again. It was too late for that.

"It's not there," Lenny Collins said.

"What's not there?"

"Macimer's name. Look for yourself. He never registered here."

"Let me see that. Are you sure you've got the right date?"

They were in a storage room behind the office in the High 5 Motel, located on Interstate 5 just north of Fresno, California. The register Collins had dug out of a cardboard storage file covered the period from April 1, 1981, to September 30 of the same year. Collins pointed at the handwritten date at the top of the page to which the register was opened: August 28, 1981.

"He never registered," Collins said again.

"That doesn't mean anything—"

"It's what we're looking for. Somebody who wasn't where he was supposed to be that day. Whatever Brea is afraid of in the missing file has to be something like this, something small and ordinary and easily overlooked."

"Macimer could have made an arrangement with the motel manager so he didn't have to register."

"According to his own daily report, he registered here and waited in the room for two hours for this informant who never showed up."

Garvey stood and opened the back door of the stifling little storage room and stared out across a field of strawberries in neat, orderly, endless rows. Twenty-five or thirty workers in the field were bent over the plants in a posture almost as old as man, laboriously hand-picking the berries.

"That's why he gave us those orders to report only to him," Collins said, his tone flat, speaking to Garvey's stubborn back.

"I don't believe it."

"Personal feelings have nothing to do with this—"

"You've got to decide who to trust," Garvey said. "Why would Macimer have started us digging into these assignments if he knew he was only going to expose himself?"

"He didn't have a choice. He couldn't postpone it any longer." Because this wasn't convincing, Collins added, "He didn't think we'd get this far, or maybe he didn't think the new management would have kept these old registers. The place changed hands a year ago."

"Keep going," Garvey said. "You haven't started to make sense yet."

Collins joined him in the doorway, still carrying the dusty register. Like Garvey he found his gaze drawn across the open field to the stooped figures of the pickers. They seemed not to have changed position since he first saw them. "There, but for the grace of God, and Abraham Lincoln," Collins murmured. "Okay, Garv, what's your theory? What's bugging you?"

"Maybe the register has been tampered with."

"To frame Macimer?" Collins scoffed. "That's reaching."

"Maybe. But the former manager of this place stayed on after it was sold until March this year. Then he suddenly quit and moved away, leaving no forwarding address. Don't you think that's strange?"

"What's strange? Motel managers aren't the most steady lot."

"I don't like the coincidence," Garvey persisted. "There's someone we could question about the register and even about Macimer. And he's nowhere to be found. I think we should find out where he is, and talk to him. And we ought to have the lab look at this register. At least analyze the pages for the twenty-seventh, twenty-eighth and twenty-ninth of August 1981. The paper and the ink."

Collins was silent a moment, considering the bent backs of the field workers. The sun was an egg frying in a polished skillet. "I'll give you this much," he said. "Those pages are removable, so it could've been done. I'll go along with you that far. But we also do one more thing."

"What's that?" Garvey asked, knowing the answer.

"We send a report to Headquarters on what we've found. Marked urgent."

25

There were two calls clocked on Macimer's answer-phone. The first caller had hung up without responding to his tape-recorded greeting. The second was Erika Halbig. "Paul? This is Erika. I know what you think, and I'm sorry. There are some things you don't know . . ." She sounded distraught, her voice rising to a high, keen edge. "Paul, please call me! It's important! I'm still at the Pook's Hill apartment, but you don't have to worry about anyone else listening. Not now."

Not now.

He resisted a feeling of compassion. Vivid memory of Erika sinking to her knees before him, the very image of passionate imploring—properly positioned for the nearest camera lens.

But his skepticism failed to silence curiosity. He replayed Erika's message. This time, attending only to her voice, not the words, he heard an almost inaudible quivering, like the tremor of a wire stretched too tight. Was it merely fine-tuned acting, like the previous night's performance, or was she genuinely distressed?

Like a wire about to break, he thought.

He picked up the phone and dialed the number of the Pook's Hill apartment. He let it ring for a long time before hanging up.

At three minutes past seven o'clock that evening, while Macimer was slipping a plastic envelope containing frozen chipped beef into the top of a double boiler, Jan's call came. Just after five o'clock Phoenix time; Linda's plane had arrived on schedule. He heard Jan's voice with mingled pleasure and relief. Then she asked sharply, "What happened, Paul? Where's Linda?"

An invisible hand caught him by the throat. "What do you mean? I put her on the one o'clock United flight. Has it been delayed?"

"No, I was there to meet her. She wasn't on board." Macimer heard the quick catch of Jan's breath. "Did you see her get on the plane?"

"I watched it take off," Macimer said, hearing the lie of omission in the words. *I was downstairs looking at some photos of Erika Halbig and myself when I should have been watching Linda until she was safely on the plane.*

"Then something happened afterward. Oh my God, Paul, where is she?"

"Now take it easy. She could have got off in Dallas—there was a layover." He knew he was grasping at straws. "Are you sure you met the right plane? Flight 27?"

"Of course I'm sure!"

He stalled, fighting his own panic. Linda would have had no reason to get off the plane in Dallas unless she was running away, and he didn't believe that. At Dulles he had been momentarily uneasy about the timing of the message that took him away from the departure gate, but the shock and anger aroused by the photographs had sidetracked him. And he had been too ready to accept the flight attendant's reassurances that Linda was on board, that only one male passenger was missing from the passenger list.

Someone else had flown in her place.

But how had she been lured away? By another message? The attendant would have been aware of any disturbance. And Macimer's FBI credentials would have been enough to alert the attendant if he had noticed anything unusual near the gate.

"Paul, are you there? Answer me!"

"I'm here, honey."

"Why would anyone want to hurt Linda? Does it have anything to do with Carole? Is this what you were afraid of?"

"We don't know for sure that anything has happened—"

"Don't patronize me, Paul! You're not telling me the truth! You know more than you're saying."

"I'll see what I can find out from the airline," he said, trying to sound calm. "I'll get back to you as soon as I can. Go back to your parents' place and stay there, so I know where to reach you. And . . . try not to worry."

"That's easy for you to say." The familiar line was caustic rather than humorous, but his reassuring tone had had some effect.

"Not as easy as you think."

Airport and airline security is dominated by former Special Agents of the Federal Bureau of Investigation. At almost every major U.S. airline, the security director and his top administrators and investigators are former FBI men. They form a loose "Old Boy Network" which Macimer had sometimes found valuable during investigations.

A United investigator stationed in Phoenix confirmed the fact that the passenger listed as Linda Macimer had been on the plane all the way through to Phoenix. Macimer asked about the flight attendants who had worked the coach section. Two of them, he learned, had caught another plane to Los Angeles, due in at L.A. International within a few minutes.

Another former agent named Frank Murphy was now with United security in Los Angeles. Macimer had once worked with Murphy in the Atlanta office. "You still chasin' stewardesses, Paul?" Murphy asked amiably, when Macimer had told him what he wanted.

"At least I'm not making a career out of it."

Murphy laughed. "That flight from Phoenix just touched down, so the girls should be along in a few minutes. Let me get back to you, okay?"

"Thanks, Murphy. This is important."

"Figured it might be."

Five minutes later Murphy was back on the phone. "I've got the flight attendant you're looking for, Paul, standing right here. Name of Melissa Powell. Let me know if there's anything else I can do."

The young woman sounded tired but cooperative. Macimer explained briefly what he was concerned about. "As far as I know, Linda got on the plane in Washington and she didn't get off in Dallas. But she wasn't on the plane when it landed in Phoenix. My wife was there to meet her."

"We had a full house," Melissa Powell said dubiously. "I don't remember any no-shows. It was one of our economy coach runs, and they're usually full up." She broke off a moment. "Wait a minute . . . yes, there was one man who didn't fly. But that was the only empty seat until we got to Dallas."

"Try to remember, Miss Powell. I know it's asking a lot with so many passengers to take care of, but . . . Linda is seventeen, slim, about one hundred and ten pounds, five feet six, wore gray slacks and a blue knit pullover with a cowl neckline."

"Doesn't ring any bells, Mr. Macimer. Hey, just a sec—Linda! I remember now. Got on at the last minute at Dulles. I remember thinking that Linda was right for her, you know, but her last name wasn't, and she wasn't wearing a gold band."

"I don't follow you."

"She was Mexican, I think. Long black hair and those deep brown eyes. Does that sound like your daughter, Mr. Macimer?"

"No. Linda has ash-blond hair, shoulder length, and blue eyes."

"I'm sorry, sir. I could be wrong, but . . . I don't recall anyone like that. And I do remember the Mexican girl was called Linda. I don't suppose that helps."

"Maybe it does," said Macimer. Was it too farfetched to presume that the slim young girl who had taken part in the robbery at his house and the beating of Joe Gerella had been enlisted in one more of Brea's maneuvers?

"There is one other thing," Melissa Powell said. "She wasn't alone. There was a young man with her, in the next seat. I think he was Mexican too."

One of the agents on night duty at the FBI Resident Agent's office at Dulles International answered Macimer's call. Five minutes later he was back on the phone, having obtained a copy of the passenger list for the United Dallas–Phoenix flight 27 that afternoon. Linda Macimer had been assigned seat Y66 on the aisle. The passenger in the seat immediately adjoining hers was listed as Francisco Perez.

Francisco Xavier Perez was one of the three names on the list Agents Rodriguez and Singleton had come up with, the names of three young Cuban refugees who fitted the profile which had evolved from a semen stain found on a sheet in Macimer's bedroom.

Jerry Russell, the ASAC, was still in the Washington Field

Office. Macimer told him what he wanted: FBI Headquarters to be notified that the two suspects had flown to Phoenix. The Phoenix office to be asked to begin an immediate search. The U.S. Border Patrol to be alerted in the event that the two Cubans tried to escape into Mexico. And Agents Rodriguez and Singleton to catch the first available plane to Phoenix to participate in the apprehension of the fugitives.

"I'll get right on it," Russell said. "But we have something else going, too—I've been trying to reach you but your line was busy." He hesitated a moment and Macimer realized that he sounded worried. "Molter has disappeared from his apartment. We had the surveillance set up for tonight, but he's gone. Taliaferro is trying to find out when he left. We think he's running."

Russell was a fine number two man, Macimer thought, one of the best ASACs around, but he didn't like having all the responsibility on his own shoulders.

"That means the surveillance is blown," Macimer said. "How?"

"We don't know. But there's been talk about a leak out of the New York office. When we called them to follow Molter last week, that could have opened it up. Before that Molter wasn't suspicious, just careful."

Macimer made the decision. "Tell Taliaferro to move in and search the apartment with a warrant. Alert both of the airport RA's—Molter may try to get to his friends in New York. And get right on to the desk super in Internal Security who's been handling this case, Jerry—Headquarters will want to coordinate this one all the way. Recommend that Alexandria move in fast on the print shop and shut it down."

"You want me to call Headquarters?" Russell sounded surprised.

"Yours isn't the only case that's breaking," Macimer said. "I need to keep my phone open."

He didn't elaborate but it wasn't necessary. Jerry Russell got the message. There was a moment's silence before Russell said, apologetically, "I'm sorry we blew it with Molter."

"We can't win 'em all. Anyway, it's a long way from a total loss. We're closing down an information leak in ERDA. We're shutting down a drop in Alexandria and we may catch a few fish in that net if we close it up fast enough. And we're getting another possible line on the leak out of New York. We've been after that one for a long time." Macimer paused. "You stay on the Molter case, Jerry. Get hold of Harrison Stearns and pull him in. I want him on the desk in the Special squad room. Brief him on what's happening in Phoenix."

"You want him all night?"

"If necessary."

The house was on Tracy Place in the prestigious Kalorama section of the District, close to Georgetown and Foggy Bottom, minutes from downtown Washington. The area was hilly, the old streets too narrow, the houses gracefully weathered. The house Russell Halbig sought was of gray stone, almost hidden behind a high wrought-iron fence and even higher hedges. The decorative iron gates were open, and the shallow circular drive was crowded with cars.

Halbig rang the bell and heard distant chimes. The door was opened onto a marble-floored foyer by a muscular young man with watchful eyes. The eyes became respectful when they recognized Halbig. "Good evening, sir. Is the Director expecting you?"

"Yes."

"You'll find them in the library."

The library had a high ceiling held up by walls of bookcases, a large fieldstone fireplace, leather furniture, french doors facing a private garden. It was a solid, warm, comfortable room in which John Landers seemed at home. There was a game table in one corner with four chairs upholstered in red leather drawn around it. The air was blue with cigar smoke.

Landers rose from one of the chairs. The other three chairs remained filled. Halbig nodded at Jim Caughey and Frank Magnuson—SAC of the New York Field Office—and stiffened visibly even before the silver-haired fourth man turned.

"You know the senator, I'm sure," John Landers said.

"Yes . . . of course. Good to see you, Senator."

Charles Sederholm smiled expansively and puffed on his Havana. What did his presence mean? Halbig felt the impact of four pairs of eyes all watching him, and he had the sensation of having interrupted a private conversation. Landers, Caughey, Magnuson— and Sederholm. Why was the senator there? And Magnuson, what of him? Was he there because he was in line for a new position of power at Headquarters? These were all big, powerful men of action. The three senior FBI officials had spent most of their careers in the field, and each had at one time or another bossed some of the Bureau's busiest field offices. Sederholm with his bulk was an even more imposing physical presence than the others, and he had the charismatic politician's ability to dominate any group. Confronting four such men Halbig felt oddly diminished.

"I was just filling the senator in on the latest developments in the Brea case," John Landers said. "I thought it was about time." Did he know that Halbig had already briefed Sederholm on the affair? The senator's eyes were hooded, and Landers' expression was unreadable. "Will you have something to drink, Russ? You look as if you could use one."

Landers handed him a stiff scotch over rocks and eyed him appraisingly. "Suppose you tell us the whole story," he said. "I got the gist of it from what you said on the phone, but I'd like you to fill us in on the details." When he saw Halbig's glance stray toward the senator, the Director added, "Under the circumstances I think it's important for everyone here to have the full story. In confidence. Isn't that right, Senator?"

"Of course, Director."

Halbig took a deep swallow of his scotch. What he had to say was a confession of failure. For someone of his rank in the Bureau, failure in his personal life was not something that could be compartmented, kept separate from his Bureau life.

"We've had Macimer under surveillance, as you know," Halbig said. "Last night two agents followed him to Bethesda. He turned up at Pook's Hill and parked in the lot outside the Linden Hill Hotel. Our agents arrived in time to see him enter a private tennis and racquetball club on the grounds. They didn't think it was possible to follow Macimer inside without being spotted. The assumption was that Macimer was a member, or was meeting someone who was a member. He was gone for about thirty-five minutes. The agents had called for a backup car. When Macimer reappeared, one of the cars followed him home. The other agents stayed behind to question attendants in the club." Halbig paused, his throat dry. "Macimer hadn't met anyone. He hadn't used the facility. He had simply walked through it and out a back door. Obviously he knew he was being followed, and he used the tennis club to lose the surveillance." Halbig felt an absurd impulse toward tears. He seemed to be shrinking inside his suit, and he was drenched in sweat.

He told the rest of his story without a break, the four men in the library listening in silence, puffing their cigars. On the assumption that Macimer had come to meet someone in or near the Linden Hill Hotel, the agents spent Friday questioning people at the tennis club and in the hotel. The club's guest and membership lists had been scrutinized, especially those who had been present Friday evening. No link to Macimer could be established. Late in the day the intensive search had focused on the Pook's Hill Lodge, an apartment hotel in the vicinity, and the Marriott, which was back down the hill but an easy walk from the Linden Hill's parking lot. Nothing had come of the questioning until a night clerk had arrived for duty at the Pook's Hill Lodge. He had seen Macimer come into the hotel and take one of the elevators Thursday evening. Because the lodge was a twelve-story building with a large number of permanent and transient residents, it had taken some time to discover which apartment Macimer had visited. The attention of agents was finally drawn to one of the apartments on the eleventh floor whose owner was out of town. The apartment was occasionally visited by a friend of the owner, a woman who looked in on the place while the owner was away.

There was no answer when one of the agents knocked on the door to the apartment. The floor maid produced a key . . .

Halbig's voice broke. "If the agents hadn't entered the apartment when they did . . ." He struggled to finish the statement but choked up. For some time no one spoke. When Halbig at last regained his composure, he said, "As you know, the woman in the apartment was my wife. She was found in the bedroom, unconscious. She had apparently taken an overdose of sleeping pills. An ambulance was summoned and I was notified. And, of course, I immediately telephoned you, Director."

Halbig drained his glass and stared at the ice cubes, as if he might find some meaning in them, like a subliminal message in the illustration for a whiskey advertisement.

"I appreciate how difficult this has been for you," Landers said quietly. "However, without jumping to any conclusions, I think we must ask ourselves if what has happened has any connection with the Brea investigation." He paused. "You've just come from the hospital?"

"Yes." Halbig's response was barely audible.

"How is Erika now?"

"She's out of danger. She's under sedation . . ."

"Good. Perhaps she'll be able to tell us more in the morning, if not before. In the meanwhile, if you feel up to it, Russ, perhaps you'll join us for a while. There are some decisions to be made."

There was a long silence. Halbig felt them all watching him, waiting. With an effort he pulled himself together. What surprised him was that his decision was not even difficult, though it went against all of the care and caution and single-minded concern for his own self-interest that had brought him to his present high position in the Bureau. "I don't think you need me to help you with those decisions, Director. And I feel I should be there when Erika wakes up. I *want* to be there. I feel . . . responsible for what has happened."

There it was. Now the Director would also see him as diminished, unreliable, a man who went to pieces in a crisis. Halbig's vision dimmed. He nodded toward the three blurred figures around the game table and at Landers.

The Director stopped him. "I understand, Russ, you should be there. Besides, what she has to say may be important. But before you go, I'd like your feel for this situation. You know Macimer and everyone else involved. But I don't think you know about the report from Agent Collins—it came in to Headquarters a short while ago by teletype." Landers tersely described what the two agents working on the investigation in California had learned at the motel outside Fresno. "In the light of everything else, do you think that means what it seems to mean?"

Halbig thought of Macimer's visit to the Pook's Hill Lodge where Erika had gone, where she had been during the past twenty-four hours while he worried, not knowing where she had gone. A man who was capable of one kind of betrayal was surely capable of another. And yet . . .

Landers was waiting. He wanted an honest answer. Not a jealous husband's bitter accusation, not a wild guess. Halbig said, "I'm not sure. Something about it . . . it's too pat. And too stupid a mistake for Macimer to make if he *wasn't* in Fresno that day, three years ago. I'm just not sure."

There was a glint in John Landers' eyes that Halbig couldn't read. "Neither am I," the Director said. "Good night, Russ . . . and thanks for coming."

The room was silent after Halbig walked out, as if the four men were waiting for the remote sound of the front door closing behind him. When it did, John Landers said enigmatically, "Perhaps I was wrong about him." No one knew exactly what he meant. Then Landers shook off a scowl and resumed his place at the poker table. "It may be a long night, gentlemen. We might as well make good use of it. I believe it's your deal, Senator."

Charles Sederholm smiled blandly, his big hands deftly scooping up the cards and shuffling them with machinelike precision. "Party time's over, so you'd all better count your chips. It's time for a man's game."

Macimer waited, a prisoner of the silent telephone. He knew that, sooner or later, a call would come. A call from Brea.

He stayed close to the phone, drinking hot coffee and going over the events of recent weeks, since the night he was called to the scene of a stolen FBI vehicle recovery, the first time he had ever seen Brea's name. The logic of events all along had argued the possibility of a large-scale conspiracy involving key figures in the Bureau, possibly even the Director himself. Something stubborn in Macimer continued to resist that logic.

Not a conspiracy. One man gone bad.

Who had kidnapped Linda.

There could be only one reason.

From the kitchen came a moaning sound, followed by an intermittent squeal that mimicked a puppy's cry. Macimer listened for a moment before he identified the labored moan and following squeal as coming from the refrigerator. With the arrival of hot weather the refrigerator was struggling. One of these days the fan motor would burn out.

Macimer gave a rueful shake of his head. The everyday trivia of living had a way of intruding upon the gravest crisis. What did it matter if some food spoiled in the refrigerator?

He felt jittery from too much coffee. Pushing his mug away, he slowly crossed the family room, carefully stepping around furniture in the darkness. Earlier he had turned off all the lights. Standing by the sliding glass doors, he stared out at the deep shadows that made of the familiar yard a mysterious cave with dark, threatening pockets. It occurred to him that someone could easily be watching him from those shadows. Someone who had killed and killed again to hide an ugly secret. In recent weeks Macimer had seen one man blown up, another drowned, a woman brutally sacrificed. But he did not fear for his own life.

Not yet. No bullet would fly from the shadows for him as long as Brea thought he had Vernon Lippert's file. And that could be the only reason for taking Linda hostage.

There were many ways to threaten a man with a wife and children. That was why Macimer had wanted Jan and the kids safely out of the way. His instincts had been accurate, he simply hadn't been quick enough. Now Brea had Linda.

Now he would call. All Macimer could do was wait.

The game broke up at three in the morning. Jim Caughey was the first to leave. Frank Magnuson, in town from New York, was staying over at the Director's home in one of the guest bedrooms. These two, along with Henry Szymanski and John Landers, would meet again in an emergency executive conference at FBI Headquarters in a few hours.

When Magnuson had gone upstairs Charles Sederholm and Landers were alone in the foyer. "I appreciate your frankness, John," Sederholm said. "In something like this, it's important that the Senate committee isn't kept completely in the dark."

"I agree, Senator," Landers said.

"You understand that there will have to be full public hearings when this thing breaks."

"Understood. And you'll know as soon as it happens."

"I hope that's before Monday. It would be a very effective way to open the hearings."

"I think I can promise you that, Senator."

Sederholm smiled. They were in agreement. Sederholm would have his bombshell to release to the media, live on television. John Landers needn't worry about his confirmation as Director of the FBI. "I don't much care who it is," the senator said. "Just give me Brea's head on a platter by Monday morning."

Landers opened the door for him. Sederholm's chauffeur waited at the foot of the steps, door open to the back seat of a black Lincoln Continental. Sederholm's California constituents might drive Toyotas and Datsuns, but they preferred him to ride in an Ameri-

258 *Louis Charbonneau*

can car. Landers glanced toward the street. The night was quiet. No insomniac reporters lurked outside the gates.

"Good night, Senator. Glad you could come."

"Good night, John. Enjoyed the game."

Landers watched the long black car slide along the driveway and turn onto the quiet street.

Macimer woke suddenly, clammy with sweat, his heart pounding. He lay rigid on the sofa in the family room, where he had dozed off. For a moment he listened intently. Then he fell back.

He had been dreaming. And the cry which had awakened him had not come from a young girl's throat. It was the squeal of the laboring refrigerator.

He sat up, his muscles stiff from lying in an awkward position, an ache at the back of his skull. He stared out the sliding glass door into the yard. The tendrils of the weeping willow trailed downward like a woman's hair. The dark shadows of night were gone.

26

Harrison Stearns, bleary-eyed at his desk in the Special squad room at the Washington Field Office, took the call from Alice Volker early Saturday morning. He checked the time as he logged the call: 7:01 A.M. An efficient woman. She had probably told herself she would call at seven.

"It arrived yesterday afternoon in the mail," the woman said. "We don't have locked boxes, you know, and Mr. Macimer said I should report anything unusual. I tried to call him at home last night but there was just one of the those answer things. I suppose he's away on a case?" she suggested brightly.

"What was unusual about this letter, Mrs. Volker?"

She hesitated. "Well . . . it looks like Raymond's own handwriting. I mean, I recognized it. And the letter is postmarked Monday. It was mailed right here in Washington," she added. "And it took five whole days to get here."

Stearns looked around the squad room, trying to pick out someone to send to Raymond Shoup's boardinghouse. Then he changed his mind. He'd been up all night and needed to get out of the office for some breakfast. Besides, this was something he wanted.

"Is there anything else unusual about the envelope, Mrs. Volker?"

"Well . . . I think there's a key inside."

Monday, Stearns thought. The day Raymond Shoup was killed. Why would he have mailed a key to himself on that particular day?

"I'll be there as soon as I can, Mrs. Volker." His excitement communicated itself as a sense of urgency. "Lock your doors and don't talk to anyone until I get there."

"Do you think . . . I mean, surely no one would . . ." A quaver of fear was audible. Alice Volker had not considered the possibility of danger for herself.

"Someone killed Raymond for what's in that envelope," Stearns said grimly. He knew he was frightening the woman but he wanted to impress on her the importance of not talking to anyone else. "Hide it, and don't open your door. I'll be there in fifteen minutes."

It took him nineteen minutes, and two more to convince Alice Volker through the locked door of her apartment that he was the agent she had talked to.

When he opened the envelope he found a key to a baggage locker at the Greyhound Bus Terminal.

"Mrs. Volker," Harrison Stearns said shakily, "can I use your telephone?"

Macimer's instructions were brief and explicit, his voice calm, but there was an edge to it that Agent Stearns was certain he did not imagine. Like Stearns, Macimer believed this was the break they had been waiting for.

"I can't leave here right now," Macimer said, "but in any event I'll meet you there in an hour, or as close to that as I can make it. Get some breakfast in the meanwhile. And Stearns . . ."

"Yes, sir?"

"Make sure you're alone."

Paul Macimer found himself going through the motions of preparing for another day. A shower, with three minutes under cold water at the end of it to banish the last fuzziness from his brain. A quick shave, listening always for the sound of the telephone. Dressing methodically, thinking about Harrsion Stearns's call and the key in the envelope. Raymond Shoup had foolishly tried to bargain with Brea, holding out his trump card—the missing pieces of the Brea file. What had he told Brea? What mistake had he made to trigger Brea's killing rage?

In the kitchen Macimer had some orange juice, put on a fresh pot of coffee. The file gave him what he needed—something to barter with for Linda's life. Brea seemed to believe that Macimer already had the file. But why hadn't he called?

When the phone in the den finally rang, Macimer's nerves jumped. He ran into the room, snatched up the phone and spoke without thinking, raw nerves and anger exploding. "Is that you, Halbig? If you've hurt Linda, you son of a bitch—"

"Get out of the house," a muffled voice answered sharply. He gave Macimer a phone number, Maryland area code. "Call me from a pay phone. Now!"

The unexpected demand cooled Macimer's rage. After a moment's hesitation he left the house and drove the short distance to the nearby gas station, where he found an empty phone booth. He had a pocketful of dimes and quarters—a veteran FBI agent's habit—more than enough to cover the charges.

When the phone was answered Macimer heard a soft chuckle. "You've got it wrong, Macimer. This isn't Halbig."

"I didn't get the blackmail message wrong. You should have known I wouldn't trade the file for those pictures. I don't care what you do with them."

There was a brief silence before the caller chuckled again. "I didn't think the photos would work, but it was worth a try. I didn't even have to work on Erika very hard. She always had a thing for you."

Macimer felt a twinge of something—suspicion, intuition, a blind hunch. *I didn't have to work on Erika very hard.* That didn't sound like Halbig. The words were not even those of someone carrying out Halbig's orders. They had a boastful, proprietary ring. They were also slightly contemptuous of a woman so easily used.

The voice could have been anyone's. For the first time Macimer sensed that it was not merely muffled, as if a handkerchief had been placed over the mouthpiece; the caller's voice was being electronically altered, disguised beyond recognition.

But it was not Russ Halbig's voice. Someone other than Halbig had used Erika. The truth, more subtle and devious than Macimer had guessed, teased the periphery of his consciousness.

"I figured the photos might not do it," the caller said. "But I have something else you want."

A band of pressure tightened painfully at the back of Macimer's neck. He spoke harshly. "If Linda is harmed in any way, the next time you see that file will be on the front page of the *Post*."

After a moment's silence the caller said, "So you do have it."

"Yes, I've got it."

"All right, we make a deal. That's what we both want. I tell you where to come to find your daughter. You bring the file with you. And come alone." There was a break for emphasis before the filtered voice added, "If you bring anyone else, you won't like what you find."

The threat was more frightening because it was made so calmly. Macimer had to wait before he could trust himself to match that control. Then he said, "You're Brea."

"Could be."

"The price of the file comes too high for me to keep it. You win."

"We both win, Macimer. You don't want that story released any more than I do. That's why you've been sitting on it. That's why you wouldn't give Oliver Packard any fresh dirt to shovel."

"Maybe."

"You know I'm right. So you'll come, and you'll bring the file. And you and your daughter can just walk away clean."

"Tell me where." There was no point in arguing, no point in saying that no one would come away from this affair clean.

Brea chuckled softly. "Uh-uh. No names and addresses. And don't bother checking on this phone number. It's a public phone and I won't be here. And it won't tell you where I'm going."

"As long as you have Linda, I play it your way."

"Now you're being sensible." Brea then gave brief instructions, assigning what would be the first of a series of stations on the way north where Macimer was to wait for another call, each time at a public phone. There would be no way for the calls to be monitored, no way for Macimer to know where he was going. "Get started now, Macimer. And if you've got company, you'd better lose them." The line went dead, just as the operator broke in to say that three minutes were up.

The phone booth was close and hot, but Macimer stood motionless, not wanting to jar the delicate balance of intuition, knowing that he trembled on the edge of discovery. That electronically filtered voice was one Macimer had heard before. It belonged to the man who had impersonated a private eye named Antonelli. The voice was disguised either because Brea was afraid Macimer might recognize it, or because Brea took no risk of having his real voice recorded for later analysis and identification. Voiceprints were as individual as fingerprints.

Macimer had heard that voice Monday night on the phone in Hogate's lounge. Erika Halbig's presence there that night now became something other than coincidence. She would do whatever Brea wanted. *I didn't even have to work on her very hard.* What had been her role that night? Probably nothing more than that of a lookout, someone who knew Macimer and could confirm that he had shown up alone. And who could provide a diversion while Brea met Raymond Shoup on Roosevelt Island.

Until that night Brea must not have been sure who had the contents of Vernon Lippert's file, Macimer or Raymond Shoup. First he had suspected Macimer, as evidenced by the staged robbery and subsequent electronic surveillance. Then he had learned about the items sent to Joseph Gerella. But when Brea finally confronted Raymond Shoup, the youth must have said or done something to indicate that he had stolen only part of the file. So Shoup had died, and suspicion tilted back toward Macimer.

And Brea believed that Macimer had been withholding the file, even from his superiors, because he didn't want the truth to come out. What made Brea so sure of him?

That's why you wouldn't give Oliver Packard any fresh dirt to shovel.

Macimer stumbled out of the hot phone booth. Like an organism rejecting an alien substance forced upon it, his mind twisted away from the truth, hurling up objections and denials, questioning the accuracy of his memory.

But there was no mistake. The call from Packard had come on Macimer's private line in his den on Sunday night, less than two hours after that phone had been cleared of bugs and taps. There had been no opportunity for anyone to get at the phone again. A bug had been left in place. Brea had heard Macimer's conversation with Oliver Packard.

And suddenly everything fell into place. It was even obvious how Linda had been lured away from Dulles International without making a scene. It was the only possible way, and Macimer would

have seen it sooner if he hadn't been resisting an answer that
brought with it too much pain.

She would only have gone with someone she recognized. Someone she knew and trusted. Someone who could make plausible an
abrupt change of plan about her Phoenix flight. Someone who had
bounced her on his knee before she was old enough to walk.

Her "Uncle Gordon."

Macimer drove back to the house. When he picked up the
phone to make the call to Phoenix he was calmer, though it was a
call he dreaded making. Then Jan surprised him, and he realized
that she had always surprised him by her strength in any genuine
crisis. Uncertainty demoralized her, but when she knew what she
had to face she had always been able to call on a core of resiliency
that carried her through.

He didn't hedge or try to soften the blow. Some things couldn't
be softened. I want a divorce. Your father is dead. Your child has
been kidnapped. You could only say the words.

He spoke on through a heavy silence, telling Jan as much of the
story of the Brea file as he could cram into a terse summary while
still making sense. He ended with Brea's call and the arrangements
for their meeting. He tried to make it sound like a simple trade-
off, the Brea file for Linda, but he knew that Jan was not so easily
fooled. "I'll bring her back," he promised. "I'm responsible for
what's happened to her."

"Responsible . . . it's an old-fashioned word now, isn't it?
You'll bring her back to the shelter because that's what parents
are supposed to do. We owe it to her."

"I'm not sure that's what the friendly neighborhood psychiatrist
would say."

"I know. It's everyone for himself."

"Sometimes you sound almost sensible." He wished she were
not so far away at this moment.

"Only when you're listening."

There was another long silence. Macimer felt unexpectedly
calm, confident, in spite of what lay ahead of him. Jan had always
been able to do that for him, he thought. Maybe he shouldn't have
needed that kind of support, but why not? Why was it so important not to need anyone? Going it alone wasn't even the normal
human condition.

"I'll give it my best shot," he said at last.

"I know you will."

Macimer almost smiled. "There's nothing like a vote of confidence."

"Paul . . ."

"Yes?"

"Do you know who it is? Do you know who Brea is?"

He took a deep breath, reluctant to answer. "I wasn't sure until this morning. Now I am." He waited for the next question but it never came. Perhaps she didn't want to know. "Jan . . . maybe this isn't the right time but there's something else I need to have settled. Before I hang up." It was the only hint he gave that his encounter with Brea might not be a simple trade-off. "What about us? You're not . . . locked in. Nobody believes that anymore."

"Aren't I?" Her tone was wry. "Oh, I've thought about our breaking up—believe me, I've thought about it. But you and I . . . we didn't go into it with that in mind."

"No." When they were married he had had this image at the back of his mind, vague and blurry like a photograph out of focus, of the two of them walking along a beach somewhere, hand in hand, fifty years later, white-haired and worn and content with each other.

"I guess I am locked in, sort of."

"Do you wish you weren't?" He heard the refrigerator groan as the fan cycled on. He waited for the puppy squeal of the failing mechanism. Nothing lasted as long anymore.

Her answer, when it came, was as painful for her to say as it was for him to hear. "Sometimes."

After a short pause he said, "Well, that's honest."

"Do *you* still want us to be together?"

"I've never wanted anything else."

"It will have to be different, Paul, in some ways. I need to . . . to explore myself a little more. I want to be surer of what I'm giving the rest of my life to." She paused. "We don't have so much more time."

"We have time enough," he said. "You were never more of a woman than you are right now, and I'm not about to lose out on the best of you after I've put in all this time."

"You make me sound like an unfinished product."

"You are," said Macimer. "You sure as hell are."

27

The emergency executive conference had convened at seven that Saturday morning in the Director's office on the seventh floor of the J. Edgar Hoover FBI Building. In addition to the Director and two of his Executive Assistant Directors, Jim Caughey and Henry Szymanski, present at the meeting were Frank Magnuson, SAC of the New York office; Fred Valentine, the Bureau's Counsel for Professional Responsibility; and Anthony Tartaglia, Russ Halbig's assistant, who had the rank of Inspector. Tartaglia had been supervising the surveillance of Paul Macimer on Halbig's instructions, and a line was open to the communications center.

Landers reviewed the events of the previous evening, including developments in the Molter case and Macimer's involvement, the fact that Macimer's daughter had apparently disappeared from a scheduled airline flight from Washington to Phoenix, and the search currently under way, at Macimer's instigation, for two Latinos who had been on the same Phoenix flight. One of those Latinos, a male named Francisco Perez, had been tentatively identified as being on a suspect list of those who had burglarized Macimer's home about a month ago. "It was Macimer's theory," Landers said, "that the robbers were looking for the Brea file."

"All that doesn't sound like a man who's covering up for himself," Caughey said.

"There's more," said Landers.

During the night Special Agent Leonard Collins had flown to Washington with the 1981 guest register for the High 5 Motel outside Fresno, California—a register which had suddenly become another question hanging over Paul Macimer's head. Forensic specialists in the FBI Lab, working in the early hours of the morning, had tested the chemical structure of inks on various pages of the register, as well as the paper itself. Henry Szymanski had brought the preliminary reports of those tests with him to the emergency conference.

"We tested the pages for dates from August 27 to August 30, 1981," Szymanski explained, "on the theory that the entry for August 28 might have been altered or a page substituted. The pages, by the way, are removable. The results for three of those pages— the 27th through the 29th—are unequivocal. The inks used on each page were the same. The papers are also identical in composition, age, fibers, color and texture. This becomes significant because, contrary to his activity report for August 28, Paul Macimer's name does not appear on the motel register."

"What about the fourth page?" Caughey persisted.

"Well . . . there are some differences there," Szymanski admitted, looking uncomfortable. He liked to have all his ducks lined up in a row, and one of them didn't fit in. "The paper is the same, but not cut from the same roll as the other three pages were. And the ink used was not the same."

"That means nothing is proven."

"I think a change in paper filling out a complete register is perfectly plausible," Szymanski said stiffly.

"Yeah, sure, and a change in pens at the same time." Jim Caughey leaned forward truculently, a broad hand beating time on the top of the Director's desk to emphasize his words. "I'd like to see more tests—more pages, before and after the dates you've already looked at. If someone was going to make a switch to make Macimer look bad, and if that someone was a Bureau man, he'd damned well be smart enough to change more than the one page. He'd figure you for doing exactly what you did. The only thing he didn't count on was that extra page."

Landers intervened as his two assistants glared at each other. "I'm sure additional tests are no problem," he said. "I take it, Jim, you're still convinced about Macimer. You don't think he's our man Brea."

"Do you, Director?"

Landers was slow to respond. Instead he rose from behind his desk and stood for a moment at a window which looked eastward toward the Capitol dome. He swung around to stare at Caughey. "I've been thinking about that call to Macimer last night from the WFO about the Molter case. You can tell a lot about a man by the way he acts in a crisis. Macimer's daughter is missing, and he's under extreme pressure. But you'd never have known it from the way he handled that call. When you put that together with his request for a pickup on those two young Latinos . . ." John Landers shook his head slowly. "If you're asking me for a gut feeling, Jim, then I think we've been barking up the wrong tree. It wasn't Paul Macimer that day in San Timoteo, poking a rifle out of a window and pulling the trigger. My gut tells me Macimer isn't Brea." He smiled thinly. "But that isn't proof, either."

Two men had upset his calculations in the last twenty-four hours, Landers thought, by reacting to pressure in unpredictable ways. At a critical moment Macimer had put the Bureau's needs ahead of his private anguish. And Russell Halbig, the duty-bound ice man, had walked away from a breaking case because his wife needed him. Each man in his own way had revealed a balance that was often lacking, the kind of balance John Landers looked for in a good agent.

Landers surveyed the men grouped around his office, all watching him. He realized that he missed Halbig's presence, his efficient, orderly management of information. The one reservation he had had about Halbig was that he simply didn't completely trust a cold, unemotional man. Now Halbig had shown unexpected depths. Perhaps he was the right man to be the Associate Director of the FBI, after all. And if Landers made that decision, he could then bring Magnuson in from New York to take Halbig's spot in Administration. Thinking of the possibility, Landers surprised the watching group by suddenly grinning. Magnuson had been needling him about turning into a politician last night in his handling of Senator Sederholm. Let's see how Frank likes it, Landers thought, at the seat of government.

"Want to let us in on the joke, John?" Magnuson asked. He was probably the only man in the entire Bureau who still had the temerity to address his old friend by his first name.

"In good time, Frank. All in good—"

Landers broke off as a voice crackled on the open line from the communications center. It was an agent calling from a public telephone, his call being patched directly through to the Director's office. He was part of the surveillance team assigned to Paul Macimer, and he was reporting by phone rather than using one of the Bureau's private radio frequencies because Macimer, if he drove his own FBI vehicle, would be able to monitor any radio communications.

The reporting agent's brief message electrified the men in Landers' office: Macimer had left his house. He was heading for Washington.

In the tense silence John Landers said, "Whatever is going down, gentlemen, I think this is it. We'll soon have our answers!"

Unlike most major cities, Washington is not a weekend place. Hotels offer special weekend packages to entice visitors to stay over the quiet days when the Congress is not in session. On this Saturday morning Macimer had no trouble finding a parking place on the street near the Lincoln Memorial. He caught a tour shuttle bus proceeding east along the south side of the Mall. At this early hour it was half empty.

Macimer got off the bus in front of the Smithsonian and strolled across the broad grass promenade. To his left the Washington Monument thrust aggressively skyward. To his right, at the far end of the Mall, rose the massive splendor of the Capitol. Pausing near a refreshment stand, Macimer watched some youngsters throwing a Frisbee. He assumed there was a team of trackers covering him, allowing one or more to drop off and others to pick up the tail. Standard Bureau procedure. What he did not understand was why, if his conclusion about Gordon Ruhle was correct, the Bureau was following *him*.

As Macimer strolled on he paused several times and glanced around like a curious tourist, trying to memorize the faces he saw, the color of a shirt or slacks or suit. It was a hot morning for the sandy-haired man in the blue cord suit, for instance. Perhaps, like Macimer himself, he needed the coat to cover up a hip holster.

Macimer ducked down the stairs of the Metro station just west of the Freer Gallery. He had to wait nearly five minutes for the train. By then Blue Cord Suit was looking unhappy. He knew that he had been spotted. He would have to drop out of the chase or switch places with one of the agents in a surveillance vehicle.

At Metro Center, Macimer caught another train on the Red

Line. He got off at Union Station, crossed over the walkway and doubled back. He stayed on the next train as far as Farragut North. Emerging onto K Street, Macimer crossed the boulevard against a red light and broke into a run. A block south he swerved sharply into the entrance of Farragut West.

This time he was in luck. A train had just pulled in as he ran down the steps. He made it an instant before the doors closed.

The train pulled smoothly away. The Metro, Macimer had once heard an agent say, was about the only thing in Washington that delivered as promised. The agent was Gordon Ruhle.

When the train stopped at McPherson Square, Macimer watched the faces of the boarders. None seemed familiar. No one paid even sidelong attention to him. By this time he was fairly sure he had lost his surveillance, but he remained uneasy when he debarked once more from the Blue Line train back at Metro Center. He mingled with the crowds going up the escalator and came out on G Street.

Macimer walked over to 11th Street and turned the corner. He waited in the entry of a Chinese restaurant—closed at this early hour—for a full five minutes. No one charged around the corner. There was no available parking along the street. No cars cruised slowly past or circled the block.

Satisfied at last, Macimer started walking north. He was sweating under his suit coat but he couldn't take it off. He was, in any event, only two blocks from the Greyhound Bus Terminal.

Harrison Stearns was waiting in a corner of the coffee shop, looking as rumpled and hollow-eyed as many of the bus passengers who were trying to wake up with coffee after all-night rides. Macimer slipped into the tiny booth across from him. The weary young agent tried to sit up alertly.

"Have you read it?" Macimer asked, taking the thick manila folder Stearns pushed across the table.

"Yes, sir. It . . . it's a bit of a shock."

Macimer made no comment. He riffled quickly through the pages of Vernon Lippert's file on Brea. He found what he was looking for on the last two entries. One listed four agents who had worked undercover in northern California in the summer of 1981 as a special team directly supervised by Special Agent Carey

McWilliams. Because of their clandestine assignments, none of the four had been carried on the roll of the PRC Task Force.

The last page was a brief report of Vernon Lippert's inquiries into the movements of the four men on August 28, 1981. Lippert had been able to verify the activities of three of those agents.

The name of the fourth undercover agent was Gordon Ruhle.

Macimer leaned back in the booth, his features carved in stone. He had known what he would find, but the physical proof still left him sickened rather than triumphant. "Volunteers," he murmured after a moment.

"Sir?"

He met Stearns's eager young eyes with an effort. "The PRC Task Force. Most of them were volunteers. It's a question I should have asked myself but never did. Gordon Ruhle was always a world-class volunteer. Why wasn't he there?"

Stearns wondered how close Macimer and Ruhle had been.

Macimer sighed. "Good work, Stearns. Did you have time to make a copy?"

"Yes, sir."

"I'll take this one, then. You look as if you could use some sleep about now."

"I'm fine, sir."

Macimer smiled. "You can do one more thing for me—two things, actually. Did you drive downtown?"

"Yes. My car's on the street."

"I'd like your keys, and I'd like a half hour. Then you hand-carry your copy of the Brea file to Headquarters. I want you to deliver it personally to the Director, no one else."

For the first time Stearns appeared overwhelmed. "Uh . . . will he be there, Mr. Macimer? Isn't he supposed to address the graduating class today down at Quantico?"

"He'll be there. And this is what I want you to tell him . . ."

For the men gathered in the Director's office at FBI Headquarters it was a period of tense waiting. During the interval Anthony Tartaglia left the office briefly to check on arrangements for a helicopter to fly Landers to Quantico at noon. He would wait until the last possible moment. Halbig would already have had the flight scheduled down to the second, Landers thought.

Tartaglia was coming through the door when another message

came through on the open line from the communications center. There was a brief, garbled transmission. Then an agent's voice came on loud and clear. "I'm sorry, Director, but . . . we've lost him."

"You've lost him!"

"Yes, sir. We had eight men following Macimer on foot, leap-frogging each other so he wouldn't tumble how we had him covered, and three surveillance vehicles. He pulled a subway switch and lost them."

There was a long silence. Then, in a tone as unforgiving as his square jaw, Landers asked, "What about his car?"

"We're watching it, but I don't think he'll be back. He's sure acting like a guilty man, sir."

"If I want your opinion I'll ask for it," Landers snapped. He turned toward Anthony Tartaglia, frozen in the doorway, his face turning pale as he listened to the report from his surveillance team. "Put as many men in the street as you can find," the Director said. "And the Metro lines. No telling where Macimer is now or where he's going. But find him!"

At a telephone booth next to a filling station northwest of Washington, Macimer waited for the first of his calls from Brea. When the phone rang he picked it up quickly and heard Brea's muffled tones. He listened without comment to the terse directions to his next stop. Following them Brea asked only a single question: "Have you got it with you?"

"Yes."

Macimer headed north on Highway 270. Traffic was light but he kept the speedometer needle of the plain blue Fairmont sedan steady at fifty miles per hour. He didn't want to be stopped for speeding now.

"Mr. Halbig is on his way here from the hospital now," Anthony Tartaglia told John Landers. Tartaglia, still shame-faced over the failure to keep Paul Macimer under surveillance, looked as if he wished he were somewhere else—anywhere else.

"Why didn't he telephone?" Landers said with a frown.

"I don't know, Director. His wife is conscious now, but apparently what she told Halbig is something he wants to report to you personally."

The Director grunted, the crease staying in place between his eyes. "What about the car rental agencies?" he asked suddenly. "Macimer isn't running on foot."

"We're checking them all," Tartaglia said. "There are quite a few—"

"I don't want any more excuses," Landers said grimly. "I want to know what's going—" He broke off as his private telephone line buzzed. He had told his secretary to hold all calls that weren't directly related to the executive conference. He pressed the button on the phone and said, "What is it, Mary?"

"There's an agent to see you, Director. He insists that he cannot talk to anyone else. His name is Stearns."

Landers exchanged quick glances with Jim Caughey and Frank Magnuson. Then he said, "Send him in."

The young agent who entered the office appeared weary but excited. He approached Landers' big desk with nervous sidelong glances at the other men in the office. He was carrying a thick manila envelope, sealed with a clasp. He held it with both hands as if afraid someone might try to snatch it from him.

"I hope this is important, Stearns."

"It is, Director. Mr. Macimer wanted me to give you this personally—"

"Macimer! You've seen him?"

"Yes, sir. About . . . forty minutes ago. He knew you'd want to have this."

"Never mind that, where is he now?"

"I don't know, Director." The young agent's hands were shaking but there was a resoluteness in his eyes.

Slowly John Landers held out his hand and took the thick envelope from Stearns. He undid the clasp and removed a yellow folder. Landers' glance flicked up at Stearns. "What's this?"

"It's the Brea file, sir."

The FBI Director studied the agent's face. Determination, he thought, not defiance. "All right, Stearns," he said quietly. "Suppose you tell us everything you know."

Two hours after leaving the Washington area, Paul Macimer stopped for gasoline and coffee on the outskirts of Hagerstown, Maryland. He was hungry but knew that he wouldn't be able to eat. Besides, a hungry man was more alert, able to think and move faster.

After another brief phone message from Brea he drove north again for fifteen miles. He turned west along a two-lane paved road that climbed quickly into the Appalachians.

By now, he thought, the Director would have heard the full story of the Brea file from Harrison Stearns. And the search for Gordon Ruhle—and Macimer himself—would pull out all stops. He was glad to get off the main highway. Borrowing an FBI vehicle had been a calculated risk, but renting a car would have taken extra time and provided only minimal delay once scores of agents hit the streets.

Ruhle would have evaluated Macimer's skills in evading surveillance and making his run northward undetected. His calculations had been close, even daring. Macimer knew he would not have been able to travel much farther on the main highway without being spotted.

Macimer had five minutes to spare when he reached the outskirts of Wheeler, a small mountain community where Gordon Ruhle's next call would come at noon. The town was one of those forgotten by progress, little changed from what it had been a century ago. Steep-roofed brick and frame houses with snow catchers protruding from the roofs. Wide porches. A turn-of-the-century ice cream parlor, crowded on this Saturday. Red's Diner, just off the road at the west end of town, looked as if it had been there from the beginning.

A phone booth stood by itself at one corner of the diner. Macimer stepped inside, relieved to find the booth unoccupied. He had been there only a few seconds when the phone rang.

Gordon Ruhle, his voice still disguised, wasted no time as usual. His final directions were terse and specific. Without waiting for Macimer to acknowledge them, he hung up.

Macimer stepped out of the booth. He stood there for a long moment at the side of the road, aware of a tingling sensation. He was being watched.

There were three people visible at window tables in the diner. All of them were staring at him. Local people, he judged, curious about any stranger. Macimer shrugged. It was possible that Gordon had had him take the last call from this telephone because it was one he could watch—and make certain that Macimer had come alone.

As he drove west out of the tiny town, he watched the car's speedometer, clocking the mileage. He found a one-lane dirt road precisely where Ruhle had told him to look for it. The narrow track climbed through a stand of pines and emerged onto a long, narrow shelf.

Macimer drove slowly across this flat meadow, a turgid cloud of dust drifting behind him in the hot, still air. The colors of the scene were vivid, primary. The dense green of the grassy meadow, enriched by recent rains. A mass of brown, sculptured bluffs rising to a knife-edge ridge. The black trunks of blue-green pines spaced tightly behind the line of the ridge. The piercing blue of the cloudless sky, draining toward the land like thin paint, lighter as it ran toward the horizon.

And, alone in all this color-saturated space, the bleached starkness of a cabin on the ridge, like a solitary abandoned house in a Wyeth painting.

A safe place to keep a hostage, Macimer thought, staring up at the cabin. Isolated, and so situated that there was no way to approach it without being seen from a long way off.

Completely isolated. There were no telephone lines visible. Ruhle could not have made his calls from the cabin. The sensation of being watched back at the diner was not a case of nerves, then. Ruhle had been in town, stationed where he could watch the booth outside Red's Diner.

Macimer's heart raced faster. If Ruhle was behind him, Linda was alone in the cabin.

Was there another route to the cabin on the ridge? A back road shorter than the one he had been directed to take? A shortcut that would put Gordon at the cabin ahead of him?

Sometimes there was no possibility of a clandestine approach, Ruhle had once told Macimer. All you can do is bore right in and deal with what you find when you get there. If a man in a hideout is smart, Gordon had pointed out, that's the way he'll set it up. He'll make sure you're out front where he can see you, and if there's an escape hole out back he'll take it if he doesn't like what he sees. Maybe you won't like going in that way, naked, but that's what you'll do.

The narrow dirt lane left the meadow and began to climb

slowly toward the ridge, cutting through a thin line of spruce that thickened toward the top of the climb. Detouring around a huge rock shoulder, the road abruptly tunneled through a pine forest as solid to the eye as a wall. The track was rough, hardly more than two ruts cut into the soft earth, its span so narrow that pine branches slapped at both sides of the car.

Macimer drove suddenly into a clearing and braked hard.

The old cabin, sun-dried and gray as an unpainted barn, stood alone near the rim. The view to the south across stepped, tree-covered spines of the mountain range was spectacular. And strangely desolate. Except for the narrow ribbon of road below the ridge, there was no evidence of human habitation or activity.

He swung the blue Fairmont in a circle, leaving the tracks of the approach road and coming about until the car faced down the road at the edge of the woods. He was not sure exactly what lay ahead, but he wanted the car ready for a fast escape if needed.

Macimer turned off the engine and stepped out of the car, carrying his black vinyl briefcase. The thump of the car door was loud in the stillness.

He walked slowly toward the cabin. No other car was in sight. There was no sign of life. No sound came from the cabin. It had a neglected, abandoned air, grass and weeds grown knee high across the entire clearing right up to the foundations of the cabin. On three sides, dense pine woods framed the clearing. Only the ridge-line was open.

He paused at the cabin door. He thought he heard a faint sound from within but could not be sure. He reached out and turned the rusty knob. The door was not locked.

Unoiled hinges creaked as the door swung inward. Macimer's sun-drenched eyes saw only dim shadows as he stepped over the threshold.

That was when Linda screamed.

28

"Daddy—don't come any closer! It . . . it's booby-trapped—the whole place!"

Her voice quavered. Macimer heard both the fear and the struggle to control it. A feeling of wonder filled him. This was his child, his daughter. Battered physically and psychologically in these recent weeks, she had not come apart. Instead she crouched in terror at the edge of a loft overlooking the main room of the cabin—and her thought was not for herself, but for him.

"I'm all right," she called out. "I just can't move."

A fierce pride stung his eyes.

As if she wanted to make certain that Macimer understood, she explained that she had tried to climb down from the loft after she was left alone. A ladder provided the only access. When her foot touched the first rung she heard a wire snap. She looked down anxiously. Dangling in the open space a few inches from her foot, attached somehow to the rungs of the ladder by wires, its familiar pineapple shape ugly and menacing, was a hand grenade.

She had remained frozen in place for long, terrified minutes, too scared to go up or down. "I . . . I don't know how long I stayed there. I couldn't move. Like a fly stuck on paper."

Macimer peered across the room as his eyes adjusted to the dimness. The grenade was suspended in midair, attached by a network of fine wires to the rungs of the ladder and to a wooden beam underneath the loft. The web of wires was so arranged that another careless step would pull the pin of the grenade. The wire broken by Linda's first step had been a warning signal.

"Don't touch anything, Daddy," Linda warned him. "He told me there are bombs and things all over—in the radio, in the light switch, maybe inside the toaster or the clock or anywhere. He wouldn't tell me where they all were, so I . . . I was afraid to touch anything."

Macimer nodded, still unable to speak. The dangling grenade had been designed to frighten and immobilize the girl when she had to be left alone in the cabin. Why not simply tie her up? Was her panic meant to impress Macimer? Or was the threat of other bombs meant to deny him access to her?

"He didn't hurt me," Linda said anxiously, as if she were defending her gallant kidnapper.

"No, he wouldn't hurt you," Macimer said, finding his voice at last.

After all, he was her "Uncle Gordon." So he wouldn't hurt her. He would only stake her out as bait in a trap. The grenade and other bombs were necessary to keep her there, like the bars on a child's crib. It would not be Gordon Ruhle's fault if she didn't stay put, if she tried to escape and triggered an explosion that blew off an arm or half a face. If she did what she was told, she wouldn't be harmed.

Gordon would have worked that all out. He was doing what had to be done.

Like setting up the People's Revolutionary Committee for a wipe-out because they were the enemy, using the unwitting police to function as his booby trap. Not nice, Gordon would say, but necessary. We're not here to be nice.

"Stay where you are," Macimer told Linda quietly. "I'll see what I can do to get you down."

First he had to get safely across the cabin. It was possible that the grenade was a dud, the warning of other bombs a ruse. Macimer thought about Gordon Ruhle and decided that one or more on the threats were real. Gordon didn't fight only with blanks.

He examined the cabin cautiously. It was essentially a single large room with a bedroom alcove at the back on the left, a small bathroom—its door was open—sandwiched between the sleeping area and a tiny kitchenette on the right. The simple furnishings of unfinished pine were minimal but appeared comfortable enough.

The air smelled musty and stale, and dust lay thick where it had not been disturbed. The comfortable interior of the cabin belied its exterior neglect. It was either a summer house, unoccupied during the long winter, or it was an unobtrusive hideaway.

In the center of the main room was an oval multicolored rug. Macimer knelt and cautiously lifted one edge of the rug. Slowly he lowered it again. There was a pressure mat beneath the rug. A relay could be used to ignite a bomb either by opening or closing a switch. No way of telling whether the pressure mat would react to the weight of a footstep bearing down on it or, conversely, to the release of pressure if the rug were lifted from the mat. A bomb might be triggered either way.

Gordon Ruhle was challenging him, Macimer thought. He still thought of it as a kind of game, even when the stakes were life and death. In some ways Ruhle, with his rigid code on the one hand, his reckless disregard of rules on the other, was like a boy playing a man's game.

Macimer carefully circled the floor rug, using hands as well as eyes to search out any stray thread of nylon or wire. He sidled past a chair and a small table rather than move either. It took him five minutes to reach the foot of the ladder that led to the loft.

The ladder was attached to the wall and climbed straight up. With the tips of his fingers Macimer lightly traced the network of wires supporting the grenade. To distract Linda he talked as he worked. "Do you know where Gordon is now?"

"No. He . . . he left about two hours ago."

Macimer nodded thoughtfully. "Has anyone else been here?"

"No."

Not a conspiracy, Macimer thought. A lone killer.

"Tell me what happened at the airport."

While she talked he gently separated two wires leading to the pin of the grenade. He didn't have to listen closely to what Linda said. He knew fairly well what had occurred at the airport. Linda had been surprised but not alarmed when Gordon Ruhle appeared a moment after Macimer was called away. She had followed Gordon unquestioningly to his car in the parking lot, believing that Macimer was there and plans for her flight had had to be changed. Once in Gordon's car, she was helpless. Ruhle had driven directly to the mountain cabin, where she had been kept overnight.

With a sigh of relief Macimer disengaged the last wire supporting the grenade. "You can come down now. Just watch your step —and don't touch anything but the ladder. I'll help you."

He caught her in his arms before she reached the bottom rung and swung her clear, holding her. Her arms tightened around his neck and a sob burst from her throat. "Oh, Daddy, I was so . . . so scared!"

"You had reason to be. But you're not alone anymore."

"What . . . what's going to happen?"

"We're going to get you out of here. Come on."

As they turned toward the door a sharp crackling stopped them. Macimer gripped Linda tightly by the arm so she would not move. All of his senses were acutely alive, quivering and sniffing and listening for some signal that would identify the scratching sound.

Then Gordon Ruhle's voice, harsh and metallic over an open intercom, said, "I wouldn't try it, son. I got a bead on that door. No way anyone's gonna come through it whole."

John L. Landers glanced at the wall clock, a century-old Seth Thomas, as it slowly chimed the noon hour. As the last chime died away he looked at Russ Halbig, seated in the green leather chair facing Landers' big desk. The two men were alone.

Halbig seemed to have himself well in hand, Landers thought. His wife was out of danger, and she had confirmed what was now a growing body of evidence of Gordon Ruhle's involvement in the Brea matter. Erika Halbig, however, knew nothing about the case. She had confessed to Halbig a previous affair with Ruhle as well as other sexual liaisons. Ruhle knew of them and had taken the trouble to acquire proof. He had used that evidence to force her to meet Macimer at the Pook's Hill Lodge. Photographs of their meeting had been taken by means of concealed cameras. She was not sure why Ruhle had wanted her to do it; he had acted as if it were a kind of joke. She had wanted to believe that, knowing Ruhle's long friendship with Macimer. She had tried to talk herself into believing it—and failed. "She knew in her heart that Ruhle had used her contemptuously," Halbig said without intonation. "I suppose she despised herself for that. And she was afraid that, with the hold he had over her, he would use her again if he wanted to. She found sleeping pills in the medicine cabinet of the apartment . . ."

After a moment's silence Landers said, "She didn't want you to know, Russ. That must tell you something."

"Yes . . ." Halbig seemed about to say more, the mask of control slipping, but he recovered. Then he said quietly, "The helicopter is standing by, Director."

"I know. I suppose I'll have to leave shortly, but . . . damn it, where is Macimer? An FBI vehicle shouldn't take this long to spot!" Landers glowered, relieved to take the discussion away from private anguish. "Keep trying to raise him on the radio. He should know better than to play the lone wolf."

"It's his daughter, sir. Almost certainly Ruhle kidnapped her, or arranged it, and is holding her. Apparently he's convinced that Macimer has been holding the Brea file, and Ruhle is using the girl to force him to turn it over. Macimer won't answer the radio signal—he's probably not even listening—if he believes our involvement would risk the girl's life."

"I know, I know . . ."

Landers' thoughts lurched back over Gordon Ruhle's three-year pattern of treachery, from the betrayal of Ruhle's informant in the PRC massacre to the murders necessary to cover up what he had done. He would not hesitate to kill again.

"I wonder why he waited so long," Landers muttered aloud.

"For what, sir?"

"To kill Tim Callahan."

Halbig considered the question coolly, methodically. "He took out McWilliams early because he perceived him as a clear risk of exposure. McWilliams may even have become suspicious. But apparently Ruhle didn't perceive Callahan as an immediate threat to him until Vernon Lippert opened up the Brea investigation. Once questions began to be asked about a maverick agent involved in the PRC affair, Callahan became dangerous. He knew about the undercover agents McWilliams was running." Halbig paused, frowning as he pursued his line of thought.

"What is it?" Landers asked.

"There is one thing we haven't considered, Director."

"What might that be?"

"Ruhle may believe you are also a risk to him. He eliminated those who could have identified him as Brea in a really intensive investigation, specifically the men in command of the PRC Task Force. First McWilliams, then Callahan. But they both worked under you. How could Ruhle be certain you weren't kept informed of all operations, including the use of undercover agents?"

John Landers regarded Halbig thoughtfully. Finally he said, "That's academic now, isn't it?"

"I suppose it is." Halbig did not appear satisfied. "I'd like to go down to Quantico with you, Director."

Landers shook his head. "No, I want you to stay here and keep on top of the search for Macimer and Ruhle. You can maintain radio contact with me. I want to know the minute anything breaks."

"Of course, Director."

Halbig seemed puzzled about something, and Landers guessed his perplexity had to do more with the events of last night than this morning. What had Halbig expected when he reported this morning to Headquarters? Evidently what he had *not* anticipated was having everything as it was before, his temporary defection overlooked, even condoned, his wife's questionable conduct not held against him.

A cool, methodical man, Landers thought, but human after all. And because of that perception Landers found it easier to talk to Halbig. Hell, the man had intimidated him before!

"It was going to be a proud day," Landers said after a moment. The class of new agents graduating from the Academy was the first he was to address as Acting Director. "Now, with this Brea case about to go public . . . it's not so proud a day for the Bureau. One of those times when some of the mud will stick."

"It comes off," Halbig said.

"Yes . . ." Landers scrubbed his face with a big square hand. Abruptly he pushed out of his swivel chair, his movements suddenly brisk. As he prepared to leave his office to go up to the rooftop helicopter pad, Landers appeared to be struck by an afterthought. He swung back toward Halbig, a thin smile bending the tight line of his mouth. "By the way, Russ . . . you're on good terms with Senator Sederholm, I believe. It might be a good idea if you got in touch with him. He'll want to know what's happening."

Landers saw the color rise on Halbig's neck as the Director ushered his assistant out of the office. As he rode up to the roof in the elevator, Landers' smile widened. It was certainly easier to like a man, he thought, when you knew his weaknesses as well as his strengths.

"How long have you known?" Gordon Ruhle asked amiably over the intercom. He could be anywhere nearby, Macimer thought, probably in a car or in the woods surrounding the clearing. No wires were visible, but communication could be something as simple as a portable walkie-talkie with a matching unit, its switches open, in the cabin.

"Not until this morning. I should have guessed earlier about the switch at Dulles when you had one of the your Cuban thugs take Linda's place. She would only have left with someone she knew."

"They're not thugs, they're patriots," Ruhle said.

"I can imagine what kind of story you must have told them."

"You never figured out it was me from Lippert's file?" Ruhle sounded genuinely puzzled.

"Raymond Shoup had the file," said Macimer. "I never put my hands on it until this morning. By that time I didn't need it. What tipped me was something you said on the phone—about Oliver Packard and what I'd said to him about shoveling dirt. That call came on the phone in my den last Sunday, just a couple of hours after you had supposedly cleared that phone. I knew you weren't that careless. That meant you were involved."

Gordon Ruhle chuckled. "I slipped up there."

"Maybe you didn't much care by then if I knew," Macimer suggested. "You wanted me up here anyway."

Ruhle's silence told Macimer his hunch was accurate. Then Gordon said, "I'm sorry it had to be you, Paul, but when I thought you had got hold of that file I didn't have much choice."

"Why not?"

"Don't you know yet? The Bureau thinks it was you! The brass, the high muckety-mucks, Halbig and Landers and the others—they think *you* were Brea."

"That's crazy." But suddenly Macimer knew that it wasn't crazy. It explained the surveillance; nothing else did. *Not a conspiracy, a lone killer.*

"Is it? You were in that area, Paul, when it all went down. Except that on the day the PRC bought it, you were supposed to be off in Fresno on some wild-goose chase. There's no evidence you were ever there, Paul."

"I registered at a motel," Macimer pointed out. "I was supposed to meet an informant, but . . ."

"Uh-uh. There's no entry for you on that register. I took care of that."

Macimer felt hairs stir on the back of his neck. "You made that anonymous call. *You* sent me to Fresno!"

"I didn't want you in the way, that's all. At least I thought that's why I was doing it at the time. I never meant to make it look like you could be Brea—not then. That came later, after Vernon Lippert wouldn't leave well enough alone and I couldn't find all the stuff he'd dug up. Then I saw the brass would start wondering about you—especially if they suspected you had the file and were sitting on it." Ruhle paused. "It's kind of eerie, I mean the way it all began to fit together, even that old register that didn't show you being where you said you were."

There was no remorse in the explanation, Macimer saw, no feeling of guilt. Gordon Ruhle had moved beyond that, shaping his own world with its own set of rules.

"Why would the Bureau suspect me?" he asked. "Why not you?"

"Without the file, and with no one alive to say otherwise, there's no proof I was ever there, Paul. Oh, I think our old pal Halbig would like to believe I was in on it, or maybe that we pulled it off together. But I doubt he thinks that anymore. The fact is, you look guilty as hell, Paul. You recovered those boxes of documents—and the Brea file was missing. You investigated the WFO bombing when McWilliams was killed—and you came up empty. You were there at Quantico the morning Callahan finally shut up. That robbery at your house even looked like a phony setup to divert suspicion. And that reporter, the one who was beaten up, you were the one he was hounding. When the snoopers put all that together with the idea that you lied about being in Fresno the day of the PRC blowout . . . well, you're Brea, Paul."

"It won't hold up, Gordon, because none of it is true. I didn't do all those things, you did." He thought of another question, one that had continued to puzzle him. "Why did you kill Carole Baumgartner? She was no threat to you."

"She saw me with Erika," Gordon Ruhle answered curtly.

Linda began to sob softly, uncontrollably, tears streaming down her cheeks. Macimer tried to soothe her with the grip of his hands, as if he might pour strength into her by holding her more tightly.

"She didn't even know you," Macimer said.

"I couldn't be sure of that. You've got that snapshot of us on the wall at home. She could've recognized me from that."

And everyone who knew, or guessed, or might in any way threaten to expose Ruhle's sinister secret had to be silenced. Everyone.

"It won't hold up, Gordon," Macimer said. "And you've forgotten someone—the Director. There's a good chance he knew about the undercover operation against the PRC. McWilliams wouldn't have launched that without approval. And Landers won't rest until he has the names."

"I didn't forget him."

Ruhle was calm again, and the pronouncement was matter-of-fact, but it brought a new chill of fear. Landers! What had Ruhle done to guarantee *his* silence?

Macimer tried to keep his turmoil out of his voice. "Landers is alive."

"He's giving the big speech to the new agents today down at Quantico. Remember how it was in the old days, Paul? A new agent never forgot shaking hands with J. Edgar Hoover the day he got his badge." Ruhle chuckled. "Believe me, nobody's ever going to forget this graduation ceremony."

"You're crazy, Gordon!" Macimer shouted. "Listen to yourself! You make murder a joke—you're mad!"

The outburst silenced the man outside. As the seconds dragged by Macimer re-examined the cabin, considering the few options open to him, trying to see the cabin, its openings, its setting, its vulnerabilities through Gordon Ruhle's eyes.

"Maybe you're right, Paul," Ruhle said at last. His tone was flat, the earlier sense of casual banter, even friendliness, wiped away. "But I won't be crucified over something that had to be done. I won't see my name used like it was something you'd spit on—not after all these years. Landers is the last link between Brea and me. Him and the file—and you brought that with you. I knew you would—you had to. So there's nothing left to point to me." Another pause, and Macimer felt the coldness in it, the implacable determination. "The way it will look, Paul, is you found that file and tried to bury it. Because you were Brea. And when you saw that a cover-up wouldn't work . . ."

"I took my own life, is that it?"

Linda gave a small whimpering cry. Like a frightened child she burrowed deeper into the shelter of Macimer's arms.

"Now you've got it."

Hearing his own death sentence, the words finally said, Macimer was strangely calmed by them. Fear remained, but it was for others—for Linda, and for John L. Landers. And if he was to save them both he had to find a way for her to get away. Nothing else mattered.

He wondered when it had started to go bad for someone like Gordon Ruhle. The man Ruhle had been when Macimer first joined the Bureau could not have plotted the death of a friend, any more than he could have planned and carried out a scheme of wholesale murder. He had had to be conditioned for it. By the bitter realization that the people he served, those who had always paid him honor and respect, no longer trusted and admired him. By years of involvement in "sanctioned" crimes. The arguments that justified a poison-pen letter against a Klansman, a false tip to a journalist, lies and scams against black militants, break-ins and arson and the rest, were the same arguments that must have been in Ruhle's mind when the idea of the PRC massacre was born. The difference must have seemed to him one of degree, not of kind.

The temptation was always there, Macimer thought. We watch too many crooks go free. We see too many terrorists flaunt their savagery because we're hamstrung by our own rules. The temptation to skirt the law a little, to overlook this small elasticity, to employ the tools and tactics of viciousness against the vicious (just this once) was always there, always insidious. It had always to be resisted.

But Macimer knew there was no way to convince Gordon Ruhle that the Bureau he loved was hurt far more by cover-ups, dirty tricks, fanatical loyalties than by the truth. Argument was useless—but talk was essential. He had to keep Gordon talking.

Macimer studied his daughter intently. Would she be able to do what he asked of her? It was a chance he had to take. He tightened his grip on her arm as he called out, "We had a deal about Linda. Her life for the file. Are you backing out on that, Gordon? Is she to be sacrificed like the hostages who were in that house with the PRC? Like your own informant? Like the FBI men who trusted you?"

"Sometimes you have to do things you don't want to do," Ruhle said coldly. "Sometimes innocent people get in the way and they get hurt, just like any war. You can't let that stop you. I buried the PRC—nobody else could do it. They were trying to destroy this country. You had a goddamn army out there in California that summer and you couldn't stop them. Well, I did, and that scared the shit out of a lot of other chicken-livered would-be terrorists who didn't like what they saw on their TV screens that day. Innocent people are alive today because of what I did, and the country is safer for it. I don't apologize for it, not by a damned sight!"

Still white-faced, Linda seemed to grow calmer as she listened to Gordon Ruhle's self-serving harangue. Macimer bent down, bringing his lips close to her ear, using the rasp of Ruhle's voice over the intercom to cover his urgent whisper. "When I tell you, go straight out the door. You'll see a car over near the trees, a blue Ford." He handed her the keys. "Don't stop for anything until you get to the bottom of the hill. Then use the car radio, station 5. It's an FBI network code number. Keep driving, but keep calling on the radio until you raise someone. Tell them who you are and where—the nearest town is Wheeler, about five miles up the road. Use my name and ask for an urgent message to be given to James Caughey or Russ Halbig at FBI Headquarters. Say that the Director must not give his speech at the Academy!"

She shook her head. "I . . . I can't."

"You've got to! It's our only chance, Linda."

"I'm sorry about Linda," Gordon Ruhle said. "If there'd been another way to get you here with that file, I'd have taken it. But there wasn't. As it is . . . her being here makes the whole thing look stronger. You knew the game was up and you flipped out, that's all. And took your daughter with you."

"Please!" Macimer whispered to Linda.

"No!" The girl was as fiercely determined as he was. "I won't leave you alone!"

Macimer saw in her eyes something he had not recognized before. Not merely terror but a stubborn loyalty. It almost broke him.

"It's over, Paul," Gordon Ruhle said.

"That's right, Gordon—it *is* over. It has been since I left Washington this morning. I had copies made of the Brea file."

"Nice try, Paul," Ruhle said. "But I don't believe you. You wouldn't do that to the Bureau any more than I would. You'd die before you'd turn that file loose."

Macimer felt a twinge of pity for his old friend. Ruhle's justifications for what he had done were self-serving, a denial of guilt to himself as well as to others. But all along he had probably been motivated as much, if not more, by his desire to protect the Bureau he had given his life to. Wondering if he could still tap that well of feeling, Macimer made a last try at getting Ruhle to believe him. "You're wrong, Gordon. I had one of my agents hand-deliver a copy of the file to the Director after I left. What's done is done, but the truth can't just be buried and forgotten. It has to come out."

"No—people don't understand! Sometimes you have to cut corners. Damn it, it's for their own good!"

"Killing people isn't cutting corners, Gordon. It's murder."

"You damned fool!" Gordon Ruhle raged. "Don't you know what you've done!"

Macimer had led Linda carefully around the booby-trapped rug on the floor. Near the door he faced her, pleading with his eyes. "Count three after I go out the window. Then go through that door as fast as you can. *You must radio that message!*"

Without waiting for her protest, he turned toward the single window in the east wall of the cabin. He folded his arms protectively over his face and hurled himself at the window.

29

"Border Patrol agents have stopped the two Cuban youngsters at the Arizona border, trying to cross over to Nogales." Russ Halbig's voice on the radio from FBI Headquarters was barely audible over the beat of the chopper's blades, and John Landers had to strain to hear. "They're being questioned now. I don't think it will take long to get the identity of the third man, the leader. He probably recruited the two young ones. And when we have him, he'll point us back to Gordon Ruhle. It's only a matter of time."

"It's all falling into place," Landers said.

The helicopter started a slow, wheeling turn, and the FBI Director saw the blocky towers of the dormitories at the Academy above the treetops to the south, surrounded by brown fields stripped of their greenery.

"Yes, Director. Except that we don't know . . ." The following words were lost in the chopper's roar as it began to descend. Landers heard only the last word. ". . . alive." It seemed born more of hope than conviction.

The crash of the window breaking out was a small explosion. Macimer sailed through the opening head first. One trailing leg caught a shard of glass in passing. It ripped the trouser fabric cleanly and slashed Macimer's calf. He didn't even feel it. He landed in the grass, rolled and came to his feet on the run.

Crouching low, Macimer ran in a zigzag path toward the woods behind the cabin. Twenty yards to cover. It might as well have been a mile.

Glance over his shoulder. Blur of color bobbing above the tall grass—Linda's blue pullover. She was running toward the blue Fairmont at the edge of the clearing. Good girl!

The brief euphoria broke like a bubble. If he could see Linda, so could Gordon Ruhle. Then, belatedly, his brain grasped what he had seen out of the corner of his eye: another car blocking the narrow road where it tunneled into the woods. Gordon had anticipated his maneuver. Linda could not escape.

There was a harsh burst of gunfire, an exploding thought—oh God, Linda!—and a glancing blow, as if someone had nudged his shoulder.

Macimer felt surprise as he was flung off balance and thrown to the ground. He skidded in the long grass. He had a glimpse of red streaking the green spears where he had fallen, slick and bright as new paint. Why did he feel no pain?

Macimer crawled, worming low in the tall grass, his heart thudding. Experience prepared him for the pain to come. But he was mobile. He could move his left arm in spite of the stain spreading over his left shoulder. And the grenade used to frighten Linda was in his hand. It might give him an edge. He lifted his head cautiously. How close to the woods?

Macimer froze. Inches from his eyes was a thin, taut strand of copper wire. He lay very still.

Gordon Ruhle had expected him to break for the trees. Either through the side window or out the small window of the bathroom. Gordon had counted on blind panic, a headlong flight. If Macimer hadn't fallen when he did—if he had hit that trip wire with his leg on the run . . .

But he hadn't fallen. He had been shot down—before he reached the wire. Deliberately? Or by freak chance?

Maybe Gordon hadn't wanted too easy a victory. He wanted it to be a contest.

Macimer tried to track the path of the wire through the grass. It disappeared, heading for the trees to the left of where he lay, snaking across the open space to his right. Macimer had little doubt there were other wires strategically placed, leading to other packed explosives buried in the ground. Always use a backup,

Gordon would say. Never rely completely on the enemy doing the expected thing.

The enemy . . .

Macimer crawled parallel with the wire. Where had the burst of fire come from? The trees? Which direction?

He should have told Linda to keep running if the car was blocked or disabled. Gordon was outthinking him.

Macimer identified something that had been tugging at his brain. Gordon Ruhle could not have failed to see Linda, but he had not fired at her. Either because he knew she could not escape in the car and was therefore no immediate threat to him, or because he could not bring himself to squeeze the trigger. Did that much of the man Macimer had admired still live?

There was pain now, a delayed reaction. A cool sensation where his left leg had been cut, a hard throbbing in his left shoulder. Not as bad as he might have expected. He had caught only one bullet and it had not struck bone.

Macimer dragged a handkerchief from his hip pocket and stuffed it under his shirt at the shoulder to stanch the bleeding. He ignored the wound in his leg.

He scanned the line of trees once more.

A dozen yards away, at the edge of the woods, Gordon Ruhle stared back at him.

Macimer dropped flat as a hail of fire rattled over his head. He felt the visceral lash of panic as he scrambled through the grass. Ruhle was armed with a Thompson submachine gun. At this short range it could cut a man in half. Macimer wondered if Ruhle had made a conscious choice of a weapon that had been so much identified with the early years of the FBI. That was like him.

Macimer flipped onto his back, caught the pin of the grenade between his teeth and pulled. He lobbed the grenade toward the spot where Ruhle had been and flattened himself against the ground.

Silence. And then—low but clear—mocking laughter. The grenade was a dud.

Ruhle had known it.

Macimer rolled again, his .38 Special in his hand now, and fired blindly through the grass in Ruhle's direction. Then he flopped back where he had been, reversing direction. Bullets spat into the ground where he had been moving. They stitched an erratic line across the rain-soft earth.

Again Macimer changed course, scurrying back over the ground where the stream of bullets had pockmarked the earth, trying to outguess the deadly marksman who had taught him much of what he knew about this kind of a fire fight. Another harsh burst from the machine gun, another singing line of bullets passed over him.

Almost over. He felt the tug at his buttock and yelled involuntarily, as much in surprise as pain.

Then he lay still. His right arm was folded under his body as he lay on his belly. His hand gripped the Smith & Wesson.

He heard the grassy whisper of Gordon Ruhle's deliberate approach. Macimer remembered watching coyotes at dusk on a golf course in California, gliding out of the hills and moving swiftly across a shadowed green fairway, circling carefully, warily, never moving in a straight line, closing in on some prey. With the same caution Gordon Ruhle circled the spot in the grass where Macimer lay, slowly tightening the noose.

He came in behind Macimer and stood over him, the Thompson submachine gun aimed at the spot in the center of the prone man's spine. "Bring your right hand out nice and slow, Paul," he said softly. "Make sure it's empty."

Macimer released the breath he had been holding. Very slowly he withdrew his right hand. He could feel the revolver hard against his ribs.

"Almost," Gordon Ruhle said. "But almost is still a loser."

"He stopped for gas before heading north out of Hagerstown," Anthony Tartaglia said. "Our agent there picked up on the license plate number of the car Macimer took from Stearns. It was on the receipt."

Russ Halbig nodded curtly. Tartaglia would receive no praise for his work this day. "Anything else?"

"He got a phone call at a pay station. We're trying to run that down with the phone company now. If it was long-distance—"

"Wait a minute!" Halbig waved him silent. "Don't we have a safe house in the mountains up that way? Northwest of Hagerstown?"

"Yes, that's right. But I don't know if Ruhle would know about it."

"You can bet he does. Find out the name of the nearest town and check with the phone company on long-distance calls from there this morning. There can't have been very many."

"Yes, sir!"

"And tell our man in Hagerstown to get up to that house as fast as he can drive."

Macimer twisted his neck to peer over his shoulder at Gordon Ruhle. The familiar face stared down at him impassively. We expect the face of murder to look different, Macimer thought. It rarely does.

"Were you telling it straight, Paul? About making a copy of that file?"

"Yes."

"Damn you, why? Why couldn't you let it die?"

"It was all going to come out sooner or later. Better now, this way. If you've been bitten by a snake, you don't wait for the poison to spread. You cut where the bite is."

"You've turned into a goddamn bleeding heart."

"And you turned into a murderer."

For a moment longer Gordon Ruhle glared down at Macimer, something baffled in his eyes. Macimer realized that Ruhle simply didn't understand. Even now he believed that he was right, that he had done what had to be done. Madness was only implausible to the sane.

"Sorry, Paul."

In one searing moment Macimer heard Linda's scream and saw Gordon's finger tighten on the trigger of the machine gun. It was an instant in which time stopped, like a reel of film arrested. Macimer's body contracted in a reflex reaction against a blow that never came.

Gordon's lips twisted in an angry snarl. *The gun had jammed!*

Macimer dug for his revolver. He twisted away from the barrel of the machine gun as it chopped down at his head. The barrel slammed into the ground. The blow was so hard that the stock shattered in Gordon Ruhle's hands. Macimer's fingers closed around the butt of his gun. He rolled onto his back as Gordon threw the broken shoulder stock away and dove on top of him.

Macimer never got the muzzle of the revolver around in time to fire. Gordon Ruhle caught his arm and the two men struggled wordlessly in the deep grass. But Ruhle was on top, and he stayed there. He was stronger—all those years of lifting weights, Macimer thought—and he was positioned for greater leverage. Slowly Macimer felt his right arm being bent back, his grip on the revolver weakening.

He did the only thing left to him. He threw the gun as far off into the grass as his limited arm movement allowed.

There was an instant when the two men were motionless, locked in place, staring into each other's eyes. Deep within Gordon Ruhle's dark eyes a familiar light danced, as if any second he would break into mocking laughter. But there was no sound but the two men's ragged breathing.

Then Ruhle got an arm free and smashed his fist into Macimer's face. He jumped to his feet and lunged after the revolver.

Had Ruhle forgotten the trip wire he had hidden in the deep grass? Macimer would always wonder. At the time there was only the shock of the explosion, the ground heaving and the stunning burst of the bomb. Gordon Ruhle was lifted into the air, an arm and a shoulder and part of his face dissolving like ashes in the wind. Then mud and grass and bits of human debris blinded Paul Macimer.

And tears.

Macimer pushed drunkenly to his feet. He felt heavy, clumsy. His feet dragged as he tried to move, and one toe kicked the drum magazine of the Thompson submachine gun on the ground. Bending slowly and painfully, he picked up the weapon by the rear pistol grip. Except for the broken butt stock, the gun appeared to be undamaged. As Macimer stared down at it, his gaze was riveted on the bolt.

It was forward.

The gun was uncocked.

"Damn you, Gordon," he whispered. "You knew!"

In a spasm of pain Macimer jerked the barrel of the machine gun upward, aiming at a single small spruce thirty feet away. The rocker pivot was set on full automatic. He retracted the bolt, braced himself against the recoil and squeezed the trigger. He held it down long after the deafening roar of automatic fire had diminished to the impotent rattle of an empty magazine.

The narrow trunk of the spruce disintegrated at a point waist-high. The top half of the tree toppled forward as the long burst of fire cut the trunk in half.

Macimer stared numbly at the crumpled shape in the grass where Gordon Ruhle had fallen. It didn't jam, he thought. *It didn't jam.*

He threw the weapon to the ground and stumbled toward the cabin. He was beyond pain, beyond grief, the organism adjusting instinctively to enable itself to survive. He felt nothing until the small hard shape of his daughter's body hurtled against him, and his arms went around her, holding on.

"This is WFO 172," Macimer said into the car microphone, identifying the FBI vehicle's call number. "WFO 172. Do you read me?"

He kept repeating the message over and over. He was beginning to despair when there was an abrupt response, loud and clear, "HGN 15, HGN 15, I read you, WFO 172. Where are you?"

Macimer felt a leap of hope. "This is Special Agent Paul Macimer. I'm five miles east of Wheeler, Maryland. Repeat, five miles east of Wheeler. It's a state road—"

"I'm heading up toward Wheeler now. You at the cabin?"

"Yes," said Macimer, stunned.

"It's a safe house," the agent from Hagerstown said. "Supposed to be empty. Are you all right, Mr. Macimer?"

"I'm fine, never mind me. Can you patch me through to Washington?"

"I can get a message through the Hagerstown RA's office. We're out of range for Washington."

"Send it urgent, priority A." Macimer took a deep breath, hoping that he was not too late, and began to talk.

The graduating class of new agents from the spring session of the FBI Academy milled around restlessly in the corridor outside the main auditorium. The doors to the auditorium remained locked, as they had for nearly twenty minutes, and there was much curious speculation in the corridor, one rumor leading to another, wilder one.

Twenty minutes earlier, a team of grim-faced FBI men and a squad of uniformed Marines had charged through the Academy on the run, emptied the auditorium and locked the doors. Shortly afterward the Director himself had arrived, shouldering his way along the corridor like a ship plowing its way along a narrow channel, scattering waves of new agents on either side. He disappeared behind the same closed doors.

John L. Landers had come to address the graduates and to shake the hand of each new agent in a time-honored ritual. It was the moment they had all been waiting for. Now it was being delayed, and no one knew why.

"I heard they were bomb-disposal specialists," one of the graduates said.

No one joked about the rumor, as they might have only a few weeks ago. The memory of Timothy Callahan's death was too fresh.

Without warning the doors to the auditorium were thrown open. The new agents were directed to their seats, and the big modern auditorium quickly filled. A buzz of excited conversation continued for several minutes, during which time a number of the graduates noted that the podium from which the Director would normally have addressed them was missing from the stage.

At last the solid, familiar figure of John L. Landers stepped into view from the right wing and strode slowly toward center stage. The moment was electric, fed by curiosity and anticipation and unchecked rumor. As one mass the entire class of new agents came to their feet, and a spontaneous roll of applause began to build.